FIRE AND ICE

A RICK HOLDEN NOVEL

Also by George Galdorisi

Fiction
For Duty and Honor
The Coronado Conspiracy
Tom Clancy's Op-Center: Dark Zone
Tom Clancy's Op-Center: Scorched Earth
Tom Clancy's Op-Center: Into the Fire
Tom Clancy's Op-Center: Out of the Ashes
Tom Clancy Presents: Act of Valor

Non-Fiction
AI at War: How Big Data, Artificial Intelligence and Machine Learning Are Changing Naval Warfare
When the Killer Man Comes: Eliminating Terrorists as a Special Operations Sniper
Networking the Global Maritime Partnership
The Kissing Sailor
Leave No Man Behind
Beyond the Law of the Sea
The United States and the 1982 Law of the Sea Convention: The Cases Pro and Con

FIRE AND ICE

A RICK HOLDEN NOVEL
by George Galdorisi

BOOKS

Aura Libertatis Spirat

Fire and Ice

Copyright © 2020 by George Galdorisi

3rd Edition

Braveship Books

www.braveshipbooks.com

Aura Libertatis Spirat

Cover Design by Rossitsa Atanassova

ISBN-13: 978-1-64062-123-7
Library of Congress Control Number: 2020925358
Printed in the United States of America

For our two adult children, Brian and Laura, who are both "safe for solo" and raising their own families. You both make us proud and continue to amaze us not just with your manifest accomplishments, but with what good people you are. Your goodness is reflected in the children you are raising.

Acknowledgements

Many people have the impression that those of us who write isolate ourselves from the rest of humanity for some long period and then produce an opus that is sent out to the world. For some with enormous talent that far exceeds mine, that may be the case.

For this book, and all others I have written, I depend on close friends and colleagues to be part of this process. For *Fire and Ice*, these include Ken Curtis, Chris O'Connor, Jim Stavridis, Rolf Yngve and Neil Zerbe. Their thoughtful and on-point feedback has made this book vastly better.

Special thanks go to former squadronmate and fellow writer Kevin McDonald. An accomplished author of fiction and nonfiction, his books, *Inside the Dead Man's Curve* and *A Nation Interrupted*, are the best-practices examples for anyone wishing to embark on a writing career. He has served as muse, sounding board, confidant, editor, copyeditor and other roles too numerous to mention in shepherding this book to its final state. This book is our collective product.

Finally, books like these would not be possible without the ongoing steadfast and heroic work demonstrated every day by the men and women of the U.S. military. No one who writes in the political-military-technology arena can do so without observing the day-to-day exploits of these heroes. They all deserve our thanks and admiration.

Author's Introduction

For over seven decades, the only existential threat to humanity has been the peril posed by nuclear weapons. Nuclear non-proliferation remains a quest, and a challenge, to this day. For much of that time, it was the West versus the East—with the West led by the United States and its NATO allies, and the East led by the Soviet Union and its Warsaw Pact subject states. And while these two competing blocs had massive conventional forces, what most feared might happen was a nuclear exchange between the two superpowers. With almost seventy thousand nuclear weapons in play, the threat was real and terrifying.

When the Berlin Wall came down, the Soviet Union imploded, and the Cold War ended abruptly. National leaders looked at this as an opportunity to reduce the number of nuclear weapons that held their countries hostage to the threat of "mutually assured destruction," aptly captured in the acronym MAD. Through one of the provisions of the 1995 Nuclear Non-Proliferation Treaty, three former Soviet republics, Belarus, Kazakhstan and Ukraine, agreed to return to Russia all the nuclear weapons on their territory that once belonged to the Soviet Union. Over six thousand warheads were taken out of their bunkers to make the journey to their new masters.

This was a time when Russia was in economic free-fall, a once mighty power reduced to near-third-world status. That nation's new leaders were eager to gain favor with the West to help their country claw its way back toward some moderate approximation of prosperity. The kleptocrats who were now taking power, many of them energy industry oligarchs, counted on the Russian military to accept, disassemble and render safe all these nuclear weapons.

Senior Russian military officers considered this a mundane task, not worthy of much, if any, of their attention.

Once numbering over five million troops in uniform, the Russian military was now a drain on a struggling economy. The nation's leaders began to trim the number of troops dramatically. That was fine as far as it went, but those who once held high power, especially Russian military officials and generals, saw their livelihoods in danger of ending. Some with the means, motive and opportunity began to cast about for a safety net to allow them to flee the country and begin a new life in the West. One easy way to do this was to look the other way when returned nuclear weapons were counted.

You had to give credit to the kleptocrats and their new leader, Vladimir Vladimirovich Putin. They mostly kept their promises. As energy prices soared in the late twentieth and early twenty-first century, they leveraged Russia's vast oil and gas reserves to become an important and trusted supplier of energy, especially to Europe. They cheered every time a crisis in the Arabian Gulf made people think twice about depending on *those* nations to be the first choice to keep energy flowing around the world.

It all worked until it didn't. When energy prices tanked, so did the Russian economy. The kleptocrats and their mercurial leader were now blamed for the country's rapidly deteriorating economic condition. Putin and his cronies did what any national leaders might do to divert their people's attention from their internal woes. They became resurgent abroad. Russia bullied Georgia and Estonia, annexed Crimea and invaded Ukraine.

And Russia *was* still Russia. As Winston Churchill famously said in 1939, "Russia is a riddle wrapped in a mystery inside an enigma." Western leaders hoped the rising nation and Putin, its latter-day czar, would play nice with others. But as one wag once put it, "Hope is not a strategy." Not to put too fine a point on it, but Sir John Slessor probably got it right over six decades ago in his 1954 book, *Strategy for the West*, when he asked:

> How can one expect any sort of respect for normal international agreements from a regime that in thirty-seven years since the Revolution, has shot as spies and traitors, amongst others, all the members of their first Inner Cabinet and all members of the party Politburo as constituted after Lenin's death except Stalin; forty-three out of fifty-three Secretaries of the Soviet War Council; three out of every five marshals; and about sixty percent of the generals of the Soviet Army?

And then there is Russia's leader, Vladimir Putin. As of this writing, Putin has been in power for well over two decades, longer than some of Russia's czars. The former KGB officer could turn on the charm and seduce the unwary. Witness President George W. Bush's comments after his first meeting with Putin in 2001:

> I looked the man in the eye. I found him to be very straightforward and trustworthy. We had a very good dialogue. I was able to get a sense of his soul; a man deeply committed to his country and the best interests of his country.

But the former KGB officer was still what he was—a ruthless autocrat who, with his cronies, wasn't "committed to his country and the best interests of his country," but to holding onto power at all costs and, in the process, becoming a billionaire many times over. Perhaps former Secretary of Defense, Robert Gates, put it most accurately in his 2014 book, *Duty*, when he wrote, "I looked into Putin's eyes and I saw a stone-cold killer."

Russia's resurgence and Vladimir Putin's naked ambition have been on a collision course with the West, and especially with the United States, for the last several years. And, like a turkey wishbone being tugged on by two determined parties, it had to give sometime. That tug-of-war is happening today in Eastern Europe—and something is about to break.

CHAPTER ONE

Mayor's Residence, Saint Petersburg, Russia
(September 6, 2130 Moscow Standard Time)

"I'm worried about Marta."

"You worry too much," Pavel Safronov, Saint Petersburg's mayor, replied with a sigh as he put down his tablet and looked up at his wife.

"She's our daughter, Pavel, someone has to worry about her, and you never have time."

Safronov paused a moment before replying. Olga was right. Perhaps he *was* spending too much time on his duties as mayor of Saint Petersburg and all but ignoring their only child. And maybe if he was more open with his wife about the pressures he was under, she would understand why he was working hellish hours to please his mentor, Vladimir Putin, a former high official in this city.

Safronov rose from his overstuffed chair and walked the short distance to where Olga was seated on the loveseat in the sitting room of their dacha overlooking the Neva River.

"You're right. We both should worry about her," he began, taking her hands in his. "It's that boy, isn't it?"

"It is. She's still in secondary school, and he's halfway through university."

"But he's from a good family. You know that, don't you?"

"He is, but even Marta admits he's a leader of the student protest movement. I don't want her to get caught up in that."

"We won't let that happen," Safronov replied as he gave her hands a gentle squeeze.

The mention of student protests made his stomach churn. And the fact that these protests were happening here, in the city where he had been mayor for just over a year, troubled him deeply. He had known only achievement and accomplishment for all his two-decade-plus political life. But that success was eluding him as mayor of Russia's second-largest city and the most westernized one in the nation.

Maybe that was the problem. There was too much westernization. Petersburg, as Russians referred to the city founded by Tsar Peter the Great, was only six hundred and fifty kilometers from Moscow but vastly more distant in so many ways. There was one thing that *did* unite the citizens of the two cities. The crash in the price of oil, Russia's biggest export, along with increasingly tight western sanctions, had made life harsher throughout Russia.

Life had become so untenable that the citizens of Petersburg had taken to the streets in greater numbers than those in any other city in Russia to demand more food and other necessities. That certainly was true when he compared his city to Moscow, where that city's mayor, no doubt with not-so-gentle prodding from Russia's president, had to deal with fewer and smaller protests and seemed to better hold things in check. Putin constantly demanded that Safronov do more to stamp out the protests in Petersburg, but he wasn't here on the firing line where the city's underfunded police force couldn't seem to keep a lid on things.

Safronov put his work woes behind him for a moment. He loved Olga and Marta unconditionally and wanted to do the right thing for his family. "You're right, dear. Maybe we should talk with Marta and explain the dangers of being with a boy who has taken such a wrong path. She's upstairs studying. Let's go talk with her."

His admission that they needed to do something, *anything*, brought a small smile to Olga's face. She withdrew her hands and replied, "I'll do it, Pavel. She doesn't like us ganging up on her."

As Olga walked up the long, curved, staircase, Safronov settled into his chair and returned to his tablet, where he was reading an e-mail from his chief of police. It wasn't a good one. He was just two paragraphs into the report when he heard the shout.

"Pavel!" Olga cried from the top of the steps, "She's not here!"

At that moment, Marta was hurrying toward Palace Square, Petersburg's main plaza and the location of the Winter Palace.

A year ago, Marta Safronov would have been in her room, where her parents had expected to find her. She would have been studying for yet another examination at Petersburg's exclusive International Academy, following the course her parents had mapped out for her. It was a path similar to that chosen by the parents of Russia's other privileged children: exclusive, expensive private K-12 education in Russia; higher education in Europe, with a concentration on honing the extensive English-language skills learned throughout their earlier schooling; an advanced degree, perhaps in the United States, but more likely at Oxford or Cambridge; and a comfortable job in one of Russia's thriving businesses.

But that had changed on a gorgeous summer day in Petersburg two months ago. That afternoon, her father's chauffer was returning Marta to their expansive state-owned dacha at the end of the school day. He had been lazy and hadn't checked traffic alerts on his mobile phone. They ran right into a food protest, where police were jostling with young people who looked, to Marta, to be not much older than she was.

Their limo was stuck for the moment as the crowds boxed them in. The protesters surged forward, and the police, all clad in riot gear, pushed back. Marta looked on in horror as a policeman savagely beat a young woman, striking her repeatedly with his baton, and then left her bleeding as he chased another protestor, who was in full flight.

Moments later, the protestors moved down the street, and the way was clear. The chauffer started to move, but Marta shouted, "Stop—we need to help her!"

His concern for the injured woman and Marta's request had not been enough to trump the man's instructions from Petersburg's mayor to keep his daughter safe at all costs. He had sped away, ignoring Marta's increasingly insistent pleas.

That night, at dinner, her parents had noticed Marta was sullen and uncommunicative. Questions like, "What's wrong, dear?" were met by stony silence. Seventeen years as a pampered princess flashed before her as she leapt up from her chair and bolted for the stairs. Her mother had started to get up and go after her, but her father held her arm and said, "She's a teenager, we need to give her some space."

In her bottled-up rage, Marta had interpreted *that* as her parents not caring for the lives of the overwhelming majority of Russians who didn't enjoy their indulgent lifestyle. Her parents didn't care—but she did.

Tonight, she was going to meet her boyfriend, Gavrill, and join the protest. He had encouraged her to stay home, anticipating that the demonstrations would be sizeable. The police, who had been routed by protestors in a large riot a week ago, had been active on social media, announcing stringent actions they planned to use to tamp down rallies.

Carried along by the swelling stream of people walking with her, Marta texted Gavrill. *On the way to meet u. Coming to join the protests.*

Her phone chirped within seconds. *Where r u?*

On Ul Tkachey. Heading to Palace Square. Where r u?

Told u these protests tonight will be large and might get violent. Please don't come.

Want to help. Can't just stay home when everyone else is out there.

Please stay away!

Gavrill waited for another text as the crowd in Palace Square swelled around him. The throng of students was even larger than he had hoped it would be. Finally, his phone chirped. It was Marta. He trusted that she had heeded his warnings and would say she was going home. What he saw shocked him.

Fuck Dostoevsky, suffering doesn't have to be our lot. Everything is too expensive. Even I know that. The US and EU sanctions, fuck them too. And Putin's response, banning EU food imports, fuck that. No one cares. Have to do something. Coming whether you like it or not!

Gavrill stared at his phone for a tiny eternity. She was right, and he knew her well enough to know that nothing he could say would deter her. *Look for me a few meters south of the alexander column. Meet me there and be careful.*

Should be there in a few minutes.

Marta slid her phone into the pocket of her jeans and picked up her pace. In less than a minute, her phone chirped again. It was her father.

Where r u? Your mother and I are worried.

Dammit! She had told them she was going to study and then go to bed early. She had turned off the lights in her room before she slipped out the second-story window and climbed down the dacha's rough stone exterior. Why had they come into her room?

Don't worry daddy, u always told me to stand up for what I believe in, and I believe in what I'm doing tonight.

She slipped the phone back into her pocket and ignored the next chirp.

———

Petersburg's police chief waited impatiently for a report from his senior captain in Palace Square. Sitting in his headquarters on Liteyny Avenue, Sergey Krasilnikov reminded himself of the official name for his police force: the Main Administration for Internal Affairs of the City of St. Petersburg. Internal Affairs indeed. These were just kids who couldn't buy the bare necessities of life.

As Krasilnikov stewed, he groused about how many bosses he had to placate. It wasn't just Petersburg's mayor. No, he routinely got gratuitous advice from the bureaucrat who appointed him, the Governor of Petersburg, as well as from the head of the Petersburg Legislative Assembly. He even had to endure constant badgering from Russia's president, who just a week ago had reminded him that he had recommended him for this job and could withdraw his support at any time.

The most recent unhelpful call from Vladimir Putin had come less than an hour after his force had been overwhelmed by student protestors. Videos of the protestors pushing through police barricades and routing the hapless squad he had sent to take control had gone viral. The fucking cowards had run away from the protesters like scared little girls. Putin's call had been followed a short time later by one from a fuming Safronov, no doubt inspired by Putin chewing *him* out.

Krasilnikov didn't consider himself a genius, but he was smart enough to follow instructions and not let another protest get out of hand. He knew that if this student demonstration spiraled out of control, he would likely be the shortest-tenured police chief in Petersburg's history. His phone rang, and he looked at the name on the screen. It was his captain, Valery Umnov.

"What's going on in the square, Valery?"

"This mob of protestors is the biggest one we've seen. We're in position on the north side of Alexander Column, but if they push toward the Winter Palace, I don't know if we can stop them. I think you need to send more men."

Krasilnikov paused before replying. Umnov was his best captain, and he was capitulating to a mob of *kids*. He knew he should have gone there himself and taken control of things; but now it was too late.

The Main Department of Internal Affairs had infiltrated one of the student protest groups and had learned that this large demonstration was going to begin as just another of a seemingly endless stream of protests for more food. But once they had assembled a huge mob, the students intended to rush the Winter Palace and occupy it. Then, no doubt, they would stream their "victory" on social media for the world to see.

Krasilnikov had gotten it loud and clear from Safronov. If that happened, he wouldn't be asked to clean out his office—someone would do it for him. He would not see the inside of his headquarters again and probably would never see his pension.

"Valery, there are no more men. You've got the whole force there. You have trucks and water cannons and other equipment we have borrowed from the outlying districts. You have tear gas, and you have the dogs. Use what you have, or I'll send someone to relieve you who will."

While Krasilnikov spoke in measured terms, his boss's direction wasn't lost on Umnov. He merely said "yes, sir" and ended the call.

Dogs? We've never used dogs before. Do these idiots want that on some video that goes viral? Umnov trudged toward his front lines wondering if he was in control of anything.

———

As Marta Safronov converged on Palace Square, she had her phone in her hand. She needed to find Gavrill and was about to send him a text when her phone chirped. It was another text from her father.

Your mother and I need you to come home now. The people in Moscow want these protests broken. The police are authorized to use deadly force if necessary. Please don't go there.

Marta deleted the text and composed one to Gavrill. *In the square now. Where r u?*

His reply came seconds later. *Still close to alexander column. Next to two women with a large white banner that says food and freedom.*

Marta quickened her pace, and seconds later, her phone rang. *No one calls anymore*, she thought as she looked at the name on the display. It was her mother.

"Marta, please come home. You're in danger," her mother said between sobs. "It's too dangerous. Please, please come home."

"Mama, don't worry. I know what I'm doing," she snapped. Seconds later, she turned off her phone.

———————————

Valery Umnov didn't like the orders he was getting from his chief, but his first loyalty was to his men. He walked along the long line of his policemen arrayed in riot gear. God, they all looked like children playing war. Umnov climbed up on the trucks carrying the water cannons and talked with the dog handlers, as well as with the rest of his force. He offered words of encouragement to no one in particular.

"These kids aren't armed; hold your ground and they'll disperse.

"You know what our rules of engagement are.

"They just need to feel they've done something. It's getting colder by the minute. They'll go home soon."

Umnov was about to walk by one dog handler when he stopped. "What's your name, son?"

"Egor Mineyev, sir."

"And your dog's name?"

8

"Irinushka, Captain. It means 'Woman of Peace.'"

Woman of Peace, indeed. He suppressed a laugh at the irony of the dog's name.

"How old are you?"

"Eighteen."

"Be strong; this will all be over soon."

As Umnov walked away, he wondered if he should have asked the youngster how long he had been handling the enormous German Shepherd. The beast must weigh as much as her handler. He decided he really didn't want to know the answer.

———

Marta spied Gavrill and rushed up and embraced him. "I know you told me not to come, but you're here, and this is where I want to be."

Gavrill knew it was no use arguing with her. "Just stay by my side. My friends are up there. We're going to meet them." Gavrill paused a moment before continuing. "While we continue to chant, that group over there," he said, pointing to a spot along the front lines of the protestors, "they'll put on their gas masks and make for the Winter Palace."

"They're going to occupy it?" Marta asked.

"Yes, I told you tonight might get violent. We've been protesting for months, and nothing has changed. They need to know we're serious."

Gavrill grasped Marta's hand as they pushed their way through the chanting crowd and up toward the front of the protest lines.

———

As the chanting, singing crowd swelled and began throwing rocks at the police arrayed in front of them, Umnov scurried from spot to spot and tried to buck up his men.

"If they surge forward, shoot at their feet," he commanded to the man on top of a truck with his finger on the trigger of his water cannon. "That will spill them over fastest."

"Fire the gas at their front lines if they break and run toward us," he continued, gesturing to his men with the tear gas launchers, "but don your own gas masks first."

"Fire rubber bullets only if you're in danger," he added as he pointed his finger at a group of men holding rifles at the ready.

At the far end of the police line, Egor Mineyev had both hands on Irinushka's leash as he tried to control the huge Shepherd. His class had been rushed through handler school and "graduated" three weeks early because there weren't enough dog teams to control the rapidly proliferating protests around their city. He wondered if something he missed in his truncated training would have helped him learn how to restrain his bucking dog. For now, he just hung on to Irinushka for dear life.

———

Gavrill held Marta's left arm with both hands as the protestors' chanting grew louder and as they hurled more rocks at the police, most of which bounced harmlessly off their reinforced Plexiglas shields. They were at the leading edge of the protestors. The group that was going to rush the Winter Place was to their left, donning their masks to deal with the gas that was sure to come.

It all happened in a blink of an eye. As the four dozen students Gavrill had pointed out bolted toward the Winter Palace, the police began to fire tear gas while water cannon trucks maneuvered toward the charging group.

As the commotion built toward a crescendo, Egor Mineyev lost control of Irinushka and the dog ran toward the chanting students. Marta was in the front of the line, and the dog leapt on her, violently pulling her out of Gavrill's grasp. She went down with a thud, and the Shepherd, seventy-five pounds of sinew and muscle, was all over her.

Gavrill kicked wildly at the dog, trying to get it off Marta, but the beast was unfazed.

Marta thrashed at the Shepherd, trying to ward it off, but her rail-thin arms had little effect.

Gavrill jumped on Irinushka's back and tried to pull the Shepherd off Marta; but the dog yanked its head around, bit into his left forearm, and ripped his flesh to the bone. Gavrill rolled off the dog and fell to the ground, writhing in pain and holding his arm, trying to stop the torrent of blood.

The Shepherd was on Marta again as she kicked her legs and flailed her arms. The circle of protestors around her grew wider. They had seen what the dog had done to Gavrill, who was still on the ground holding his arm.

Marta mustered what little energy she had left and rammed her fist into Irinushka's snout. But that blow sapped the last of her strength, and as her arms fell away, the Shepherd did what its training and instincts told it to do, it went for Marta's neck and dug in hard.

She tried to jerk her head away—anything to get out of the dog's grip—but as she did, the beast, crazed by the blood gushing from her neck, continued to attack and bit into Marta's face.

Blood spurted everywhere, and that triggered some deep, primal instinct in Irinushka. She continued to chew Marta's face to shreds. The crowd of students dispersed as they feared the dog would attack them next.

Irinushka finally responded to the silent dog whistle and bounded back toward the police lines.

Gavrill crawled to Marta, bent over her body and wept unashamedly. He knew she was dead. Several other protestors, responding to Gavrill's cries for help, converged on them, lifted

11

Marta off the bloody cobblestones, and carried her body toward the back of the protestors' lines.

CHAPTER TWO

Supreme Allied Commander Europe (SACEUR) Headquarters, Mons, Belgium
(September 7, 0730 Central European Time)

Lieutenant Laura Peters sat at her desk outside of U.S. Navy Rear Admiral Ruth Morton's office, multitasking as she usually did. As aide to the senior intelligence officer in the U.S.-only cell attached to Supreme Allied Commander Europe (SACEUR), Peters had to run hard to fulfill a myriad of duties.

Located in an old nuclear bunker outside the main SACEUR building, the small group's spaces were modest, cramped and dingy. The U.S. cell coordinated with the larger, multinational SACEUR intelligence directorate, which worked in the main headquarters building. While there was constant coordination on most issues, there were more sensitive matters that were kept strictly within U.S. circles.

Peters was accustomed to running hard, and she had done so in all her previous assignments. But SACEUR was a bigger stage and one that challenged her. Like most military officers, she had a strong desire to serve her nation and had the additional motivation of being the only child of a Navy chief petty officer father who had aspired to join the officer ranks. That goal had eluded him, and he had encouraged his daughter to apply for a Navy ROTC scholarship.

She won one of those coveted slots and had excelled academically and athletically at the University of Virginia. When it

13

came time to select a career field, she did her due diligence and saw that, while the Navy had made some strides, it had not yet fully accepted women as equal partners commanding ships and aircraft squadrons. Therefore, she had selected the intelligence field upon graduation, suspecting that it would provide a more level professional playing field and afford her the opportunity to prove herself.

Peters had distinguished herself in a number of prior tours, most notably as a brand-new lieutenant assigned to U.S. Southern Command, where she had worked with Navy SEAL Rick Holden to uncover a military plot to try to impeach the U.S. president. That, and strong performance in a follow-on tour with a Joint U.S. military intelligence detachment at Camp Zama, Japan, had identified her as an up-and-coming professional. She had opted for back-to-back overseas assignments so she could serve in Europe.

While the Navy typically balked at sending its officers and sailors on successive tours outside the continental United States, it often made exceptions for officers who were single. It was all about the math: It cost much more to move, and then house, families on overseas assignments. And in her quiet moments, Peters did have to admit that she had applied a significant bit of charm on her detailing officer at the Navy's personnel command in order to seal this deal.

The man was on the fence about assigning her to SACEUR until Peters took personal leave to visit the Bureau of Naval Personal in Millington, Tennessee, and lobby for the assignment. Her detailer didn't know whether it was her persistence, or having the five-foot, eight-inch, athletic-looking woman in her crisp khakis standing in front of his desk, riveting him with her eyes. But whatever it was, it finally swayed him to not only write her orders to SACEUR, but to put her in a package of officers to be interviewed to serve as Morton's aide.

SACEUR, headed by U.S. Army General Davis O'Sullivan, was easily the most complex and diverse of all the United States combatant commands. O'Sullivan held the second-highest military position within NATO, below only the chairman of the NATO Military Committee. He was responsible for the military efforts of the twenty-nine NATO nations and had several million active and reserve military personnel under his command.

Morton's role (and, by extension, Peters') was to coordinate the all-source intelligence needed to support NATO operations. Morton was a fair, but demanding, boss with a taciturn manner. She typically summoned Peters to her office with an insistent text message.

Peters was working her way through the morning e-mail queue, sorting through the hundreds of e-mails Morton got each day and sending her boss only those of importance, when her secure cell phone chirped with a familiar text.

Need you.

Peters walked the few feet to the door of Morton's office, knocked twice, entered, and came to attention a few feet in front of Morton's desk.

Morton rose and asked, "How's your day going so far, Lieutenant?"

It was only 0730, and the question perplexed Peters, so she replied with a safe, "Just fine, Admiral."

Morton worked her face up into a fierce frown and said, "Well, it's about to get worse. You're fired."

Peters couldn't hide her shock as she felt her jaw grow slack and her knees begin to buckle. Her mind went into overdrive: What had she screwed up? What had she neglected to do? What had she done to make Morton angry? She had worked for her for four months and had received nothing but praise. It was muted praise to be sure. Morton wasn't anyone's idea of a warm and mentoring leader, but it was praise nonetheless.

15

Despite summoning all the self-control she could muster, Peters began to shake.

Morton moved from behind her desk and motioned for Peters to sit in one of the two chairs in front of it. The admiral took the other chair. The chairs were several feet apart, and Morton moved hers closer to Peters so their knees were almost touching.

Peters braced herself for what was coming next, undoubtedly Morton telling her what offense had caused this firing.

Morton reached out and took Peters' two hands in hers.

The fact that her aloof boss was holding her hands shocked her, but what she heard next ratcheted that surprise up to another level.

"Laura," Morton began.

In the four months working for the admiral, her boss had never addressed her by her first name.

A broad smile formed on Morton's face. "You're fired as my aide because I have a more important assignment for you."

Peters let out a sigh of relief, but her head was spinning nonetheless.

"Look, Laura, you've done a fantastic job as my aide. You know the reason I selected you had nothing to do with you being a woman and my favoring females over males and trying to give a junior woman a career leg up. You completely outshined the other three officers I interviewed for this assignment."

"Yes, ma'am, but I don't—"

"You don't get it, I know," Morton interrupted. "I can find a qualified, but less-capable, officer to sort through my message queue, manage my appointments, arrange my travel plans and take care of all the things that go with being a flag aide.

"But keeping you in this billet doesn't fully leverage what you bring to the table. I've gone through your service record in detail. And I have also gotten feedback from my senior staff officers. They tell me that when I've been on leave or have otherwise not needed you, you've always taken it upon yourself to show up at Lieutenant

Colonel Sauter's anticipatory intelligence cell to lend a hand. Candidly, he tells me he counts on you as much as any of his permanently assigned officers. The colonel is a Marine and doesn't offer praise lightly."

"But all his billets are covered already. He doesn't have space for another officer. It's a pretty small cell," Peters replied.

"He didn't, until now. Air Force Captain Fred Warren has been a mainstay of that cell for almost two years and has requested early transfer back to the States because he has an exceptional family member who needs ongoing medical treatment in the States. We want to honor that request, and we would rather fill that spot with you, if you're willing."

Peters was still trying to get her brain around the fact that Morton was acting like a human being and not a robot. The surprised lieutenant was also having trouble processing what this opportunity might mean. While Morton didn't emit a great deal of warmth, she did treat her fairly. Additionally, being the flag aide to a two-star admiral meant that she accompanied her boss to a plethora of important meetings where weighty matters were discussed and where vital decisions were made.

Peters knew those opportunities would pay off in spades as she worked her way up through the ranks. However, at the end of the day, she had to admit that working as a flag aide involved just being always available and not really doing anything she considered important. Peters wanted action—not a job as a benchwarmer.

She knew she would have all the action she could handle if she worked full-time in the anticipatory intelligence cell that Lieutenant Colonel Martin Sauter had stewardship over. The small cell had been established in 2009, during the tenure of the then-SACEUR commander, Admiral James Stavridis. The unit had proven itself invaluable in its relatively short history by harnessing the power of a state-of-the-art computing infrastructure, mining well-curated big data, and applying artificial intelligence and machine learning to provide anticipatory, actionable intelligence.

These advanced technologies, combined with specially designed collation architectures and algorithms, could electronically filter all-source raw intelligence data and distill the basic elements of a problem faster than even the best analysts. Over the past decade-plus, this information had provided vital early warning of a variety of impending crises. It was fascinating work, and Peters had reveled in it every time she could steal away and spend some time there as a part-time helper.

Now she was being offered the opportunity to be a member of this high-octane team. Peters was as ambitious as any junior military officer. She didn't consider herself a climber, but she craved the professional respect that came with taking on the toughest assignments. As the daughter of a Navy chief petty officer, Peters knew that strong performance equaled career success. In a still-male-dominated U.S. military, she felt, rightly or wrongly, that she had to outperform her male counterparts just to keep pace.

"I know that you have your top-secret clearance and Colonel Sauter has let you participate in some of his cell's activities," Morton continued, "but we will have to get you read into some compartmentalized programs so you can make the biggest possible contribution. Even though that cell is of vital importance to this command, it is still thinly manned, so everyone has to be ready to pull their weight."

"Yes, Admiral. I will, and thank you so much—"

Morton cut her off. "Laura, don't thank me. You've gotten a taste of the cell as you've helped out from time to time. But with all the crap Russia has been pulling lately, every member of that group is overworked and stressed out. You're going to earn your keep, believe me. Tomorrow, I start interviewing candidates to replace you, so get back to your desk and start writing up a pass-down file for your relief. Otherwise, you'll be a hostage with me."

"Yes, Admiral—right away," Peters responded as she beat a hasty retreat. She couldn't hide her smile; this could be the best thing that ever happened to her professionally. She had put relationships on hold as she had focused almost exclusively on her career and had accepted back-to-back overseas assignments. Now, with this high-intensity job about to begin, she knew she would have to put anything resembling a normal social life on hold a bit longer.

CHAPTER THREE

**Office of the Russian Federation President, The Kremlin,
Moscow, Russia
(September 7, 1145 Moscow Standard Time)**

Vladimir Putin sat at his desk in the Senate Building of the Kremlin
complex. The office of the president of the Russian Federation and
supreme commander in chief was opulent by any standard. *Ironic*,
Putin thought to himself. The Communist regime he had served as a
KGB officer for many years sang the praises of their predecessors
who had overthrown the czar a century ago; but he could imagine
the last Russian czar, Nicholas II, feeling at home at his desk in this
well-appointed room.

None of that mattered at the moment as he sat and stewed,
sipping a cup of strong tea. He insisted that his staff upload
whatever it was they wanted to tell him to his tablet before asking
for a meeting. His chief of staff had done just that, and now Putin
flipped through the pages of the report. It was a disaster by any
measure. Finally, he buzzed his secretary and told her to send in his
chief of staff.

The man knew this was not going to be a pleasant meeting; far
from it. He had been Putin's chief of staff and alter ego for just over
two years. He recalled how his predecessor had been sacked for not
carrying out the Russian president's orders, or at least not carrying
them out to his boss's satisfaction.

"Talk to me," Putin said as his chief of staff approached his
desk.

"Mr. President, I think you've read the reports about the student protests in Petersburg last night."

"Are you sure they were students and not just agitators?" Putin snapped.

"The police arrested about four dozen people. All of them were young," he began, and then added, "But they kept them out of the Winter Palace."

"Your report said there were several policemen injured, and two are in critical condition. Were any killed?"

"No, thankfully none were. Petersburg's police chief is on his way to Mariinsky Hospital to visit the men who were injured."

"I want Pavel to send me a report about the injured men soon, this morning," Putin commanded.

His chief of staff stood in shocked silence. The report had highlighted the fact that Pavel Safronov's daughter had been among the student protestors killed, and in a most horrific way. He knew that Putin was Safronov's mentor. Petersburg's mayor had been in this very office many times, paying courtesy calls on the Russian president. Safronov had as close a relationship with Putin as his aloof and detached boss allowed. The president had to know the man needed to grieve, not spend time feeding him information.

"Mr. President, I noted in my report that Mayor Safronov's daughter was one of the students killed."

"Yes, I read that. There were three students killed and about two dozen injured, right?"

"Yes, sir."

"Safronov's daughter shouldn't have been there protesting. If he couldn't control her, that's not my worry. He's the mayor. I want my report, and I insist on knowing immediately if any of those policemen in critical condition die."

"I'll see to it."

"That's all. I have other things I need to worry about."

His chief of staff left quickly, knowing he would be the target of Putin's anger if he stayed a moment longer.

The chief of staff was unquestionably loyal to his boss, but he was no sycophant. Sure, Putin had helped Safronov's career, but Petersburg's mayor had paid it back many times over. Couldn't he muster a little compassion? The man had just lost his only child.

He had reconciled himself to Putin's increasing moodiness. While he had only been his chief of staff for two years, he had aligned himself with Vladimir Vladimirovich Putin for over two decades, beginning in 2000, when Putin was first elected president of the Russian Federation. He had guessed then that Putin's goal was to be a latter-day Russian czar who would never relinquish power, and he had been right. He had worked for the Russian president and prime minister in a long series of increasingly important jobs. Now he was as close to the seat of power as it got.

The moodiness: he *got* that. Putin's first presidency was marked by spectacular economic growth as the Russian economy, fueled by the commodities boom and high oil prices, soared for over a decade. Putin had made *all* Russians happy as the country's GDP rose rapidly and they saw their purchasing power skyrocket. And more importantly, he had made a new class of Russian oligarchs fabulously wealthy. They cheered him and rewarded him generously.

That seemed a lifetime ago. The crash in oil prices, along with Western sanctions imposed as a result of Russia's annexation of Crimea and military intervention in Eastern Ukraine, had dumped Russia's economy into a recession. The statistics didn't lie. More than twenty million Russians, over fifteen percent of the population, lived in poverty, and the numbers were growing. The oligarchs who once applauded Putin now had nothing but contempt for the man. As Russia's economy continued to sag, his support was melting away just as quickly.

While all this troubled Putin, his chief of staff knew that these issues were not his biggest worry. What the Russian president was focused on, almost obsessively so, was the unrest within his country. Yes, the average citizen in Russia was suffering a significantly diminished quality of life. Hell, call it what it was, life in the *Rodina* (homeland) was starting to feel like that of a third-world country. Food was becoming as scarce as it was in the worst days of the Communist regime, and what *was* available was offered at inflated prices. But food protests and riots in many of Russia's largest cities? It was unbelievable. Was this his Russia?

While Putin was embarrassed that his fellow citizens couldn't suck it up and wait for Russia's economy to turn around, as his ministers told him it would, what was driving him over the edge was that his security forces couldn't control the protests. His long service in Russia's KGB told him this was nothing more than a failure of nerve by those in charge, especially the mayors of Russia's cities and their police chiefs and other security forces. Pavel Safronov had lost control too? He was the man he had mentored. And now he had lost his daughter in one of those demonstrations. Maybe that would bring him to his senses and help him get a grip on his city.

Later that day, Pavel and Olga Safronov were in Petersburg's morgue. It was the same grim place where, in the fall of 2015, the bodies of those killed in the Metrojet Flight 9268 crash in Egypt had been brought.

Marta Safronov had been whisked away from Palace Square in an ambulance. They knew she was dead, but there were procedures. Gavrill had sprinted to the Safronov dacha. Seeing the bruised and battered man with a huge bandage wrapped around his bloody left forearm, the housekeeper had enough sense to call the mayor, not his wife, to the door.

Safronov stood in shocked silence as Gavrill delivered his breathless report, or as much as he could blurt out between sobs. After roughly dismissing Gavrill, Safronov had trudged into their sitting room and broken the news to his wife. Olga's wails and cries had brought the household staff on the run, and with a nod from Safronov, their butler had called the family physician. The man arrived within a half hour and, over Olga's protests, administered a strong sedative.

By the time his wife awoke in midmorning, Safronov had learned the full details of their daughter's death: how the dog had shredded her face beyond recognition; how the doctors at Mariinsky Hospital had done heroic things to try to save her, but had failed; how his police chief had already cashiered his captain who had been in charge in Palace Square; and how he had the entire dog team under investigation and the team's leader under arrest—as well as a dozen other details. None of these explanations assuaged his grief or that of his wife.

His deputy mayor had the foresight to call the morgue and ask what needed to happen to identify Marta's body. The chief medical examiner had suggested, in the strongest possible terms, that the mayor not bring his wife when he came to identify their daughter. He told him that, no matter what miracles he tried to work, there was no way he could reconstruct her face to bear any resemblance to the beautiful young girl she once was. Safronov had begged his wife not to come, but she was insistent.

Now, they were here. The chief medical examiner greeted them outside the morgue and assured them that, using DNA, they were able to identify their daughter's body and there was no need to complete the gruesome task of looking at her mutilated corpse. Safronov agreed, but Olga was adamant. "I want to see my daughter!" she shouted.

The chief medical examiner had no choice but to usher them into the bowels of the morgue. Petersburg's mayor and his wife stood there as the chief medical examiner signaled his assistant to open the curtain of the window separating them from Marta's lifeless body. As the curtain was pulled back, Olga shrieked in horror and collapsed in Safronov's arms. At that moment, it all changed for him.

———————

Vladimir Putin finished reading the report the Director of the Federal Security Service of the Russian Federation (the FSB) had sent him, put down his tablet, and shook his head in disgust. The successor agency of the USSR's Committee of State Security (the KGB), where he had spent the early years of his career and risen to the rank of lieutenant colonel, continued to disappoint. He would make the FSB's director, General Aleksandr Bortnikov, wait in his outer offices for another hour just to remind him who determined his fate.

He was sure Bortnikov would have all manner of excuses: the FSB had suffered steep budget cuts, the local police in Russia's largest cities were woefully undermanned, the internet and social media had made it difficult for the FSB to do much of anything without scrutiny, what passed for a free press had them under a microscope, and a long list of other reasons. Feeble excuses. Bornikov's FSB had virtually unlimited power to enforce internal security, but he had made hash of that responsibility. This would never have happened in *his* KGB.

Putin busied himself with a dozen small tasks, whatever it took to ensure Bortnikov had to cool his heels and worry, before finally buzzing his secretary and having the general ushered into his office.

"Mr. President," the general began as he approached Putin's desk. "You wanted to see me? I sent you a report; was it satisfactory?"

Stiff and officious as usual, Putin found himself thinking. *Maybe if he would shed some of his tin soldier qualities, the man could actually make something happen.*

Putin got out of his chair and stood behind his desk, scowling. He didn't invite the general to sit.

"Your report was satisfactory, General. The results you are getting are anything but," he hissed.

"Mr. President—" Bortnikov countered.

"Stop!" Putin interrupted. "You've made all your excuses in your report. I don't need you repeating them."

Bortnikov paused before responding. He knew Putin could dismiss him at a whim, as he had done with many others during his almost two decades as president and as prime minister of Russia. He began carefully. "Mr. President, as you know, the protests in some of our biggest cities—not only Petersburg, but also Novosibirsk, Yekaterinburg and others—have been growing, surpassing some of our worst fears. And then there are..."

Putin looked down at his desk as Bortnikov droned on, making excuse after excuse. The KGB would have rounded up the student protest leaders long ago and sent them to the gulag. Did he have to run the damn FSB himself? Finally, after several minutes of this drivel, he'd had enough.

"General Bortnikov, you disappointment me. If I thought there was anyone in your organization capable of doing anything right, I'd relieve you on the spot. Sadly, they're all just as inept as you—"

"Mr. President!" Bortnikov interrupted, though as soon as those words left his lips, he began to have second thoughts. "If you no longer need my services, I will resign immediately."

"I'm not letting you get off that easy. Use the power you have and shut down these protests for good. And stop sending me reports—I don't need them. I've got this mess with Belarus I need to deal with. Now get out of my sight and send in my chief of staff."

Bortnikov departed, and Putin's chief of staff entered his office and closed the door.

———————

The ground floor of the White House West Wing houses, what is beyond question, the most intense five thousand square feet in the frenetic city of Washington, D.C. The White House Situation Room, the Sit Room for short, is where a small staff composed of the brightest minds from the U.S. intelligence agencies—DIA, CIA, NSA, NGA and the rest—ingest mountains of information and prepare daily reports for the president. The Sit Room also contains two secure video teleconference rooms, where the president and his closest advisors monitor actions in the field and speak with U.S. combatant commanders, ambassadors, and others across the globe.

The Sit Room staff had been mining troves of data, some of it at the highest levels of classification, but most of it from international news media feeds, on the violent student demonstrations and riots in Saint Petersburg. These staffers passed this information to the Sit Room watch floor, as well as to those senior staff responsible for writing the President's Daily Brief. As the most senior staffer on duty pulled the report together on his secure tablet, weighing which events around the globe needed to be brought to the president's immediate attention and which didn't, the events in Palace Square were consigned to a footnote.

———————

Later that day, a stream of Vladimir Putin's most senior intelligence, security and military officers, as well as ministers and advisors, made their way to the Security Council Meeting Hall in the Kremlin compound. Officially "The Moscow Kremlin," but usually referred to as the Kremlin, the fortified complex in the heart of Moscow overlooked the Moskva River to the south, Saint Basil's Cathedral and Red Square to the east, and the Alexander Garden to the west. It had been the seat of power in Russia since the days of the czars in the fifteenth century.

As their armored limousines converged on the headquarters of the government of the Russian Federation and the official residence of its president, the Kremlin's imposing walls reminded each of them that the name Kremlin means, "Fortress Inside a City."

Their staffs had been briefed on the reason for the summons, and each organization had worked feverishly to prepare its principal for the meeting.

Inside the work zone of the Senate Palace, those whom Putin had summoned arrived at the Security Council Meeting Hall. As they entered the palatial room, the officials were dwarfed beneath the two-tiered chandelier that hung from the arched ceiling. The towering white walls were embedded with more than a dozen dark gray marble columns, each decorated with an ornate gilded cap where it met the crown molding at the base of the ceiling. As the officials took their assigned positions at the long table, each had talking points to address the questions they anticipated the president of the Russian Federation would ask.

Once they were all in place behind their chairs, Putin entered and stood at the head of the table. He began without preamble: "The President of Belarus can't control her country, and now terrorists are strangling our oil transshipment pipelines. My staff has asked each of yours to come up with options to stop this."

Putin paused a long moment and scanned the sea of faces around the table. Then he continued. "Let me be clear; the only options I want to hear are those that involve us taking action inside Belarus. Now sit down, and let's get to work."

As the assembled group of Putin's most senior advisers took their seats, they knew it would be a long meeting—and likely a fateful one.

CHAPTER FOUR

Office of the President of Belarus, Republic Palace, Minsk, Belarus
(September 8, 0830 Eastern European Time)

The subject of Putin's urgent meeting was in her office in the government administrative grounds in Minsk, the capital of the Republic of Belarus. Independent since 1990 when it broke away from the dissolving Soviet Union, with a land area of just over two hundred thousand square kilometers and a population of less than ten million, Belarus was one of the smaller countries in Europe—and one surrounded by powerful neighbors.

Maria Sechenov, president of the Republic of Belarus, felt that smallness acutely as she read the report from her minister of state security and gauged the impact recent events would have on her biggest neighbor, Russia. The president of the Russian Federation had been unambiguous with his threats: Stop Belarusian vigilantes from sabotaging the oil pipelines that delivered Russian oil not just to Belarus, but to many other European nations as well, or he would be forced take action to stop them.

President Sechenov wasn't a religious woman, but she had been raised in the Russian Orthodox Church and bible study had been part of her upbringing. The quote from Galatians 6:7: *Be not deceived; God is not mocked: for whatsoever a man soweth, that shall he also reap* was something that now dominated her thoughts.

Sechenov was part of the tiny Russian minority that made up less than ten percent of the population of her country. But while they were just a sliver of the nation's nine and a half million people, the Russian descendants in Belarus held the whip hand. In much the same way that Saddam Hussein's Sunni faction had dominated Shias in Iraq, or as the Assad family's Alawite clan still rules the Sunnis in Syria, the Russian minority that populated the eastern part of Belarus bordering Russia held onto power ruthlessly.

Sechenov had grown up in that privileged minority and clawed her way to the top of the government. In every assignment during that climb, she ensured that ethnic Russians had all the privileges and the Belarusian majority, which made up almost ninety percent of the population, got less food, less energy, and less of just about any other necessity. In a nation with a per capita income of just seven thousand U.S. dollars, that meant that the majority of her citizens lived below what Western nations had dubbed the "poverty line."

Maria Sechenov had been in office for less than a year since unseating her predecessor, an autocrat who had cozied too close to Russia and who was cast out by Belarusians wanting to preserve their national identity. But she was walking an increasingly precarious fine line. She tried not to alarm her Russian supporters by giving too much to the ethnic Belarusians, but she had to do something to try to placate the country's majority. Her predecessors should have been able to predict the results of what they had sowed.

The Belarusian majority wanted two things: a more equitable distribution of their nation's limited assets and integration with the European Union rather than being absorbed into the Russian Federation's Eurasian Economic Union. Sechenov knew from where her support came, and would never let the first thing happen. She also knew that the best way to prosperity for her nation was to join the EU.

But things had spiraled downward too quickly for her to even think about pulling further away from the Russian Federation. All she could do at the moment was react to events. The Belarusian majority had been increasingly vehement in demanding food and energy, and while her security forces had managed to maintain control and her government had officially dismissed the demonstrations as events fomented by "agitators," *that* played into the hands of the leaders of the uprising. The Belarusian majority knew that her power was tied to that of the president of the Russian Federation, and they knew where the pressure points were.

The attacks on the oil pipelines had started only two months ago, but they were already having a dramatic effect. While the price of oil had crashed, it still remained a primary source of income for Russia, and Europe was its biggest customer.

The Belarusian vigilantes planned their attacks on the pipelines skillfully. As the Belarusian security forces, the Internal Troops, reached the site of a breech, the rebels attacked another location. With thousands of kilometers of pipelines snaking their way across the country, defending them was an impossible task for the over-stretched Belarusian brigades. Angry energy ministers in European capitals threatened to cancel their contracts for Russian oil if Moscow could not deliver.

But worse, it was a two-front war for Sechenov's Internal Troops. Even with three independent brigades and seven separate battalions, there simply were not enough of them to combat vigilantes *and* enforce crowd control in protests that seemed to be springing up everywhere. While a militia of hardcore ethnic Belarusians conducted the attacks on the pipelines, there were increasingly large and violent demonstrations in Minsk, as well as in the nation's smaller cities. Two nights ago, more than forty thousand demonstrators had massed in Minsk's Independence Square.

Maria Sechenov wanted answers, but none of her ministers or assistants were giving her any. She knew it was only a matter of time before Vladimir Putin's limited patience would be exhausted.

———

That night, Patricia Bailey, a reporter for CNN's Eastern Europe and Russia division, was shouting to be heard over the din of the protestors massing and chanting in Minsk's Independence Square. At his anchor desk in CNN's Atlanta headquarters, veteran news anchor Robert Wright looked at the swelling crowd as Bailey's live stream appeared on his screen.

"Bob, I think you can see Independence Square behind me. We reported from here two nights ago, and the protests were loud; but eventually, the estimated forty thousand people who massed here drifted away peacefully. Tonight, conservative estimates put the numbers in the square north of seventy-five thousand."

"Patricia, would you remind our viewers why these people are protesting and how the government of President Maria Sechenov is reacting?"

Wright and Bailey had teed up this question an hour before the broadcast, and Bailey had written down and rehearsed a detailed response. She had practiced it enough times that she was certain she could make it sound spontaneous while what she had written rolled on the teleprompter one of her assistants held.

Bailey cared not one whit that the protest swelling behind her might result in violence and that people might actually die. She didn't ask to be in Minsk; she had been promised Russia—either Moscow or Saint Petersburg. But when the new assignments had come out, she had been consigned to this third-world shithole.

She understood the Moscow assignment. That went to a veteran reporter who had been with CNN for over two decades, spoke fluent Russian, and had a trove of broadcasting awards. But Saint Petersburg? That...that *bitch*...Sandra Collins had gotten that, and she had no creds. Hell, she had been with CNN less than half the time Bailey had been with the network. What middle-aged executive in a loveless marriage who inhabited one of CNN's corner offices was she sleeping with?

And it was getting worse. That slut's reporting during Saint Petersburg's recent riots had gotten rave reviews. Collins was fast becoming the network's golden girl. If Bailey was going to claw her way over and past her, she had to hit it out of the park. Tonight might be her night.

Bailey's ego was so enormous that she chose to forget why she was hired by CNN in the first place. Her father, Senator John Bailey, had been chairman of the powerful Senate Commerce Committee that had oversight over the Federal Communications Commission and, by extension, all U.S. media companies.

When Patricia Bailey was looking for an internship during her senior year at Georgetown, CNN was eager to please Senator Bailey and offered her a prime position. They ensured that she wasn't assigned to do any of the drudge work typically assigned to interns. When she graduated a year later—mindful of the Senator's frequent inquires as to "how's my girl doing?"—they hired her permanently.

As the teleprompter rolled, Bailey laid pipe for the *why* behind the protests: The Belarusian economy was still mired in recession, the government of Maria Sechenov had made promises during her election campaign they could not possibly keep, the ethnic Russians in Belarus were getting an even bigger slice of a still-shrinking pie, the protestors were becoming increasingly emboldened by the tepid response from the Minsk police and the Internal Troops, and a host of other factors.

Wright interrupted Bailey while she was in midsentence. "Patricia, I see smoke behind you—and are those gunshots I hear?"

Bailey jerked her head around and then turned back toward the camera. She began breathlessly. "Bob, we talked with protest

33

leaders this morning as we watched them bring steel barricades into Independence Square. One of their spokeswomen said they had broken into an armory on the outskirts of this city and stolen scores of gas masks and a cache of tear gas and gas launchers. I see that the protestors are firing tear gas at the police and the police are firing at them."

"Patricia, they're shooting rubber bullets, aren't they?" Wright asked hopefully.

"Bob!" she shouted, "I see at least a half dozen…no…make it more than a dozen protestors down. The police are rushing forward, and the protestors are pushing them back. Wait! Here come some military vehicles. They're crashing into the protestors' barriers …they're…they're flipping them over and…and…my God, Bob, they're crushing the people…oh the humanity!" Bailey finished with a flourish, liberally borrowing a reporter's words from the Hindenburg disaster over eight decades ago.

Bailey continued her breathless and frantic reporting, describing what she saw and embellishing it where she needed. She hoped that bitch Collins was drinking it all in. We'd see who CNN's golden girl was going to be now.

As the battle in Independence Square raged and more and more limp bodies littered the cobblestones, Bailey found that she no longer had to hype her report. The carnage shocked even her icy persona.

CHAPTER FIVE

**Naval Special Warfare Command, Coronado, California
(September 9, 0645, Pacific Daylight Time)**

It was early morning in Coronado, California, and the marine layer chilled the air. Rick Holden looked at the twenty-seven Navy SEAL candidates of Class 335, who had spent the last forty-five minutes in the surf, and shook his head. They were a sorry-looking lot, but as one man struggled to emerge from the surf, another man lent him a hand. *They all just might make it*, he thought.

Holden was new to the Naval Special Warfare Command, NSWC for short, and was the Training Component Phase One officer. He had been with these men, as well as their fellow SEAL candidates who had washed out, for most of the summer. Class 335 had begun with 145 men, men carefully screened for Basic Underwater Demolition/SEAL training, or BUD/S. Twenty-nine from that class had made it through "hell week," but two were too battered to continue. Past experience said that not all the twenty-seven survivors would make it through the six-month BUD/S ordeal and then complete the seven months of SEAL Qualification Training.

"You've been here for over two years, Senior Chief," Holden began. "How does this class measure up to others you've seen?"

Senior Chief Petty Officer Alex Wilson rubbed his shaved head and replied, "I think they're a bit better, sir. The Navy has stepped up their screening process to weed out the men who come here for the wrong reasons, and they're mostly doing a pretty good job."

"Mostly?"

"Well, *El Tee* [LT]," Wilson began, using the common moniker derived from the Navy's official abbreviation for lieutenant, "I think it's a lot easier with the enlisted. They come from other parts of the Navy, and they get it right between the running lights about not wasting the Navy's time if they aren't really serious about becoming SEALs...."

Wilson's voice trailed off.

"And the officers?" Holden prodded.

"Well, sir, the officers come right out of college or the Naval Academy. Most of them are jocks and...and...."

"*And*, Senior?"

"It's like this, sir. No disrespect to you officers, but some of these men have egos as deep and wide as the Grand Canyon. See that officer over there, that guy who's really ripped." Wilson pointed to an officer trainee struggling to do one more pushup. "My bet is he's gonna ring the bell before the day's over."

"Ensign Franklin?" Holden asked, his voice and body language conveying astonishment. "He was starting fullback at the Naval Academy last year. He's one tough kid."

"Mind and body, sir...mind and body. He looks like Adonis, but that won't be enough to get him through."

As if on cue, the struggling trainee stood up and walked over to the brass ship's bell lashed to a stanchion outside the BUD/S training office. He made no move, just standing and staring at the bell.

"You had enough of this, Mister Franklin?" Wilson asked.

Franklin didn't respond, but just stood there shivering, his eyes locked on the bell.

"Look, sir, here's the deal," Wilson continued. "You either want to do this or you don't. Either ring the frickin' bell or get your sorry ass back out there and keep pushing them out."

BUD/S candidate Franklin looked at Wilson, then Holden, and then Wilson again, seeking sympathy or encouragement. There was none. Franklin shrugged the shrug of a defeated man. He grabbed the braded lanyard tied to the bell's clapper.

CLANG! CLANG! CLANG!

The other trainees doing pushups in the sand looked up to see who of their number had quit.

"What the fuck are you girls looking at?" Wilson shouted. "Get your heads down and keep pumping!"

So ended the attempt of yet another physically, but maybe not mentally, capable young man to become a Navy SEAL. Head down, he turned and walked off the grinder.

Ringing the bell was the way a SEAL trainee let everyone know he'd had enough of the torture that was Navy SEAL training. That was why the shiny brass bell sat in a prominent place on the grinder, within easy reach of any recruit who wanted to quit. Franklin would not be the last trainee from this class to "ring out."

"I've got it from here, El Tee. I know you've got your meeting with Commander Rowley. I'll get these guys cleaned up and ready for their next event."

"Thanks, Senior," Holden replied as he headed to the training building.

Talking with Wilson reminded Holden that he had once worn the chief's anchors. But that was the only way their backgrounds were similar.

Holden had not begun his career in the Navy, but rather in the CIA. He had been a covert operator with the Special Activities Division, or SAD (later renamed the Special Activities Center), and had been deployed to Eastern Europe, where the Agency leveraged his extensive language skills. He had successfully plied his trade until an operation in Ukraine went terribly wrong.

After that, it was too dangerous to keep him in the field for other Special Activities Division operations, so the Agency gave him three choices: end his employment with the CIA, return to Langley for a desk assignment, or go somewhere outside the CIA and perform useful work until the Agency felt it was necessary to call him back.

Holden rejected the first option out of hand. A second-generation American and the only son of a Polish father and Czech mother who had emigrated to America when the Iron Curtin fell on Eastern Europe, he wanted to serve the country that had given his parents a second chance. And to no one's surprise, he never considered taking a desk assignment at Langley.

Holden picked the final option; and, thanks to a handshake agreement between the CIA and the Department of Defense, the service record of Navy Reserve Chief Petty Officer Richard Holden "materialized" in the Navy's personnel bureau.

It didn't take long for his new masters to realize two things: Holden wouldn't be happy in an administrative or clerical role, and that his SAD-developed skill set would make him a natural fit for the part of the Navy that most resembled the Special Activities Division, the Navy SEALs. It helped that Holden *looked* like a SEAL. A full six feet, two inches tall and a finely muscled 180 pounds, Holden had remained as fit as he was when he played tennis competitively: first at the University of Virginia, and later on the professional satellite tour.

The Navy SEAL community is small, and a great deal of finesse was required to ensure that Holden blended in and his cover was maintained. Navy Reserve Chief Rick Holden was assigned to a new unit where virtually all the men were strangers to one another.

While no one was able to tease out the fact that Holden wasn't a career SEAL who had worked his way up through the ranks in the Reserves, that was as far as being undercover went. He was drawn into intense action as a SEAL chief aboard USS *Coronado*, and subsequently as a SEAL officer embarked in USS *Carl Vinson*.

That was enough for the Agency, and they insisted that he be assigned somewhere where there would not be any action. Shore duty at the Naval Special Warfare Command Training Component seemed like the best choice.

While he enjoyed his life as a Navy SEAL, especially the opportunity to work with men who were warriors, this assignment would not have been his choice. Putting other men through the brutal torture of SEAL training that he himself had never had to endure grated against his sense of fair play. But he wasn't calling the shots; the Agency was.

He was also worried that this assignment might blow his cover. While most civilians broke the ice with a new acquaintance by asking where the person was from or what school they had attended, the typical way that SEALs self-identified was by naming their BUD/S class.

Holden's handlers had worked with the Navy to select a class that was appropriate for someone his age, and one where most of the graduates had left the service. That decreased the chances of anyone connecting the dots and finding out he was not a career SEAL. But now that he was on the front lines of pushing BUD/S candidates, he was constantly on guard, and the fact that he had to perpetuate a lie troubled him deeply.

Holden had no idea when, or even if, he would be called back to the CIA's Special Activities Center, but as his father had told him whenever he faced a tough challenge, "Just put your head down and swim, Rick." He also had to admit to himself that after back-to-back operational assignments where he had been drawn into caldrons that almost cost him his life, having some time to decompress on shore duty wasn't a bad thing.

All he knew was that he was not to inquire—he would be called. A unique ring tone on his phone would be the first indication that the Agency needed him again. And while the uncertainty of not knowing when he would be yanked out of his current assignment and sent who knows where by the Agency would be a stressor for most, as a single man with no serious girlfriend, Holden was not troubled by the same sorts of things that bothered most people.

One former girlfriend had even called him a "Goody Two-shoes," and sometimes he wondered if what he learned serving as an altar boy and being an Eagle Scout still dominated how he approached the world. For now, he'd just do the best job he could and ensure that as many as possible of the right men made it through SEAL training.

CHAPTER SIX

Home of the Russian Ambassador, Minsk, Belarus (September 10, 0815 Eastern European Time)

Inside her enormous residence in the Trinity Hill neighborhood of Minsk, hard by the Svislach River, Russia's ambassador to Belarus sat in her kitchen. Iskra Baryshev watched as her husband dripped some honey into their simmering cups of tea. "Are you trying to make me sweeter for today's meetings?" she asked, her full lips breaking into a slight smile.

"Only to begin your meetings, dear; only to begin," he replied.

Baryshev considered this for a moment. "Sweet" wasn't the first impression men usually had when they met her. "Gorgeous" was more like it. "*Hot*," one aging and horny bureaucrat had blurted out when he first met her at a party in Moscow a decade ago.

Iskra Baryshev was a classic Slav beauty. Tall, lean in all the right places, less so in more noticeable ones, with high cheekbones, crystal blue eyes and cascading red hair, she turned heads wherever she went.

Baryshev had gone along with her mother's wishes and had entered beauty and talent contests from her earliest days. But while her competitors had showcased talents like singing, dancing, gymnastics and the like, Iskra would have none of that.

Her grandmother had cautioned her against being nothing but eye candy. She had constantly reminded her of something she had heard the now-dead American comedian, Joan Rivers, say: "Beauty fades; dumb is forever."

41

Baryshev had determined not to be a bimbo, but to out-work and out-think everyone else. The talent she displayed in those contests was passionately recounting long passages from Russia's most famous writers: Dostoyevsky, Tolstoy, Chekhov, Pushkin and others. While people admired her stunning good looks, they were equally impressed by her ability to memorize and narrate the best passages from Russian literature. She delivered paragraphs from these classics with such power and conviction that, even while she was in secondary school, her admirers told her she had a future in politics.

Iskra Baryshev wasn't interested in the gutter politics that were an ingrained part of the Moscow political system. No, she was interested in international relations and issues that determined the fate of nations and societies. To achieve this goal, she attended Moscow State Institute of International Relations for both her undergraduate and graduate studies and set her sights on working for the Russian Foreign Ministry, known officially as the Ministry of Foreign Affairs of the Russian Federation.

Baryshev had won internships in the Ministry of Foreign Affairs during each year of her university studies and did all she could to prepare for a happy landing there once she completed her advanced degree. She was not above using her considerable charms to flirt with officials in this male-dominated bureaucracy, leaving each of them with the impression they could bed her eventually.

But as one horny minister after another had tried to get too close, she charmed an even higher-placed one, and set her sights on the most senior officials in the Ministry of Foreign Affairs.

In some cultures, if an aged, unfit and altogether unhandsome man had a young, beautiful assistant or intern, he would keep it as much of a secret as he could. But Russian men flaunted it. During the final year of her graduate studies, the senior minister Baryshev was interning with had a meeting with Russia's president and brought her along. Baryshev had used the brief encounter to turn on the charm—on steroids. Vladimir Putin noticed. The day after the meeting, Putin had called the minister and told him to ensure there was a place for Iskra Baryshev in the Foreign Ministry the moment she finished her advanced degree.

Baryshev had begun her career by starting her first job in the Foreign Ministry in a position that was typically held by someone five years her senior. She rose rapidly through the ranks of the ministry bureaucracy by dazzling her colleagues with her intelligence and sometimes, when necessary, charming her male colleagues with visions of a potential liaison.

But that was something that never happened, even with Putin, whom she skillfully engineered ways to meet on every possible occasion through the normal course of her work at the Foreign Ministry, as well as at social events attended by Russia's privileged elites.

Now, at age thirty-seven, she was Ambassador to Belarus.

"Just the first step, Iskra," Putin had whispered as he embraced her after the ceremony naming her ambassador.

"Busy day today?" her husband asked absently, not taking his eyes off his tablet as he scrolled through the morning news. He was an ordinary looking man, and people often did a double take when they saw the couple together. But he was happy with their marriage of convenience. The son of a wealthy Russian oligarch, he knew that while Iskra brought beauty and brains, he brought money, and lots of it. She kept him happy in ways that mattered to him, so he couldn't care less what others might say.

"Yes, as usual. I have a normal day at the embassy in the morning, with never-ending meetings. Then in the afternoon, I must deliver yet another one of Vladi's threats to that incompetent Sechenov. I'm running out of ways to say, 'Why can't you control your damn country?' She thinks Vladi is bluffing. She can't be that stupid, can she?"

Her husband paused a moment before responding. He knew his wife disdained anyone who wasn't an ethnic Russian and that she considered the non-Russian citizens of Belarus almost a lower life form. The fact that Maria Sechenov, who *was* an ethnic Russian, couldn't control this…this…*rabble* was driving his wife over the edge. "Maybe she is. But don't worry; you said we wouldn't be posted here long."

"And Vladi better keep his fucking promise!" she shouted as she shot her arm forward, almost knocking over her teacup. "Nothing good is going to happen in this joke of a country, and I'll be damned if hanging around here too long is going to derail my career."

Her cell phone chirped. It was her executive assistant. The car had just pulled up to take her the short distance to the Russian Embassy.

———————

While Iskra Baryshev sat in the back seat of her heavily-armored Sukhoi limousine, her executive assistant (EA) held his tablet in front of her and scrolled through the day's upcoming events. Across the street and a half block from the Russian Embassy, on Navavilenskaja Vulica Street, another man was also busy.

On streets in this section of Minsk, which contained many of the embassies and missions of the hundred-plus nations that had diplomatic relations with Belarus, a vehicle that didn't belong was quickly noticed and dealt with.

But the man had planned well. In the early hours of the morning, he had shorted out the electrical circuit breakers of a neighboring embassy and set up a well-concealed *Stingray II* switching device in the shrubbery along the embassy's fence. Once the first of that embassy's staff had arrived and used a cell phone to call in the outage, the device intercepted the call and sent it to him. He had responded that he would be there shortly.

That was over an hour ago. He had arrived, spoken with the embassy staff, and then unloaded equipment from his panel van and begun his "troubleshooting." He had donned his hard hat and placed orange cones around the van, which had a convincing electrical contractor logo. He had leaned his ladder against the power pole in the street, strewn tools and equipment around the van, and busied himself as he waited.

His cell phone chirped, and he looked at the text. Within a minute, he closed the back door of the van and got behind the wheel, leaving his ladder, tools and other material on the sidewalk.

Iskra Baryshev was only half-listening as her EA detailed the minutia of the day's early events. She was already rehearing for what she anticipated would be an unpleasant meeting with Maria Sechenov that afternoon. She had picked one of her most expensive and revealing dresses, and had worn her highest heels and most expensive jewelry. She knew it would make the short, plain-looking president of the Republic of Belarus jealous and put her at a disadvantage during what Baryshev was sure would be a testy meeting.

"Madam Ambassador," her EA said in his efficient, clipped voice, "that wraps up today's schedule of events. Do you have any questions?"

"Yes. Any idea what frumpy outfit that dowdy bitch, Sechenov, will be wearing today?" Baryshev asked, leaning toward her EA and smiling as she revealed a generous amount of cleavage.

Her EA was used to this game and smiled slightly as he replied, "I'm certain it will be something off the rack, Madam Ambassador."

"Ha!" she laughed as she threw her head back and punched him playfully on the shoulder. "There's a reason I keep you around."

45

Turning back to business, her EA continued. "You know that the police strike in Minsk still isn't resolved; but the chief of staff has arranged for extra security around the embassy."

"Yes, he's as efficient as you are," she began. Then leaning into him again, this time dumping cleavage just inches from his face, she continued. "Just remember, you keep making me happy this way, and when Vladi pulls me out of this shithole and back to Moscow, I'll bring you with me."

Minutes later, the ambassador's limo pulled up to the front gate of the four-story Russian Embassy. In a well-choreographed routine they had performed many times, a guard outside the gate walked up to the limousine as the driver opened his window and presented his creds. The guard nodded and spoke into his mic. The security force monitoring the grounds from the tower deck on the roof of the embassy activated the switch that swung the enormous security gate open.

Suddenly, there was a huge explosion near the southeast corner of the embassy fence. Surprised, the security force stopped the fence's movement, leaving it open only a few feet, and not enough for the Sukhoi to continue into the embassy's grounds.

The startled driver sat there with his foot on the brake. Should he wait for the gate to continue opening and then drive onto the grounds? What if the embassy was under attack? Should he drive away? He looked at the security man in the front passenger seat, but the man appeared as confused as the driver felt.

Baryshev's EA saw it first and shouted at the limo's driver, "Move, MOVE!" But it was too late. The panel van smashed into the Sukhoi's left, rear quarter, pinning the limo against the embassy fence as it did. The force of the crash bent the limo's frame just enough that one of the rear bulletproof windows shattered under the force of tempered steel squeezing it from all sides, spewing glass everywhere.

Baryshev and her EA were dazed but conscious, waiting for the driver to do something. Then they looked into the front seat in horror as they saw blood spurting from the driver's head, which was imbedded into the front windshield. Then, they saw the security man's head lolling to the side.

Baryshev's EA was no hero, but he reacted as well as anyone could. The driver was dead; they weren't going to move. The gate was open several feet and the safety of the compound was so close. He reached across the ambassador, flung open her door, and shoved her out of the limo. "We've got to get inside the compound, Iskra! Make for the gate!"

He jumped out of the limo right behind her, grabbed her arm forcefully, and started to pull her to safety inside the compound, which was rapidly filling with the embassy security forces.

Just then, the door of the van flew open, and the driver leapt out. He leveled his AK-101 Kalashnikov assault rifle and pointed it at the fleeing pair. The weapon, on full-automatic, spat out a steady stream of spent shells from the chamber as its deadly 5.56 mm bullets found their mark, chewing into Baryshev and her EA. It was over in seconds. The van's driver sprinted away on foot as the embassy security forces converged on the torn-up bodies.

Baryshev's EA was dead, and the ambassador looked dead; but when a security guard placed his two fingers on her neck, he felt a pulse. Minutes later, she was rushed to the trauma center at Hospital No. 1, less than two kilometers away.

CHAPTER SEVEN

Office of the President of Belarus, Republic Palace, Minsk, Belarus
(September 10, 1230 Eastern European Time)

Several hours after the assassination attempt on Iskra Baryshev, Maria Sechenov sat at her desk, glowering at the three men sitting in front of her.

Within days of assuming office as president of the Republic of Belarus, the five-foot, four-inch tall Sechenov had ordered workers to install a specially built executive chair in her office. The gun metal chair matched her enormous, rectangular desk and was built on a platform that lifted her body up to an imposing height. She had also had the legs on her guest chairs shortened by several inches.

Her deputy president, the head of her Internal Troops and the mayor of Minsk now sat in three of those chairs. They had just finished telling her what she did not want to hear: They didn't know why local security outside of the Russian Embassy had broken down. They could not understand why no one had thought it odd that a neighboring embassy had completely lost power. They were baffled as to why no one thought to ask for some identification from the driver of the panel van parked in this supposedly secure neighborhood. And, most damningly, they had no idea where the assassin was now.

They had told their story once, and she had blasted them as incompetents and worse. They had come up with every alibi and excuse under the sun. She was about to inject another dose of expletive-laden venom when her secretary burst into her office.

Sechenov turned her simmering rage on the man. "I told you, we weren't to be disturbed!" she shouted.

The secretary stopped dead in his tracks. "Madam President, President Putin is on the phone. He insists on speaking with you right now."

She pushed her round body up from the chair and waved her right hand at her three visitors. "Leave!" she hissed.

As the men left, she scowled at her secretary and said, "Send the call in, and then get back here and take notes."

Seconds later, the phone rang. Sechenov took two deep breaths and picked it up on the third ring. She had no doubts about the reason for the call. Before the president of the Russian Federation could say a word, she began. "President Putin, I am shocked and saddened about this assassination attempt against Ambassador Baryshev. I assure you we are doing everything we—"

Putin interrupted. "I'm not interested in your flaccid condolences, Maria. When a country that borders mine is out of control, it concerns me and worries all of our citizens."

The plain looking and diminutive president of the Republic of Belarus hadn't gotten to this high position by allowing people to bully her, and she wouldn't let it happen now. "Nothing here is out of control, Vladi, you can be sure of that. We will handle the investigation and catch who did this."

That was all it took to trigger Putin. He began shouting, recounting the numerous ways she was not controlling Belarus: the increasingly frequent attacks on her country's pipelines carrying *his* energy, the violent demonstrations in Minsk and other cities in Belarus, any number of other failings he could think of, and now this—his ambassador in a medically induced coma and not expected to live.

Sechenov endured the withering attack, her mind racing to form a response. Her secretary looked on in horror; he could hear Putin's voice clearly.

When Putin finally stopped his loud harangue, Sechenov began to speak, but the line went dead.

Laura Peters had spent enough time as a part-timer in SACEUR's anticipatory intelligence cell that it didn't take Lieutenant Colonel Sauter long to bring her up to speed and insert her into the watch rotation. The recent events in the command's area of responsibility had made for long days and nights, and even as she leveraged her prior experience, she still felt that she was getting the proverbial fire hose treatment as she tried to absorb everything going on around her.

Now, she was huddled in Sauter's office with the rest of the cell members. Individually, as well as in their two-person watch teams, they had been "what-iffing" what might happen in the wake of the assassination attempt against Ambassador Baryshev through the prism of what they already knew about the tension between Russia and Belarus. The cell was especially concerned over Vladimir Putin's and Maria Sechenov's mutual distaste for one another. They considered what their feeds from the intelligence community were suggesting and then weighed that against what their anticipatory intelligence algorithms were telling them.

Sauter had brought them together as a group to exploit what they knew and, more importantly, to learn what they thought might happen next.

"Tell me what you're thinking, Pat," Sauter asked his number two, Army Major Pat Cook.

"This does it for me, Colonel. You wanted us to look for dots connecting, and they're not just connecting—they're colliding. The demonstrations in Russia, Putin squeezing Belarus about terrorist vigilantes attacking their oil pipelines, Maria Sechenov showing no signs of folding up, the riots in Minsk, and now this assassination attempt. I think this is the straw that will break whatever patience President Putin has left. I think something is going to happen soon."

"I can't disagree with anything you said, but we need to find out whatever we can and get ahead of the problem. General O'Sullivan meets with NATO's secretary general tomorrow, and we need to arm him with everything we've got."

Sauter paused and turned toward Peters. "Lieutenant Peters, you're our newest person, and you're not burdened by whatever baggage and groupthink the rest of us carry. What do you think?"

Talk about being thrown into the fire, Peters thought. *What do I know yet?*

"Ahhh...Colonel...I think I basically agree with Major Cook," Peters began, her green eyes unblinking. "The food riots in Russia are unprecedented, and Putin will need to do something to divert attention from the crisis in his country. Now he has a tailor-made excuse to move into Belarus," she continued, mindful that she was brand new and choosing her words carefully, "and if that happens, his troops can bump right up against the borders of Poland, Lithuania and Latvia. I think the EU would be apoplectic if that happened."

Sauter paused a moment before breaking into a broad smile. "Peters," he said nodding, "I think you just might work out here."

Early the next day, Maria Sechenov was still simmering over her dressing-down by Russia's president. She was no fool; she had seen what Putin had done in Crimea, as well as in Ukraine, a country that dwarfed hers and had a population five times that of Belarus. It pained her to admit it, but Putin had a point.

She knew Vladimir Vladimirovich Putin well enough that she felt she understood what mattered to him most. The food riots in his country were embarrassing but were merely a blip. And the assassination attempt on his ambassador? Sure, that was a problem, but he would eventually get over it. Sechenov knew that what angered Putin most were the attacks on the oil pipelines. Those hit him where it hurt—in his pocketbook. She knew the oligarchs who ran Russia's oil companies were in danger of losing their contracts with many European nations if they couldn't guarantee delivery.

She needed to get her army into the field to help the Internal Troops stop the attacks on the pipelines. Her chief of staff had set up a meeting with two of her generals that afternoon. Sechenov wondered if she should have someone on her staff saw another inch or two off the legs of her visitor chairs.

CHAPTER EIGHT

Office of the Russian Federation President, The Kremlin, Moscow, Russia
(September 13, 0930 Moscow Standard Time)

Alexi Pankov sat in the outer office of the president of the Russian Federation with his thin briefcase perched on his lap. The Belarusian ambassador had been summoned here on no notice two hours ago and had been cooling his heels for over an hour. The fact that he was accustomed to this kind of treatment from Vladimir Putin didn't make his wait any easier.

He had received a secret cable from the Belarus foreign ministry relating the details of the angry phone call between Putin and President Sechenov several days ago. The cable laid out Putin's demands and told him what Sechenov was, as well as what she wasn't, going to do to comply with them.

He was glad she was trying to do more to stop the attacks on the pipelines, but he had trouble digesting the rest. When he inquired as to whether she was going to make a public apology for the assassination attempt on Russia's ambassador to Belarus, he was told, in no uncertain terms, "When hell freezes over."

After waiting for another fifteen minutes, Pankov was finally ushered into Putin's office. As he entered, he saw two other men sitting there. One he recognized—he was Putin's chief of staff. The other man was a general, but Pankov didn't know him.

"Mr. President," Pankov said as he approached Putin's desk. "How may I be of service to you today?"

The President of the Russian Federation didn't stand, something to which Pankov had long ago grown accustomed. The ambassador wasn't invited to sit.

"Mr. Ambassador, I can't seem to communicate with your president. I speak, but she doesn't listen. Now I need your help."

"Of course, Mr. President."

Putin rose, pointed his finger at Pankov, and began a long screed that the ambassador knew was coming: the riots, the pipelines, the failure to take any action, the assassination attempt against the ambassador, cozying up to the EU. Pankov endured the harangue with diplomatic equanimity, waiting patiently for his opportunity to respond. Finally, Putin stopped, picked a piece of paper off his desk, and handed it to Pankov.

"Since your president won't listen to me, and I'm unsure if you can properly convey my demands verbally, I want you to give this to President Sechenov. I don't want you to scan it and send it to her via cable, and I don't want you to read it to her over the phone. I want you to deliver it in person. Can you do that?"

Pankov was accustomed to Putin being blunt, but this was over the top. He mustered all the self-control he could and replied, "Certainly, Mr. President."

The ambassador took the proffered paper and began reading:

Madam President. I am mindful that your neighbors to the west are anxious to continue receiving the oil that we ship through your nation, and I know as well that your own people are suffering because they can't receive our energy due to the outlaw attacks on your energy infrastructure.

I am also aware that your Internal Troops and your military are stretched thin and are unable to deal with the terrorists conducting these attacks. My military can help, and I have already put them on standby to assist you.

In the spirit of cooperation, I offer you the following:

- *A division of our Orlan-10 unmanned aerial vehicles, all with multispectral capability, to help monitor your pipelines day and night*
- *A squadron of our most-capable Mil Mi-26 helicopters to rapidly transport forces to locations where these attacks are taking place*
- *As many of our OZM-72 land mines as needed to lay along the entirety of the pipelines snaking through your country*
- *Up to two hundred of our highly capable robots with advanced sensors to monitor the pipelines from ground level*

These systems are state-of-the-art and require significant expertise to operate. It would take too long to train your troops, so my soldiers will operate and maintain them.

Madam President, let me be clear. Continued attacks on these pipelines are not acceptable. I urge you to agree to this help immediately.

Pankov finished reading and looked at Putin. For a moment, there was silence.

"Ambassador Pankov, why are you still standing there?"

"I...I...will convey this to my president," he stammered.

Putin stared at him with a look that was at once questioning, but also unambiguous. *Get out.*

After Pankov departed, Putin's chief of staff said, "I think you have offered President Sechenov a generous amount of help. You made it easy for her to say yes and accept your proposal to have our military guard the pipelines."

Putin paused before speaking as a broad smile filled his face. "Don't worry, she won't accept it."

He turned to his general. "Do you have any questions about your orders?"

"None, sir."

Putin stood up; the two men rose with him and then left his office.

CHAPTER NINE

**Supreme Allied Commander Europe (SACEUR) Headquarters
(September 14, 0730 Central European Time)**

Lieutenant Laura Peters and Air Force Captain Charles Johnson were halfway through their watch rotation in the anticipatory intelligence cell and were in earnest conversation. They had been running potential scenarios and simulations to try to make sense of what might happen next, given the volatile situation in Eastern Europe.

For Peters, it was both exhilarating and exhausting work. She had never shied away from challenges in her career, but her brief visits to the cell while she was Morton's aide hadn't prepared her for the full-time pressure of holding down a watch rotation. However, she had to admit that working with a team was something she enjoyed more than the one-on-one relationship an aide had with his or her principal.

While their small cell, jokingly called the "nerd nook" by others on the SACEUR staff, had access to computing power and anticipatory algorithms that rivaled anything else in the U.S. military, their responsibility involved more than just taking what their system spit out. They also had to sift through what the U.S. intelligence community (the IC) offered, to say nothing of the intelligence agencies of the twenty-eight other NATO nations.

But beyond the curated data they mined, they had to apply their own professional expertise. Sauter had built his cell carefully to ensure that he had officers and senior enlisted from all the services, as well as from various professional disciplines. It wasn't lost on

Peters that she was only one of two U.S. Navy officers assigned to the cell, and the only intelligence officer among her peers.

She had been working with Johnson for just a few days, but she knew him well enough to know that when he started clicking his pen in rapid succession that meant he was trying to get his brain around something.

"What's up, Charlie? Something on your mind?" she asked.

"Is it that obvious?"

"You've been here longer than almost anyone else in the cell. I can almost see your brain sorting through this drama between Russia and Belarus."

"When we had that staff meeting a few days ago, Pat Cook laid out a pretty compelling case that Russia was somehow going to move against Belarus. But even though the IC has stepped up collection operations, they haven't sniffed anything out."

"I know, and I'm surprised," Peters replied. "I don't have the security clearances yet to be read into everything our algorithms are capable of telling us, but every professional instinct I have is that we need to know about any communications between Putin and Sechenov. I'd bet the ranch he'll threaten her. How she responds will likely determine things one way or the other."

Johnson liked Peters, but he also liked keeping his job. He knew what the worm they had secretly inserted into the Kremlin's communications nets had revealed, as well as what their algorithms were telling them, but he couldn't share that with her—at least not yet.

"I guess we'll have to wait and see," was his tepid reply.

———————

Following protocol, Ambassador Pankov had alerted Maria Sechenov of his summons to the office of the president of the Russian Federation. She directed him to call her immediately after he returned to the Belarusian Embassy.

Pankov did as instructed. He called on a secure line and started to tell Sechenov about how quickly he could be on a flight from Moscow to Minsk. He was in the middle of spilling out his itinerary when she stopped him abruptly.

"You don't take orders from Putin; you take them from me. Read me the letter."

"Madam President, as I said, I can be on a flight in less than two— "

Sechenov cut him off. "Read me the damn letter, Alexi."

In addition to the computing power and analytical capability Colonel Sauter's nerd nook brought to SACEUR's tool kit, the cell had large-screen displays on their watch floor that presented information in an easy-to-absorb and compelling way. This enabled analysts and decision makers to make the right call simply because they could digest the information faster and better.

It was late afternoon, and Sauter's number two had assembled the rest of the group and had then asked his boss to come to the watch floor to get an update on the crisis brewing between Russia and Belarus.

"Boss, we wanted to show you this," Pat Cook began as he stood in front of the LED display that dominated one wall. The massive screen had a map of Eastern Europe and Russia and was centered on the long border between Russia and Belarus. "Captain Johnson is going to walk you through what's worrying us."

Johnson strode to the screen and hovered his laser pointer for emphasis. "You've read the reports we have been sending you, but it's hard to connect the dots without using a map. After you gave us the go-ahead to use our systems to monitor the comms nets we needed to hack…I mean dig into…in Russia and Belarus, we turned up some worrisome stuff, much of it still emerging in real time."

Johnson recounted the details of the phone call between the president of Belarus and her ambassador to Russia, emphasizing Sechenov's angry rejection of Putin's demands. He then segued to the reports on Russia the IC had been feeding them. There had been no hints of troop movements toward the border with Belarus, and Johnson used his pointer to identify the closest Russian military bases to the Belarusian border. There were no indications of more intense activity by Russian ground troops or aircraft.

"Great report, thank you," Sauter said. "Now we know what they're *not* doing. Any ideas as to what they might be planning?"

"It's hard to believe Putin will take Sechenov telling him to shove it lying down," Cook offered. "We know he is most concerned about keeping the oil moving to Europe, but Ambassador Baryshev being gunned down gives him a trigger to retaliate in a forceful way."

"And you recall that in our report," Peters added, "there is some evidence Putin's relationship with Iskra Baryshev is more than just professional."

"It's always a drama with Russia," Cook added.

"It will take me a while to process all this," Sauter replied. "For now, what's your best guess as to how Russia might move against Belarus? I'd like to give General O'Sullivan something solid to share when he meets with the NATO Military Committee tomorrow afternoon."

Cook nodded in the direction of Johnson, who began, "Colonel, this is what we think…." He paused as Peters zoomed in on the area around Moscow.

"You can see these buildings on the outskirts of Moscow. One is about eight klicks southeast of the ring road, and the other is about fifteen klicks north of it." Johnson paused again as Peters drew red electronic circles around both buildings.

"The IC did a deep dive after the cyberattacks on Estonia in 2007, as well as similar attacks on Georgia and Azerbaijan in 2008.

They had strong suspicions, though no proof, that the attacks were directed from one, or both, of these buildings. But right after the Russian *Snake* cyberweapon played havoc with Ukrainian government systems, there was compelling evidence the attacks came from them.

"Shortly after that, Russia also spied on NATO and EU computers," Cook added. "After that, the IC ramped up their surveillance, and they are certain that the attack on the Ukrainian power grid in late 2015 came from this building, here," he continued as Johnson jiggled the laser pointer at the northern building.

Sauter was silent for a moment as *he* connected the dots in his head. "I think what you all are telling me is that the first hint of a Russian move against Belarus could likely be a cyberattack."

CHAPTER TEN

Belarus Army Command Center Outside of the City of Barysaw
(September 16, 0930 Eastern European Time)

Northeast of Minsk, Major Anton Yurevich sat with his feet on the watch table in one of the six Belarus Army command centers. Yurevich hated the 2000 to 0600 watch and was bored to tears. He busied himself by playing a video game on his secure tablet. The device was supposed to be used strictly for army business, but the idiots who made those rules didn't have to stand watch in a damn concrete bunker. He couldn't wait for this assignment to end. He had already received his orders to the 103rd Guards Airborne Division. He was counting the days.

"Major!" The shout came from a soldier sitting a few feet away and manning one of the command-and-control consoles.

"What?" Yurevich asked, as his feet clunked on the concrete floor and he moved the few feet to look over the man's shoulder.

"Sir, my screen's gone blank, but right before that, the picture went haywire."

Yurevich jerked his head to the right and looked at a soldier sitting a few feet away. "Sergeant, is your picture okay?"

"No, Major. It just went blank too."

Yurevich walked back and forth, looking at the other screens in the command center.

"Should we call Minsk?" his assistant watch commander asked.

"Yes, dammit!"

Lieutenant Colonel Martin Sauter admitted to himself that, for all the brainpower and high-tech wizardry his anticipatory intelligence cell could muster, sometimes luck was a good thing to have. As Belarusian military installations absorbed the massive Russian cyberattacks, an American geosynchronous signals intelligence (SIGINT) satellite was soaring over Russia. It was travelling over seventeen thousand miles an hour, twenty-four thousand miles above earth, and the satellite's wide footprint just happened to be over the suspect building fifteen klicks north of Moscow's ring road.

It was a slam dunk. Russia's cyber-hackers did their evil work secretly over the internet, and the results they achieved in attacking Belarus exceeded even their most optimistic hopes. One corporal was so pleased that he stepped outside the building to take a smoke break, threw all security regulations to the wind, and used his cell phone to call a comrade at another facility to report their results in glorious detail. The conversation emanating from outside that building triggered the satellite's sensors at the same time that Russia's information warfare officers and enlisted were wreaking havoc with the Belarusian military command centers.

Moments after confirming the information, Sauter was in the office of General O'Sullivan's chief of staff. Minutes after that, they were standing in front of the SACEUR commander's desk, where Sauter poured out the story. They watched as O'Sullivan composed a secure text message to the NATO Military Committee. The short text ended with the following assessment: "We think this is a prelude to a Russian invasion."

Once his chief of staff and Sauter left, O'Sullivan glanced at the line of clocks on his wall. One told him that it was 0315 in Washington, D.C. He had two calls to make: one to the National

Military Command Center and another to the White House Situation Room.

———————

Hours after the cyberattacks on their military command centers, Maria Sechenov's senior generals unleashed legions of military and civilian technicians to attempt to restore them to full capability.

For the Belarusian military, the country's dated technology, which might otherwise have been considered a disadvantage, turned out to be a small blessing in disguise. Some military officers had lobbied for newer technology to keep pace with potential adversaries. But after Russia's cyberattacks on Estonia, Georgia and Ukraine, the advantages of having systems not completely dependent on the cloud, and ones that were air-gapped in many places, dashed those modernization initiatives.

The antiquated technology in many of the Belarusian Army command centers was less vulnerable to cyberattacks than that in military headquarters in most advanced nations. Within a matter of hours, most of the nation's military command centers were operating at near-full capability.

———————

The next morning, Lieutenant General Pyotr Tikhonovsky, Belarus's most senior field officer and junior only to the country's minister of defense, was in his secure bunker northwest of Minsk. He shook his head at the irony of the situation. For decades, as part of the Warsaw Pact, his nation was united with the Soviet Union and was poised to repel an attack by NATO. Even more than three decades after the Berlin Wall had come down, a large percentage of his nation's military bases were still in the western part of the country facing a threat he knew would never evolve in his lifetime.

But that meant there were fewer bases facing east, toward the more likely threat: Russia. He had lost count of how many times he and his uniformed colleagues had lobbied Belarus's civilian leaders to shift assets from western bases to eastern bases—and to build more of the latter. But their requests were always denied. An annual military budget of less than two billion U.S. dollars a year didn't buy much.

For the moment, his assistants were bringing him reports of the status of his far-flung command and control centers. He knew what a cyberattack could portend, and he needed answers.

"Major, has our command center north of Viciebsk reported in in the last hour?"

The man scrolled through his tablet and then replied. "No, General."

"Then call them. I want a status report on their radars."

Before the man could respond, Tikhonovsky called out to an officer sitting to his left. "Captain, what about Gomel? Have they checked in?"

"Yes, General. They are back up and operating."

"Good."

The interrogation and the reports continued, and General Tikhonovsky became a bit more confident he would get advance warning if there was an incursion across Belarus's lightly-guarded border.

Tikhonovsky had been in his command center for almost ten hours, and fatigue was starting to set in. But duty was duty. He would stay there until the immediate crisis was resolved.

It was shortly before midnight, and he was still processing information flowing in from multiple sources when his deputy called out to him. "General, it's the watch commander at Labkovicy on the secure line. He says it's urgent he speak with you."

Tikhonovsky walked the short distance to where the secure phone hung on a bare concrete wall. "Yes?" he asked, as a picture of that command center, three hundred kilometers due east of Minsk and near the Russia-Belarus border, formed in his brain. He had been there many times and knew what the radars, ground sensors and other surveillance assets could see.

All eyes in the command center were riveted on Tikhonovsky as he received the report. They watched his face sag and heard the thud as he sat down hard in a chair at the command console adjacent to the phone.

———

The report General Tikhonovsky had received was a manifestation of his worst nightmare—Russian armor was rolling across the border. Soon after he received the initial alert, the calls from the watch commander at Labkovicy became more frantic. Tikhonovsky knew that the command center outside that city would be one of their first targets.

The spearhead of the massive Russian armored column that was piercing the Russia-Belarus border at Labkovicy, as well as at several other locations along the more than six-hundred-kilometer-long frontier, was the T-90 tank. The T-90, Russia's third-generation main battle tank, was a beast, weighing almost fifty tons, and was the most advanced tank in service with the Russian Army. What was most impressive about the T-90 was its highly accurate 125 mm smooth-bore gun, and secondarily, it's 12.7 mm Kord heavy machine gun. First built in the early 1990s but continuously upgraded since then, the T-90 could travel at a top speed of sixty kilometers per hour.

It was doing just that as it attacked the Belarusian Army outposts along the border. The Labkovicy command center was one of the first targets to be blasted by the tank's armor-piercing discarding sabot projectiles. Soon after that command center was obliterated, the few Belarusian Army tanks in the area, primarily old Russian-manufactured T-54s and T-55s, surged forward to meet the onslaught.

Belarusian Army Captain Taras Klimovich was the commander of the small division of four T-55 and three T-54 tanks. While their tanks were old, they were simple and robust, which meant they were reliable. Their D-10T 100 mm rifled gun was inferior to most tank guns in the West or Russia, but it could pump out a half dozen rounds per minute and hit a target sixteen thousand meters away.

But the most important advantage for Klimovich and his small division had nothing to do with armor or armament. They knew the terrain and had drilled endlessly in war games anticipating just what was happening now. While they remained out of range of the Russian tank column, Klimovich had his seven tanks split up and dash through the foothills west of Labkovicy, hiding from any Russian air cover that might be working with the T-90 column.

The Belarus tank division was supported by an Altair UAV, purchased from Germany. Flying fourteen kilometers overhead and two kilometers to the east, the Altair, a European version of the American Predator, had a clear view of the enemy tanks surging west as they emerged from the pine forest on the Russian side of the border.

"They're almost in range," Klimovich said to his gunner, Vlad Garmash. "We can wait until they come to within twelve thousand meters, then we'll come out of the hills and meet them head-on."

"Good, I like it when we don't fire at max range. These guns are old."

"They're good enough!" Klimovich snapped. "Call the others on the secure net. We'll form a column and ambush them when they come into range."

The Russian tank column pressed forward. They didn't have air cover, but they did have their own UAV up, a rotary wing Kamov

Ka-137. Smaller and nimbler than the Altair, the Kamov had scouted ahead and observed Klimovich's division dashing through the foothills.

The little drone piped its picture back to the commander of the T-90 division. He did some simple math, taking into account their position, the location of the enemy tanks, and the range of their tanks' guns. He estimated to within a half kilometer where the Belarus tanks would make their stand.

As the Russian armored column came over a small rise, Taras Klimovich could taste victory. The Russian T-90s would be running down an incline and would likely have their guns' muzzles depressed below an effective firing angle for at least a minute, maybe two. He planned on letting about a half dozen of the enemy start down the hill before opening fire.

"Now?" Garmash asked.

Klimovich could tell his gunner's trigger finger was getting itchy.

"Not yet," he replied, looking at the feed from the Altair. "Only the first two are on the slope. Give it another thirty seconds."

Thirty seconds came and went.

"NOW?" Garmash shouted.

"Yes, NOW!" Klimovich commanded. Then over the radio, "All units, commence firing, COMMENCE FIRING!"

The D-10T rifled gun began spitting out 100 mm shells that roared toward the Russian tanks at a thousand meters per second. Now just over eleven thousand meters away, the attackers were well within the gun's effective range.

Within seconds of seeing the first muzzle flash from the Belarusian tanks, the Russian tankers activated their *Arena* countermeasure systems. The *Arena* system used its Doppler radar to detect the incoming projectiles and then automatically fired defensive rockets. The rockets soared into the sky and, as programed, exploded a few meters in front of the incoming shells.

Shrapnel flew everywhere as shell after shell was ripped apart by the Arena rockets. A few shells made it through the defensive barrage and found their mark. First one, then another, T-90 stopped suddenly as D-10T shells cut through their defensive armor. But behind them, more than two dozen T-90s surged forward and were back on level ground, their 125 mm guns blazing.

Taras Klimovich knew their fire was accurate and they had hit at least a half-dozen of the Russian tanks, perhaps more. He had heard that the *Arena* system was only effective against missiles, and he had counted on that—but the reality was altogether different. A recent software upgrade to the system, using stolen Western technology, had made *Arena* almost as effective against projectiles like tank shells.

They had closed the Russian tanks to within seven thousand meters and now there was no retreat. His division was still intact. They would attrite as many of the Russians as they could, slow down their advance, and wait for their fellow tankers from other bases in the surrounding area to join the fight.

"Continue firing, maximum rate, don't save any ammo!" Klimovich shouted over the secure radio.

It wasn't a fight—it was a slaughter. The T-90's *Arena* systems continued to shrug off most of the D-10T's shells as they opened up with their own 9M119M *Reflecks* anti-tank guided missiles and high explosive fragmentation ammunition. The Russian shells ripped through the handful of Belarus T-54s and T-55s and left them smoking hulks.

General Tikhonovsky received reports from his command centers along the border before they were blasted by the Russian tanks or overrun by Russian troops advancing behind the tanks in their BMP-3 infantry fighting vehicles and BTR-82A armored personnel carriers. As he processed the reports, an alarming picture formed in his mind. This multi-pronged attack was advancing on Minsk.

An ashen-faced Tikhonovsky turned to his watch commander and said, "Get the Minister of Defense on the line, and do it in a hurry."

Patricia Bailey groped for her cell phone as it vibrated and nearly levitated on her bedside table. It was a text from Danik, a young officer in the Belarus Internal Troops brigade stationed in Minsk. *What time is it, 0415?*

Danik was one of the many sources Bailey had established since she arrived in Minsk. He was young, handsome, dashing, and came from money. She had convinced herself that sleeping with him was something she would have done anyway, even if he hadn't agreed to alert her to emerging events that involved the Internal Troops or Belarus's regular army.

She read his text: *The Russian Army has crossed the border at multiple places. We think their armored columns are headed to Minsk.*

Bailey replied to the text and then composed one to her cameraman. *Meet me in front of my apartment in ten minutes and bring all your stuff.*

She dashed into her closet and pulled on her clothes. Then it was into the bathroom to pull her hair back into a long ponytail. She grabbed her makeup bag and headed for the stairwell. *The elevators in this dump are too damn slow,* she reminded herself as she anticipated her biggest story yet.

Three hundred and fifty kilometers from where the assault he had unleashed was chewing up enormous swaths of the Belarus countryside and quickly enveloping the eastern part of that nation, the president of the Russian Federation sat in his office with his chief of staff. The reports Putin had received about the attack pleased him, and the man could see the relief on his face.

"You're happy with the progress of the attack?" his chief of staff asked.

"Yes," Putin replied, "more than pleased."

"There is little resistance from their army, just as we expected."

"They haven't been able to upgrade their forces," Putin continued. "Our generals have war-gamed this to death. They thought they could do this, but perhaps not so easily."

"Do you think they can cover all of the pipelines in less than a week as they've planned?"

"With luck, maybe less."

The two men continued their conversation, discussing the rest of their plan, anticipating international condemnation, but hedging against it in so many ways. Putin was under enormous pressure from Russian energy oligarchs to ensure that their oil got to the thirsty markets in the West, to say nothing of his need to keep Europe dependent on Russian oil and gas. Now he was delivering. The thousands of Russian troops surging into Belarus were going to take up stations along the nation's network of oil pipelines to do what the government of President Maria Sechenov proved completely incapable of doing: protect those pipelines.

Two decades of serving his master had honed his chief of staff's instincts. The man knew his boss had wanted to find an inciting incident to justify this massive invasion. Putin's senior advisors had suggested one idea after another—all of which the Russian president had shot down. His chief of staff remembered it like it was minutes ago when Putin came up with that incident on his own. He would have agents from the FSB inserted into Belarus and have them assassinate the woman he had once been linked to romantically—Russia's ambassador to Belarus, Iskra Baryshev.

His chief of staff had blanched when Putin put this to him, but the president of the Russian Federation was firm and unemotional in his decision: Baryshev was expendable. The FSB carried out his orders, and the Belarusian authorities were still looking for the perpetrator of the attack, likely a member of one of the nation's opposition groups they assumed.

General O'Sullivan's text to the head of the NATO Military Committee had, predictably, triggered a cascading avalanche of meetings, phone calls and other frenetic action. But it was action without purpose; it was mostly hand-wringing.

As he spoke with a plethora of officials, O'Sullivan recounted what was known about the crisis, including how quickly Russian forces were deploying throughout Belarus, where their advance was continuing, and where it was stopping. He explained where NATO's Response Force and its Very High Readiness Joint Task Force were located, how close those forces were to the Belarus border, and what U.S. troops were available—including those on the ground in Europe, as well as those at sea in the Baltic or elsewhere.

The results of these extended conversations were not encouraging. No one could see any near-term way to stop the Russian advance, let alone push it back, and many questioned whether, or if, NATO should do anything but lodge a diplomatic protest.

"Where do we go now?" Patricia Bailey's cameraman had asked when he picked her up on the dark and deserted street outside her flat in Minsk's Tsentranly District.

The diligent and well-prepared Bailey had initially been stunned. This was not something she'd ever thought about. She had finally snapped out of it and said, "Go to the Belarus Ministry of Defense. It's on Kommunisticheskaya Street."

Her cameraman had complied and had driven as fast as he could, though not fast enough for Bailey, who had continuously urged him, "Faster, dammit, faster!" as she had furiously texted Danik and asked him to tell her more, anything, that would help her put together a compelling story of the invasion.

Danik had balanced what he could tell her—without grossly breaking every security tenet he had ever learned—with what he thought she wanted to know and finally told her what he assumed would soon be obvious. The Russian armored pincers were aimed, like a dagger, at the heart of Belarus—at their capital of Minsk.

It was still dark as Patricia Bailey stood on Kommunisticheskaya Street, the Belarus Defense Ministry behind her, and began her breathless reporting. She told the CNN anchor desk in Atlanta what she knew, what she surmised, and without naming them, how great her sources were. She finished with a flourish. "Reliable and highly placed sources within the Belarus military and intelligence services indicate this Russian assault is aimed at this city and may well be in Minsk's outskirts in the next twenty-four hours."

General Andrei Ravkov, the Belarusian Minister of Defense, had been surprised by the call from his Russian counterpart. Their countries were at war, and it was long past the time for talking. It was now just over thirty-six hours since Russian armor had crossed the Belarusian frontier with overwhelming force. Outmanned, outgunned and completely overmatched, the few Belarusian Army units that had not been completely obliterated were in full flight, heading west.

His generals had planned for and war-gamed a Russian attack; it was the pacing threat, after all. And they knew their capital, Minsk, would be the target of a Russian assault in much the same way that Paris had been the target of the Nazis more than seven decades ago. They knew this, but then things changed in a perplexing way.

As General Ravkov's army units fell back to form a ring of steel around their capital city, the Russian advance stopped pointing at Minsk and the Russian units began fanning out throughout the Belarusian countryside like a giant amoeba. While he had imperfect intelligence, General Ravkov was finally able to discern exactly what the Russian invasion was all about—they were taking up station along the oil pipelines snaking through his country.

Patricia Bailey was sitting inside her favorite coffee shop, the GURU Coffee Club on Michajlaŭski Zavulak, just blocks from her apartment, when she received the text from Danik. Each report she had filed since the beginning of the invasion had been more wildly speculative than the one before it as to the terror that would be the lot of the citizens of Minsk when Russian artillery shells began raining down on the city. But contrary to her reporting outside the Belarusian Defense Ministry the night before, as well as her follow-up coverage throughout the day, military-to-military talks had revealed that the Belarusian capital would not be attacked.

She stared at the text for a nano-second. "*SHIT!*" she shouted loud enough to be heard by everyone in the coffee shop.

CHAPTER ELEVEN

Office of the President of Belarus, Republic Palace, Minsk, Belarus
(September 19, 0930 Eastern European Time)

Only hours after the Russian invasion, Maria Sechenov had tried to call her Russian counterpart. From inside the Kremlin, underling after underling had told her that the president of the Russian Federation was indisposed. Sechenov had tried everything: threats, cajoling, imploring, and all else her decades in politics had taught her to do, if what to do when your country was being invaded was something that could be taught.

But once her generals told her what they had learned from their Russian counterparts, she calmed, if only a bit. Horrific visions of her capital city and its two million citizens under siege by the Russian Army melted away. It was now clear just why Vladimir Putin had overrun her country and what his troops were trying to accomplish.

But that didn't change the fact that her nation had been invaded. The European Union and the United States had protested bitterly and had demanded an urgent meeting of the United Nations Security Council, as if that would accomplish anything. Sechenov didn't like the words "fait accompli," but that was precisely what this looked like.

Finally, a full three days after the invasion, Putin deigned to take her call.

"President Sechenov," Putin began. "I am sorry I have been so hard to reach. I imagine we have both been preoccupied a bit as our two countries work out their differences."

Sechenov had consulted with her advisors, and especially with her generals, and knew that Russian troops would leave only when Vladimir Putin damned well felt like pulling them out. She knew when to fight and when to listen.

"Mr. President, I wish this was something we had discussed and agreed to in advance. We regret that we have not been able to secure our oil pipelines properly. We will accept your temporary help."

Putin smiled and paused before responding. "Good, Madam President. We don't want to stay any longer than needed. I urge you to continue to do whatever you can to stop these vigilante attacks by using your own troops. The perpetrators need to know my soldiers will not arrest anyone who attacks these pipelines. We will eliminate them. An assault on that vital infrastructure is now an attack on my troops and my country. Have I made myself clear?"

Maria Sechenov began to respond, but the line went dead.

Rick Holden and his fellow SEAL lieutenant, Paul Lee, sat at an outside table in Coronado's Tent City restaurant. The place was a frequent lunch spot for Naval Special Warfare Command SEALs, as it was just ten minutes from their BUDS training facility. Holden and Lee were both single, while many of their fellow SEAL officers were married, and they had formed a natural bond.

Holden continued to be bothered by the fact that he was putting SEAL candidates through the torture he had never endured and was casting about for another assignment with NSWC. He knew what Lee did, so he offered to buy him lunch so he could learn more regarding what Lee's duties entailed.

"How goes it with BUD/S Class 335?" Lee asked. "Gonna have anyone left after you all are done?"

"I think so. We probably have attrited out the ones who didn't want it bad enough. If anyone else doesn't make it through, it will likely be from an injury and we can roll them back into the next class."

"Yep, that makes sense—just like when you and I went through this a jillion years ago."

Holden was on guard, so he continued carefully.

"You've told me a little bit about the shoot house training you run in the advanced course. But other than seeing you and your trainees get into a van and head up to Camp Pendleton every other week or so, I don't know exactly what you do or how you do it."

"It is hands-on, realistic training, the best I've ever been exposed to. And that has nothing to do with the fact that I'm running it. The Marines at Camp Pendleton just finished building this state-of-the-art facility, and it allows us to conduct some awesome simulations. We're lucky we get to use it."

Lee went on to describe the details of how the men he was training used the facility to conduct simulated takedowns of houses, as well as hostage rescues. As Lee spoke, Holden pictured the killing of Osama bin Laden in Abbottabad, Pakistan, in 2011.

"That sounds like righteous work, Paul. Any chance I could tag along sometime just to see how you do what you do?

"Sure, anytime. You thinking of asking for a reassignment or something?"

"I just might be."

"Okay, I'm pretty stoked about what we do there. You might be too. I think our next window to use the place comes up in about two weeks. I'll let you know."

CHAPTER TWELVE

The Oval Office, White House West Wing, Washington, D.C. (September 22, 1115 Eastern Daylight Time)

Ryan Garrett had first met then-Senator James Miller soon after the Florida lawmaker had announced his candidacy for president. Even after over a decade in the Senate, Miller had little foreign policy experience. His focus was on domestic issues and, of course, bringing home the bacon to the grateful people of Florida.

Other than a stint as a Navy surface warfare officer to pay off his ROTC commitment after his graduation from the University of Florida, Miller had little military experience. However, he was mindful of how many jobs Florida's vast array of military bases provided to the citizens of his state. He had learned just enough about how crucial each base in Florida was to the defense of the nation so he could ensure that those posts were spared the budget axe as military funding continued to decline after the Cold War ended.

Garrett had been one of just a few people who sought to be an advisor for Miller's long-shot presidential campaign. The Florida senator found the man's international relations, national security, military, and how-to-get-things-done-in-Washington credentials irresistible.

Soon, the talking heads who held forth on the presidential campaign were marveling at Senator James Miller's command of national security issues. Within hours of his election night victory, Miller had offered Garrett the coveted job of national security advisor. Garrett had accepted on one condition: that he have an input in selecting the rest of the president-elect's national and domestic security appointees and advisors. Miller agreed immediately; and, together, they had assembled a dream team.

Now, less than a year into Miller's first term, Garrett was pulsing the rest of the national security team to try to decide how to deal with the emerging crises in Eastern Europe. General O'Sullivan had given the president early warning of the impending Russian attack on Belarus. Now, almost a week after Russia's initial cyberattack against their neighboring nation, the president and his national security advisor wrestled with what the United States should do next to deal with the Russian aggression.

"Ryan, I've read the memos and taken the briefings you've set up. It's been almost a week since Russia invaded Belarus, but I'm at a loss as to what we can, or even should, do about it."

Garrett had been with the president long enough to know that even though James Miller was couching what he said in temperate terminology, he was frustrated and angry. The reemerging and unpredictable superpower had ruthlessly invaded a neighboring country, and all the United States had done about it was to lodge a protest with the United Nations and put U.S. military forces in Europe on a higher alert level. Was it any wonder that Russia's president seemed increasingly emboldened to do what he damned well pleased in Europe?

Garrett considered the president's query for a long while before addressing a question to which there was really no answer. "Mr. President, as General O'Sullivan has briefed us, the NATO secretary general is still evaluating how quickly he can get NATO's Response Force or its Very High Readiness Joint Task Force to the Belarus border. They've had readiness issues with their transport aircraft, and the report we got two days ago said they were looking at ground transport options."

"Readiness issues," Miller huffed. "What a surprise."

Garrett knew that there was nothing to be gained by reviewing all the issues the United States had with its NATO allies: their meager military budgets that averaged less than two-percent of Europe's massive twenty trillion U.S. dollars GDP, as well as Europe's abject dependence on Russian energy. And he knew it would only anger Miller if he reminded him how long the United States had been enabling this wretched behavior by propping up their so-called allies who did little on their own to dissuade Russia from intimidating all of Europe.

Soon after Miller had taken office, Garrett had provided thick briefing books to show the president where the more than thirty-five thousand U.S. military troops were stationed in Europe, mostly in garrisons that had been established at the beginning of the Cold War. "That's too damn many. I'll talk with SECDEF, and we'll do something about it," the president had said.

But nothing had happened, just as Garrett could have predicted. The United States continued to enable its NATO allies by maintaining massive numbers of troops and equipment on their soil. Was it any wonder that the term that most often came to his mind when Garrett thought about Europe's military capability was, "pathetic?"

None of this mattered at the moment. His president wanted answers, and it was Garrett's job to try to provide them. He sat with the president and tried to be a good sounding board. He gently, but firmly, reminded him of the enormous stakes the United States had in Asia and the Middle East. Garrett knew, and he suspected the president knew also, that the last thing the nation needed was to be drawn into a conflict in Europe, especially when it meant bailing out those countries once again.

After an extended conversation, Garrett had validated for the president what James Miller knew but had to be convinced of anyway: No one was going to try to push Russia out of Belarus.

The only way to put pressure on Vladimir Putin to withdraw his troops was to hit Russia with even harsher economic sanctions.

Marik Rybak and his ragtag group of vigilantes crouched in the bushes fifty meters south of the oil pipeline near the city of Vileyka. Situated on the Viliya River, the regional capital was one hundred kilometers north of Minsk, near where the pipeline crossed the P29 Highway. As he looked through his Orion 8 x 26 compact binoculars, he spoke to the man next to him. "I think I count two, no three, Russian soldiers. Two guys are standing there smoking, and the other one is sitting on his ass, probably sleeping."

The man nodded a reply and waited for his leader to tell them what to do next. They had been attacking and crippling these pipelines for several months. They had laughed as the inept Belarusian Internal Troops had tried to catch them. They had operated with near impunity.

These Russians presented a more serious threat, but from Rybak's reckoning, Russia hadn't surged enough troops to adequately guard what they had come to protect. Two nights ago, another band of vigilantes had blown up a section of pipeline right under the noses of the Russian troops. They hadn't intended to kill any of them, but when the Russians shot at them, they fired back, and two Russian soldiers had died in the melee. Maybe these Russians were as inept as Belarus's Internal Troops.

Rybak trained his binoculars a bit to the west and saw a section of the pipeline where there didn't appear to be any troops. He put his binocs in his pouch and slung his German-made StG 45(M) Mauser assault rifle over his shoulder. He jerked his head to the left and moved through the heavy brush, his half-dozen confederates on his heels.

The night was overcast, and there were no moon or stars to illuminate the pipeline as Rybak once again peered through his binoculars. The coast was clear, and he motioned to two of his men to take the satchel charges out of their backpacks. There was no need to say anything; they had done this so many times before. The two men with explosives would rush the pipeline while the others covered them with their guns. Once the charges were fastened onto the massive pipe, they would melt back into the wooded area and detonate the explosives remotely. Then, they would be in the wind.

The vigilantes emerged, and as two men rushed the pipeline, the others stood and searched for threats with their infrared optics.

Suddenly, the night air was broken by the loud, unmistakable, pulsating rumble of an approaching helicopter. As the vigilantes reoriented their attention toward the night sky, had they been able to see through the thick clouds, they would have seen two Russian Mil Mi-24 *Hind* helicopter gunships screaming toward them at almost three hundred kilometers per hour at low altitude.

The *Hind*, in service with the Russian (formerly Soviet) Air Force for over four decades, had been continuously upgraded and improved and was now one of the world's most effective attack helicopters. It was little wonder then that well over two thousand *Hinds* had been produced, or that Russia exported this helo to over thirty nations. While it could carry up to eight troops, the *Hind's* nickname, the flying tank, best described its primary purpose: It was a high-end attack helicopter and killing machine.

As the *Hinds* spied the vigilantes through their infrared sights, they both opened fire with their 12.7 x 108 mm Yak-B four-barrel Gatling guns. As the Yak-B's spinning barrels spat out rounds, the *Hind* pilots adjusted the sights of their KPS-53AV under-nose sighting system and walked the line of bullets up to the fleeing men. The rounds from the Yak-B's guns tore into their bodies and tumbled each vigilante to the ground. Then, the *Hinds* did a version of a wingover and lined up for a second pass, but a call from the

Russian captain on the ground in the nearby woods waved them off. They had done their deadly work.

A platoon of Russian troops emerged from the woods north of the pipeline where they had been watching the vigilantes' movements and coordinating the attack by the Hinds. His men followed behind him as their captain kicked each of the fallen vigilantes to ensure he was dead. All were, except one man who was moaning and trying to staunch the flow of blood from his multiple wounds.

The captain turned to a group of his men who were dragging boards of rough-hewn lumber behind them. "We have our orders, and you know what to do," he commanded. "Crucify them—this one first," he said, pointing at the wounded man.

As the soldiers began their gruesome task, listening to the agonizing cries of the wounded vigilante as they drove huge spikes through his hands to secure him to the board, another soldier was filming the macabre scene. After all the bodies were nailed to the crosses and each cross was stood up and sunk into the deep holes the soldiers had dug, the Russian troops melted back into the forest and uploaded the video to a website.

Laura Peters was standing watch with Major Pat Cook when Lieutenant Colonel Martin Sauter entered the anticipatory intelligence cell.

"Attention on deck," Peters reflexively said as she stood up. Cook followed suit.

"Whoa, Lieutenant, at ease," Sauter said, smiling. "I recruited you based on your background and what you showed us when you joined us as a part-time helper. Now I need you to get into the flow of our team. Jumping up and trying to out-Marine me breaks up the battle rhythm I need you all to have."

Peters smiled. "Roger that, Colonel."

"It's been almost a week since Russia invaded Belarus. I suspect you and Major Cook have been giving our algorithms a workout trying to intuit what Russia will do next."

"It looks like the Russians are doing what they came to do," Peters began. "Our best estimates are that over fifteen thousand Russian troops are now in Belarus, along with a massive amount of equipment. It seems like the President of Belarus is just rolling over and letting them do what they need to do to guard the pipelines."

"It doesn't look like she has much choice," Cook offered.

"I think you're right," Sauter replied. "What do you two think NATO will do in response?"

Cook was senior to her, so Peters looked to him to answer the question, but Cook merely said, "Beats the hell out of me, Boss."

"Colonel," Peters added, "Like Major Cook says, that's a tough call. Belarus isn't a NATO member, so there's no Article Five collective defense agreement. But look at this, sir," Peters said as she maneuvered her mouse and brought up a video on the large screen display.

The grainy video showed crucified men with Russian troops pointing and smiling.

Sauter recoiled in horror. "Those bastards," he growled.

"It looks like they're serious about protecting those pipelines, Colonel. But these crucifixions are beyond the pale. I think the EU, and maybe the United States, are going to hit Russia with massive sanctions."

"I think you're on to something Peters. Why don't you feed what you're thinking into our algorithms and see if we can narrow this down a bit?"

"Will do, Colonel."

"And remember—no popping out of your chair and hollering when I come in here next time."

"Roger that, sir."

Sauter left as quickly as he had arrived. Once he was gone, Cook turned to Peters.

"Well, I guess I dropped the ball not briefing you on the CONOPS for our cell. Colonel Sauter is all-Marine, but he insists we keep things informal. He thinks it helps the process, and I tend to agree."

"I got the message loud and clear."

"There is something I've been meaning to ask you, but the question keeps getting lost in the intensity of what has been going on for the past week. Why did you agree to take this assignment?"

Peters was on guard. Cook was Sauter's number two, making him her executive officer. Throughout her career, she had recognized the importance of presenting an upbeat and buoyant persona to those she worked for. There was no place for doubt or showing any kind of weakness. But there was something about Cook's easy manner and welcoming attitude that caused her to let down her guard, if only a bit.

"I enjoy working here, and as I recall, Admiral Morton really didn't give me a choice—"

"Ah, that's just Ruth's...I mean Admiral Morton's...way," Cook interrupted. "She got the feedback about how much you were contributing here as a part-timer, and she just wanted to honor that."

"I think she was kind to do that."

"But here's what I don't get," Cook continued. "The scuttlebutt around the staff is that Admiral Morton is a lock to get her third star, and that she's being considered for the J2 spot on the joint staff. If you had continued working for her, she would've likely pulled you back there, and you know what they say—careers are made in Washington and lost in the field."

Peters had considered precisely what Cook had just described. He was being open and honest with her, and she let down her guard even more.

"I hear what you're saying, and I appreciate it. But here's why I want to be here, and why I *need* to be here. Intelligence officers typically spend their careers in a box, and often a pretty small box. We analyze the data we have, present it to our seniors, and get a nice pat on the fanny for doing so.

"But I didn't join the Navy to do that. I wanted to be in the middle of the action. My dad was a Navy chief petty officer and saw combat during the Gulf War. This is a huge staff, but what we are responsible for puts us smack in the middle of the action in dealing with this crisis. Working here is like oxygen for me."

Cook paused before responding, and then a broad smile crossed his face."

"I recall Colonel Sauter saying, 'Peters, I think you just might work out here,' when you first joined our cell. I believe he was right."

"Thanks. That means a lot to me."

"Okay, before we get all misty eyed about this, let's do what the colonel asked and put our algorithms to work."

CHAPTER THIRTEEN

NATO's North Atlantic Council Headquarters, Brussels, Belgium
(September 24, 1045 Central European Time)

Two days later, in Brussels, Belgium, the NATO secretary general was in a meeting with a few of his closest advisors. He had just presided over, if presided were the right word, organized chaos, a fractious meeting of NATO's North Atlantic Council. The Permanent Representatives of the NAC, the principal political decision-making body of the NATO alliance, had been in near-continuous session for three days.

They had consulted with the SACEUR commander, General O'Sullivan, and had asked, pleaded really, for more American help. The NAC had looked at the options and had finally come to the unhappy conclusion that their military logistics infrastructure was in such a bad state of disrepair that they could not get their Very High Readiness Joint Task Force to the Belarusian border for at least a week to even signal to the Russians that they *might* intervene.

The American general had reminded them, as diplomatically as possible, that since Belarus wasn't a NATO Treaty member, there was no Article Five requirement for collective defense. A NATO member had not been attacked, and the United States wasn't going to rush in and deal with what O'Sullivan not-so-gently explained was a European problem.

Now, with his core personal staff, most from his home country of Denmark, Magnus Pedersen allowed himself to relax a bit and shed his public persona of an in-control NATO secretary general. He sat at the head of the small conference table and rested his chin on his steepled hands. His eyes were bloodshot as he looked at the half dozen people to his left and right.

One advisor after another told him what he already knew. When they looked at the risk-reward curves of intervening militarily in Belarus, those trap lines were pointing in the wrong direction. And this was far worse than Crimea, which was over one thousand kilometers away and as much Asian as it was European. After Belarus, what was next: Latvia? Lithuania? Poland?

Another advisor had reminded him about the seriousness of Russia's intent. Unlike Russia's move into Ukraine, where the so-called "little green men," Russian military or para-military forces in civilian garb, had been used to thinly disguise Russia's meddling there, Russia's move into Belarus, one of the former Soviet republics, was nothing less than naked military aggression.

After an interminable silence, one of his youngest advisors offered something to try to break the gloom. "Well, now that the Russians are firmly in control of the pipelines, at least our oil shipments are back to normal."

It cheered the NATO secretary general little. He knew that all the nations of Europe could do now was to protest diplomatically and to push the European Union to levy even harsher food, trade and banking sanctions on Russia. He hoped the representatives who made up the voting members of the twenty-eight EU states would have the backbone to do so. He knew the European Parliament had been in session for several days, and he thought a decision would be imminent.

───────────

Even though the video of the crucified Belarusian vigilantes had gone viral, Patricia Bailey had decided that this was *her* story. Once she had seen the video of the crucifixions in Vileyka, she insisted her cameraman drive her there so she could do her own reporting.

The man had covered the hundred kilometers over poor roads in record, death-defying time in the dead of night, and now Bailey waited for sunrise so she could begin filming the corpses on their crosses. She fussed with placing her cameraman in just the right position so she would be framed by the rising sun with the crosses in the background.

During the long nighttime journey, Bailey had wondered if they were wasting a trip. Would the Russian troops standing guard let outsiders, especially Americans, near the pipeline? They had wagered it was a fifty-fifty chance, at best. But when they finally arrived in the early morning hours, what they saw shocked them.

The rotting bodies still hung on the crosses, and the Russian soldiers were doing nothing to shoo away onlookers. On the contrary, those troops stepped into the background as family members and curious onlookers approached the grisly scene.

Soon after her cameraman set up his equipment, Bailey approached an old woman who was standing at the foot of one of the crosses. Even with her limited command of the native language, Bailey determined the woman was the mother of the dead man. As the sun rose and framed Bailey's face, that cross and the grieving mother were captured by her cameraman's high-powered lens as Bailey began her reporting.

But even as she talked, her mind was in overdrive. Describing what was happening was one thing, but she had an idea that would make her subsequent reporting at the feet of these crosses even more memorable. She had paid it forward with enough of her CNN colleagues that she knew she could call in favors, and she needed those favors now, and quickly.

———

Two days later, a grim-faced Erich Becker sat in his office in the New Europa Building, the European Council's headquarters in

Brussels, Belgium. Established as an informal body in 1975, the council was formalized as an institution in 2009 when the Treaty of Lisbon entered into force. Now it was Europe's chief crisis-solving body and Becker was its president and principal spokesman.

As the high-intensity lights clicked on and the director began the countdown to the camera's rolling, Becker recalled his predecessor's announcement of sanctions on Russia in the wake of their annexation of Crimea and military intervention in Ukraine. Somehow, that now seemed like a million years ago. What was all too immediate were the series of intense meetings he had chaired over the past week, trying to hammer out a decision on what sanctions to levy on Russia for its invasion of Belarus.

Becker smiled inwardly at the irony of it all. Now that Russia had invaded Belarus and taken draconian measures, Europeans *were* relieved to be receiving Russian energy again. He had expected the ministers from the Eastern European nations that were once part of the Warsaw Pact to be especially cheered, as their nations were vastly more dependent on this oil and gas than nations like France and Spain.

There was a natural reluctance on the part of many European nations to levy harsh sanctions on Russia now that Putin had his thumb on the Belarusian pipelines. While "sanctions on Russia" made for good press and better sound bites, Becker was mindful that restricting EU countries from doing business with Russia hurt those nations' foreign trade. The German minister had reminded him pointedly that Germany's exports to Russia totaled well north of thirty billion Euros a year. It was one thing to punish Russia; but it was quite another to cripple European businesses by putting a massive dent in their export market.

Despite these legitimate qualms, the European Council had finally hammered out an agreement that its member nations could, if not applaud, at least live with. Becker nervously adjusted his tie and cleared his throat. The world press had been alerted that he would be making an address this morning, and his public affairs people had told him to anticipate a worldwide audience of over a billion people. As the director counted down on the fingers of his right hand and pointed, Becker began his prepared remarks.

"Good morning," he began, looking directly at the camera. "As most of you listening to me know, the European Council was established long ago to deal with crises affecting the European Union. Our charge is to address emergencies impacting the security and prosperity of the EU member states."

Becker paused as the camera zoomed in. "Russia's naked aggression, invading the peace-loving nation of Belarus, has shocked and saddened all of our member states and the world. Later today, President Miller will announce U.S. sanctions against Russia that are designed to complement ours. But let there be no mistake—though Belarus is not an EU member state, we stand behind her people and demand that Russian troops immediately withdraw.

"We give President Putin ninety-six hours to begin this withdrawal in earnest. If we do not see strong evidence of that by the end of this period, we will impose the following sanctions...."

Becker returned to his notes and began reading a long list of new sanctions, on top of those that already been levied in response to Russia annexing Crimea and intervening militarily in Ukraine. These new measures included: a complete ban on Russia's banks, restricting them from raising loans from the EU; a total ban on the export of any oil or gas exploration or drilling equipment; a ban on direct investment in Russia by any EU nation; and many other sanctions on Russian oligarchs and institutions.

But Becker saved his final sanction for last. As planned, the camera locked in even tighter as he clenched his jaw and began: "If Russia refuses to withdraw from Belarus, we will impose a complete and total ban on the export of *any* vehicles, *any* machinery, *any* electronic equipment and *any* pharmaceuticals to Russia. The United States is considering similar bans. While the industries in some EU nations will see a decline in their revenue as a result of these strong measures, we feel this is necessary to ensure the territorial integrity and security of the people of Belarus, who are suffering as a result of Russian atrocities."

As Becker uttered the word "atrocities," a clip of Patricia Bailey's reporting from Vileyka played on a screen to his right. And while the images of crucified vigilantes were shocking, it was Bailey's high-pitched voiceover, condemning Russia's "brutality and complete disregard for humanity" as she embraced the mother of one of the dead men, which garnered the most attention.

As Bailey finished her last sentence, her face faded out, and a movie-quality video appeared on the screen. She had called in substantial favors with her colleagues who worked in CNN's video archives. The film bore the title "Mass Murder: Yesterday and Today."

It began with images of Armenians being exterminated in Turkey, shifted to Stalin's forced famine in the Soviet Union, segued to the Nanking genocide, and then showed scenes from Hitler's extermination camps at Belzec, Treblinka, Majdanek, Auschwitz-Birkenau and others. It then moved to more contemporary exterminations: the Cambodian genocide in the 1970s, the Rwandan exterminations in the 1990s, and the Darfur, Sudan and Myanmar genocides in the 2000s. Bailey's voiceover reminded viewers what they were witnessing.

All of the scenes were brutal and repulsive, purposely so, but it was the final seconds of the video that were the most impactful. It showed a split-screen, with crucified Belarusian vigilantes on one side and the smiling image of Vladimir Putin on the other. As the video faded out, Bailey asked, "Who will stop today's Hitler, today's Pol Pot, today's killer—Vladimir Putin?

In his Kremlin office with his chief of staff, Vladimir Putin was one of the billion-plus people watching the broadcast of Erich Becker's speech. The FSB had a network of informants buried in the European Council's staff, and the sanctions Becker had just listed came as no surprise. But there was something about hearing them announced to the world that cemented for Putin the actions he had discussed during intense meetings with his closest advisors over the past week.

As Becker finished his remarks, Bailey's video wrapped up, and the cameras faded out, Putin threw the remote down on his desk and huffed, "Just as we anticipated. I've heard enough. We need to do what we said we would do if the EU and the United States go through with these sanctions."

"We haven't heard from President Miller yet," his chief of staff offered. "That won't happen until later today."

"Fair enough; but we know he will go along with Europe."

"Yes—" his chief of staff started to reply.

Putin cut him off. "We've looked at what these new sanctions will do to our economy. There's no question they will dump us into a recession, maybe worse—"

"But all we have to do is withdraw from Belarus, and there won't be sanctions," his chief of staff blurted out.

Putin paused for a moment before continuing. "I won't give them that satisfaction now that they've shown their hand. We'll leave Belarus when I'm damned ready to. Once we put *our* sanctions in place, what happens to those pipelines won't matter anymore."

His chief of staff knew precisely what Russia's president was about to put in motion. While he had absolute confidence in Putin's abilities, a step like this could bring Europe to its knees—or it could fail spectacularly. He just didn't know which.

His chief of staff was about to leave when Putin called out, "Wait."

"Yes, sir?" he asked, as he stopped dead in his tracks.

"I've heard about enough from this CNN reporter. What's her name?"

"Bailey, sir. Patricia Bailey."

"Bailey!" he shouted. "Get Bortnikov in here. I want her dealt with."

"Right away, sir."

His chief of staff left to call General Bortnikov.

Although the watch floor of the anticipatory intelligence cell was one of the most secure spaces in SACEUR, and Lieutenant Colonel Sauter trusted his talented team absolutely, the sensitivity of tapping into the Kremlin's phone conversations took the need for secrecy and security to an entirely new level. After consultation with Admiral Morton and General O'Sullivan, Sauter had arranged for the new server racks where that information was collected, collated and stored to be installed in an alcove off to the side of his watch floor. The highly sensitive information was piped to a single computer workstation next to those racks.

Colonel Sauter, Major Cook, Charles Johnson, Laura Peters and two other cell members were the only ones read into this hacking program, and they organized themselves in a watch rotation so the stream of Kremlin conversations could be monitored continuously. The high-end software not only translated the Russian into English, but also converted the voice recordings into text and displayed them on the monitor in chronological order.

Sauter had borrowed SACEUR's most talented IT specialists to train the nerd nook's algorithms to look for certain key words and highlight the text when one of them was found. In short order, whoever was manning that watch station knew what was contained in each call coming out of, or going into, the Kremlin.

Twenty minutes after being dispatched to "get Bortnikov in here right away," his chief of staff was back in Vladimir Putin's office.

"Sir, I checked with General Bortnikov's staff. He's on an inspection trip to Nizhny Novgorod. But we have him on the line in your secretary's office. Shall I have her send the call in?"

"Yes," Putin replied.

Putin settled into his chair and picked up the phone. "General, we have a problem in Belarus," the Russian president began, "and I need you to deal with it—but discretely." Putin then launched into a detailed recounting of why he wanted Bailey silenced.

The general asked no questions. He just kept saying, "*Da.*"

Putin stressed that he wanted no witnesses or fingerprints pointing back to the Kremlin.

"I will do so immediately, Mr. President!" Bortnikov shouted.

The Russian president did a slow boil. *What part of "discretely" doesn't Bortnikov get?* He needed to replace him, but not now. Just shut Bailey up. That was job one. He tried again to make Bortnikov understand. "Pay attention, General—*discretely! Understood?* I won't tell you how to do your job, but I want this done right, and I have some ideas."

Putin painted a clear picture of what he wanted Bortnikov to do. After ten minutes he stopped talking, eliciting a simple "*da*" from his general.

———

It was 0330 when the cyber-worm Sauter's team had used to hack the Kremlin's phone calls pushed the call between Vladimir Putin and General Bortnikov into the anticipatory intelligence cell. The translation software immediately converted it to English. Soon after that, the digital transcription of that conversation scrolled down the screen of the workstation in the alcove off the cell's watch floor.

Lieutenant Laura Peters and Staff Sergeant John Sundstrum were near the end of their four-hour watch rotation, and both were fighting fatigue. Peters had been read into the hacking effort and was the one monitoring that single screen. After reading just the first few paragraphs of the Putin-Bortnikov conversation, she feared the worst. Once she read the entire exchange, those fears were confirmed.

Peters blurted out, "Staff Sergeant, call our command center. Tell them we need to speak with Admiral Morton, as well as with General O'Sullivan's chief of staff, immediately."

"Ma'am, it's still the middle of the night," Sundstrum replied.

"I know that. Just do it."

CHAPTER FOURTEEN

Security Council Meeting Hall, Senate Palace, The Kremlin, Moscow, Russia
(September 28, 1030 Moscow Standard Time)

They had been meeting here every day for ten hours a day. The economic sanctions imposed by Europe and the United States hadn't had time to cause real damage, at least not yet. But it didn't take a Nobel economist to predict that it would not be long before Russia's economy took a severe nose dive. The quality of life for the average Russian would go into the sewer.

If anyone thought the recent protests and riots in the *Rodina* were bad before, things could easily spin out of control now. The Russian president had made it clear that he would not pull out of Belarus until he was damn good and ready. Now, he needed to do something to force Europe's hand and break the back of these sanctions. He thought he had the right lever, but he wanted to be certain.

Vladimir Putin had summoned them here and asked them for the answer to one question: If Russia turned off the energy spigot to Europe, what other markets were available and what would be the impact on Russia's oil and gas conglomerates?

The question didn't linger for long before voices rose in protest. The oligarchs running Russia's biggest oil and gas corporations: *Rosneft Gazprom*, *Lukoil* and others were the first to complain—and loudly—how they needed the European market to keep their businesses afloat. Putin's energy minister added his voice to the chorus of protests, predicting dire—even apocalyptic—results if

Russia took these draconian steps.

"Mr. President," the energy minister had begun, startling everyone as he bolted out of his chair. "Europe buys more than seventy percent of our crude oil and almost ninety percent of our natural gas. Those exports make up well over half of our federal budget!" he shouted. "We can't possibly make that up with other markets. This is outrageous; I will resign before I'll be a party to this lunacy."

The others at the table looked toward Putin, waiting for a reaction, but he sat there impassively.

That emboldened the naysayers and others piled on, and for most of the first day, it seemed clear that the Russian president's question would be answered quickly: If Russia stopped selling energy to Europe, it would crush the Russian economy, which had recently slipped behind Italy in gross domestic product.

But that was before others whom Putin had invited to this summit had their say. One after another, his foreign minister, his longest-serving economist, the head of his foreign intelligence service, his former ambassador to China, and his former ambassador to North Korea weighed in with impressive statistics, mind-numbing slide presentations, and thick briefing books. They presented their information over the course of several days, overwhelming their comrades with graphs, pie charts and spreadsheets.

What they presented was a compelling story, one that was unknown to most in the room. All the data pointed to the fact that China had weathered its short economic downturn, if GDP growth of 7 percent could be called a downturn, and China's economy was growing at a double-digit rate once again. Chinese heavy industries needed oil and gas, and they needed it now. Add to that the previously closely held fact that North Korea, even with Chinese help, was proving utterly incapable of exploiting its vast energy reserves under the Yellow Sea. China had counted on buying that energy at a discount, but it simply was not going to be available.

And then there was India. What many had been predicting for years, even a decade, was finally happening. India's economy was booming at a rate that exceeded even the most optimistic predictions. And while India wasn't nearly as invested in so-called "smokestack industries" as China was and didn't need energy as desperately to keep its factories going, it needed energy for another reason. Ask any lower-middle-class Indian what he or she wanted above all else, and the answer was always the same—an automobile. With a population of over 1.3 billion and a booming economy, India was once again building and importing cars as fast as it could, and gas prices were spiking. It was a market made in heaven.

The list went on. Leveraging China's growth, a number of Southeast Asian nations—Indonesia, Malaysia, Vietnam, the Philippines and others—were growing at record rates, and they all needed energy. What's more, these countries had been burned before by interruptions in oil deliveries from the Arabian Gulf. For them, Russia was a much more dependable supplier.

After kicking off this group's meetings with his open question and then leaving them to their deliberations, telling them he would return only when they had come up with a solution, Putin was invited back to the Security Council Meeting Hall at 1000 the next morning. He wondered if he had finally worn them down.

The three-dozen-plus stakeholders the Russian president had sequestered here had collectively decided to make the head of Russia's Ministry of Economic Development their spokesperson. As Putin took his seat at the head of the table, the woman began. "Mr. President, I have no slides, graphs or charts. There is no data we need to present. We have reached consensus, and we have come to the conclusion that alternate markets for our energy are robust today and growing rapidly tomorrow. We are no longer dependent on Europe to buy our oil and gas."

The Russian president had expected a long series of briefings and more data than he cared to absorb. He was astonished by the cut-and-dried presentation, if one could call it that, and consensus conclusion. Once he recovered from the surprise, he asked, "How soon can I cut off Europe's energy?"

"Today, sir. Immediately."

"Good, thank you," Putin replied. Then shifting his gaze halfway down the table to his energy minister, he continued. "Mr. Minister, I'll expect your resignation today."

———————

After Sauter's anticipatory intelligence cell had alerted their SACEUR chain of command about Putin's order to "deal with" CNN reporter Patricia Bailey, General O'Sullivan had waited until it was morning in Washington, D.C., and had personally called the chairman of the Joint Chiefs of Staff, the secretary of defense, and the White House Situation Room.

Those calls were just the prelude to a series of meetings chaired by the National Security Council. While there was an urgency to ensuring that a high-profile American reporter was not in harm's way, at the end of the day, no one in the executive branch of the U.S. government had the power to order Patricia Bailey to leave Belarus. It was left to U.S. Attorney General Clare Finley to try to use professional suasion on Bailey's employer.

Soon after Attorney General Finley had alerted CNN's leadership about the threat to Bailey, the cable network's leaders were in action. Calls back and forth between the CEO, Brian Nelson; the head of the network's European regional headquarters in London, Alice Milligan; and Bill Sanders, its station chief in Minsk, were heated and increasingly divergent.

Patricia Bailey's reporting from Belarus had been a boon to CNN's ratings. Her report from Vileyka had garnered more hits on CNN's website than any event since 9/11. The network was flooded

100

with the same request from its millions of viewers: When was Bailey going to report again?

Nelson had finally insisted that the one-on-one conversations end and that all the principals, as well as Bailey, get on a conference call. It was 1400 in Atlanta and early evening in London and Minsk when the call kicked off.

Nelson had heard the warnings directly from the attorney general and argued for safety: Bring Bailey home—ratings be damned. But Milligan and Sanders had been insistent: Bailey was on a ratings roll, and pulling her would disappoint CNN's viewers. Bailey weighed in too, insisting—almost pleading—to be left in the field.

Finally, a compromise emerged. Sanders would hire high-end private security to watch Bailey around the clock and would also alert Minsk police officials to keep an eye on her apartment and tag along when she went into the field. Bailey bristled at the hand-holding but was roughly told she didn't get a vote.

Nelson ended the call with one proviso to Milligan and Sanders: "Make sure she gets a tracking chip."

———

General O'Sullivan had been backfilled on the plan to leave Patricia Bailey in Belarus and protect her with private security. He didn't like it, but he was powerless to do anything about it. Like any good leader, O'Sullivan communicated the decision to his staff.

Lieutenant Colonel Sauter and his anticipatory intelligence cell were especially disappointed with the decision, as was Admiral Morton. They had read and deconstructed the Putin-Bortnikov conversation and feared the Russian leader's orders would be carried out with ruthless precision.

Sauter directed his cell do what they did best: harness their algorithms to try to intuit what would happen and suggest what they could do to either avert her capture or, if that were not possible, rescue Bailey and return her to safety.

Even with the most advanced hardware and software and the best minds in the U.S. military, Sauter's team couldn't come up with a good option and was relegated to sorting through a selection of bad ones. The only thing they knew for certain was that if Bailey was kidnapped by the Russians, the complicated situation in Belarus would suddenly become impossibly complex.

———————

It took Vladimir Putin's media people a few hours before they found video footage sufficiently compelling to satisfy the president of the Russian Federation. They had dropped hints about an upcoming address by Russia's leader and waited only for him to approve what would be shown over his shoulder during his speech.

Each of Russia's largest television networks (the Russian language RBC TY, the English language RT network, the Russian language Russia 24 network, and several others) were committed to carrying the impending speech. Finally, the Kremlin's media office announced that the president of the Russian Federation would make an important address at 2000 Moscow Standard Time, the timing designed to reach most of Europe during the dinner hour.

Vladimir Putin sat at his desk with a dour look on his face and with a single sheet of paper in his hand. At precisely 2000, the director pointed, and Russia's president began speaking in a clipped, measured voice.

"Good evening. Tonight, I call upon the European Union and the United States to end these unlawful sanctions against the peaceful people of the Russian Federation. Our security forces entered Belarus for one reason and one reason alone: to ensure that the nations and citizens of Europe continued to receive the energy they need to run their businesses, to heat their homes, and to power their transportation.

"We have accomplished just that—in spite of raids by

Belarusian vigilante groups who have attacked our security forces. Behind me, you see the faces of Daichi Grankin and Sergei Mishin, both killed while peacefully guarding the pipelines that bring needed energy to you. Daichi Grankin was the only child of his widowed mother, and Sergei Mishin leaves behind a grieving wife and three small children."

The picture on the screen behind him changed, and Putin continued. "And what have your sanctions accomplished? You have cut the Russian people off from buying your vehicles, machinery, electronic equipment and pharmaceuticals. This is economic warfare, and it is genocide!"

Putin paused for effect, and then continued, "This picture is the dialysis ward of the Russian Children's Clinical Hospital, here in Moscow. Look at these children. The pharmaceuticals you used to send us have kept them alive and have prevented their kidneys from failing. They will soon start dying. And now you threaten us with further sanctions and a cutoff of all drugs. More children will die, as will aged people needing heart medication, diabetics needing insulin, as well as many others. Have you no shame?"

Putin continued his harangue, getting more and more worked up. *"Finally,"* he finished with a flourish, "it pains me to admit that we need the goods you produce, but we do. However, you need our oil and gas. Effective immediately, we are suspending all energy shipments of any kind to the members of your so-called European Union. You hold us hostage by not shipping your manufactured goods to us, and you have forced our hand. While it is currently balmy in your countries, winter is coming. Soon, you will beg for our energy."

With that, the camera shifted its focus from Putin, and the picture of the Russian Children's Clinical Hospital's dialysis ward filled the screen for another minute. Then, the screen went black.

CHAPTER FIFTEEN

**Remarka Apartments, Minsk's Tsentranly District
(September 30, 1030 Eastern European Time)**

Patricia Bailey was a fighter, but she knew when continuing to fight was a pyrrhic victory at best, a defeat at worst. She had used every argument she could think of to try to persuade her boss, Bill Sanders, to hire just a single rent-a-cop who could maintain a discrete distance from her and her cameraman while they worked. Sanders could always lie to his superior, telling her that he was hiring high-end security to protect CNN's rising star. After all, Alice Milligan, head of the network's European regional headquarters, was far removed in London. She would never know the difference.

When Sanders had rebuffed those arguments, Bailey had tried charm on the fifty-something, short, bald and recently divorced Sanders, but *that* didn't work either.

Bailey finally had to resign herself to having three "minders," all former U.S. special operators working for DynCorp, with her at all times. One "goon," as she called them, was stationed in the hallway outside her apartment whenever she was there, while two others were in a car outside her building trying unsuccessfully to look inconspicuous. When her cameraman came to pick her up each day, the hallway minder got in the car with them and the two other goons followed in their car.

After a few days of this hand-holding, Bailey finally had to admit that, while it did cramp her style, it kept peace with her network and it kept her mother, and especially her father, who was now Senate majority leader and a close ally of President Miller, happy. And she had to admit that she enjoyed the light banter with a young former Army Ranger who was often in her hallway at night. His given name was John Reed, but Bailey simply called him "Hallway Johnny."

Laura Peters had never shied away from challenges, but as the newest member of SACEUR's anticipatory intelligence cell, she was feeling overwhelmed. Even harnessing their world-class technology and leveraging the best brainpower their cell—as well as others in SACEUR—could bring to bear, they had nothing that was actionable. Their combined puzzle-solving efforts had generated many more questions than answers.

Now that Vladimir Putin had turned on a dime and shut down the pipelines that carried Russian energy to Europe, his primary reason for invading Belarus had evaporated overnight. But he wasn't withdrawing his troops. While Sauter's cell waited in near-suspended animation for that crisis to resolve one way or another, they switched their focus to one American, Patricia Bailey.

In the hours after Peters had first read the worrisome conversation between Putin and Bortnikov, the nerd nook had come alive. When Sauter and Morton had initially briefed General O'Sullivan, they couched what they said in temperate terminology, but they had firmly laid out the downside of the U.S. military getting involved in any attempt to rescue an American kidnapped in Belarus. And it might not happen, they explained, as all they had to go on was a call between Putin and the head of his FSB. But the call had been ominous, and they feared the worst.

Soon after the meeting with O'Sullivan, Sauter had brought his cell together to tell them that the general had agreed with their analysis that it was beyond SACEUR's scope of responsibilities to organize a rescue effort should Patricia Bailey be taken hostage.

But while Sauter understood the constraints under which his commander needed to work, *his* team had been the ones who had learned of Putin's plans, and every professional instinct told him the former KGB colonel would have them carried out. He refused to walk away from the challenge and do nothing.

After he related the details of his meeting with the SACEUR commander, Sauter continued, "I'm a bit conflicted about how we might help should Ms. Bailey get snatched. I'd like to hear what you all are thinking."

"Boss," Pat Cook began. "We know what security measures CNN has put in place to protect her, and to be honest with you, they're pretty weak. It's a half-ass compromise at best. If Putin follows through with his plans, and we're betting he will, she's going to be taken."

"All right, I think we agree on that," Sauter replied. "But Americans have been taken hostage all around the world, and in most cases, we've done nothing. Sometimes their families have paid huge ransoms to get them back."

"There's no way her family can buy Putin off. This is personal for him," Cook replied.

After a few moments of silence in the room, Peters chimed in. "Colonel, I think it's worth remembering that Patricia Bailey's father is the Senate majority leader and is one of President Miller's closest friends. If she's taken hostage, I think we should anticipate a personal appeal from Senator Bailey to rescue his daughter, and I doubt that the president will turn him down."

"I agree with you," Sauter replied. "Are you thinking he'll have one of the three-letter agencies try to rescue her if she's grabbed?"

"That would be my strong suspicion," Peters replied.

"Most likely CIA?" Sauter asked.

"Yes, sir."

"I concur."

Sauter turned to his number two. "Pat, who's our CIA liaison officer?"

Cook scrolled through a few pages on his tablet and replied, "Steve Dolan, Boss."

"Peters, can you reach out to him and see what, if anything, he knows about any contingency plans?"

"Will do, Colonel."

Laura Peters' role was expanding, and she thought she had a line on how she might help.

––––––––

President James Miller had met with his agency heads at State, Defense, Commerce, Treasury, Energy and others almost continuously over the past several days. It didn't take his advisors long to reach a consensus: The United States should begin shipping more energy to Europe and do so immediately.

In any government, there are typically competing priorities that make many decisions difficult and some impossibly so, leaving leaders no choice but to select from the least-bad of a list of choices. But this wasn't the case with regard to selling additional oil and gas to Europe in the wake of the Russian announcement. The reasons were straightforward.

Despite U.S. commitments in Asia and the Middle East, the United States was still wedded to Europe for a host of reasons: culturally, economically, militarily and in a number of other ways. There was no question that the United States needed to prop up its European allies before they succumbed to Russian blackmail.

And then there were the domestic issues. The midterm elections were next year. While the recent slump in energy prices was a boon for the American consumer, it had decimated the U.S. shale oil industry. Massive layoffs of oil workers had depressed the economies of a significant number of U.S. states, among them: Texas, Oklahoma, Arkansas, Michigan, Ohio and Illinois. All were states James Miller had won in the last election, and his party needed to carry those states again in the midterms. The cost of oil was still low, but Europe would pay a premium for it, and that would push the price up enough to make it profitable for U.S. oil companies to ramp up production and, more importantly, re-hire hundreds of thousands of laid-off workers. The electoral math was simple and straightforward.

The president rarely spoke to the nation from the Oval Office, preferring the White House Press Room for most of his addresses. But if the issue was important, and he wanted to covey that significance, the Oval was his first choice.

"My fellow Americans," the president began. "I'm speaking to you this evening about an issue of national security. As you know, Russia has stopped its shipments of oil and gas to the European Union. To put it plainly, Russia has declared economic warfare on the seven hundred and fifty million citizens of Europe. Our commitment to our NATO allies is absolute. We will not let them be held hostage by the capricious actions of another nation...."

The president continued as he detailed how a complete cutoff of Russian energy would cripple the economies of the EU nations. He laid out facts and figures his National Security Council staff had provided, alternately glancing at his notes and reading from the teleprompter. He likened Europe's plight to the emergency immediately after World War II, when the United States had put the Marshall Plan into effect to help restore Europe's devastated economies. Finally, he put down his paper and looked directly at the camera.

"Effective immediately, the United States will begin shipping more oil and gas to Europe. We will more than make up for the thirty percent of Europe's energy that comes from Russia. We will ramp up production and refining immediately and, if necessary, reduce our shipments to other markets. During the time it takes us to ramp up our production, we will also decrease the amount of energy we supply to our domestic markets and will institute conservation measures to enable our citizens to cope with the temporary reductions to our internal energy sources."

The president paused again as the camera moved in tighter. "Well over a half-century ago, another American president, John Fitzgerald Kennedy, stood on a platform on the steps of *Rathaus Schoneberg* and famously said, '*Ich bin ein Berliner.*' [I am a Berliner.] Today we are all Europeans."

———

Within minutes of the president's midday Oval Office address, U.S. markets surged, with the Dow jumping over eight hundred points and energy futures soaring. And soon after that, U.S. oil and gas producers posted immediate job openings. That evening, the talking heads on America's broadcast and cable networks were predicting a surge in the U.S. economy unrivaled in a generation.

———

A far less happy scene was playing out in the Kremlin. Days ago, they had watched the spot price of oil soar within hours of Putin's announcing Russia would stop pumping oil and gas to Europe. The Russian president had reassured Russia's energy oligarchs that they could weather the storm until the EU lifted their sanctions. Now, however, Vladimir Putin and his close aides viewed the U.S. president's speech as a threat to their well-crafted plans.

Putin and his close circle of advisors had gamed it well. Prices soared so high immediately after they cut off Europe from their oil and gas that they were able to offer energy at a discount to their new markets in China, Southeast Asia and India. They would not only be able to cover surging demand in those nations, but were optimistic that they could elbow out several long-term suppliers from OPEC and elsewhere.

Granted, there was the issue of building temporary pipelines needed to get additional energy to Russia's ports so it could be shipped overseas, but Putin's senior advisors had all worked in the Soviet Union when it was a command economy, and they knew how to get things done.

They also had the benefit of leveraging the several years of brutal work already done when the Power of Siberia pipeline, linking Siberian gas production centers with China's northern industrial hubs, was built. There was no need to cut a new path through the swamps, mountains and permafrost; that had been done when *Gazprom* had laid down that gas pipeline. Now it was a relatively simple matter of putting an oil pipeline adjacent to the one carrying gas.

And they knew money talked. They offered generous terms, as well as substantial bribes to the right officials, to nations like Greece, Japan, Singapore and others whose tanker fleets had been operating at far less than full capacity ever since the 2008 recession and the 2020 Covid-19 crisis.

Russia had a bullet-proof plan to dominate world oil markets in ways about which they and others had only dreamed. Putin was not surprised by the actions the United States planned to take. In fact, he had anticipated them. But more importantly, he knew his next moves would put a brake on those intended actions.

CHAPTER SIXTEEN

Supreme Allied Commander Europe (SACEUR) Headquarters (October 1, 0730 Central European Time)

Within minutes of their anticipatory intelligence cell meeting breaking up, Laura Peters had called the SACEUR CIA liaison officer to set up a meeting.

A secretary had answered the phone and told her that Steve Dolan was out of the office, but would be back in the morning.

Peters was waiting outside his office when he arrived at work.

"Hello," Dolan said as he saw a woman he didn't know standing there.

"Hi," Peters began, extending her hand. "We haven't met. My name is Laura Peters. I work for Colonel Sauter in our intelligence division. He asked me to speak with you. I called yesterday, but you weren't in."

Dolan was still cradling his Yeti coffee mug and hadn't anticipated a first-thing-in-the-morning crisis. And this woman was sounding extremely hyped up.

"Right, I had some personal business yesterday afternoon. What is it you wanted to talk about?"

"I think we need to speak in a secure space. Do you all have a SCIF here?" she asked, referring to a Sensitive Compartmented Information Facility, a secure room where top secret discussions could be held.

"Sure, we have one down the hallway—follow me," Dolan replied, still perplexed by this early-morning visit.

The Belarusian vigilante attacks on their nation's oil and gas pipelines had begun spontaneously throughout the country with almost no coordination, or even interaction, between these multiple independent groups. And for a while, while they were dealing with the inept Belarusian Internal Troops, no organization was needed.

But as the Belarusian Army, and now the Russians, got involved and started catching and crucifying their comrades, they realized their freelancing was becoming too dangerous. They needed to somehow get organized.

Ilia Novik emerged as the leader of all the vigilante groups. A former special forces captain in the Belarusian Army, Novik had the leadership attributes, organizational skills and passion for his mission that convinced even the independent-minded leaders of disparate vigilante groups throughout the country to agree to his leadership.

Novik had asked the leaders of the other vigilante groups to meet him in an abandoned warehouse on the outskirts of Minsk to assess where they stood and what their next moves should be. Even though Putin had announced that energy shipments through the pipelines they had been attacking for the past several months would cease and was carrying through on his threats, no one trusted Russia's capricious leader, and they knew he could start using these pipelines again at any time.

It was early morning when the men, as well as two women, were assembled. There were almost two dozen in all, and each of them had much to say. They agreed that the attacks on the pipelines should continue, but that their task was becoming impossibly dangerous. But it was the report by the leader of a group operating in the southeastern part of the country, near Homel, that was the most sobering.

The man reported that the night before, three of his team, including one woman, had been captured as they attempted to blow up a section of pipeline. His group had tried to rescue their comrades, only to be driven back by the heavy weapons the Russians had used against them. Two of his men had been killed, and several more had been wounded, in that effort.

Novik had finally heard enough. He needed to level the playing field. He turned to one man, "Didn't you tell me that you had a new man who joined you a week ago and that he was a conscript in the Belarus Army, but recently deserted?"

"Yes, he was, and he did. He was being brutalized by the sergeants and other older soldiers. He slipped out of his barracks one night and ultimately joined us."

"I want to talk with him—and soon. We need better weapons to even the score with these bastards, and I'll bet he knows where we can get them."

"I can have him here in a day," the man replied.

"No, not here. It's not secure enough. We're moving our base to Astravets. We'll meet there. Bring him as soon as you can."

———

They had deposited their cell phones in the lock boxes outside the SCIF, signed in, and were now seated in a small conference room.

Steve Dolan's body language shouted impatience, and it was clear to Laura Peters that she needed to get to the point. She had done her homework and knew that Dolan sat in on General O'Sullivan's morning briefings, so he was likely up to speed on the situation with Patricia Bailey.

"Steve, I'm sure that you know about Putin's threats to snatch Patricia Bailey and that no one thinks a military rescue would be in the cards if she's taken."

"That seems pretty clear from the briefings I've heard and the reports I've read."

"Our cell is thinking that the president will be under enormous pressure to rescue her if that happens, and it's likely to be assigned to the CIA to execute."

Dolan was still trying to get his brain around why some Navy lieutenant, and one who seemed hell bent for leather to speak with him *right now*, was here in the first place.

"I suspect it might—*if* she is kidnapped, and *if* someone decides that she needs to be rescued, and *if* it falls to my organization to do it. That's a lot of 'ifs,' Lieutenant."

While Peters had received glowing fitness reports throughout her career, when she had pressed her commanding officers for areas where she could improve, she always received the same advice: Try not being so direct and all-business with seniors and juniors, and especially with peers. Treat them as the imperfect humans we all are. One of her skippers had even told her, "Try not to be so in-your-face with people."

Peters wasn't a psychologist, but she did not have to be to tell that Dolan had no intention of making her concerns his unless she tried another approach. She was trying to use a modicum of charm and develop some rapport by using his first name, and he was addressing her as "Lieutenant." Maybe she could try to see the world from his point of view.

"Steve, I'm coming to you as a colleague, asking you a pretty straightforward question. I'm just doing what my boss asked me to do. We're in a secure space, and I have all the clearance tickets, so we can have an open, professional discussion. All I'm asking is if you have gotten wind of contingency plans to rescue Ms. Bailey if the Russians grab her. I'm not trying to get you cross-threaded with your chain of command. I'll keep anything you tell me in confidence. I think we both want the same thing: getting our fellow American back if she's snatched."

Even though he was frustrated by the intrusion, and was still angry that he had initially gotten a face-full of attitude from Peters,

114

Dolan was happy that she was backing off of what had started as an interrogation. He was enough of a professional that he decided to try to do the best he could to help.

"Look, Lieutenant, I think you all have a term in the military, 'way above my pay grade,' and that certainly applies here. You have likely noticed that I'm an army of one on this staff. My sole function is to serve as a conduit between the SACEUR commander and CIA headquarters at Langley. I'm not a field operator—I'm a desk jockey." Dolan continued, describing how he had no clout on their staff and was little more than a walking Wikipedia to explain CIA functions to General O'Sullivan.

Hearing how powerless he really was and realizing that treating him as a human, not just as a means to an end, was a better course to take caused Peters to continue to soften her approach. "Okay, Steve, I get it. Thanks for being so open and candid. I think what you're telling me is that any action to rescue Ms. Bailey would likely be instigated and directed by Langley and that you wouldn't be involved."

"Exactly, and I'd bet my next paycheck that I wouldn't even be informed an op was going down—and I doubt your commander would either. That all gets done by our Special Activities Center, and *believe me*, I've been with the Agency long enough to know they make it a point not to let anyone know what they're doing."

"You probably can't tell me this, but do they have operatives in place in Belarus, or nearby, in the event they need to move quickly in a case like this?"

"I can't tell you—mainly because I don't know. But all I've seen in the years I've been at the CIA has been budget cuts. I think, if we did anything, we'd have to surge those folks from the States."

"But wouldn't those people have to have some knowledge of where they were deploying to so they could get the job done?"

"Again—above my pay grade. But my guess would be they would likely have to start from scratch, get a team together, bring them up to speed and all that. I may be wrong, but I couldn't see anything happening for weeks."

"You're kidding?"

"I wish I were. These budget cuts have really sucked; and in the time I've been with the Agency, I've seen us try to do more with less—only to get people killed. I get that there will be pressure to rescue this woman if she's taken, but I'd be the last one to try to rush a bunch of folks into Belarus without the skills to get her out."

After a few more minutes of generally frustrating discussion, Peters decided that Dolan wasn't going to help solve her problem.

They left the SCIF and went their separate ways. But as they did, she decided to reach out to the one person she thought could help her.

———————

Vladimir Putin hoped that his moves to strangle Europe's energy supplies were going to have the impact he desired. Externally, things were all moving in the right direction. Internally, however, he was far from satisfied.

He had leaned on Moscow's mayor and forced help on him to quell the riots in Russia's capital, and it had largely worked. While there were occasional flare-ups, there was nothing bad enough to pique the interest of the international media.

That was not the case in Petersburg. Rioting there had gotten worse, more people had died, and the city's police force was a laughingstock.

It was late in the day when he summoned his chief of staff. As the man entered his office, he could tell that Putin was in a foul mood.

"Have you read this?" Putin asked, shoving his tablet in the man's face.

"Yes, I have. The demonstrations in Petersburg are getting worse, and the western media is all over it."

"Is Mayor Safronov that fucking inept? Doesn't he understand that his job is to control his damn city?"

Putin's chief of staff knew it was a rhetorical question and didn't reply. He waited for his boss to continue.

"You've listened in each time I've called him. Haven't I made my expectations crystal-clear?"

"You have, Mr. President. I can't fathom why he hasn't taken your advice and why he's letting these demonstrations spiral out of control."

"Get him here. I want him in my office tomorrow. I don't care what else he's doing. Safronov is going to find out how thin the ice is that he's skating on."

Putin's chief of staff knew better than to remind his boss that it had been less than a month since Safronov's daughter had died in a riot in Petersburg, or that Safronov's wife had had a psychotic breakdown and was under the close care of a psychiatrist and heavily medicated, so he merely said, "I'll see to it, Mr. President."

CHAPTER SEVENTEEN

The Oval Office, The White House, Washington, D.C.
(October 3, 1430, Eastern Daylight Time)

President Miller knew his Oval Office address would trigger action, and he was not disappointed. The financial markets continued to surge, and his approval rating soared to heights he had never thought possible.

But it was the meeting his secretary of energy had requested that was about to cheer him the most. The day before, the man had presided over a multi-location VTC (video teleconference) where he had spoken with the CEOs of America's largest energy companies. Now, he was in the Oval to report the results.

Miller was fearing the worst. He had told the nation what he wanted to do, but he was completely dependent on these business leaders to make it happen. He wasn't a businessman, but he knew all too well that CEOs had a fiduciary responsibility to their shareholders that trumped all else. Whether Europeans shivered during the coming winter was not their concern.

He steeled himself for what he thought his energy secretary would have to report: grudging cooperation and only half measures to fulfill Europe's new energy needs.

The man began cautiously enough. "Mr. President, I convened the meeting you asked me to and spoke with our energy industry leaders—"

"And?" Miller prodded.

"In a sentence, sir, these people are patriots. They simply want to know how fast you want to start shipping more energy. They are ramping up their production already."

"That's great news. Once they secure their initial contracts and have a schedule for the first shipment of additional oil or LNG, let me know. I want to go to that port and tell the nation how proud we are of our energy leaders."

"I'll do that, Mr. President, and I don't think it will be long before you'll be making that speech."

Even though they had worked together to derail a plot to try to impeach the U.S. president a few years ago, Rick Holden and Laura Peters had gone their separate ways after that. The U.S. military had assigned them to commands half a world away. They e-mailed or texted occasionally but were only casual friends.

Holden had been out on the grinder with Class 335 when he had gotten a text from Peters that simply said, *Need to speak with u urgently. Please call me.*

Caught off guard, he had to think a while before he punched the "call" button. It was just past noon in Coronado, and he knew she was assigned to EUCOM, so he guessed that it was evening in Germany.

Their call was brief, with Peters simply telling him, "Rick, I need to talk with you—but on a secure line. You're at Naval Special Warfare Command, aren't you? Do they have a SCIF?"

"Yes, but isn't it night where you are? Can you access one?"

"I'm in the Intel Directorate at SACEUR. I can get to one anytime. Text me the info so I can call you. Can you get to a SCIF in, say, thirty minutes?"

"Make it an hour, would you? It will take me that long to get a call set up."

"All right—but sooner if you can."

Ilia Novik had asked to see the Belarus Army deserter soon, and his comrades did not disappoint him. The man who had escaped the ambush outside of the city of Vileyka brought a young man to an abandoned farmhouse outside of Astravets, just fifteen kilometers east of the Polish border. Novik now used this remote location to coordinate their efforts. It was within striking distance of both the main Yamal-Europe pipeline, as well as the Jamal pipeline that went due west into Poland and then on to Germany. It was also close enough to the border of Poland that they had a good escape route if the Belarus Army, or more likely the Russians, closed in on them.

The man they had brought to meet their leader was the former Belarus army conscript. He had told the members of that group a convincing tale of where they could get heavy weapons from lightly defended army bases in their country. Now, they needed him to tell Novik the same story.

Novik considered the short, reed-thin man sitting in front of him at the large table in the dining room of the farmhouse. The man, a boy really, couldn't be more than eighteen. After months of fighting a government, and a now a foreign power, both of which were trying to crush his movement with everything they had, Novik didn't have a shred of trust left and proceeded carefully.

"My comrades tell me you used to be in the army, but you fled and want to join our cause," he began. Then he leaned close to the man and looked him dead in the eye. "Help me understand why you want to do that."

The man who had brought him to Novik had asked that same question, and had listened to the conscript's sobbing story. He wondered if he would hold it together in this interrogation.

"I...I...didn't want to join the army. My mother tried to protect me. But I was made to join and was assigned to the motor pool. I'm not a mechanic, so they made me a driver. I was one of the youngest and newest soldiers, and one of the sergeants said I was his...his...bitch—"

"He made you have sex with him?" Novik interrupted.

"Not just him—but others too. I tried to fight back once, but then they just gang-raped me," he said. He started crying uncontrollably.

"They did unspeakable things," the man who brought him to Novik said.

Novik waited for the sobbing and blubbering to subside and then put his hand on the man's shoulder. "The same men who did this to you are working with the Russian pigs who are murdering, and even crucifying, my comrades. Do you want to help us?"

"Yes...yes...more than anything."

"Good. I'm told you have information that can help us fight back."

With that, the man who had brought the former conscript to Novik laid an old military map on the table. The young man began a detailed recounting of what he knew about the military bases in the western part of Belarus. Many of them were Cold War relics. He explained what he had learned during his military training and what Novik already knew. At the height of the Cold War, the nation's armed forces numbered well more than a quarter million. Now those numbers had been dramatically reduced to something closer to fifty thousand.

In the process of scaling back the size of the Belarusian Army, many weapons were taken out of service, and a number of bases were closed and shuttered—or reduced to inactive status. A handful of soldiers guarded mothballed equipment at those outposts that were no longer active. From his experience as a motor pool driver delivering essentials to those bases, the young man had learned that some of them housed deactivated, but still useful, heavy weapons. That was precisely what Novik was hoping to hear.

The former conscript stood up, leaned over the map, and jabbed his finger at a spot. "I think here is where you'll find a large supply of the kind of weapons you're looking for," he began. "And this one too." He stabbed his finger at an army base a few dozen kilometers away. "One of the corporals told me this one was guarded by a skeleton crew as more troops were pulled out to put down the protests and guard the pipelines."

Novik smiled as the man continued to pour out what he knew. Once he finished, he put his arm on the young man's shoulder again. "This is valuable information, and I am ready to make you one of us. Can you shoot?"

"Only if I'm shooting at a soldier from our army—or a Russian."

"Good! That's the spirit."

Rick Holden sat in the SCIF at Naval Special Warfare Command headquarters waiting for Laura Peters' call. The phone rang at precisely the time she had set up.

"Holden," he said as he picked up the secure phone.

"Rick, it's Laura. Thank you for taking the call."

"I have to admit you were a bit mysterious when I called to answer your text. It's been a long time since we talked. What's up?"

Peters poured out her story. Even talking on a secure line, with both of them sitting in rooms designed for top secret conversations, she began carefully, explaining what her cell at SACEUR did, what they had discovered, what she thought would happen, and why she anticipated the Agency would be tasked with a rescue mission.

Holden took it all in and resisted the urge to ask what all this had to do with him. He had been seconded to the SEALs for several years without even a vague indication that the Agency would pull him back. There were so many unknowns in the story she was relating. He shared those thoughts with her, but Peters persisted nonetheless.

"Rick, don't you see? DoD won't do a thing; it will have to be the CIA. But our CIA rep here at SACEUR told me how long it would take to pull together and train a team before they'd send them to Belarus on a mission like this.

"You told me about your work, years ago in Eastern Europe, with the Special Activities Division. You know the countries, you know many of the languages, and you had a team of men you worked with and could trust. They likely could reconstitute you all in a short time."

They continued to talk, Holden asking questions and Peters describing why she thought he was uniquely qualified to do what she was certain would need to be done.

He wasn't sure whether he was convinced by her arguments or just worn down, but he finally said, "Laura, look, I'm not averse to anything you're suggesting, but the Agency made it crystal clear that I'm not to contact them except under the direst circumstances."

"But you did contact them when we uncovered the plot to try to impeach the president, and they helped us fight our way to the Capitol."

"You're right, they did. But I can't push being yanked back to Langley from this end. There has to be a pull. They would have to call me."

"I may have a way to make that happen. Are you willing take on this mission if asked?"

"We all serve 'at the pleasure,' so the answer is *yes*."

They ended their call, and Peters left the SCIF. She headed straight for the SACEUR duty office to get the emergency contact number for Steve Dolan.

———

Pavel Safronov knew why he had been summoned to Vladimir Putin's office. Putin's chief of staff had not minced words and had told him that Russia's president wanted him to restore order to his city or he would find someone else who would.

Safronov had expected to be kept waiting in Putin's outer office, and he was. Putin hadn't conveyed a scintilla of empathy for the loss of his daughter or for his wife's medical situation. Yes, Putin had mentored him and helped his political career along, but Safronov had paid him back many times over.

Now Safronov had nothing but contempt for Putin. He would listen to what Russia's president had to say, but he wasn't Putin's man any longer.

Putin's chief of staff finally ushered him into the Russian president's office. Safronov was surprised when the chief of staff, who typically was part of meetings with Putin, departed and closed the door behind him.

Putin began cordially enough. "Pavel, I think you know why I asked you to come here."

"Your chief of staff made that abundantly clear, Mr. President."

"Can you help me understand why the demonstrations in your city are continuing to fester and even get worse? You have to know that your city is making our nation look like we can't take care of our internal matters."

Safronov knew what Putin expected: excuses, then groveling, and then promises to try harder and do better. He wasn't going to give it to him. "Mr. President, I know you are displeased. What I don't think you understand is how bad conditions are in Petersburg, as well as throughout Russia. The overwhelming majority of demonstrators in my city are students. They're kids who can't afford to buy the necessities of life…."

Safronov continued, laying out statistics about the dire economic conditions in Russia and especially in Petersburg. He knew Putin understood all this, but he laid it on him anyway. None of this was what Russia's president wanted to hear, but Safronov no longer cared.

Predictably, Putin pounced.

"Mayor Safronov, I don't need a lesson from you, or from anyone else. I read the reports. Trust me, I know all this. But I also know how many tourists visit Petersburg every year and help pump up your economy. Do you have any idea what these demonstrations are doing to wreck that?"

Safronov mustered every ounce of self-control he possessed and said, "I know all too well, President Putin."

"Well, if you know, why don't you do something about it?" Putin yelled.

Safronov lashed back, "If I continue to disappoint you, perhaps I'm not the right man for this job."

That jolted Putin. He had helped manage Safronov's rise in politics. The man was once as ambitious as any other politician, but now he was sitting there like a sullen, whipped puppy.

"I have helped only a few people rise in politics. I mentored men, and women as well, who had what I thought it took to vie for my job one day in the future. You were one of them. So was Maria Sechenov. But she became expendable. Don't let that happen to you."

"Expendable?" Safronov asked.

"Pavel, sometimes I feel you have good political instincts, but other times your naiveté troubles me. Maria was expendable, and here is why…."

Safronov sat spellbound as Putin freely related what had happened to his ambassador to Belarus. Putin swore him to secrecy, and the mayor promised to comply. But if he had any second thoughts about what he was planning to do next, they were now indelibly erased.

CHAPTER EIGHTEEN

Remarka Apartments, Minsk's Tsentranly District
(October 4, 0630 Eastern European Time)

Patricia Bailey was on cloud nine. Her reporting from Minsk during the riots, and especially her coverage of the Russian atrocities against the Belarusian vigilantes who continued to attack the pipeline even after the Russian invasion, had garnered international attention. What happened outside the city of Vileyka had been repeated in other locations, and Bailey had captured it all. And the video her CNN colleagues had made comparing Putin to Hitler, Pol Pot and all the others who had perpetrated crimes against humanity had gone viral.

She had received e-mail congratulations from a number of mentors and colleagues and had even gotten one from the head of CNN's European regional headquarters in London. The last line of Alice Milligan's e-mail had made her giddy: *We have another posting in mind for you once you wrap up your outstanding reporting in Belarus.*

This morning, Danik had tipped her off that Russian troops had captured three vigilantes who had attacked a section of pipeline a few kilometers west of Minsk, and that one of them was a woman. The Russian invaders had announced that they would interrogate them to extract every bit of information they could about the vigilante organization, and then would crucify them on a hill overlooking the city. She had to get there before reporters from rival networks did.

Her cameraman had texted her that he was waiting outside her apartment and asked her to hurry the hell up. *So, he's finally feeling it*, she thought to herself.

As she stepped out of her apartment, she didn't see Hallway Johnny, her minder who usually had this early morning watch. *Horny fucker*, she thought. There were several single women on her floor, and Johnny must have taken a shine to one of them. *To each his own.* The idea of an early morning quickie didn't appeal to her.

Hurry up, Bailey, she found herself thinking as she turned to double-lock her door. She heard steps, started to turn around, and suddenly it was all violence. A heavy, gloved hand clamped over her mouth and a thick arm wrapped around her torso, pinning her arms and crushing her breasts. Within seconds, the first pair of hands roughly stuck a large piece of duct tape over her mouth and another pair of hands scooped up her feet.

Bailey tried desperately to free her arms and kick her legs, but the two hooded men just squeezed her harder and pinned her limbs against their bodies. She continued to struggle until the one holding her upper body hissed, "Be still, bitch, or we'll break all of your bones one by one."

Once she was horizontal, she looked in horror as another hooded man unrolled a large carpet. The two men carrying Bailey dropped her onto the carpet and then rolled her up in it. One man led the way to the stairwell, as the other two hefted the carpet-Bailey burrito onto their shoulders. They hurried down the stairwell, dashed into the alley behind the apartment building, threw their prey into the back of a van, and disappeared into the Minsk morning.

Bailey's kidnapping was unknown to anyone at SACEUR when Laura Peters and Steve Dolan arrived at the SCIF at 0730. They went through the normal procedures and were directed to a small conference room.

Peters wasn't opposed to using a bit of charm and even flattery to get the results she needed. She had listened when Dolan explained how underutilized he was at SACEUR and how he wanted to make more of a contribution. She would use that.

"Steve," she began, "I couldn't say much when I called you last night, but this has to do with what we talked about right here a few days ago. You explained how long it would take to assemble and train a team to rescue Patricia Bailey, and I listened. I thought I might have a solution, but it involved an individual I knew some time ago, and I had to be sure he was willing to step up. He is, and you can help make that happen."

Peters spared no detail, explaining Rick Holden's background with the Agency, how he had wound up with the SEALs, how they had worked together, and why he might be their only chance to get to Bailey in a hurry if the worst happened.

Dolan listened impassively, his mind in overdrive as he processed her story. She had only stopped talking for seconds before he replied, "I'll call Langley."

———

Her cameraman had gotten tired of waiting, and had texted Bailey multiple times with no response. He sat in his car and stewed. It was always "hurry up and wait" with this high-strung reporter.

He finally climbed out of his car, waited for someone to come out of her apartment building, and let himself in. *That* triggered the two security men outside, and they were on his heels in seconds.

After a quick exchange of creds, the three men sprinted up the stairwell to Bailey's floor. They opened the fire door, turned the corner, spied her open apartment door, and almost tripped over Hallway Johnny's prostrate body.

Minutes after the first call from Bailey's security detail to CNN's Minsk offices, a long series of calls across multiple time zones passed the news.

It was just after noon as Laura Peters and Captain Charles Johnson began their watch rotation in SACEUR's anticipatory intelligence cell. Peters was manning the bank of phones and the secure e-mail queue on the watch desk, while Johnson manned the computer workstation that monitored the stream of Kremlin conversations. Things had been relatively quiet for the past several days, and Johnson was slumped in his, chair looking a bit dazed.

"Hey Charlie, you awake over there?" Peters joked.

"Yeah, I don't care how high up in the food chain these damn Russians are. All they talk about are women and booze."

"Don't listen to anything your mama wouldn't want you to—"

Johnson cut her off midsentence. "Laura, come here and read this. Bortnikov just called Putin. They have Bailey!"

Peters leapt out of her chair and read the transcription. She dashed back to the watch desk, and Johnson followed. They both grabbed phones and began punching in numbers.

Word of Patricia Bailey's capture rocketed up U.S. military and diplomatic chains. Within thirty minutes of Johnson and Peters making their initial calls, national security advisor Ryan Garrett was standing in front of President Miller's desk in the Oval.

Garrett knew how close the president was to Senator John Bailey. He was the first sitting senator to endorse Miller at the start of his long-shot presidential bid. And he knew the president well enough to know that he would be consumed by guilt for letting CNN convince him, and everyone else for that matter, that they could protect his friend's daughter with private security guards.

He began as gently as he could. "Mr. President, we knew something like this could happen, and we did our best and let the people who employ Senator Bailey's daughter step up and—"

"But she's an American citizen, dammit; we could have ordered her home." Dejected, the president held his head in his hands. "Oh, I can't believe this has happened. What are we going to do, Ryan?"

Garrett could see the president's eyes misting up. He dared not remind him that his National Security Council had recommended ordering Bailey home, but that the president had been convinced that CNN could handle protecting her.

"Mr. President, when we discussed this, I think we all agreed that the using U.S. military assets to rescue Ms. Bailey wasn't the right solution, but that the CIA would have to be the ones to mount the effort to get her. After that conversation, I spoke with Director Simmons and asked him to begin drawing up a contingency plan should we need to try to rescue her. Shall I get him on the phone so you can tell him to put those plans in motion?"

Yes, but not yet. I need to tell John Bailey first. Can you get him on the line?"

"Of course, Mr. President.

At CIA Headquarters in Langley, Virginia, Steve Dolan's call to his boss in the operations directorate had precipitated a series of meetings, each bubbling up to a higher echelon.

While having to organize a rescue effort was still only a possibility, albeit a strong one, the Agency prided itself on its readiness and determined to lean in should they be called. The operations director had endorsed the idea of not just recalling Holden, but of rebuilding his team around him.

The ops directorate's staff had done their due diligence and located Holden's five former teammates. One had left the Agency, three had desk jobs at Langley, and one was assigned in Costa Rica. That man was on an Agency Gulfstream in an hour.

CHAPTER NINETEEN

**Shoot House, Camp Pendleton Marine Corps Base, California
(October 5, 0915 Pacific Daylight Time)**

Rick Holden stood on the catwalk with his fellow SEAL, Paul Lee, waiting for Lee's team to take their trainees through their paces. Though it was daylight outside, inside the sealed-up house, it was pitch black, and the two men stared at the floor below, where things were about to happen.

"Watch how my senior chief kicks this off," Lee whispered to Holden. "He lives for this stuff; it's almost like crack for an addict."

The two men watched as the silence below them was broken by the flash-bang grenade that kicked off the IBT (initiative-base tactics) exercise. The explosion signaled violence, but it was controlled violence. It was all about moving and shooting, or not shooting, depending on the threat and the target.

Two teams emerged from a kicked-down door and moved through the shoot house like a well-choreographed ballet company.

"Coming up."

"Clear left."

"Next man up."

"Moving right."

"Clear in here."

"Moving now."

"Clear right."

Each man spoke into his lip mic, and that signaled others to work through the maze of moveable partitions made of heavy-rubber, bullet-absorbent material.

Suddenly, paper targets showing dark-complexioned men holding guns popped up in several places, as did another paper target of a woman shielding a small child. Each trainee assessed the targets in the green glow of his night-vision goggles, and it was game-on.

Shots rang out as the trainees took out the gun-wielding men with their Heckler & Koch HK416 assault rifles and then pressed forward again.

"Clear here."

"Two enemy down."

"I'm moving up."

"Clear."

The controlled chatter continued as the trainees took out the simulated terrorists, but also one civilian, as the two teams swept the entire house and finally carried out the single simulated hostage hidden in a corner.

As the lights came on and they took off their sound-suppressing headgear, Lee turned to Holden. "It's going to be a rough debrief. They did okay, but took out a target that was clearly a civilian. I'm heading down to try to buck them up a bit after Senior Chief chews their asses."

"That was awesome training. I'll wait for you outside while I try to get my heart to stop pounding," Holden replied.

———

Rick Holden had been leaning on the exterior of the shoot house for a short time when he heard his cell phone chirp. It was a sound he hadn't heard for years. It was Langley.

He pulled the phone from his back pocket and answered, "Holden."

The voice on the other end identified himself as the CIA's deputy operations director. The man was short and to the point, even blunt. Holden was being recalled to the Agency. His old team was being reconstituted, and they had a mission.

Had he and Laura Peters not discussed this likelihood, the call would have been a complete shock. But while he knew it was a possibility that he would be pulled back to the Agency, and was prepared to some extent, the reality of it still hit him. His life was about to change dramatically.

"How soon?" Holden asked.

"Thirty-six hours, tops. Sooner would be better."

After he learned that Patricia Bailey had been snatched, President Miller wrestled with whether to tell his friend, Senator John Bailey, on the phone or in person. His national security advisor had urged the latter and arranged for a car to pick up the senator and bring him to the Oval.

It had been a wretched meeting, with Bailey weeping unashamedly and Miller struggling mightily to console his friend while assuring him that the full force of the United States government was already being mobilized to rescue his daughter.

The president gave Bailey enough time to compose himself. He was ready to escort his friend to the door and tell him again that the United States would stop at nothing to get his daughter back, when Bailey grasped his arm and began shaking his head from side-to-side.

Miller tried to hide his shock as Bailey began, "Mr. President, I'm afraid this involves more than just rescuing the daughter of a friend. Patricia knows things she shouldn't know, and if she's tortured and reveals any of it, I'm afraid our national security will be compromised."

"What does she know?"

"I'll tell you, Mr. President, but I think you should have your national security advisor here when I do."

Fifteen kilometers west-northwest of Minsk, in a walled villa outside Tarasava, Belarus, a hooded, gagged and bound Patricia Bailey had no more tears. She had begged her captors to release her, promising them huge sums from CNN, even making up examples of cases where the network had paid an exorbitant amount of money to rescue one of its captured reporters in the field.

The man who was the leader of the three-person team holding her hostage had pretended to listen and then had asked her to repeat her made-up story of a captured colleague who had been ransomed by CNN. He had another man put those details into his tablet and do a search and, unsurprisingly, it had turned up nothing.

That had led to the first of many beatings, all designed to wear her down in advance of trying to extract any useful information she might have but not mar her face.

That had been bad, but it was nothing compared to what happened when they scanned her and found the tracking chip that had been implanted in her right shoulder blade at the insistence of her CNN bosses. The size of a grain of rice, and inserted via a relatively painless injection by a doctor, it came out when one of her captors used a pen knife to roughly snatch it out of her body. The shock and pain caused her to pass out.

Now, the normally confident and feisty Bailey sat there, whimpering—no longer able to control her emotions. The more she sobbed, the more gleeful her captors became.

"When does President Putin want us to set up the video communication?" one of the captors asked.

"He'll let us know," their leader replied. "In the meantime, you two go buy what he told us to get. There's a lumber yard just a few kilometers east of here. And hurry it up; we don't know when he'll want to talk with her."

General Bortnikov had called Vladimir Putin and told him of Patricia Bailey's capture, but he still wanted the Russian president to shower him with congratulations in person, so he bullied Putin's staff into arranging a short-fused meeting.

Bortnikov related the details of Bailey's capture in excruciating detail. Putin only half-listened. He was already planning how to extract retribution from the captured reporter. It was not lost on the Russian leader that Bailey was the daughter of a prominent United States senator, and he intended to leverage the fact that he had her under his control to put pressure on the United States and the EU to lift sanctions on his nation.

Once Bortnikov stopped talking, Putin started issuing orders.

The president and his national security advisor sat in rapt attention as Senator Bailey poured out his story about what his daughter knew. It was worse than either of them could have anticipated.

Patricia Bailey's first assignment working for CNN had been in Moscow, doing the normal jobs given to a new employee. But even at this entry-level position, she wanted to cultivate her own sources.

She began dating, and was soon sleeping with, the senior U.S. Marine Corps attaché in Moscow. Over pillow talk, he revealed that one of his duties was to manage the extraction plan for a number of CIA operatives in and around Moscow. He explained that if their cover ever became compromised and they were in danger of being rounded up by the Russians, he was responsible for getting them out of the country.

Her Marine Corps friend had a secure laptop in his apartment. After a night of recreational sex, as he slept soundly, Bailey's curiosity got the best of her. She poked around his computer, trying to find information that would help her gain an edge over other reporters.

What she discovered shocked her. She found the emergency extraction information for all CIA operatives in Moscow. Bailey found their names, addresses, and pickup points throughout the city. She made cryptic notes on a piece of paper and stuffed it into her purse. She didn't know how, or if, she would ever use the information, but as a brand-new reporter, knowing something her colleagues didn't know felt like a coup.

Months later, while she was home on leave, Bailey began to have second thoughts about what she had seen on the secure laptop. She revealed this to her father, and after wrestling with his conscience, Senator Bailey told her to keep the information to herself.

Now, sitting with the president and his national security advisor, Bailey realized how wrong his decision had been.

"Mr. President, I know I should have insisted she tell her attaché friend this critical information had been compromised—"

"That's for damn sure!" Garrett interrupted.

"Let him finish, Ryan," the president said.

"I know, I know, Mr. President. But she told me he was violating security procedures having that laptop in his apartment in the first place and that his career would be ruined. It's all my fault, but none of us can change any of that. But if she's tortured, and if her captors extract that information, it will be a disaster...." Bailey continued talking, and the president let him finish his story.

The president paused before speaking, and then said firmly, "John, thank you for telling us this. We'll get Patricia back; you can count on that. But clearly, we've got some other work to do."

"I understand, Mr. President. And I'm sorry."

The president grasped Bailey's shoulder and gave it a reassuring squeeze, but there was ice in his voice as he said, "Ryan will show you out."

A minute later, Garrett was back in the Oval.

"Unbelievable…and from a senior senator!"

"I know, Ryan. He's handed us a shit sandwich for sure. This changes nothing as far as trying to rescue her, but we need to let the CIA director know what has happened."

"I'll take care of that, Mr. President."

"I know you've already got your staff working with the CIA on rescuing Ms. Bailey. Do you need me to talk with the president of Belarus?"

"I was going to ask you to do that."

"Good—just give me some talking points. We want her cooperation, but we don't want to tell her everything." Miller paused for a moment.

"There's another thing, Ryan. I know I said I wanted to go to the first port that would be shipping energy to Europe and give a speech, but I can't do that now—not with John's daughter being taken and this possible compromise of CIA operatives. What should we do?"

As always, Garrett had a backup plan. "The vice president can give that speech. He heads your energy council. He's the logical choice to do it."

"Good idea. But talk to him first. I don't want some milquetoast speech. Now that we know what these Russians are capable of, I don't want him to just talk about helping our European allies. I want him to let Putin know we're sticking it to him."

"I'll see to it."

After his wife's breakdown, Pavel Safronov had given his butler, the senior member of his household staff, additional authority and had begun to use him as his personal executive assistant. The man was up to the task and handled his duties with dispatch and, when needed, compassion.

Safronov returned from work at his usual time, and as was his new custom, asked their butler to tell him how the day had gone. That was always code for asking him how Olga Safronov was doing.

The man replied, "About the same, Mr. Mayor."

"I see," Safronov replied. "I will need your help, as well as that of the rest of the staff, getting us packed up to attend the international mayor's conference in Vienna next week. My wife will need help picking out her clothes. Even before her troubles, that was always a challenge."

The man could not hide his shock, "Mr. Mayor...Mrs. Safronov's condition...I mean...are you certain?"

"I appreciate the fact that you care, but that is my decision. The conference is relatively short, and I have already arranged for help for Mrs. Safronov while we are there."

"Very well, sir."

CHAPTER TWENTY

Operations Director's Office, CIA Headquarters, Langley, Virginia
(October 7, 0830 Eastern Daylight Time)

Rick Holden had taken a direct flight from San Diego to Washington's Dulles International Airport and had arrived at 0100 in the morning. A car and driver sent by the CIA's director of operations picked him up and whisked him to a hotel in nearby Tyson's Corner. He was told to be dressed and ready for pickup at 0615 for a 0700 meeting with the ops director and his deputy.

The two men briefed him on the need to rescue Patricia Bailey, laid out the plans for the mission, and told him that none of the members of his old team had been told anything other than to kit up and wait for him to arrive. They also told him that he was going to have a new team member, Mia Yaeger, a former Air Force civilian Global Hawk operator who was also well versed in Eastern European languages.

The ops director was candid in telling Holden that the decision to rescue Bailey was made by the president himself, in spite of the strong objections of the CIA director. That was now water under the dam, he explained. He also briefed Holden that the CIA had no ready assets to provide intelligence on Bailey's location, but that the director had a handshake agreement with the secretary of defense to have SACEUR provide needed intelligence. As part of that intelligence and reconnaissance support, Holden and his team would have access to one or two Global Hawk unmanned aerial vehicles assigned to SACEUR.

The ops director ushered Holden to a nearby conference room. There were handshakes all around as Holden greeted the four members from his old team and his new addition, Mia Yaeger. Then they all sat. His team took the chairs around the table and the ops director sat in the corner. Holden then related the details of their mission as it had been explained to him.

There were numerous questions. Holden was able to answer most of them, but the ops director had to chime in a few times. When there were no more questions, the ops director exited—but not before saying, "I know this is a challenging mission, and we don't have the luxury of letting you take the time that you really need to prepare. But I have confidence in Rick and in all of you. Bring her home."

Holden knew the challenges of this emergent mission, but as he surveyed the faces around the table, his confidence grew. He had worked with them, all but Yaeger, in several operations in Eastern Europe and knew their strengths and weaknesses. More importantly, he knew how they complemented each other and how they operated under stress, especially when an operation went bad.

There was Jim Folga, known to his teammates as Jimbo. Mississippi born and bred, he was the oldest member of the team and had found his way to the CIA during his senior year at Mississippi State, when the Agency set up a booth at a job fair on campus. He had been with the CIA for two decades and was an expert in large and small caliber weapons. He also was the one who had a mellowing effect on the high-strung individuals who made up the rest of the team. His typical response when one or the other of his teammates was going high-order was, "It'll be all right." Jimbo and his family were evangelical Christians, and Holden had met Folga's wife and three kids—two girls and a boy—at an operations directorate social event years ago when they first worked together. He swore he had never heard more "yes, sirs" in his life. Jimbo's only known hobby was fly fishing.

Blake Mason was a Northern California native who held a high-end engineering degree from Cal Poly San Luis Obispo. He had worked for a series of dot-com startups in Silicon Valley, labored eighty hours a week, made a ton of money, and burned out at age twenty-seven. He found his way to the Agency the way many did, looking to do something more meaningful than getting rich. The skills he had developed in the tech industry were put to good use on Holden's original team, as Mason was the one they counted on to set up the communications networks that enabled groups under the thumb of authoritarian governments to communicate with the West. He lived with his girlfriend from Cal Poly days, who was a professional staffer for a senate committee. They had no children and could be found most weekends participating in tough-mudder competitions.

Darko Markovic was a first-generation American. The son of a Serbian father and Macedonian mother, his family had immigrated to the United States when he was three and had settled in the Cobble Hill section of Brooklyn. He had grown up in an expat community that included a wide range of Eastern Europeans: Romanians, Ukrainians, Moldavians, Latvians and others. He had eye-watering language skills by age twelve, skills he honed in high school. With few job prospects after high school, he worked as an Uber driver. He took night classes at City College of New York, where he graduated in the top ninety percent of his class. His lack of academic pedigree would have disqualified him from even a casual look by the Agency were it not for his dazzling language skills, something Holden had seen in action many times when they worked together previously. "Dark Mark," as he was jokingly referred to by his teammates, wasn't married and had no known hobbies. He was also a regular in the D.C.-area club scene.

Hector "Chapo" Chavez was Holden's one former team member who had not been manning a desk at the Agency when the team was recalled. He had been pulled out of an op in Costa Rica.

Chavez grew up on the south side of Chicago, where a rural experience was the trash-strewn vacant lot where the kids played baseball and hid from the local merchants after they'd boosted a video game or sweatshirt from their store. Chapo was born in Puerto Rico and came to Chicago with his mother and father when he was six. Both his parents worked multiple jobs, and Chapo and his three brothers were left alone after school. All four Chavez boys flirted with gangs. One brother was dead, killed in a drive-by. Another was doing time in the Dixon Correctional Center in the northwest corner of the state. Chapo might have been pulled into the gang life but for a youth club mentor who introduced him to Muay Thai fighting, also called Thai kick boxing. He was small, compact and quick. Chapo eventually got his GED degree, worked his way through Chicago State University, and ultimately joined the Agency. Chapo and his wife had three girls, on whom he doted, and were avid bingo players at the MGM Casino in National Harbor, Maryland.

Finally, there was Holden's new team member, and a complete unknown, Mia Yaeger. Her CIA dossier was straightforward enough. She had earned an Air Force ROTC scholarship and graduated from Notre Dame with a degree in aeronautics. She didn't qualify for flight training, but took the next-best assignment and became a Global Hawk operator. Sitting in a windowless room for hours on end while flying an unmanned aircraft didn't float her professional boat, and she left the Air Force as soon as she had served enough years to pay off her ROTC commitment. She found her way to the Agency, was hired as an analyst, but had applied multiple times to work for the operations directorate. Her ability to control a Global Hawk and her easy facility with Eastern European languages made her a natural choice to join Holden's team. Yaeger had a long-distance relationship with a former Air Force ROTC classmate, who was flying C-130s at McChord Air Force Base outside of Tacoma, Washington. She lived on Capitol Hill and spent most of her personal time as a gym rat.

Holden surveyed the team around him and considered their experience, as well as his history with them. He chose his words carefully. "I know you don't need a stay-focused, stay-professional speech from me. You've been there, you know the deal, and you're all professionals. Not only is getting Ms. Bailey out of Belarus alive a presidential imperative, but she's one of ours, and she's a pawn in Putin's designs to poke us in the eye.

"I know you've said goodbye to your families and loved ones already, and now it's time to compartmentalize. When we leave, we need total, front-sight focus on the mission. The bus to The Farm is waiting outside," he continued, referring to the CIA training facility at Camp Peary, near Williamsburg, Virginia. "We may have a day to train, maybe two, and then we head straight to Andrews and get on the big bird flying us east. Grab you gear and follow me."

———

The plush VRBO villa the FSB men had rented using an offshore account met their needs perfectly. Secluded, with no nearby neighbors and with high walls and plenty of greenery, the mini-estate was the perfect place to hold their hostage. General Bortnikov had sent them a secure text from FSB headquarters, congratulating them on their successful capture of the CNN reporter and assuring them that Russia's president was more than pleased.

They had done what they'd been asked to do and tortured her to determine if she had any useful information. They learned nothing of value, but weren't disappointed. What *was* important to Russia's president was what they were finally going to do to her.

It wasn't that they found the final task he had for them off-putting or gruesome in any way; they had seen and done worse. They just wanted to get it over with and get home. And they especially wanted to get away from the wailing and whimpering woman.

Finally, the text from Bortnikov had come. The president of the Russian Federation would initiate a video connection late that afternoon. They were to have Bailey positioned in a chair facing the sixty-inch LCD television in the villa's great room. Their only other instruction was to ensure that they could turn her chair to face the villa's expansive back yard.

CHAPTER TWENTY-ONE

Port of Corpus Christi
(October 8, 0830 Central Daylight Time)

The vice president stood on a hastily constructed platform in the grassy commons area in front of the Port of Corpus Christi's administration building. Positioned on the western side of the Gulf of Mexico—with a long, deep channel—and at the nexus of three railroads and two interstate highways, this facility was the fourth largest port in the United States and one of the primary energy transshipment facilities in the nation.

Though it was an early fall morning, the Texas sun was bright, and the vice president squinted as he looked out at the throngs of employees gathered to celebrate the fact that they would load their oil onto the first ship that would deliver U.S. energy to Europe. Patriotism ran deep in this state, and what would have otherwise been a routine speech had been hyped to a high level. Local and national media had the event blanketed.

The vice president was no orator and had been given a tight script. The address had been fashioned by his staff and reviewed by the national security advisor, as well as by the president's speech writer. After extending the president's regrets for not being there in person, he gave an acceptable speech; but then, inexplicably, he yanked the microphone out of its holder, stepped out to the center of the platform, and went off-script.

"Over eight decades ago, another dictator attempted to conquer and dominate our European allies and friends. This nation mobilized to beat him back and free hundreds of millions of captive people!" he shouted, thrusting his right arm in the air.

"Today, Vladimir Putin is holding Europeans hostage by cutting off the energy that heats their homes, enables their manufacturing, and powers their transportation. He is an international outlaw who has violated every possible norm of human decency, crucifying countless Belarusian partisans. He must be stopped, and you, all of you standing here, are the ones who will do it!"

The assembled crowd of workers, administrators and others clapped, cheered and stomped their feet in appreciation as the media filed their stories.

Erich Becker had been alerted that the vice president would make an address at the Port of Corpus Christi and had prepared his remarks in advance. The European Council president's speech was carried live or only slightly delayed throughout Europe during the evening news hour.

Becker's speech was short and to the point, but then, like the U.S. vice president, *he* went off-script, his anger at the Russian president taking over his emotions. "...and finally, I say this to President Putin. You will no longer hold the peoples of Europe hostage. Your crimes against humanity make you an international pariah. The United States has come to our aid, and you will regret what you have tried to do. We intend to impose additional sanctions on Russia as follows...."

Becker spit out the words as he ad-libbed whatever he could think of to stick it to the Russian president as his ashen-faced staff stood in the wings.

Russia's leaders had a well-developed network of spies and multiple ways to electronically eavesdrop on the conversations of whatever enemies were giving them trouble.

147

Neither the U.S. vice president's speech nor that of the European Council's president were unanticipated, and the personal attacks rolled off Vladimir Putin's back. His focus now was on what he had to do to stop those energy shipments.

"Get my chief of staff in here!" he shouted to his secretary.

President Miller had called Belarusian President Maria Sechenov and asked for her cooperation in "rescuing an American citizen in distress."

Sechenov had countered that her Internal Troops or military could conduct this rescue, but Miller was insistent: This needed to be a U.S. operation.

The president of Belarus was astute enough to know this wasn't a battle she needed to fight. She listened impassively as Miller told her what was needed: landing rights at Minsk International Airport, a secure hangar, no interference by customs officials, and three Dartz Nagel Dakkar SUVs.

"Of course, Mr. President. I will ensure that you have what you need. All I ask is that you let me know when your operation is complete."

"Of course, Madam President."

CHAPTER TWENTY-TWO

**Onboard the CIA Gulfstream V Over the North Sea
(October 9, 1730 Eastern European Time)**

Rick Holden had used the limited time at Camp Peary to prepare his team for their mission to rescue Patricia Bailey. They were facing a host of unknowns, not the least of which was any sense of where she was being held. Holden was counting on SACEUR to provide whatever intelligence they could to help locate Bailey, and he had established a secure chat room with Laura Peters to obtain that intel in real-time.

Holden and his team had launched from Andrews Air Force Base the night before. The Special Activities Center pilots had told them to expect stiff headwinds, as well as a needed stop for refueling, and hence a longer-than-normal flight. Holden had let his exhausted team sleep for the first six hours of the journey.

Now over the North Sea and just an hour-plus from Minsk International, he reviewed the bidding with his team.

"Here's the deal," he began. "The intel we've gotten from SACEUR strongly suggests these guys don't intend to kill Ms. Bailey, at least not right away. They think Putin wants to stick it to CNN and to the United States for her reporting from outside of Minsk—especially for that video she produced comparing Putin to other mass murderers. They will likely lay up somewhere in or near Minsk and wait for orders."

"That video was kick-ass, Boss," Chapo Chavez offered.

"Yeah, it was, Chapo," Holden replied. "And it likely pushed Putin over the edge and made him decide to snatch her."

"But what about that tracking chip we were told CNN had inserted in her?" Blake Mason asked. Mason was the team's comms specialist, and Holden knew this was in his wheelhouse. "Do you know if the device they gave us to locate the chip will work?"

"I don't know," Holden replied. "And my guess is that unless Putin had her snatched by total amateurs, and that's doubtful, they've already dug it out of her and destroyed it."

"Roger that."

"Tell me about our wheels, Darko?" Holden asked.

Darko Markovic was the team's logistical guru, and Holden knew getting the right gear was his forte.

"Once we pull into the secure hangar at the airport, we'll have three Dartz Nagel Dakkar SUVs waiting for us—"

"Wait," Jimbo Folga interrupted, "I thought we were supposed to buy American." Folga had always been the guy who'd lightened the mood when they had worked together before, and Holden was happy to see that hadn't changed.

Markovic paused and scowled, using his best schoolmarm look. "Maybe for you we can get a used Ford Pinto, but for the rest of us, it's the Dartz Nagel Dakkar. It's the slightly smaller cousin of the Dartz Black Shark, the up-armored SUV favored by Russian billionaires. They'll give us the upper hand if we need to duke it out with Ms. Bailey's captors."

"Good, Darko," Holden replied.

"Mia, tell me what you've got set up with the Global Hawk," Holden continued.

"Sure. The folks at the 9th Reconnaissance Wing at Beale Air Force Base provide two Global Hawks to SACEUR. They promised to dedicate one to us and let us fly it where we need it. Once we get on the ground, I can control it from this," Yaeger replied, holding up a military-grade Getac T800 tablet. "The Global Hawk won't help much if they have Bailey in a building in central Minsk; it's damn dense there. But if they're holding her somewhere in the countryside, it may be our ace in the hole."

Holden raised his eyebrows, and Yaeger read him well. He was skeptical that the Air Force squadron at Beale would cede control of their asset.

"I know you're thinking the Air Force wants to keep close control of their Global Hawks, especially after Iran shot one down in the Gulf, but this is new technology that they're beta testing. I think they trust me to try it out because I've worked with them for so long."

"They must," Holden replied.

"Don't worry. If this tablet doesn't do all the things it's advertised to do, Beale can take control of the bird, and I can talk to them real-time via secure SATCOM," she replied, referring to satellite communications.

"I know that the Global Hawk is a high-altitude, strategic surveillance asset," Holden began, "and a Reaper or Sentinel drone might better meet our needs. But tell me again why we can't get access to one of those."

"It's actually pretty simple," Yeager replied. "Neither of those are available to SACEUR because they're being used twenty-four-seven in the Middle East. What we have is what we have."

"Okay, I get it. I'm no expert in these unmanned aircraft, but I think the Global Hawk will give us an edge," Holden replied. Then, turning to Markovic, he asked, "Darko, once we're loaded up in the SUVs, where do we head to lay up?"

"I think here," he replied, pulling up a map on his tablet. "We got word that neither the Belarusian military nor their intelligence services had anything that could serve as a safe house. Since that wasn't an option, I Airbnb'd six places in Minsk proper and the burbs. We have no idea where Ms. Bailey is yet, so I picked this villa in the southern part of the city. It's near the intersection of the

P1 highway and the M9 ring road. It's a mini-estate with a barn, where we can hide our SUVs so they don't attract lookie-loos."

"Sounds good," Holden replied. "Anything I forgot? Anyone have any saved rounds?"

"I think we're good, Boss," Folga replied. He had more experience than anyone else on the team and was Holden's de facto number two.

"I have a question," Markovic added.

"Yes, Darko?" Holden replied.

"Will we have time to stop for *draniki* and tea?"

"*Draniki?*"

Markovic let out a heavy sigh, "It's a local breakfast specialty, a fried potato pancake."

"Once we get Ms. Bailey back, I'll buy," Holden replied.

At SACEUR headquarters, Laura Peters and her colleagues were frustrated beyond words. Colonel Sauter had reorganized their watch teams and had pressed his IT specialists to tune up their anticipatory intelligence programs to try to intuit where Patricia Bailey was being held. Thus far, they hadn't uncovered a scintilla of useful information.

Peters felt it most acutely since she was the person who had set the wheels in motion to have Holden and his team embark on this mission. They had a secure chat room open, and all she was able to send was a constant stream of messages saying she had nothing to report.

Sauter, as well as the rest of his team, believed that their ability to find Patricia Bailey hinged on how well and how quickly they could read communications between the Kremlin and whoever was holding her. They banked on the fact that her now-viral video had attacked Putin so viciously that the Russian president would communicate directly with her captors.

To that end, the nerd nook now had two monitors where watchstanders could read the digital transcripts of Kremlin phone conversations. Two more people were read into the program, and now those communications were able to be read in near-real time.

Among Ryan Garrett's manifest talents was his ability to anticipate events and to get out in front of potential problems before they materialized. That was what had vaulted him to more and more important positions in the U.S. government and, ultimately, to the role of national security advisor.

While he understood the need, as well as the urgency, for the United States to ship energy to Europe, he also understood the pitfalls. He asked for a meeting with the president and brought along the homeland security advisor.

After an exchange of greetings, Garrett began. "Mr. President, we all heard the vice president's speech in Corpus Christi, and I would be lying to you if I told you I wasn't worried about how brittle this plan is."

"You've got my attention, Ryan."

Garrett continued, reading the bullet points from his issue paper. He reminded the president how Russia had attacked the Belarusian military's command centers and how Russia's offensive cyber capabilities were rivaled only by China's. He then switched gears and laid out research his staff had done regarding how vulnerable U.S. ports were to cyberattacks.

He then recounted the lack of effort by U.S. energy corporations to make their ports secure from cyber and physical attacks despite urging by various Federal government agencies (Homeland Security, Energy, Northern Command, and others) to do so.

Miller found himself agreeing with the assessment as Garrett went through his list. The national security advisor finished with a flourish. "If there's an Achilles' heel in this plan, it's these ports. I don't think there's much we can do in the short term, but I think we ought to alert U.S. Cyber Command and see what they can do, if anything, to shore them up."

"You're spot on, Ryan. Please call Admiral Scott at CYBERCOM. He's not shy about jumping into these things."

———————

Ilia Novik wasn't a patient man, but he knew what he wanted, and he was willing to move deliberately to get it.

It had been just less than a week since the young deserter had poured out his story and identified the army base at Brest as the one that contained the weapons they needed to grab to take on the Russian troops.

During that time, Novik had to quell dissention among some of his men. Now that Russia was no longer pushing energy through the pipelines running through their country, acquiring weapons to take on the well-armed and well-trained Russian troops guarding them didn't make sense to all of them.

But it did to Novik. It was no longer about protesting against the Russian minority running his country and oppressing his fellow Belarusians. Nor was it about interrupting future energy flows.

For Ilia Novik, it was now personal. The Russian pigs had murdered and crucified over two dozen of his countrymen and had gloated about it on the internet. And they had done more than that. In one small village near a pipeline that was attacked, the Russian invaders had dragged the city's mayor and his wife out of their bed in the middle of the night and crucified them in the town square as a warning to any other Belarusians who dared to harbor vigilantes.

Putin had bullied their country's president, and if she wasn't going to lift a finger to drive the Russians out of their country, he and his men would do it. Novik hoped that soon they would have the weapons they needed to outgun the Russian occupiers.

They had rented several vans from different companies in Minsk and had driven to Brest and laid up in a cheap hotel. Novik set up a watch rotation, sending two of his men at a time to observe the base day and night, watching the troops that patrolled the perimeter, looking for a weak spot. They waited, but Novik was becoming impatient.

Their landing at Minsk had been uneventful, and as promised, there were no customs officials to be seen. After the Gulfstream taxied into the hangar at the fringes of the airport, a single man in a paramilitary uniform was standing at the bottom of the aircraft's steps. He shook Markovic's hand, exchanged words in the native language, and handed him three sets of keys. From there, the team had unloaded their gear and packed it into the SUVs. Within a half hour, the Special Activities Center pilots had refueled and taken off, and Holden and his team had rolled out of the airport.

It was 2230 when the convoy of three SUVs pulled up to the small estate they had rented. Markovic punched the code into the gate, and they entered the courtyard.

"Welcome to the first stop on your luxury tour of Belarus," Markovic began. "Before you stand your quarters, seven bedrooms and five baths. The swimming pool is out back and is likely to be a bracing sixty degrees. Sadly, the butler, the maid and the houseboy are on their six-week vacation, so you'll have to tote your own bags."

"Got any food laid up, or is this the bargain basement tour?" Folga quipped.

"Ah, once we unpack, Mia and I will hit the market up the road. We speak the language, and husbands and wives typically shop together in Belarus.

Though she was new to the team, Yeager was no shrinking violet. "You mean father and daughter, don't you, Pops?"

155

"As you wish," Markovic replied with an exaggerated bow.

Holden just shook his head. He needed to get his team moving before they drove themselves crazy.

CHAPTER TWENTY-THREE

Villa Outside Tarasava, Belarus
(October 10, 1030 Eastern European Time)

Fatigue had finally overcome fear, and Patricia Bailey had lapsed into sleep in a bedroom in the villa. Her hands and feet were bound, and she was shackled to the bed with a gag in her mouth.

The door slamming open awakened her, and she looked up to see her captors pull a wooden chair into the bedroom. They unshackled and unbound her, sat her upright, and tied her securely to the chair. Then they dragged her into the great room and put the chair about eight feet in front of the massive flat-screen television.

A thousand thoughts rushed through Bailey's head as she tried to guess what would happen next. One of her captors typed commands into a keyboard. The TV came alive.

To Bailey's shock, the face of Vladimir Putin filled the screen. A small smile flitted across his face.

"Good morning, Ms. Bailey," Putin began. The smile disappeared. "We haven't met, but of course, I know of you from your breathless reporting in and around Minsk."

Through her gag, Bailey tried desperately to reply.

"Ungag her!" Putin commanded. "We have much to talk about."

One of the FSB men roughly ripped off the duct tape holding the gag in her mouth, and Bailey coughed out the cotton wad.

"That's better," Putin continued. "I see you have been able to locate the places in Belarus where these filthy vigilantes have

157

attacked the pipelines and killed our soldiers. And you have made quite a reputation capturing what we've done to them in each case. Your cameraman is quite good framing you in front of crucified bodies."

Putin paused.

Bailey's head was spinning. She knew she should say something; but what? Finally, she blurted out, "President Putin, I was just reporting on what my producers had lined up as that day's story—"

"Oh, so just following orders?" Putin interrupted.

"Why, yes, sir. You see, I'm just a junior reporter. I don't get to pick my stories. I have a producer in Minsk, and then there's—"

"Enough!" Putin snarled. "That is what the Nazis who murdered millions of Russians were fond of saying, 'Just following orders.' Are you a robot? Or perhaps a puppet?"

Bailey was momentarily lost for words, and Putin pressed ahead and poured out his venom on her, her network, the EU and the United States. His harangue lasted ten minutes.

When Putin finally stopped talking, Bailey started to speak, "President Putin, I—"

"I have matters to attend to *Patricia*," Putin interrupted, lingering on her first name, "and I'm tired of your sniveling excuses!" he shouted.

"Put her gag back in!" he commanded. Once that was done, he continued. "You seem to be quite fond of crosses, Patricia. So you don't have to chase this story, my men have brought it to you."

With that, one of the FSB men spun Bailey's chair around so it had a clear view of the villa's expansive back yard. There, in the middle of the yard, they had erected a cross.

Bailey started shrieking, the gag only partially muffling her screams.

As her screaming subsided enough for Putin to be heard, he said to the senior FSB man. "Kill the video connection and talk to me on the phone. I'll tell you what we're going to do."

Laura Peters was standing her watch at the duty desk in the anticipatory intelligence cell. A map of Belarus, centered on Minsk, dominated their large-screen display. Captain Charlie Johnson and Major Pat Cook were manning the workstations where the transcripts of Kremlin conversations were displayed.

"Holy shit!" Johnson exclaimed as he burst out of his chair.

Without prompting, Peters and the other watchstanders rushed over and looked at what Johnson had on his screen.

"Read this," Johnson said as he hovered his cursor over a conversation. "It's Putin talking to Bailey. It's a video connection. He's telling her she's 'fond of crosses,' and she's screaming at the top of her lungs."

"Freeze that," Cook replied. "Send it over to the ops desk. Her captors have to be communicating on cell phones and our info warfare guys may find a way to triangulate the cell towers they're using. We won't get a pinpoint location, but we'll be close."

As Johnson picked up the phone, Cook turned to Peters. "Tell Holden and his team we got a hit."

Rick Holden was sitting in the great room of their villa, along with most of the other members of his team, when he read Laura Peters' message. His mind went into overdrive.

"Listen up!" he shouted. "SACEUR may have a hit on Ms. Bailey's approximate location. We need to be ready to move out. They're working on triangulating cell phone towers to try to get us close to where she is."

Everyone in the room converged on their leader, and those in other parts of the house came running into the great room.

"Darko, we need to get the SUVs loaded up."

"Got it, Boss."

"Mia, tell SACEUR we want to take control of our Global Hawk now. Have it fly lazy circles over the center of Minsk. Once we get some idea of where she might be, you can direct it there."

"Will do."

"Darko, I don't know if we'll need to lay up in one of the other Airbnbs you've secured, but let me see where they are so we can plan."

As Markovic powered up his tablet, the rest of the team burst into a frenzy of activity.

At SACEUR headquarters, General O'Sullivan was cheered by the fact that they might have the means to zero in on Patricia Bailey's location. He wasn't a micromanager, but he made frequent passes through his information warfare watch center where his team was working mightily to get an approximate location of where Bailey was being held.

In the anticipatory intelligence cell, Colonel Sauter and his team were reading and re-reading the digital transcript of Putin's conversation with his FSB team in Tarasava and noodling over what they could do to help. They felt they had reached an impasse when Staff Sergeant John Sundstrum said, "Putin said something about a cross, and Ms. Bailey started screaming. We figured she is somewhere in or near Minsk and likely at some sort of secure villa. Should we be looking for a cross erected outside of a house?"

"You're spot on," Sauter replied. Looking toward Peters, he continued, "Pass that info to Holden and his team. It won't do us a lot of good until we can nail down an approximate location, but once we do, they can use the Global Hawk to look for a cross."

CHAPTER TWENTY-FOUR

Information Warfare Building, Moscow, Russia
(October 10, 1145 Moscow Standard Time)

Colonel Andrei Rykov had reason to be smug. He had made himself indispensable. While his fellow Russian Army officers got jerked around from post to post and were sometimes sent to fight in a nation Moscow used to control in better days, he had been coming to work in this nondescript building eight kilometers southeast of Moscow's ring road for almost ten years. He had gone home to his wife and two sons every night and had been promoted twice during that time.

It bothered him little that his fellow military officers made snide remarks about whether he should wear the same uniform they did, whether he knew how to fire a weapon, and even about his manhood. The thin, bespectacled and bald Rykov knew he was a geek and even reveled in it. He was part of a new cadre of Russian military officers skilled in information warfare.

Rykov and those like him had conceived and implemented cyberattacks around Russia's periphery: Estonia, Georgia, Azerbaijan and elsewhere. Most recently, they had temporarily crippled the Belarusian military's command and control nodes. Farther afield, they had conducted what were essentially nuisance cyberattacks against the United States.

The U.S. attacks were little more than proof-of-concept for their BlackEnergy malware program—but they had two positive results. First, they had successfully burrowed into several industrial control systems in U.S. water, energy and property management systems.

Second, and clearly the bigger victory, was one they could have only dreamed of. The U.S. Department of Homeland Security had announced these penetrations, flagged the issue and made recommendations. And then nothing had happened. U.S. industrial-control software remained laughably vulnerable.

While the geek in him was always keen to work more mischief, Rykov wasn't naïve about global politics. The orders that had come down through the general in charge of all Russian military information warfare forces were said to have originated from the president of the Russian Federation himself. Rykov and his fellow officers had debated this question ad nauseam in discussions typically fueled by generous amounts of vodka. Would this mean they were at war?

Over six thousand miles south-southwest of where Andrei Rykov and his team were doing their work, Mary Rosen sat at the control table at the Port of Corpus Christi operations center and stifled a yawn. It was approaching midnight, and her watch rotation would go on for another two hours. That didn't matter to Rosen. She had served as an operations specialist in the U.S. Navy for four years and had gotten her high school equivalency diploma. The single mom of a toddler had moved back in with her parents after her Navy stint, gotten her certificate in industrial controls at Texas A&M University-Corpus Christi, and landed a job with the Port of Corpus Christi as a controls specialist in their operations center. Now, eight years later, she was a shift leader in charge of a watch team.

Four junior controllers in the Port's main operations center monitored the transfer and loading process as millions of gallons of oil flowed from the facility's massive storage tanks through miles of piping. Tonight, they were monitoring that flow as the oil was loaded onto the Maersk tanker pierside in the Nueces River.

Mary was slumped in her chair, idly looking at the sea of security camera monitors, each showing various locations around the facility, and quietly humming a Sarah Bareilles song when she was jolted upright.

"Mary, the flow through Bravo Pipe is pushing through redline," one of her controllers cried out. She was looking over his shoulder within seconds.

"Trip the override harness now!" she shouted.

"Nada!" he yelled. "It's not working."

To her left, "Mary, I've got same thing, Delta Pipe!" the woman shouted.

The watch shift sprang into action and began to execute their well-rehearsed emergency procedures. Mary tried to manage the chaos as alarms clanged on and a robotic voice told them what they already knew: that the flow of oil through their piping system was exceeding the upper limits of what it could handle.

Suddenly, a huge explosion rocked their building. Rosen and the others looked up in horror at one of their monitors and saw flames leaping from a ruptured pipe and a sea of oil flooding through the port complex. Then there were sirens as the Port's fire brigade converged on the broken pipe.

"Shut the manual breakers!" Mary shouted to one of her watchstanders.

But as the man leapt up to comply, another explosion generated a shock wave and knocked him to the floor.

As Mary Rosen looked up at another monitor and saw the oil from the newly-ruptured pipe wash over a speeding fire truck and knock it sideways, she did the only thing she could do—she prayed. Soon, fire would consume their building and there was nowhere to run.

———

In the hours after the catastrophe at the Port of Corpus Christi, watch teams across the nation (at the **Department of Homeland Security, the Department of Energy, the U.S. Cyber Command, the National Counterterrorism Center** and elsewhere) all assessed and analyzed what they knew and tried to determine precisely what had happened.

All signs pointed to a cyberattack. Later, when the manager of the Port tapped into the remote server that had recorded the conversations Mary Rosen's watch team had had in the minutes before flames consumed their control center, there was no question about what had occurred. And there was little doubt, though no proof yet, about who had made these attacks.

———

Colonel Andrei Rykov and his team of information warfare officers and technicians found it satisfying beyond words as they watched the international news feeds from the smoldering remains of what was once the Port of Corpus Christi. It would have been nice to open a bottle of vodka and pour a glass, or maybe a few, in celebration. But orders were orders.

Rykov's men swung into action and hands flew over computer keyboards. Just over two thousand kilometers from where his men conducted their first cyberattack, the Calumet Industries oil refinery on the shores of Lake Superior was about to suffer a fate similar to the one the Port of Corpus Christi had just experienced.

CHAPTER TWENTY-FIVE

Supreme Allied Commander Europe (SACEUR) Headquarters (October 10, 1315 Central European Time)

Even though thousands of military and civilian officials worked at SACEUR, for the moment, the command's focus was primarily on two groups: the information warfare team led by Army Brigadier General Frank Bayliss and Colonel Sauter's anticipatory intelligence cell. It took all the discipline the latter group could muster to not badger their information warfare colleagues to tell them anything they might have found that would help narrow down Patricia Bailey's location.

Bayliss was at his command console, hovering over one of his watchstanders, when Navy Information Professional Chief Pauline Nixon shouted, "I think we found it!"

"What?" Bayliss asked.

"I've been walking back the cell phone conversations Colonel Sauter targeted for us. I started with the most recent ones and worked backwards, and I found one. It's from almost two hours ago. I triangulated on these three cell towers," she said, hovering her cursor over the screen.

"Where is that?" Bayliss asked.

"Wait one, General." Nixon pulled up an overlay on her screen. "It's somewhere in Tarasava, about twelve klicks northwest of central Minsk—"

"Any landmarks?" Bayliss interrupted.

"It's just west of the intersection of the M9 ring road and the M6 highway."

"How big is the ellipse?" one of the other watchstanders asked. Triangulating cell towers to look for the location of a cell phone was part science, part art. You never got a point location—just a more-or-less defined area.

"It's about...," Nixon began as she maneuvered her mouse, "roughly fifteen miles east to west and maybe eight to ten miles north to south."

"Great!" Bayliss exclaimed. "Pass that to Colonel Sauter's team."

———

Colonel Sauter's anticipatory intelligence command center was full. No one had left, hoping that they would get what they needed from General Bayliss's team.

Captain Johnson picked up the command phone on the first ring. He nodded and kept saying "yes, yes." When he put down the phone, he exclaimed, "We've got a location. Here's what you need to tell Holden's team...."

Laura Peters typed furiously on her tablet.

———

Rich Holden heard the distinctive "bing" on his tablet and read Laura Peters' message. He re-read it to ensure he got all the details right, then switched screens to bring up a map.

"Gather around," he shouted. "We've got an approximate location where Ms. Bailey is being held, and there's likely an identifying landmark: a cross."

The others assembled as Holden started issuing directions.

"Darko, she's here—near Tarasava," he began, pointing at the map. "Have you rented anything close to there?"

"Checking," he replied.

"Mia, how far is the Global Hawk from here?" he asked, pointing at Tarasava again.

"It's a bit northeast of Minsk; I can vector it down there now."

"Do it."

"Darko?" Holden asked impatiently.

"Here, Boss," he replied pointing at the tablet. "We have a place just north of the M6 highway and about two klicks inside the M9 ring road. It's a hell of a lot closer than where we are."

"Good, let's move out.

"Mia, ask SACEUR for their second Global Hawk. Take control of both of them and start looking for a cross."

Vladimir Putin's instructions to his senior FSB man had been explicit: Have Bailey stare at the cross, for a day and a night, and then tie her to it the next morning with her feet just inches from the ground. At sunset, they were to put raw meat right below her and then open the gates of the villa. The home's security lights were to be turned on, and their camera was to be trained on Bailey.

Their Dartz Nagel Dakkar SUVs had already been loaded, and it would take Holden and his team just over an hour to arrive at their new layup house.

Holden drove one SUV, and Mia Yeager rode shotgun. SACEUR had given them control of both Global Hawks, and Yeager was employing them in deliberate search patterns.

The RQ-4 Global Hawk is a high-altitude, remotely piloted surveillance aircraft that was designed to perform similar duties to that of the manned U-2 aircraft. The Global Hawk isn't anyone's idea of a small drone. It weighs over 30,000 pounds fully loaded, nearly as much as some military tactical aircraft.

Flying at an altitude of up to 60,000 feet, cruising at 350 knots, and with an endurance of over thirty hours, it can survey as much as forty thousand square miles of terrain a day—an area the size of

South Korea. The RQ-4 provides a broad overview and systematic surveillance using high-resolution synthetic-aperture radar and long-range electro-optical/infrared sensors.

Holden kept glancing at Yeager's tablet and marveled at how she maneuvered both unmanned aircraft. He knew she knew what she was doing, but couldn't help asking, "Any cross yet?"

"Not yet, Boss—not yet."

CHAPTER TWENTY-SIX

Belarusian Army Base Near Brest, Belarus
(October 11, 0200 Eastern European Time)

Ilia Novik had extracted everything he could from the runaway army conscript his men had brought him. He had then met with his top lieutenants to plan their attack. They had picked the weapons and equipment storage base at Brest, near the Polish border and opposite the Polish city of Terespo, as their target. It was one of the two bases the man had suggested, and this particular base had the benefit of offering them an escape route into Poland.

It was 0200, a time when Novik's reconnaissance suggested the base would be most lightly guarded. He and his team crept toward the chain link fence in the northeast corner of the base, the spot farthest from any of the army base's buildings. He had brought ten of his most trusted men with him, more than he thought he would need to overwhelm whatever number of soldiers might be guarding the base but enough to load up and carry away the weapons they hoped to seize.

Once at the fence, the men bunched up behind Novik and the man holding the wire cutters. "Cut it," the leader whispered.

Within two minutes, the man had cut a four-foot by four-foot hole in the fence. Novik was the first one through, and his men followed.

It happened in an instant. Suddenly, floodlights around the periphery of the base came on, lighting up the night with their enormous candlepower and making the landscape brighter than a night game at a soccer stadium.

Seconds later, they heard a noise. The men looked up in horror as two enormous German Shepherds bounded toward them. Before any of them could react, one dog attacked a man and latched onto his left arm. Another dog was just a few meters behind him.

"Shoot them!" Novik commanded.

Several of his men leveled their assault rifles at the Shepherds and fired on full auto. The dogs went down.

"Let's go!" Novik shouted as he rushed forward, toward the main building in the compound. They were no longer covert, and they knew that they would soon be confronting soldiers.

Seconds later, they heard the roar of an engine, looked up, and saw a Soviet-era Gaz-66 truck bearing down on them. There were soldiers in the bed of the truck, firing wildly at the intruders.

Novik's men dropped into defensive positions and fired back, shooting at the driver's windshield. The Gaz-66 continued to bear down on them and was now just fifty meters away. The soldiers in the truck continued to pour out fire. What their shooting lacked in accuracy it made up in volume. First one, and then another, of Novik's men went down.

But Novik's men fired well-aimed shots, and they found their mark. They punched through the windshield, and the bullets shattered the driver's skull. The Gaz-66 decelerated, careened wildly to the left, hit a sharp rise in the ground, and flipped over on its back, throwing the soldiers in every direction.

Within seconds, the only sounds were the hissing of steam escaping from the truck's busted radiator and the groans of one of the soldiers who was thrown from the truck.

One of Novik's men moved to the man and leveled his assault rifle at his head.

"Wait!" the leader shouted. "We need him. Check the other ones."

They examined the downed soldiers. Save for the one wounded man, they were all dead.

"Your comrades are dead," Novik began as he hovered over the wounded soldier. "We'll spare you if you tell me what we want to know. If you don't, I'll gut shoot you and your death will be worse than theirs."

"Yes...yes," the man stammered. "I'll tell you whatever you want to know."

"How many more are there, and where are they?"

"There aren't any more. We're the only ones guarding this base—"

"Don't lie to me!" Novik shouted as he jammed his assault rifle into the man's crotch. "It will be one bullet at a time, and you'll wish you died like the others."

"I swear; we're the only ones. This isn't an active base; it's just a storage site."

"Where are the weapons kept?" Novik asked.

"In that big building over there," the man replied, waving his arm toward a one-story building several hundred meters away. "They're all underground."

"Show us!" Novik shouted as he jerked the wounded soldier to his feet.

"Arrrgggh," the man cried out in agony.

Novik let him drop to the ground. It was clear he was bleeding out from his wounds and wouldn't live long enough for the attackers to drag him to the building.

"How do we get access to the weapons?"

"On the north side of the building," his prisoner gasped, spitting the words out as he fought through his pain. "There's a ramp that takes you down into the underground bunker. The doors are secured with huge locks, but they're cheap, and you can probably destroy them with the weapons you have. Once you get inside, the bunker goes down several levels."

"What about vehicles? We only have a few vans and a pickup truck. We want to carry away as much as we can."

"South of the building, near the fence line, there are armored personnel carriers and trucks that are laid up."

"Do they work?" Novik asked.

"Yes...yes," the man replied. He pawed at his left shoulder with his right hand, trying to feel what was left where the attackers' bullets had ripped into it. "We drive each one every other week to make sure they work; but otherwise, they just sit there."

Novik could see that the man was going into shock and that he had told him everything he needed to know.

"Good, my friend. You have earned a better fate than what I was going to do to you."

With that, Novik put the barrel of his Mauser on the man's forehead and pulled the trigger once.

He gathered his men around him. "We have to hurry. These soldiers likely alerted others at nearby bases. We'll come back for the wounded in a minute, but right now we need to get into that building and grab as many weapons as we can carry away."

With that, Novik got up and charged the building. His remaining men followed him, leaving their two wounded comrades to fend for themselves.

They found the incline the now-dead soldier had told them about and walked down the steep ramp, bunching up at the bottom. A huge garage-like door, secured with two massive locks, barred access.

After a nod from their leader, two of his men leveled their assault rifles at the locks. Several long bursts obliterated them.

Once that was done, another man walked forward, grabbed the strap on the bottom of the door and pulled. The door barely budged, and another man came to help. The two men tugged on the strap, and the huge door started moving on its rollers. Finally, it was full up.

Novik led his men into the enormous underground bunker, shrouded in darkness except for a few dim ceiling lights.

"Flashlight," Novik snapped.

One of his men produced a military-grade gooseneck flashlight they had taken from a dead soldier.

As they all moved forward together, Novik shined the light around the cavernous room, a space bigger than a soccer field.

Almost in unison, the men gasped in amazement as their leader moved the flashlight around the periphery of the room. What the escaped army conscript had told them would be there, and more, was stacked up on sturdy metal shelves that reached all the way to the twenty-foot ceiling.

Soviet-built recoilless rifles, machine guns, mortars and other heavy weapons sat inert on the shelves.

"Look!" one of the men shouted as Novik held his flashlight beam on a shelf. The man rushed forward and pointed at a shelf containing over a dozen *Igla* man-portable, surface-to-air missiles. "These are Soviet-made manpads," he continued, using the common abbreviation for man-portable. "Let those bastards in the Hinds come after us again."

"There are more weapons here than we can carry in the vehicles we brought. You two," he said, pointing at two of his men, "go to where that soldier said those trucks were parked. Start some of them up and make sure they work."

Then turning to another man, he continued. "Go back and take care of our wounded. Bandage them up as best you can and get them ready for a long ride. We'll need to load up quickly and get these weapons away from here."

As Novik spoke, another man found a ramp that led down to another level of the bunker. "I'm going down here to see what else we can find," he shouted to Novik over his shoulder.

"We've got plenty here, more than we can even carry," Novik snapped.

But the man's curiosity pulled him down the ramp, his flashlight lighting the way as he trudged forward. At the bottom of the ramp, he encountered a huge steel door with formidable-looking locks. He paused, wondering for a moment what he should do next. Like the others, he was excited about what they had found already. What if he was the one to find even higher-end weapons?

He leveled his assault rifle and aimed a burst at each of the four locks in succession. Three of the locks shattered, but another held.

He moved closer and fired at the recalcitrant lock on full auto. It finally burst apart. He moved forward and grabbed the large handle of the huge, vertical steel door. He put both hands on the door and yanked for all he was worth, grunting and straining. He managed to crack the door open just a few inches.

That was all it took. He dropped his flashlight and his rifle as the shrill siren assaulted his ears. The deafening noise continued, splitting the air.

When they heard the assault rifle firing, Novik and the others had started toward the noise, worried the wounded soldier had lied and that their comrade had encountered more troops in the lower reaches of the bunker. When the sirens started, they quickened their pace. They got to the bottom of the ramp and saw only their man. Another man picked up the flashlight and shined it around the frame of the door. Novik did the same thing, looking for a way to shut down the piercing sound. Novik held his flashlight on a protruding red button, and another man rushed up and mashed it.

The alarm went silent.

Three men grabbed the door's handle and pulled it open. The space inside was dark, but another man eventually found a light switch and flicked it on.

The high-intensity ceiling lights snapped on, and Novik and his men stared at the squat body with four tail fins, the first of almost a dozen other bombs.

Without a word, one of the older men in the group pushed forward and walked over to one of the bombs. It was about four feet high and six feet long and was sitting on a trolley. He ran his hand over it almost lovingly.

"I've seen these in old films showing parades in the Soviet Union. We had to watch them when I was in primary school. These are nuclear bombs."

"Are you sure?" Novik asked.

"I am," he replied.

"We don't need them, they won't help us fight against the Russian troops guarding the pipelines," one of the other men said.

"No," Novik replied. "But we can sell them on the black market. When the trucks get here, I want these loaded first!" he commanded. "I want to carry away as many of them as we can."

CHAPTER TWENTY-SEVEN

Near Tarasava, Belarus
(October 11, 0615 Eastern European Time)

It was just after dawn, and Rick Holden and team were laid up at their new location, waiting for one of the two Global Hawks Mia Yeager was controlling to get a hit on a cross. They knew they were close, but they needed to pinpoint Patricia Bailey's location before they moved out.

Laura Peters continued to feed them information as SACEUR's information warfare cell worked to refine the ellipse they had originally reported. While they were able to shrink its size slightly, it still left a huge area for the Global Hawks to search.

Holden used the time to continue to plan their mission. He thought back to his time when Paul Lee had let him observe the training at Camp Pendleton. He figured that that kind of takedown would be what was needed to rescue Patricia Bailey.

It had taken Ilia Novik and his men hours to load the nuclear bombs and other weapons on their own vehicles, as well as on several of the Belarusian Army trucks they had commandeered. Their little convoy had moved away from the base under cover of darkness. Novik's goal was to put as much distance as he could between his cadre and the base while not attracting the attention of nearby Russian troops.

They couldn't go back to the hotel where they first laid up. A mini-convoy of Belarusian Army trucks would stand out like a sore thumb. They had found a thickly wooded area and driven as deep into it as the dirt road would allow. Most of his men were happy about the conventional weapons they had gotten and envisioned taking on their Russian foes. But they were less sure about what good the nuclear bombs would do.

Novik had enough time to think about it and entered an intense conversation with his second-in-command. "The other weapons we have will help us even the odds with these Russian pigs, and we need to get them to where the others are laid up as soon as we can," Novik began.

"I agree," the man replied. "But what about the nukes? We have no way to use them. Why did you want to carry them away in the first place?"

Novik liked the man. He was fearless and had probably killed more Russians than any of his other men. But he was a coal miner from a poor family and had no concept of geopolitics or higher-level military matters.

"We can sell these on the black market, and I think I have an idea about who will pay top price for them. We're not the only ones who hate the Russians. I just have to make the right connections, and then we'll need to get to a port."

The man just shook his head. Even with his lack of education, he knew Belarus was a landlocked country. What the hell was Novik talking about?

Mia Yeager was glued to her tablet as the two Global Hawks she was controlling searched the Belarus countryside.

While the Global Hawk had infrared sensors, the scope of what it could see at night was greatly reduced. She had covered only some of the area of the ellipse during the night.

177

They were all assembled at the huge oak breakfast table in the villa, eating the *draniki* Markovic had insisted on preparing and downing cups of coffee.

Yaeger leaned her tablet on a pile of books she had grabbed from the villa's library as she held her coffee cup in one hand and shoveled *draniki* into her mouth with the other. "I've got something!" she exclaimed.

"What?" Holden and the others shouted in unison.

"Hold on," she said, "I saw something on the video feed from one of the birds, but it passed by too quickly. I've got to send it over that spot again."

The rest of the team hovered around her as she steered one of the Global Hawks to the suspicious spot. Seconds ticked by.

"There—it's a cross!" she yelled as she simultaneously put the Global Hawk in a lazy circle above the spot.

"My God!" Jimbo Folga shouted. "Is that a woman hanging on it?"

"I think it is," Chapo Chavez added. "Mia, can you zoom in with the bird's cameras?"

"Working it."

As the rest of his team stared at the tablet, Holden had already pulled the GPS coordinates off Yeager's screen and was planning their route to rescue Patricia Bailey.

CHAPTER TWENTY-EIGHT

Near Tarasava, Belarus
(October 11, 0730 Eastern European Time)

Rick Holden and his team had planned the basics of how they would rescue Patricia Bailey, but now that they had a location, they needed to assess precisely how to attack the house where she was being held.

As the Global Hawk made endless circles over the villa, it was difficult not to stare at Bailey hanging on the cross. Holden's team needed to get as much information as they could about the house itself. It was easy to see why her captors had chosen this place. It was secluded, far away from any other houses.

They needed a closer assessment. Holden and Darko Markovic drove one of their SUVs into a wooded area close to their target. They had a clear sight line to the house.

"There's a wall, and I see only one gate. How about you, Darko?"

"Yes, only one. That's pretty common in this part of Europe. They might even have a doorbell camera so they can see who's at the gate."

"Makes sense. What I don't get is what happens next. They have her hanging on the cross. We can't tell if she's dead or alive."

"I'm going with alive, Boss."

"I know, Darko; me too. We know Putin had that one video conversation with her, and Peters and her team would have told us if there was another one."

"But how long are they going to let her hang there? Do you think they'll do another connection with Putin?"

"Unknown. But you recall that the Russians streamed video of the Belarusian vigilantes they captured, killed and crucified after they attacked the pipelines. Maybe they're going to do the same thing with Bailey."

"I hope not," Markovic replied. "Something tells me she's worth more to Putin alive than dead."

"I think I agree, but do we risk waiting until night to snatch her?" Holden asked.

"That's the big question. I don't think we want to chance it. It's dicier taking the place down during the day, but I say we go in soon," Markovic replied.

"That's risky."

"Her captors might be awake, but they're likely just sitting around watching soccer matches on TV or playing video games. If we go over the wall there," Markovic said, pointing to a section of the wall on the eastern side of the villa, "we can push up against the front door of the house."

"Good call, Darko. Let's go back and get the others."

———

At infrastructure nodes across America (electricity generating stations, port facilities, hydroelectric dams, and especially nuclear power plants), operators and technicians scrambled to harden their facilities against cyberattacks as best they could. But there was little they could do to counter this new cyber-threat after decades of neglect and hoping against hope that such an attack would never come.

The Calumet Industries oil refinery on Lake Superior had worked as hard as other plants, and maybe a little harder, to take as many of their control systems out of the cloud and offline as possible. Technicians who had not used these antiquated systems in years broke out dusty manuals and dumbed down their control systems as best they could.

When the cyberattack hit, the Superior refinery wasn't bulletproof, but they weathered the attack far better than Corpus Christi had. Oil flows were diverted manually when their electrical systems began to go haywire. While two large pipes did burst as too much oil surged through them too fast, in each case, the flow was soon stopped. They would need massive cleanup and extensive repairs, but there had only been one small fire, and no one had died.

That was little consolation for the Department of Homeland Security and U.S. Cyber Command officials who were on site at Superior, as they were at every U.S. infrastructure node to which they could rush. One crippled facility could be explained away. Two plants represented a nationwide emergency. Soon, reports were rocketing up several chains of command.

CHAPTER TWENTY-NINE

Villa in Tarasava, Belarus
(October 11, 1015 Eastern European Time)

The sound of the breaching charge, as it blew in the door of the villa, was deafening. For Rick Holden and his team members, pressed against the front wall of the building, it was partially muffled by their sound suppressors.

Seconds later, it was purposeful bedlam as Holden led the team inside the home's entry hallway, each man with his HK416 assault rifle at the ready.

Inside, an FSB man, who had been playing a video game on his smart phone prior to the breach, reached for his rifle and fired off a wild shot. Alerted by the sound, the team surged forward and Chapo Chavez double-tapped the man, toppling him where he stood.

On a small rise in the woods outside the villa, where they had stashed their vehicles, Blake Mason and Mia Yaeger stood sniper overwatch, ready to take out any squirters, as well as warn of approaching threats.

Holden, Chavez, Jimbo Folga and Darko Markovic surged through the house. As they approached the great room in the back of the house, the two remaining FSB men ran into the yard in full flight. Each was met by a precise hail of fire that spun them to the ground.

Holden and his team pushed through the great room and into the yard. They were relieved to see that, although she was in physical and mental agony, Patricia Bailey was still alive. They found it odd that the cross was pounded into the earth so deep her feet almost touched the ground.

She would later tell her rescuers that the kidnappers, acting on what they told her were Vladimir Putin's direct orders, were planning on abandoning the villa that night and leaving the doors and gates open so that the wolves, wild boars, and other animals that inhabited the surrounding hills could feast on her.

As they gingerly took Bailey off the cross and assessed that she wasn't seriously injured, Holden looked toward the rise where Mason and Yeager were watching the house through their optical sights and gave them a thumbs up. The pair quickly got into their SUV and headed toward the house.

Holden turned toward the others and said, "We're not sure how many more of these guys are around. As soon as Blake and Mia get here, let's load up Ms. Bailey, head back to our house, and plan our route back to the Minsk airport. I'll let the Agency know we need our aircraft back ASAP."

"Do we know where they have it staged?" Chavez asked.

"Dunno, Chapo. I do know that it took a lot of negotiating with the Belarus government to have our aircraft land in Minsk in the first place. Leaving it at Minsk International was too big of an ask. I'm guessing it's somewhere in Europe."

"Roger that, Boss."

"For now, we just need to let them know we have Ms. Bailey and lay up. Chances are, her captors are supposed to check in with someone periodically. When they don't, things will get dicey."

"We've collected their phones. That may give us some idea of what's going on," Markovic said.

"We'll hope for the best, Darko," Holden replied. "But this country is crawling with Russian troops. Once Putin finds out that Bailey isn't under his control any longer, all hell will break loose."

Markovic echoed Holden's assessment. "That's for damn sure."

Within minutes, Mason and Yeager arrived with their SUVs. They put Bailey in the front passenger seat of one vehicle. Mason drove, and Folga and Chavez stuffed themselves in the back. Markovic drove the other SUV, Holden rode shotgun and Yeager piled into the back seat.

Holden turned toward Yeager, "Mia, drive one Global Hawk down a route toward our house. Have it fly about three to four klicks ahead of us. Let me know if you see any Russian troops"

"Will do, Boss."

In Washington, D.C., President James Miller entered the larger of the two conference rooms in the White House Sit Room. As he always did, he had conferred with his national security advisor before convening this emergency meeting of his cabinet secretaries and other senior advisors. The men and women stood behind their chairs, expecting this might be a tense meeting.

Ryan Garrett had asked the secretary of homeland security to lead the discussion. Once the president sat down at the head of the table, the others did as well. The homeland security secretary strode to the screen and began her presentation. Her first PowerPoint slide showed the charred remains of the Port of Corpus Christi.

"Mr. President, ladies and gentlemen, you all know what happened in Corpus Christi, as well as what happened at Superior. We haven't fingered who made these cyberattacks, but we will," she said, looking at the head of U.S. CYBERCOM, who nodded in agreement.

"But that's not the issue before us," she continued, advancing her slide deck to show a picture of the Superior refinery. "Superior dodged a bullet, only because they had ample warning; had some of the most antiquated and, therefore, largely immune control systems; and because they weren't pumping oil into a ship at the moment of the attack. Our other oil-shipping ports are vastly more vulnerable,

184

and here," she continued as she pulled up another slide, "is the schedule of oil and LNG tankers set to sail from our ports and head to Europe over the next two weeks."

The energy secretary gave his affirmation by adding, "And we're scheduled to ramp up in the weeks after that, Mr. President. Europe can take all the oil and gas we can ship."

"We've swarmed our refineries with our best talent, and they can do a lot to make our shipping ports less vulnerable to a cyberattack," the homeland security secretary added, "but it will take time—"

"How long?" the president interrupted.

The woman paused. She knew the president didn't want to knuckle under to what was increasingly looking like Russian blackmail to force the United States to stop shipping energy to Europe. But she was also mindful that the nation could not absorb many more Port of Corpus Christi disasters. She proceeded carefully, weaving the most optimistic spin she could.

"The short answer is, we just don't know. Perhaps as little as two to three weeks—but maybe a month or more. Inserting manual control systems and weaning those facilities off the cloud will take time and talent, as well as calling back retired workers who know how to use them...."

The woman paused as she saw a frown forming on the president's face. With a nod from the national security advisor, who had just whispered something in the president's ear, she continued.

"Mr. President, I'm mindful we don't want to cave in and stop shipping oil to our European allies, especially given who we think is behind these attacks. But the downside of continuing to pump oil and gas into ships moored at these facilities opens up more of our infrastructure to damage...or even destruction."

She continued her presentation, showing slides that illustrated just how vulnerable the port facilities were. More slides predicted how many jobs would be lost at each severely damaged or destroyed port, and still more slides contained a host of other foreboding statistics.

As the woman continued her pitch, other voices around the table chimed in, some urging the president to continue to ship energy despite the hazards and others urging caution. To a man and woman, they empathized with the president. He wasn't being asked to choose between a good and a bad alternative—only to select the least-bad option.

Finally, the president spoke. "I don't like abandoning our European allies, but I won't put more Americans at risk. We stop shipping energy now. I'll call President Becker myself. Then I want the Russian Ambassador in my office. We know who did this, and we need to stop pussy-footing around."

The day after arriving at the International Mayor's conference, Pavel Safronov had personally called the event's organizers and told them that he and his wife would not be attending the gala dinner on the conference's final evening. He cited pressing matters at home, and given the well-known news of the ongoing demonstrations in Petersburg, his hosts assured him that they understood completely.

As his fellow mayors from scores of major cities mingled at the white-tie event, Pavel and Olga Safronov slipped out of their hotel room, hailed an ordinary taxi, and headed toward Vienna International Airport, about twenty kilometers southeast of the city.

Once at the airport, they boarded their flight. It was not the return flight to Petersburg their office had booked for them. Rather, Safronov had used his own funds and purchased tickets on an Air France flight, direct from Vienna to JFK airport in New York. From there, he intended to rent a car and drive to Washington, D.C.

CHAPTER THIRTY

Near Tarasava, Belarus
(October 11, 1930 Eastern European Time)

Once they were back in their lay-up house, Rick Holden set up a watch rotation and had Mia Yeager position the Global Hawk above the villa to look for any approaching threats. They returned control of the second UAV to SACEUR.

Holden had contacted the Agency and had been told that their aircraft would head to Minsk airport soon and that he would get several hours' notice before his team needed to move out and drive the approximately sixty klicks to the airport.

Blake Mason had tried every trick he knew to hack into the cell phones they had collected from the dead FSB men but had turned up nothing useful.

Immediately after arriving at the lay-up house, Holden and the team had gotten some food and liquid into Patricia Bailey and insisted that she sleep. After she had awakened, had received some additional nourishment, and had put on a fresh set of clothing Yeager had given her, Holden had Bailey relate her story from start to finish.

That compete, Holden turned to the extremely sensitive matter of what Bailey knew regarding CIA operatives in Europe and whether the FSB men had interrogated her regarding their names and locations—and what she had revealed.

After getting over her shock that Holden knew this, she assured him that she had not been asked about those individuals. Holden told Bailey that he believed her story but that there would be more extensive debriefing once they left the country.

Now they waited.

Holden used the time to exchange texts with Laura Peters. They soon reached the point where texts were bogging down communication. He called her on his secure satellite phone.

"Rick," Peters began. "Great job rescuing Ms. Bailey. We are all tremendously relieved."

"I'm glad we were able to pull this off with none of our team killed or injured. Now we need to get out of here before the Russians try to recapture her. Are you all dialed in to our extraction plan?"

"That hasn't trickled down to our cell yet. All we know thus far is that the Agency is working on getting your aircraft to Minsk airport as soon as possible and that we left one Global Hawk under your control so you can fly it ahead of your route to look for threats."

"That tracks with what I know. But once the Russians find out we've snatched her, they will likely figure we'll try to fly out of Minsk airport and move to intercept us. We may need your help with anticipatory intelligence and anything else you can give us."

"I'll pulse my boss. More to follow."

"Thanks, Laura."

"Be careful, Rick."

———————

Tanya Volkov had only been married to her Belarusian Army husband for nine months, and they had been posted at the base at Brest for the entire time. Now pregnant with their first child, she was grateful that her husband had a routine job guarding the inactive base. He called it boring, but she was happy that she didn't need to worry about him.

Though he was only a private, he knew enough about what most of his army comrades were doing: chasing vigilantes throughout their country. He had assured her that coming home to her every night was a blessing and that they should be grateful, even though his pay was meager and their army housing was decrepit.

She *was* grateful and had busied herself with lunches with other army wives and preparing their home for their baby. One sergeant's wife had taken the nineteen-year-old woman under her wing and showed her the ropes of army life.

Tonight, when Volkov's husband didn't return for dinner as scheduled, she called the sergeant's wife and asked if something could be wrong.

The woman assured her that nothing was amiss; perhaps the officers had made the men stay late and do extra work.

Reassured, Volkov took the supper of *machanka*, a traditional pork dish, off the table and put it back in the oven.

But the sergeant's wife began to have second thoughts. Her husband hadn't returned home either. She tried texting him and then called his cell phone—nothing.

She called the base, but the phone just rang.

She called the captain's wife, who told her that her husband was on leave and visiting a sick relative. The captain's wife said she would call the regional command center and make some inquires.

At the command center, the corporal who answered the call told her he would pass the information to the watch team commander. He informed the captain's wife that he guessed they would send a vehicle to the army base to ensure all was okay.

———

Ilia Novik had become the leader of all the Belarus vigilante groups for a host of reasons, not the least of which was his ability to get things done off the books. The former Belarusian Army special forces captain was not unlike special operators in militaries worldwide. He knew there were rules, but he never let rules get in the way of getting things done.

He had despised the Russians for as long as he could remember. They were even worse than the pro-Russian masters ruling his country. That hatred fed his interest in blogs and other media, even the dark web, where anti-Russian venom was spewed.

He quickly learned that if there was one ethic group that hated Russia more than the Belarusian majority in his country, it was the one and a half million citizens of Chechnya. They would jump at the chance to buy these nukes, and he knew just where to look on the dark web to find a buyer.

───────────

The major in charge of the watch team at the 38th Mobile Brigade base was told that the wife of an army captain had called with concerns about the inactive base at Brest. Had it been a hysterical teenage wife of a junior enlisted man, he would have blown off the call.

He assigned a staff sergeant and a corporal to get a vehicle from the motor pool and drive to the base to see what might be the matter. The two soldiers took a leisurely route to the base and joked along the way about meddling wives. Still, it beat sitting in the command center under the eyes of officers.

When they arrived at the base, it took them only minutes to assess what had happened. They called the major.

Then all hell broke loose.

CHAPTER THIRTY-ONE

Washington, D.C. The Oval Office
(October 12, 0700 Eastern Standard Time)

It was early morning in Washington, D.C., as President James Miller waited for the call from European Council President Eric Becker. Their aides had scrambled to set up the hastily arranged call. The attack on the Calumet Industries oil refinery was international news, and the media talking heads had engaged in speculation regarding what the United States might do.

Becker thought he knew what the American president was going to say. He feared the worst. Miller confirmed those fears. He couched what he told Becker in the most optimistic terms, saying that, once the U.S. had hardened their facilities, energy shipments could continue. But Becker was no optimist—he was a realist.

The call ended after less than five minutes.

———

Ilia Novik knew that time was not on his side. Eventually, the Belarusian Army would discover that their base had been attacked and that these weapons, and especially the nukes, were missing. The generals who had let their thinly guarded base be attacked would hunt them down, if for no other reason, to save their own skins.

He had communicated with one Chechen, who had passed him along to another man, and then another, until he reached someone who had the power and the money to buy what he was offering for sale. At every level, he had been quizzed as to whether he really

191

knew what he had. Each time, he had rolled out his creds as a former Belarusian Army officer as a way of assuring them that he did, indeed, have nuclear weapons and was willing to sell them. But what clinched the deal each time were the pictures he sent of him posing in front of the squat bombs as he held a recent newspaper.

After what seemed like endless haggling, Novik and the Chechen principal finally agreed on a price. The man told Novik that more details would follow as to how they would transport the weapons to Chechnya.

Novik's men had watched their leader talking on his cell phone for hours. He had looked angry and had often been heard shouting into the phone.

They were relieved when he slipped his phone into his pocket, smiled, and said, "Gather round, I have something I want to tell you."

There was far less happiness in the office of the president of the Republic of Belarus. Maria Sechenov sat in her chair, glowering at her defense minister and the head of her armed forces. As the two men offered all manner of excuses for what had happened at the base at Brest, Sechenov listened, barely able to control her simmering rage.

The defense minister described how they would catch the culprits and return the weapons to the base. He assured his president that security would be stepped up at all of the country's military bases.

When Sechenov heard that, she bolted out of her chair and pointed her pudgy finger at the man. "Mr. Minister, you disappoint me! Do you have *any* idea what missing nuclear weapons mean to the international community? Do you think you can find these terrorists by unleashing thousands of your troops and not have the Russians who still occupy our country find out what's going on?

You think we are occupied now? Have you no concept of how many more Russian invaders will surge into our nation? We will be the laughingstock of the international community, no better than failed states in Africa and Asia...."

As Sechenov continued her harangue, the two men sank lower into their chairs, not knowing what they could do to placate their raving president. They soon found out.

"General!" she barked. "You will keep your troops in their barracks. You have failed me and failed your country. Get the hell out of my sight—both of you!"

Seconds after the two men had departed, Sechenov buzzed for her chief of staff. A minute later, the man was in her office.

"I need you to arrange a secure phone call with the American president. Tell whoever handles these things at his end it is extremely urgent."

"Right away, Madam President."

———

The European Council's president had listened impassively during his call with President Miller. It was not unexpected. The United States had cut and run from conflicts as far afield as Vietnam, Somalia and Iraq. The European Union was just the latest victim. Afraid to ship energy—this from the supposedly most-powerful nation on earth? It was pathetic.

Eric Becker had not gotten to this high station in life without being able to deal with surprises, even the most unpleasant ones, and turn on a dime.

Within a few hours of President Miller's call, he had convened an emergency meeting of his ministers. While there was wild speculation about when the United States might start shipping oil and LNG again, no one wanted to hazard a precise guess. To make matters worse, the nations of Europe were already tapping into their limited reserves of oil and gas, and winter was approaching.

Finally, a consensus emerged, and Becker gave the European Council's energy minister his mandate: Fly to Riyadh immediately and broker an agreement with the Saudis. Then, fly on to Tehran and make a deal with Iran. He told the minister that he was putting his personal Airbus ACJ320 corporate jet at his disposal and that it was at Brussels International Airport, fueled and ready. A Mercedes Maybach sedan, with a driver, was waiting for him outside the New Europa Building. Becker told him not to worry about packing a bag; he could buy whatever he needed in Riyadh.

His energy minister complied—to a point. He knew the greedy Saudi's would hold them up and try to force them to pay a premium for their oil. And he also knew that the Iranians, who had smarted from U.S. sanctions for years and who were eager to find some way to ship their oil to any buyer, would be eager to sell. He convinced himself that the fact that his Iranian go-between would ensure that he got a huge kickback had nothing to do with his change in priorities.

He would make a short, pro forma stop in Riyadh, to get the unpleasant task of talking with the Saudi's out of the way, and then rush to Tehran, where he would make a deal for Iran to start shipping oil immediately.

Once he was seated in the back of the Maybach and the privacy window between him and the driver was up, he called his Iranian contact.

Vladimir Putin's chief of staff had struggled with just how to tell the Russian president that Patricia Bailey had been snatched away from the clutches of his supposedly crack FSB men. He dithered for as long as he could, but finally the fear that Putin would learn from some other source that Bailey had been rescued convinced him to enter his boss's office.

"Mr. President," he began. "I have some dreadful news...."

Putin listened coolly as the man poured out his story. Even in his rage, he knew it wasn't his chief of staff's fault; it was the incompetent FSB director, General Aleksandr Bortnikov. He would fire Bortnikov before the sun set. But first, he had to deal with the issue of Bailey's escape.

"Look," Putin began after his chief of staff had finished. "There shouldn't be any question as to who snatched Bailey out from under our noses. I've got bigger fish to fry—stopping the Americans, or anyone else—from shipping energy to Europe. One reporter has little to do with that."

His chief of staff was holding his tablet, waiting for the next pronouncement.

"But I won't give the Americans the satisfaction that they can reach this close to our borders and do this. And if they went through this much effort just to rescue one American, maybe *she* knows something they don't want *us* to know—"

His chief of staff used the pause to interject, "But I'm told she was thoroughly interrogated by the FSB. They didn't discover anything of importance—"

"That's because they're fucking incompetent!" Putin bellowed. "I have other ways to interrogate her. But first, we have got to find her. Tell me again where our generals have set up their headquarters in Belarus."

The man scrolled through his tablet. "They've commandeered a dacha on the outskirts of Minsk, near Kapishcha."

"Good. Get them on the phone immediately. I want her hunted down."

———

Several hours later, in SACEUR's anticipatory intelligence cell, Colonel Sauter's team read the transcription of Vladimir Putin's conversation with his generals in Belarus.

195

Armed with that information, Laura Peters sent a secure chat message to Rick Holden.

Holden called his team together and delivered the news. For the moment, there was nothing they could do but wait.

CHAPTER THIRTY-TWO

Washington, D.C. The Oval Office
(October 13, 0930 Eastern Standard Time)

Her staff had been evasive regarding why Maria Sechenov needed to speak with President Miller so urgently. Finally, Ryan Garrett had intervened and spoken directly with Sechenov's chief of staff. He had told the man that, while the American president always wanted to honor the fact that the head of another nation—and one clearly under duress—needed to speak with him, he needed to know more. The man had complied, and the shocked Garrett agreed to set up a secure call.

The President sat in the Oval with Garrett as the only other party in the room. He picked up the phone on the first ring. Garrett listened in, silently, on another line.

"Madam President."

"Mr. President, thank you for taking my call on such short notice."

"Maria, thank you for allowing my team to enter your country and rescue Ms. Bailey. As you likely know, we're arranging to have an aircraft land at Minsk International today and fly her and my team home."

"I do, James. I suspect the Russians who still occupy our nation will try to intercept them, but we are happy to help ensure that they return to your country safely—if you need us, that is."

"We will let you know if that's the case; but for now, I understand you have a larger issue you would like to discuss."

"Yes, James. Here's the problem...."

Sechenov related her situation, telling Miller what Garrett had already told him. But hearing it from her directly helped him understand the situation better.

Miller kept saying "yes" or "I understand" as she told him everything that had happened at Brest. But she had not yet told him what she wanted him to do.

"James, those nuclear weapons should have been returned to Russia decades ago. Why, or how, they were still at that base in Brest is something that we may never know, let alone how many of them may be stored at other bases. I can find, and properly safeguard, other nuclear weapons that were never returned to Russia. My generals are discretely going to all of our active, as well as inactive, bases to inventory every last bullet, rifle and bomb. I worry about what they will find, but at least I can control what happens next."

"I see," Miller replied.

"But if I unleash our army throughout my country and turn it upside down looking for those stolen nuclear bombs, the Russians will surely find out and push their thumb down on us even more firmly. Then we'll never get them to leave, regardless of how this energy issue gets resolved."

"How can we help, Maria?"

"I don't know the composition of your team that rescued Ms. Bailey, or what part of your government they work for—and, frankly, that's none of my business. But, clearly, they are capable. Is it possible that they might find those missing nukes, discretely, and let us take control of them again?

Miller looked toward Garrett, who nodded affirmatively.

"Maria, the short answer is that we want to help and I think we can. I need to consult with my people. May I get back to you?"

"Certainly, James. And thank you."

As soon as the line went dead, Miller asked Garrett, "Can we do this, Ryan?"

"I think we can, Mr. President. But as you told President Sechenov, we need to think it through. It will likely have to be a team effort between the CIA and SACEUR. Shall I get the Director and the JCS Chairman in here?"

"Yes, and sooner rather than later."

"I'll take care of it, Mr. President."

———

The call from their CIA handler had finally come, and it had electrified Rick Holden and his team. The Agency's aircraft would land at Minsk International in three hours.

As soon as he ended the call, Holden called his team together.

"That was the call we've been waiting for. Our aircraft is landing in a few hours. Let's load up.

"We need to be careful. SACEUR told us the Russians will try to intercept us and will likely guess we'll try to extract via Minsk. But if we move quickly, we can do this."

His team started to move out, but Holden interjected. "Darko, Mia, wait one. We discussed the various routes we could take to the airport. I know we decided the most direct route had us move east and then intercept the M9 ring road."

"That's pretty much what we planned to do," Markovic replied.

"That was good *then*. But now that we know the Russians are looking for us. We need to look for concentrations of troops and even roadblocks. Mia, get the Global Hawk scouting ahead. Meanwhile, I'll circle back with SACEUR and see if they can help us."

———

Laura Peters had already been alerted that the Gulfstream was on the way to pick up the CIA team when Holden signaled her on their secure chat line. Seconds later, they were on the phone.

"Laura, as you likely know, we're breaking camp and will be outbound to dash to Minsk International. Any intel on your end as to where the Russians might be trying to intercept us?"

"Nothing that my cell has seen, and I've pulsed others in the command. You still have control of that one Global Hawk, right?"

"Right. We'll fly it ahead of our route and sweep for threats."

"Good, our ops desk has already put our one remaining Global Hawk in an orbit over Minsk International. That's where we assess the threat will be the worst."

"Got it. I'll let you know once we're on the move."

───────

The national security advisor's large staff normally handled things like setting up meetings, but because of the urgency, Ryan Garrett personally placed the calls to the CIA director and the chairman of the Joint Chiefs of Staff himself.

Now those two men sat with the president and Garrett in a secure conference room inside the White House Sit Room. The image of the SACEUR commander, General Davis O'Sullivan, filled the screen at one end of the room.

The president laid out the issue. "Gentlemen, I know your staffs have not had time to bring you fully up to speed on the situation in Belarus, but President Sechenov has asked for our help. We need to give it to her before those missing nukes fall into the wrong hands."

The CIA director was the first to respond. "Holden and his team can try to track those weapons down, but it's not a small country. We have to think the people who stole them were Belarusian vigilantes and that they will try to sell them to a foreign buyer. We'll need massive help from SACEUR with signals intercepts. Otherwise, we're just looking for a needle in a haystack."

O'Sullivan spoke up. "I hear you, Mr. Director. I've already got my command working on it. You'll get everything we can give you."

"I'm counting on it, General."

O'Sullivan continued. "There is one more thing, Mr. President. Given the concerns about what she might know, I recommend the CIA team get Ms. Bailey to Minsk International and get her out of the country before they start their hunt for the nukes."

The president nodded his head. "I agree, General."

The CIA director agreed as well. "I know they're communicating with your staff, General, so tell them to do just that—and do it ASAP."

The four men continued their conversation, with the president directing Garrett to contact the director of National Intelligence and tell him to organize the rest of his three-letter agencies to help find the stolen nukes before they could be spirited out of Belarus.

Ilia Novik had brokered what he thought was the best possible deal with the Chechens, and now he and his team waited. He feared that the Belarus Internal Troops, the Belarusian army, and the Russian troops would be combing the countryside, trying to hunt down him and his men. But thus far, they had seen no frantic activity. For now, they waited.

Laura Peters didn't bother to signal Rick Holden via secure chat. She called him on the secure sat phone. "Rick, your mission has changed and changed dramatically."

"I'm listening," Holden replied. He thought he detected a tremor in Peters' voice. As Peters updated him on the significantly changed situation, Holden's mind went into overdrive. Once she had finished, he simply said, "We're on it."

James Miller had made a political career out of being a smooth operator, a good listener, and a man with an always-calm demeanor.

It had propelled him to years in the Senate, representing the good people of Florida, and had finally helped land him in the White House.

None of those qualities were on display as an aide ushered the Russian Ambassador into the Oval.

Miller stood scowling as the ambassador approached his desk. The U.S. intelligence community had fingered Russia for the cyberattacks on U.S. energy ports. Motive had met opportunity and capability. The evidence was compelling.

"Good evening, Mr. President," the ambassador began. "How may I be of service to you today?"

The president thrust his right index finger at the ambassador and shouted, "Do you know how many Americans died in the fire at the Port of Corpus Christi?"

"Only what I read in the news reports, Mr. President. I was saddened to learn of that tragedy—"

"Saddened?" the president interrupted.

"Yes, sir—saddened and shocked. I heard your government is already taking steps to make your ports more secure."

"You're God damned right we are!" the president shouted. "But that's almost impossible if your government continues their cyberattacks against them."

"Cyberattacks? My government? Mr. President, I'm not sure I know what you are talking about."

Miller was out in front of his desk and just two feet from the man in seconds. Shocked, the Russian Ambassador took a step back.

"Don't you deny it, and don't try to tell me your president didn't personally order these attacks!"

"Mr. President, I serve at your pleasure; but I must say, I object to the nature of these personal attacks. Perhaps if you—"

Miller stepped forward, his face now just inches from the ambassador. "Mark my words. You get Putin to stop these attacks, or we'll unleash cyber-strikes on you that you will never recover from. Now get out!" he shouted. *"Get the hell out!"*

As the Russian Ambassador retreated quickly and left the door to the Oval open, Ryan Garrett entered with the head of the U.S. Cyber Command.

CHAPTER THIRTY-THREE

On the M9 Ring Road Around Minsk, Belarus
(October 14, 1415 Eastern European Time)

Rick Holden and his team were mindful that they had no idea where in the eighty thousand square miles of Belarus the missing nukes might be—if they were still in the country at all. Holden had decided he and Darko Markovic would take just one vehicle and make a dash for the Minsk International Airport. If they had taken the entire team and all three vehicles in a convoy, even the most inept Russian roadblock could have easily sniffed them out.

Holden had decided to ride shotgun and have Darko Markovic drive. If they were stopped, Darko could communicate in the native language. After apologizing to Bailey about the need to do so, they had rolled her up in a huge Persian carpet taken from the villa and put it in the back of the SUV. They took another half dozen carpets from throughout the house and piled them on top of the one holding Bailey. They would tell any Russian soldiers who stopped them that they were picking up more carpets at the airport's cargo terminal and then taking the lot of them to a distributor on the outskirts of Minsk.

They had just turned north on the M9 ring road when Mia Yaeger called Holden from the team's layup house. "Rick, the Global Hawk shows trouble up ahead, about eight klicks north. It looks like a convoy of military trucks heading south. Unknown if they'll stop and set up a roadblock."

Holden looked toward Markovic. "Whatcha think, Darko?"

"Ask Mia how fast they look like they're going."

Holden complied, and Yeager told him they were moving at high speed.

"It doesn't sound like they're looking for us. If they really wanted to set up a roadblock on a main highway, they'd have done so already. And they would spread out their assets, not bunch them up in a convoy. I say we keep going."

"Agreed," Holden replied.

They continued along the ring road and were about to intercept the east-west portion of the M2 highway when Yaeger called again.

"There's a roadblock on the M2 highway about four klicks from where it turns south. There are already several dozen cars and trucks backed up in the southbound lanes. We need to get you off that highway and onto local roads."

Holden related the conversation to Markovic and then looked at his tablet for alternate routes.

"Let's go this way," Holden offered after a minute of searching. He pointed at the map. "Take the next exit. I'll steer you from there."

As Markovic complied, Holden kept a running dialogue with Yeager, who steered the Global Hawk along the roads they were on, as well as the ones they would use next, to look for threats. Taking this circuitous route added time to their journey, but they needed to avoid intercept if they wanted to get Bailey out of the country safely and get on with the rest of their mission.

Laura Peters was accustomed to multitasking, but functioning as the primary conduit to Rick Holden and his team during Bailey's extraction was taxing, even with her talents. She had to use all the assets at SACEUR's disposal, especially the Global Hawk, to keep Holden clear of Russians around the Minsk airport. She also had to ingest all the information from outside sources, as well as their own anticipatory intelligence, to try to pinpoint where the people who had stolen the nukes, Belarusian vigilantes was everyone's best guess, were located.

Her immediate priority was Holden and Bailey and getting her safely aboard the CIA Gulfstream that was waiting at the cargo terminal on the fringes of the airport. Security and customs officials had been paid off to let the team's vehicle drive onto the tarmac, directly to their aircraft; but with Russians combing the country, just getting to the airport was anything but a certainty.

The Air Force captain driving the Global Hawk anchored over the Minsk airport had an open line to Colonel Sauter's command center and relayed continuous updates of what she saw.

As Holden and his cargo got within a few klicks of the airport, Peters didn't wait for the Air Force captain's reports. She quizzed her incessantly.

The EU energy minister had insisted that his Saudi counterpart meet him at Riyadh International Airport rather than at one of the Saudi government buildings in the city.

The Saudi minister had been taken aback, but he was eager to make what he sensed would be an extraordinarily lucrative deal. He was also planning to shake down his desperate EU counterpart for an under-the-table "brokering fee," so he complied with the minister's request.

After an exchange of pleasantries, the EU minster laid out his energy requirements.

The Saudi listened and then named his price, offering all manner of reasons for the inflated ask. He knew his initial offering was ridiculously high, but it was just his opening gambit that would kick off hours of haggling before the EU minister caved to a "compromise" price that still amounted to near-blackmail.

Once the Saudi was finished, the EU minister just shook his head and said, "I am sorry we can't agree on a deal. I wish you well, my friend."

Fifteen minutes later, his Airbus was on the taxiway and cleared for takeoff to Teheran.

Ilia Novik knew his men were getting restless while they waited in a wooded area for instructions as to what to do next with their weapons. He had explained that it was up to the Chechens to figure out where they wanted their product delivered, but that didn't allay their anxiety, or his, about what would happen next.

Novik rejected any thought that they might be instructed to take an overland route through Russia. It was a journey of over two thousand kilometers and, with the Russians trying to hunt them down already, was far too risky. He knew the Chechens didn't give a damn about his safety or that of his men, but based on how much they were willing to pay, they sure as hell wanted the weapons.

He figured that his Chechen handler would arrange for a merchant vessel to transport the weapons. He weighed the pros and cons of either driving north, through Lithuania, to a port on the Baltic or south, through Ukraine, to a port on the Black Sea. He had his ideas, but he doubted they would carry any weight.

Once the weapons were loaded on a ship, their part of the bargain was done, and they would be paid. There were advantages and disadvantages to each route, and the speculation was driving him crazy. But for now, all he and his men could do was wait.

The call from the watch officer at the SACEUR command center was insistent. They needed one of Colonel Sauter's watchstanders to come there ASAP.

Major Pat Cook was the watch commander and dispatched Charles Johnson and Laura Peters on the run.

When they arrived, the Air Force colonel manning the watch team simply said, "Listen to this."

He clicked the *Play* button on his computer monitor and played the conversation picked up by a National Reconnaissance Office (NRO) satellite between Ilia Novik and his Chechen handler. That bit of signals intelligence had been passed to the National Security Agency (NSA) and then on to SACEUR.

Even though the recorded conversation was hours old, it told them precisely what they needed to know: The Chechens wanted to buy the stolen nukes. And from what they could glean from the conversation, it appeared that the weapons were still in Belarus.

Johnson and Peters thanked their colleagues, asked to be alerted to all future conversations, and dashed back toward the nerd nook.

————

Darko Markovic's evasive driving, Rick Holden's countless route-changing audibles, and Mia Yeager's ability to sweep ahead of their SUV looking for threats had accomplished their goal. The van rolled into Minsk International Airport and up to the Gulfstream. Holden and Markovic extracted Patricia Bailey from the carpet and helped her onto the aircraft.

One of the Special Activities Center's pilots asked Holden, "Is the rest of your team coming in other vehicles?"

Holden quickly explained their situation and then got back into their SUV for the return trip to the house where they were laid up.

The Gulfstream was airborne within minutes, and as instructed, the pilot called the CIA director on a secure line, telling him Bailey was aboard.

As Yeager kept the Global Hawk searching ahead of their off-highway route, Holden got a call from Laura Peters. They now knew vastly more about their mission.

CHAPTER THIRTY-FOUR

Supreme Allied Commander Europe (SACEUR) Headquarters (October 16, 1030 Central European Time)

The activity at SACEUR Headquarters was frenetic as many centers of excellence in the command worked together to try to point to where the Belarusian vigilantes with the nukes were and, more importantly, where they were going.

While Colonel Sauter was one of the more-junior officers in charge of the effort, his cell was the one in direct contact with Holden and his team, so all information flowed to his watch floor. Sauter's team had the additional advantage of taking any raw intelligence they received and pushing it through their anticipatory intelligence algorithms.

But while the potential was there to narrow the focus of their analysis, there had not been another intercept between Novik and the Chechens for almost two days.

Russia had its own signals intercept capabilities, which rivaled those of the United States. They had started listening during the Cold War and—most recently, under the guise of combating terrorism—were monitoring communications throughout Russia and surrounding nations.

While terrorism was a legitimate concern, the effort was more about controlling free speech. Whatever was being said—at anytime, anywhere—the Kremlin wanted to know what was discussed. Now, that blanket of communications intercept capability had paid off in spades.

His intelligence chief had told Vladimir Putin that there were missing nukes in Belarus and that the Chechens were going to buy them.

The Russian president could add two and two. After the atrocities Russian troops had committed during two Chechen wars, he knew Chechnya was thirsting for revenge and had done little to try to control the disparate groups that would hold Russia hostage for concessions to which he would never agree.

Finding those who had the bombs before they were spirited out of the country became an all-consuming goal. He told his generals already in Belarus that unless they found the missing nukes in short order, he would put new officers in charge of the operation and thousands more troops would be surged into the country to assist those already there.

The EU energy minister had expected to meet with only his Iranian counterpart but was surprised when that man met him at the foot of his Airbus with a limousine and driver and told him they would be meeting with the President of Iran.

After a short but terrifying drive through Teheran's notoriously bad traffic, they arrived at the government building and were ushered into the president's office. The EU energy minister was greeted as if he were a visiting head of state. The man stated his needs, and the Iranian president named his price. The deal was done in less than twenty minutes. It was sweetened when the Iranian president said, "We know you need energy quickly, and we want the EU to know we will be your supplier of choice."

"And you are," the energy minister replied.

"Good. We have one of our large tankers loaded with oil, which put into our port of Chabahar—on our southern coast—to deliver a sick crewman who needed medical care. It was destined for Japan, but we can reroute it to you. It can steam into the Red Sea and onward to your port of choice immediately."

"That would be perfect," the minister replied.

"I know it is just one tanker, and sending it as the first one of our ships delivering oil to you is mainly symbolic. But that symbolism works for both of us, don't you think?"

"I do, Mr. President. I'm anxious to report this to President Becker. May I inquire as to the name of the vessel?"

The president looked toward his energy minister, who replied, "The ship was originally named *Sima*, but now it is called *Blossom*."

The Iranians asked the EU energy minister to stay for a celebratory dinner, but he declined, saying he needed to return to Brussels immediately to brief President Becker. He was back aboard the Airbus within an hour, and as the aircraft climbed out of Tehran International, he called Becker's office.

The secretary who took the call was a new hire with an interim security clearance. Had she been fully vetted, someone might have turned up the fact that the Russian GRU (Main Intelligence Directorate) had worked for over six months to place her in this low-paying and unfulfilling job. Once she told Becker's chief of staff that she had the energy minister on the line, she returned to her desk and discretely listened to the call.

When the conversation was over, she told another secretary that she was dying for a cigarette break. Soon, she was on the sidewalk on the east side of the New Europa Building, cell phone in hand.

———

At their layup Airbnb, Rick Holden and his team were going through the same kind of calculations Ilia Novik and his men were weighing. They knew the stolen nukes were somewhere in Belarus and that the Chechens wanted them.

Holden had pulsed his team members individually, and now he huddled with his number two, Jimbo Folga, to plan their next step. He put the tablet with the map of Belarus on the coffee table in front of them.

"The team's consensus seems to be that it's time to move. What do you think, Jimbo?"

"We know they grabbed the weapons here," he began, pointing at the location of the Brest army base in the extreme southwestern portion of the country. "And we know they eventually have to get them to Chechnya. One way is overland; do you think they'll do that?"

"Doubtful," Holden replied. "That's almost two thousand klicks on Russian roads."

"I think I agree. That means by sea, a port—here, or maybe here," Folga replied, pointing to locations on the Black Sea, as well as on the Baltic.

"If we want to intercept them, we need to get nearer to those two potential routes. Time to relocate?"

"That's for damn sure."

"Let's do it as soon as it's nightfall. I'll have Darko find us another place to lay up."

While he was not happy that the cyberattacks on U.S. port facilities had, at least for the moment, suspended America's energy shipments to Europe, the president was somewhat cheered when his national security advisor entered the Oval to report that the EU had brokered an energy deal and would soon be receiving oil from the Mideast.

President Miller was not pleased that, given the decades of animus between the United States and the Islamic Republic of Iran, Eric Becker had made a deal with Tehran. But after Ryan Garrett carefully explained Europe's near-desperation for energy from somewhere, *anywhere*, Miller decided that it was the best that could be done under the circumstances.

While Mia Yeager flew the Global Hawk ahead of their route, Rick Holden and his team rolled out of their villa in their three vehicles at 2300. Holden and Folga had wrestled with exactly where to move their location so they would be closer to the Belarusian vigilantes if or when they began a journey to some seaport.

They realized that without a signals intercept that would help narrow the location of whoever had the stolen nukes, they would never find them. But their goal was to be as close to their suspected location as they could manage. While it was still guesswork, Holden and Folga had told the rest of the team that they would next lay up in a villa outside the city of Baranavichy, midway between Minsk and Brest.

CHAPTER THIRTY-FIVE

Aboard the Blossom in the Red Sea
(October 18, 1230, East Africa Time Zone)

Captain Farid Kirmani stood on the bridge of the *Blossom*, shielding his eyes from the intense Red Sea midday sun. He considered his good fortune to be in command of the Iranian-flagged Very Large Crude Carrier, VLCC for short. One of the ways the National Iranian Tanker Company had tried to skirt sanctions in the past was to adopt English names to replace the Persian names of their ships. *Sima* was the ship's original name, and Kirmani had to admit he had liked that one better.

But none of that mattered now. Iran was shipping oil to Europe, and at a premium. He wasn't privy to the negotiations that had made this all happen; he was just proud his ship was the first one to deliver oil under this new contract and delighted that he and his crew were being paid a bonus.

After being alerted that his destination had been changed, he had asked questions but had been told that those were his orders. He advised his crew about the change in plans and put the best spin on things.

Kirmani was still trying to get his brain around why things had changed so quickly when his first mate approached him.

"Have you sailed to through the Suez Canal before, Captain?" the man asked.

"No, this will be a first for me," Kirmani replied. "Are you looking forward to seeing some of the Mediterranean?"

"Yes, and I like that these voyages will be much shorter than those we were making to China and Japan."

Kirmani paused a moment before replying. His first mate, as well as most of his crew, was single. It wasn't like it was two decades ago, when he had first signed on as a sailor. Then, Iran was an international pariah, and its economy had hit bottom. Being at sea had been a welcome relief. Now, with the Iranian economy bouncing back and with the Iranian mullahs relaxing rules about courtship, at least a bit, being a single young man in Iran wasn't such a bad thing.

He realized his first mate didn't need or want a lecture on how bad it was in the old days, so Kirmani merely said, "Me too."

Fifty miles west-southwest of Moscow, the Antonov AN-12 four-engine turboprop lumbered down the northeast runway at Kubrinka Air Base and clawed its way into the afternoon sky. Similar in size and capability to the U.S.-made C-130, and originally built during the Cold War, the old but sturdy Antonov was now in service with the Russian information warfare forces.

Once the Antonov completed its initial climb-out, the aircraft's pilots banked it around and headed due south, settling in for a long flight. In the tube of the aircraft, a small cadre of technicians tuned up their electronic warfare equipment. They had last employed their gear in Ukraine—with devastating results—and were anxious to turn it against a new foe.

The call between EU President Eric Becker and President James Miller had been preceded by countless hours of staff work to prepare both men for the conversation. While the preparation was usually necessary, in this case, it was essentially pro forma. Now that Europe had a reliable source of energy again, it was time to turn up the pressure on Russia to get its troops out of Belarus.

"President Becker," Miller began as he took the call in the Oval. "I'm told you have brokered a deal with Iran to begin shipping oil to Europe."

Becker began cautiously. He was well aware that there had been disagreements in the past between Europe and the United States regarding sanctions on Iran.

"Yes, Mr. President. We've signed an agreement with Teheran, but that is only one of many we hope to secure. The Saudi's tried to hold us up and sell to us at exorbitant prices, and we turned them down. But I am confident we will soon secure energy agreements with Iraq, Kuwait and the UAE."

"That's good," Miller replied. "And as we've discussed before, we are doing everything we can to make our ports more secure so we can begin shipping energy to you again."

"I appreciate that, Mr. President. Now that we're moving forward to meet our energy needs, there is still the issue of Russia and Belarus. We have both imposed sanctions, but Putin is still not moving his troops out. I think it's time we turned up the pressure on him and his cronies."

"I think I agree. What did you have in mind?"

Becker began laying out his plan. "Here is how I think we can apply maximum pressure…."

CHAPTER THIRTY-SIX

Outside the City of Baranavichy, Belarus
(October 18, 1415, Eastern European Time)

Holden and his crew were laid up in the large Airbnb Darko
Markovic had secured on the western outskirts of the city of
Baranavichy. They were settled in, and most of the team was
relaxing in the great room, watching soccer matches on the
enormous TV.

"Hey Darko," Chapo Chavez said, "how can I get the kind of
expense account the Agency has given you? This place is sweet."

"Rick is paying the bills. I don't want to be around once we get
back to Langley and he submits his chits."

Chavez grinned at Markovic. "Me neither. Mia," he continued,
"has your bird seen anything worth looking at in the last
whenever."

"Nothing."

"I guess that's good news," Blake Mason added. "I don't mind
hanging out in these digs, but this sure as hell isn't what we came
here to do."

As they caucused in another room of the villa, Rick Holden and
Jimbo Folga understood their team was getting restless, but there
was little they could do.

"Anything more from Peters today," Folga asked.

"No. But I do know SACEUR has gotten massive cooperation
from the three-letter agencies, and we have satellites listening and
zeroing in on what's coming out of Chechnya."

217

"Yeah, but I don't get it," Folga continued. "The Chechens want these damn things. And they have to figure either the Belarusians or the Russians are trying to get them back. Why no comms for so long?"

"I think it's the geography, Jimbo." Holden pulled up a map of Europe on his tablet. "Whoever this group in Chechnya is, they likely don't have their own ships. They have to go out on the market somewhere and find a shipper who doesn't ask questions and pay him a hell of a lot to take the job. Then they've got to get that ship to whatever port they pick, here or here," he continued, pointing to the Black Sea and the Baltic. "My guess is these guys will continue to hunker down while all that gets sorted out."

The two men continued talking and what-iffing. Waiting was not in their nature, but it was what it was for now.

_____

At SACEUR headquarters, Laura Peters was happy that her higher-level security clearance had finally come through. Without it, she would not have been sent to the SACEUR command center to hear what one of the National Reconnaissance Office satellites had picked up. She also would have been dealt out of Colonel Sauter's watch rotation.

Of all the assets in the U.S. national security arsenal, signals intercept satellites represent one of the most valuable, and most closely guarded, capabilities. As vital as the information gleaned from these billion-dollar orbiting wonders is, keeping potential adversaries from learning what those satellites can do is equally important.

Peters and the other members of Sauter's team had a direct line to the SACEUR command center, which received SIGINT information from the National Security Agency. The NRO had done everything they could to focus their satellites on conversations coming out of Chechnya, and the NSA was running their own algorithms to try to key in on conversations between the sellers and buyers of these weapons.

"Tired of waiting, Laura?" Pat Cook asked as they stood watch in the anticipatory intelligence cell.

"Yes and no," she replied. "*Yes* because we want to stop these nukes from getting into the wrong hands. But *no* because, given the distances involved and everything else, it might be too damn hard to get them from point A to point B."

Cook was years senior to Peters and had served at SACEUR for almost three years. He didn't want to give her a tutorial, but he did want to help her stay in the game.

"It might, but I think we would be well served not to underestimate the Chechens or their hatred for the Russians. I suspect you know that history as well as I do. I can't think of any people, with the exception of the Jews during the Holocaust, who were so systematically eliminated."

Cook went on to recount the atrocities Russia had committed in Chechnya: over 100,000 civilians killed, cluster bombs, air raids on Grozny with no military objective beyond terrorizing the population, the use of imprecise fuel-air explosive bombs, the use of rape as a means of torture, the indiscriminate killing of aid and relief workers, and a long list of other crimes.

Peters knew the history in general, but having Cook put it in such stark terms helped crystalize it for her.

"I've got it, Pat. Looks like they are all-in on getting those nukes, whatever it takes. Can we pulse the command center and see if the satellites have picked up anything new?

"Sure, I'll make the call."

His Chechen handler had told Ilia Novik to lay low and not contact him via phone—only text. When it was time to talk, he would call Novik—not the other way around.

He had told Novik that, when he got the call, he needed to be ready to move to a seaport. *Which one* was still being determined, but they had to move without delay when notified.

Armed with that information, Novik knew that he would have to travel through either Lithuania or Ukraine with the weapons.

Travelling in the Belarusian Army trucks they had stolen was out of the question, and none of his other vehicles could handle all of the bombs.

He had rented the largest, most beat-up camper he could find— one big enough to carry the nukes. He had also purchased a load of beach equipment: boogie boards, pop-up tents, surfboards, beach chairs and the like, and secured them onto the top of the camper. He had also asked one of the most fearless woman vigilantes to join his team.

If they were stopped by Russian or Belarusian troops, or at a border crossing, their cover story was simple and believable: They were going to a beach resort in the fall, when hotel costs were less. The woman would ride shotgun and explain that her sister was in the back of the camper nursing her infant. They weren't certain that would get them a pass, but if it didn't, Novik and the woman would be armed with the best conventional weapons they had stolen and would fight it out.

CHAPTER THIRTY-SEVEN

Lieutenant Colonel Dmitry Tsaryov was born and bred to be a Spetsnaz unit commander. Third generation Russian military, his grandfather had fought and died at Stalingrad in World War II. His father had had been posted throughout Eastern Europe at the height of the Cold War and then fought in the Soviet War in Afghanistan.

His father had been decorated for heroism after leading his Spetsnaz (special forces) squad in *Operation Storm-333*, the assault on the Tajbeg Palace, which killed Afghan President Hafizullah Amin. Most had thought he was on the fast track to rise to the rank of general in Spetsnaz, but the wounds he suffered in that assault had cut his career short. He was dead four years later from alcohol poisoning, the dirty little secret that the family kept hidden—but not before he had proudly commissioned Dmitry Tsaryov as an officer in the Russian Army.

Tsaryov had excelled in his army training and was encouraged to apply to join the elite Russian special forces. Over seventy percent of the men who entered this brutal training washed out, but at the end of it all, he was one of the few left standing.

He would be the first to admit that, even with the talent and grit he had brought to being a Spetsnaz officer, luck had played a part in his rapid rise. The units he had been assigned to always seemed to be in the right place at the right time. He had seen action in the Second Chechen war, the Beslan school siege, the intervention in Ukraine, and most recently, in the Syrian Civil War.

221

Now he was one of the youngest lieutenant colonels in Spetsnaz and commander of the 45th Guards Detached Spetsnaz Brigade. He had made more jumps with this airborne brigade than even his most seasoned non-commissioned officers. Tsaryov would not say this himself, though his men did: He led from the front.

As he watched his senior sergeant supervise his small squad in loading their gear aboard their Ilyushin IL-76 heavy transport, which was forward-staged at Kubrinka Air Base, Tsaryov considered his good fortune. Even though serving in Spetsnaz meant that he spent more time away from his wife and daughter than officers and soldiers in regular army units, those regular units were saddled with aging—even antiquated—gear. Russian special operations forces got the most up-to-date equipment money could buy. They would need it for this operation.

As the last of his men climbed aboard the Ilyushin, his senior sergeant approached him. "Colonel, we are loaded aboard. The pilots say there's a problem with the number two engine and it may not deliver full power. They asked if you want to delay launch time long enough for them to fix it."

Tsaryov's face went hard. "The senior pilot is new to Spetsnaz; he's still learning. Tell him we launch on time. Let me know if I need to speak with him or his colonel."

"Yes, sir."

"And tell him to call ahead to the base at Belbek. We're refueling there. They can have their mechs check the engine out then."

———

Captain Farid Kirmani stood on *Blossom*'s bridge as the Egyptian city of Al-Qusayr came into view on the port side, eight kilometers in the distance. He listened intently as one of his seamen spoke into *Blossom*'s general announcing system, reading from the script

Kirmani had written out. Sunset was fast-approaching, and this would be the last landmark they would see until the morning.

> *Al-Qusayr is a city in eastern Egypt, located on the Red Sea coast. Populated for approximately five thousand years, its ancient name was Leucus Limen, which means "white port" in Greek. Al-Qusayr is located one hundred and forty kilometers south of Hurghada and seventy kilometers north of the Marsa Alam International Airport. The population of Al-Qusayr is approximately fifty thousand. There are ancient ruins....*

Kirmani listened as the man continued to read the detailed script. While some of his young crew had initially balked at these "history lessons" being read throughout their voyage, they had eventually come around and now looked forward to them.

Kirmani was a devout Shia and refused to succumb to the temptation to do what other ship's captains did to keep their crews happy and wile away the endless, boring days at sea. Many captains loaded up on pornographic videos and magazines, items that were forbidden in Iran, and things that could get a man arrested and beaten by the religious police if he was caught with them. One captain had even embarked two prostitutes to service his men during a now-legendary voyage.

Kirmani would have none of it. When one of his seamen had complained and asked him to take aboard "just a little smut," he had upbraided him. "You will do nothing on my vessel your mother would not be proud to see you do."

For now, he was keeping his men happy with a taste of history and geography they had never experienced before, as well as giving them more responsibility and authority than other ship's captains did. In the same way he gave his seamen a turn reading his "lessons" and leading his crew in prayer five times a day, he ensured that even his most junior men took a turn standing watch on *Blossom*'s bridge.

"Captain," the seaman who had just finished reading the Al-Qusayr narrative said, "The first mate says I have finished my qualifications and I'm ready to stand watch on the bridge tonight—with your permission, of course."

"You are more than ready, Mohsen. I'll sleep well knowing you are in command of my bridge."

Moshen Rouhani suppressed a smile and scurried off the bridge.

———

Several hours later, the Antonov AN-12 was in position, twenty miles south of the city of Ras Mohammed on the tip of the Sinai Peninsula. The pilot was doing lazy racetracks at 20,000 feet as his crew tuned up their electronic warfare gear. The lead technician, a captain in Russia's information warfare forces, was finally satisfied they had tweaked their equipment to take best advantage of the atmospherics that evening.

"We're ready back here," the captain said over the roar of the Antonov's four turboprop engines.

"Begin jamming," the pilot commanded.

———

They had completed their refueling at Belbek, a Crimean base Russia had controlled since it invaded in 2014, and were now nearing their jump point over the Red Sea.

"Nice and tight, Colonel?" his senior sergeant yelled above the howl of the Ilyushin's engines. He jerked the lower straps of Lieutenant Colonel Dmitry Tsaryov's parachute harness, snugging it tight.

"Is that all you've got?" Tsaryov asked, loud enough for his squad to hear.

Tsaryov. The Spetsnaz commander got up, nodded, and gave the man a thumb's up.

As the senior sergeant stood up and the rest of the squad rose with him, the loadmaster activated the hydraulic crank. The enormous ramp/door at the rear of the aircraft began to grind open. As it did, the heavily laden men, their faces streaked with black and green war paint, began shuffling toward the ramp. The last two men in the squad dragged their heavy inflated boat behind them.

The Ilyushin was flying at twenty-two thousand feet, well above an altitude where someone below might see them. As the men bunched up at the ramp, the howling wind assaulted their ears. The freezing air bit into their faces as they anticipated the jump. Tsaryov walked up and down the line of the six commandos, squeezing each man's shoulders and looking him dead in the eye. His men looked back impassively. Tsaryov walked to the edge of the cargo bay, perched himself on the ramp, and waited.

The red lights on either side of the ramp winked out, and bright green lights took their place. Tsaryov ran down the ramp and leapt into the air, followed closely by his senior sergeant and the rest of his squad. Ten seconds later, the loadmaster shoved their rigid-hulled inflatable boat (RHIB) down the cargo ramp.

Had anyone below them been able to see what was happening over four miles above, they would have seen eight small parachutes blooming and two larger ones deploying a minute later. As they dropped toward the water, the eight men steered their chutes to drive themselves closer to their boat.

Minutes later, each of the commandos landed less than a hundred meters from the RHIB. A less-well-trained squad might have struggled to shed their chutes and their oxygen gear, swim to the boat, and clamber aboard. Not Tsaryov's team. In less than five minutes, they had swum to the RHIB, stored their gear, and readied their weapons. As Tsaryov extracted his tablet from its waterproof bag, his senior sergeant fired off the boat's engine. Overhead, the pilots of the Ilyushin linked them the position of the *Blossom*, just a few kilometers north of where they were surging ahead.

———

Aboard *Blossom*, Moshen Rouhani continued to monitor his navigation system and fought fatigue. The older crewman who trained him had warned him that this would happen near the end of his watch, when the drone of the ship's engines, the warm night air, and the lack of anyone to talk to could lull even the most vigilant man into lethargy and inattention.

Rouhani was pacing back and forth on the bridge, struggling to stay awake and alert, when, suddenly, his walkie-talkie came alive. It was one of his shipmates, a man he knew always fished from *Blossom's* fantail at night. "Moshen, there's a large rubber boat, and it's closing us rapidly. It is right in our wake and looks like it's going to drive right up our stern."

"Are you sure?" Rouhani asked. The man was younger than Rouhani, and the leery watchstander suspected he had smuggled weed aboard *Blossom*. Moshen would have bet a week's pay that the man's night fishing expeditions served a dual purpose—fresh fish for the crew and a stupor for him.

"Yes, *yes*, I'm sure!" the man shouted. "Pull it up on the monitor and see for yourself."

Rouhani walked the few feet to the monitor that displayed what *Blossom's* array of cameras saw. He punched the tab for the astern-facing camera. What he saw shocked him.

All action now, Rouhani grabbed the phone handset connected to *Blossom's* internal communications system and punched in the number to the captain's cabin.

The ringing jolted Farid Kirmani awake. He groped for the phone, knocked the handset to the floor, and had to flick on his reading lamp to find it. "Yes, *what?*" he said as he tried to focus on the red LED display on his bedside clock. His eyes finally adjusted and the numbers read 2:47.

"Captain, we're being attacked by pirates. There's an inflatable boat closing us at high speed, I have it here on the bridge monitor. I think I see..." Rouhani continued, the pitch of his voice growing higher and higher.

But Kirmani was no longer listening. He had thrown the phone receiver onto his bed, slipped on his sandals, and was heading toward *Blossom's* bridge at full tilt.

———

U.S. satellites had picked up the jamming the Antonov was putting into the electromagnetic spectrum and pushed this information to the Joint Staff, U.S. Space Command, U.S. Cyber Command and U.S. Central Command. Since the jamming appeared to come from the air and water space under their purview, CENTCOM had passed it to their naval component, Fifth Fleet.

At Fifth Fleet Headquarters in Manama, Bahrain, only three watchstanders manned their stations in the command center. Two intelligence analysts were posted in the top-secret secure space, monitoring a variety of intelligence nets.

Commander Megan Franks was the tactical action officer in charge of the watch team. The intelligence she could glean from her multiple systems told her the jamming was coming from somewhere in the northern Red Sea. She scanned her Global Command and Control System (GCCS), which displayed all air and sea contacts in the area, looking for U.S. naval units in the Red Sea. There were none. Satisfied there was nothing to do until the jamming stopped, she made a notation in her watch log.

———

Standing on the starboard bridge wing in his Primo Beer tee shirt, boxer shorts and sandals, Farid Kirmani may not have looked imposing, but he was definitely in charge. He looked into the bridge and yelled to Moshen Rouhani, "Tell the engine room full power now, *immediately!*"

"Yes, Captain."

Kirmani squinted through his Vanguard binoculars, trying to get a better look at the boat converging on them, now less than one kilometer in the distance. He had already sent his first mate and two seamen to the ship's weapons locker and had sent another two men to break out fire hoses.

Kirmani had read about the sophisticated anti-piracy systems some cargo ships, especially those owned by western nations, possessed: automated water cannons, barbed wire, high-frequency microwave devices, and other defensive measures. *Blossom* had none of these. But Kirmani had made the best of a bad situation and drilled his crew with what they did have: fire hoses; large metal rakes to repel boarding ladders; and a few rifles and pistols, all Iranian clones of European models.

"They won't try to board from the stern," Kirmani said to his first mate as the man and his team appeared on the bridge with their small weapons cache. "They'll try for a spot on our beam. Once they commit to our port or starboard side, go there, shelter behind a steel bulkhead just as we've practiced, turn a spotlight on them and start shooting."

"Yes, Captain," the first mate replied.

"Do the same thing with the fire hoses. Tell the men with the hoses to flake them out athwartships, as we've rehearsed, and then man the same positions they have during our drills. But remind them not to engage until the boat is close aboard."

Kirmani said a few words of encouragement to the young seamen holding the weapons. They looked scared shitless. Then, turning to the first mate, he handed him his binoculars and said, "Keep an eye on the boat and let me know as soon as they commit to one side or the other. I'm going to radio for help."

Back inside the bridge, the captain walked up to **Rouhani** and put his hands on both his shoulders. "You did the right thing to awaken me Moshen; I told you that you were ready to stand watch."

"Thank...thank you, Captain," Rouhani stammered. Kirmani couldn't decide who looked more terrified, Rouhani or the seamen he had just left on the bridge wing.

"Now that I've got our defenders ready to do what they must do, we need to get help. Who have you called so far?"

"Ca...ca...captain...I can't call anyone. The radios aren't working—"

"Not working!" Kirmani shouted. "When did this happen? What's going on?"

Rouhani related what had occurred when noise started to overwhelm the radios. He explained how he had tried to adjust the volume, change frequencies, and do any other things he could think of, all to no avail. Kirmani took it all in with disbelief.

"We have been deaf and dumb for almost two hours, and you haven't told me?"

Whatever boost to his ego from the small praise Rouhani had received moments ago melted away in an instant.

Kirmani strode to the center of the bridge and grabbed the handset of *Blossom's* marine radio. He began to speak, but as he did, a loud, high-pitched whine overwhelmed his ears. He changed frequencies and tried again, with the same result. He flung the handset down and cursed their equipment, the embargo, and anything else he could think of.

The captain turned to Rouhani and shouted, "Go to my cabin, grab my cell phone, and bring it up here!"

Kirmani ran back out to the starboard bridge wing and stood next to his first mate. "Can you see the pirates yet? How many are there?"

The first mate pulled the binoculars down and looked directly at his captain. "I can't make much out in the dark, but the boat doesn't look like any pirate boat I've seen pictures of. It looks like a military boat of some kind."

Kirmani snatched the binoculars from the first mate and looked for himself. Seconds later, Rouhani was at his side and handed him his cell phone. The captain punched in a number, but instead of a ring, he was met with the same howling sound he had heard when he tried to use the ship's radio.

He felt *Blossom* surge underneath him, straining to reach her top speed of 14 knots. He handed the binoculars to his first mate again. "When they get inside five hundred meters, hit them with the spotlight and tell me how many men are in the boat and how they're dressed."

Back inside the bridge, now inhabited by a few of his senior seamen as well as Rouhani, Kirmani barked at one of the men. "Open up the flare locker. Start firing one every two minutes."

"Yes, Captain."

Kirmani stared at the navigation display, searching for a harbor—somewhere to run where the pirates would not follow. The closest safe harbor was more than fifteen kilometers ahead. They would be boarded well before then.

Back on the bridge wing, Kirmani walked up to the first mate, stood beside him, and snapped at the two seamen there. "Leave us for a moment; go inside the bridge."

Once they were alone, Kirmani looked at his first mate and saw the fear in his eyes. "You're thinking these may not be a bunch of skinnies looking for a payday?" he began, using the common term for the young Somali pirates who had become the scourge of this part of the world.

"Not with that kind of boat," the first mate began. Then the man hesitated, struggling with what he was going to say next. "Captain, if they *are* pirates, maybe ones more well equipped and well-armed than skinnies, they want the ship, not us. Are you sure we want to start shooting at them with the few weapons we have?"

"At this point, I'm not sure of anything. I don't want to get any of our men killed, but if a few shots from us, or a blast from a fire hose, can scare them off, we might manage to get away. Let's wait until we can see who they are—then we'll decide."

The first mate considered this, figuring his captain was dreaming if he thought he could scare their attackers away. After a few seconds, he spoke. "I think they're within five hundred meters now."

"Good. Give me the binoculars and hit them with the spotlight."

The first mate handed over the binocs and spoke a few words into his walkie-talkie. Within seconds, the spotlight on the deck above the bridge came alive and the seaman controlling it slewed it astern. They found the boat converging on their ship.

The first mate saw his captain's jaw drop, just as they heard shots ring out. Seconds later, they heard shattering glass and saw the spotlight go dark. Kirmani stared at his first mate and said, "They're not skinnies."

———

When he saw *Blossom* speed up, Dmitry Tsaryov had suspected he and his men might have been seen. When the spotlight blinked on, he was sure of it. A word to his sniper and the man holding the SVDK rifle and looking through his infrared sight had sent several well-aimed 9.3 mm shells into the offending light.

"Now we know they've seen us. Turn out and head for the port side," Tsaryov commanded.

The man at the helm of their RHIB pushed the craft to full power and spun the boat to comply. It leapt ahead and made for a spot on *Blossom's* port beam, just where Captain Kirmani had predicted they would.

———

"They're making for our port side!" Kirmani shouted to his first mate.

The captain and first mate sprinted through the bridge and stood on the port bridge wing. They peered over the side and could see the RHIB now even with their stern. They heard the roar of its engine.

"Captain?" the man asked.

Silence.

"Captain, what do you want to do?"

Kirmani was still silent, staring ahead blankly. His decades at sea hadn't prepared him for anything like this.

"Captain, you told the men with the weapons to fire on the boat and the ones with the fire hoses to blast it when it gets close aboard. Do you still want to do that?"

It was happening too fast for Kirmani. Yes, he knew pirates were always a problem, and they were usually Somalis. But they typically ranged out from their coastline into the western Indian Ocean, not here in the Red Sea. Were they expanding their operating areas? And he had expected to see skinnies—young, emaciated black men wearing little more than rags in a wooden boat—not what looked like military commandos in a high-end RHIB. The more conflicting data he shoved into his brain, the more overloaded he became and the more he froze.

"*Captain?*" the first mate implored loudly and impatiently.

The first mate's insolence was enough to snap Kirmani out of his temporary lethargy. "No! Don't shoot at them—don't shoot!"

The first mate spoke rapidly into his walkie-talkie, telling their men not to shoot and not to spray water on the approaching RHIB.

———

As they approached *Blossom's* port beam, Dmitry Tsaryov gave the megaphone to the man in his squad who spoke Farsi and said, "You know what to say."

The man stood up and began, "Aboard the *Blossom*, you are violating Egyptian territorial waters and disregarding international law. Heave to and prepare for boarding and inspection. We mean you no harm, but we will not ask you again."

"Captain?" the first mate asked.

"They're not Egyptian, and we're not in their territorial waters. It must be a trick." He looked into the bridge. "Bring me the megaphone."

The RHIB was now abeam on the port side, and Kirmani could see his adversaries clearly. It was a military boat, and there were eight well-armed commandos. He knew he had no chance. He was about to speak into his megaphone when, to his horror, he saw a jet of water shooting from *Blossom* and engulfing the RHIB.

"I told you not to shoot anything!" Kirmani shouted at his first mate. "No weapons, no fire hoses—nothing!"

But it was too late. The RHIB turned away from the water stream and then surged forward, paralleling *Blossom's* course close aboard. Seconds later, automatic weapons fire saturated the port bridge wing. Kirmani dove for the steel deck and just avoided the hail of bullets, but the first mate wasn't so lucky. The captain looked on in horror as the first mate's shattered body landed on the deck just a few feet away.

Kirmani raised his head and shouted into the bridge, "Stop the ship...*stop it now!*

Dmitry Tsaryov saw *Blossom* slowing, but didn't wait for the ship to stop. He signaled his helmsman to drop back a few dozen meters until they were again on the port beam.

Once there, his squad began their well-rehearsed actions. A boarding ladder went up and latched onto *Blossom's* gunwale. Tsaryov's senior sergeant was first up, his AK-74 5.45 mm assault rifle at the ready. Once he was aboard, he surveyed the deck with

235

his infrared sight. None of the ship's crew were there. He looked down at the RHIB and gave the signal. In less than two minutes, the boat was made fast to *Blossom's* side and the eight commandos were aboard.

As the rest of his squad spread out on *Blossom's* main deck, Tsaryov and his senior sergeant made for the ship's bridge.

CHAPTER THIRTY-EIGHT

Supreme Allied Commander Europe (SACEUR) Headquarters (October 19, 0230 Central European Time)

Lieutenant Laura Peters and Staff Sergeant John Sundstrum had the 0000-0400 watch rotation in SACEUR's anticipatory intelligence cell. It was the quietest duty shift, and Peters used the time to leverage the cell's capabilities to try to intuit how the vigilantes who stole the nukes from the base at Brest were going to get them to Chechnya.

Her fellow nerd nook colleagues had fed disparate information into their system over the past several days, but she wondered if they were giving their highly capable tools the right information in the correct format. As capable as their brilliant hardware and software was, the old adage, "garbage in, garbage out," still held true.

She decided to craft a narrative that started at the beginning, on October 11, when the Belarusian Army base at Brest had been assaulted. She told Sundstrum, "Staff Sergeant, I'm going hot, dark and quiet. Keep a heads-up, okay?"

The Army sergeant smiled. He liked Peters and thought there should be more officers like her, so he happily put up with what he called "Navy brainwashing." She had explained that "hot, dark and quiet," was an old Navy term for what happened on Navy steam-powered ships when the boiler crapped out: the air conditioning went off line, the lights went out, and all ventilation noise stopped.

237

Even good officers have their little quirks, Sundstrum mused.

The National Reconnaissance Office "Mentor" satellite soared high above Russia, listening. Unlike its NRO cousins, which famously could photograph objects on the ground as small as a softball, the Mentor was a SIGINT (signals intelligence) satellite that had one role: it listened.

Anchored miles above Chechnya, its huge antenna soaked in transmissions from radios, data links, pagers, and most importantly, cellular mobile phones. It then sent gigabytes of data through highly secure links to the National Security Agency at Fort Meade, Maryland.

Responsible for the global monitoring, collection, and processing of information for foreign and domestic intelligence and counterintelligence purposes, the NSA had some of the best analysts on the planet. Automated algorithms did a great deal of the sorting, separating the wheat from the chaff, and transcribing conversations from various languages into English. But humans did the rest.

The NSA analysts knew what they were looking for, and they poured over their data around the clock. At 2330, just before her watch shift ended, a junior analyst replayed a conversation between a Chechen they had been monitoring and what sounded like the owner of a ship sailing under a Liberian flag of convenience.

She typed furiously, reporting what she had heard and what she made of it: The sums of money discussed were enormous, vastly more than one would usually pay to ship even a large amount of goods, and the insistence that the ship change its route immediately was loud and clear. Satisfied she had captured all that was important, she pushed "Send," and her report went into the queue of a senior analyst.

Rick Holden had to balance getting his team ready to intercept the Belarusian vigilantes with the stolen nuclear weapons and not being discovered by the Russians. The intercepted Kremlin conversations Laura Peters had provided them made it clear that Vladimir Putin was still outraged that Patricia Bailey had been rescued and wanted revenge against those who had snatched her.

Just after dark each evening, while Mia Yaeger maneuvered the Global Hawk ahead of their path, Holden sent two of his team members out along the local roads and major highways to try to determine the most likely routes the vigilantes would take to get their cargo to a seaport on the Baltic or Black Sea.

It was part science and part art. He was mindful that they knew their country far better than he and his team did, but he was counting on the technology he had at his command to try to get the upper hand. What complicated things was that he had to have a "plan A" and a "plan B," depending on what port the vigilantes tried to reach.

Blake Mason was the team geek, and as his teammates came back with information about roads they had traversed, he put that information into his tablet, organizing it on Excel spreadsheets cross-referenced to maps of the area. It wasn't much, but at this stage of the game, they were looking for any edge they could get.

CHAPTER THIRTY-NINE

Aboard the Iranian Ship Blossom, Red Sea
(October 19, 0345 East Africa Time Zone)

As Dmitry Tsaryov and his senior sergeant burst onto *Blossom's* bridge, the Spetsnaz commander barked, "*Gde kapitan?*" [Where is your captain?]

Farid Kirmani approached Tsaryov and said in Farsi, "I am."

The Spetsnaz commander towered over the small man wearing the Primo Beer tee shirt and considered him for a moment. Then he asked, "Do you speak English?"

"Yes," Kirmani replied as he tried to stand just a bit taller. He was still in shock from seeing his first mate blown to bits right before his eyes, but he mustered all the intestinal fortitude he had and kept eye contact with the Russian.

"Captain, it was unwise of you to try to sink our boat with your fire hoses, but I'll forgive that as the fear of the moment overcoming you and your crew—"

"What do you want with us?" Kirmani blurted out.

"A good question, Captain. With you and your crew, nothing. We simply want your vessel and its cargo. We are going to go through the Suez Canal with your ship and then enter the Mediterranean and head toward Greece, where we have a buyer. We will release you and your crew there—that is, if you give us no trouble."

Tsaryov turned to his senior sergeant and said, "Bring all of the crew up to the bridge."

Kirmani's head was spinning. Take his ship to Greece? Sell the oil and then the *Blossom* too? None of it made any sense.

"Sir," Kirmani began. "This is an Iranian-flagged vessel, delivering oil to Europe under a European Union-brokered arrangement with my government. My ship is expected to dock in Constanta, Romania. People will be alarmed if we don't arrive as scheduled. And then there is...." Kirmani continued, thinking of every possible reason to convince these intruders to leave his ship and let them alone. His courage grew just a little bit as Tsaryov stood there smiling and nodding, seemingly being convinced by his arguments.

As the two men were having this conversation, *Blossom's* bridge was becoming crowded. The rest of the crew had been brought up, their hands fastened behind their backs with snap ties. The Spetsnaz commandos stood behind them and held them under their guns.

"That's all very good, Captain—but not very interesting at the moment. Regardless of what port we ultimately pull into, we still must go through the Canal at your appointed time, wouldn't you agree?"

"Yes," Kirmani replied, thinking he might buy a bit of time.

"Good. What time is your transit scheduled?"

Kirmani figured his captors must have done their homework and knew that Suez Canal transits were strictly scheduled. And even though this was to be his first transit, he had been told that he was to make that time, precisely and without fail. Otherwise, his ship would be denied transit. If he refused to give these commandos a time, they would suffer that fate and *Blossom* would be stranded in the Gulf of Suez, making it far easier for the Iranian Navy to rescue them.

"The time...time...for our transit?" Yes, I think I've been given the time. I need to look at my navigation books," Kirmani said.

He walked to the forward part of *Blossom's* bridge, where a stack of books was spread out on a small table. He flicked on the red light above the table and began fumbling with the books while Tsaryov looked over his shoulder.

The Spetsnaz commander wasn't fooled by Kirmani's dithering and had finally had enough. "*Kapitan vremeni?*" [The time, Captain?] Tsaryov barked in Russian as all eyes on the crowded bridge, commandos and captives alike, were riveted on Kirmani.

"The time, yes...well...you see...this is my first transit of the Canal in any ship, and now I recall. I was told that I am to contact the Canal authorities later today, shortly after noon. But you see, our radios have been inoperable since earlier this morning."

"Radios inop?" Tsaryov asked, arching his eyebrows. Once they had boarded *Blossom*, Tsaryov had signaled the Antonov to stop its jamming. The Spetsnaz commander looked at the speaker above them, which was carrying the normal chatter. The Russian walked over to the switch controlling the radios and turned the volume all the way up. The loud babble overwhelmed the bridge.

Tsaryov turned the volume down a bit. Then he looked out to the port bridge wing at the first mate's prostrate body and the sea of blood surrounding it. "It is unfortunate that man had to die, Captain. But, after all, you shot fire hoses at my men first."

"It was an accident, sir, I assure you."

"I would take you at your word on that, if you hadn't lied to me about the radios, so I don't know what to believe now. The man lying on the bridge wing looks older than the rest of your crew. Your second-in-command perhaps?"

"Yes, he is...was...my first mate."

"So, your oldest crewmember, yes?"

"Yes...yes...I think so," Kirmani stammered, baffled as to where this line of questioning was going.

"Indeed. Then who is your youngest?" Tsaryov asked, scanning the line of captives on the bridge. "*And don't lie to me, Captain!*"

As he shouted, he drew his GSh-18 semi-automatic pistol and placed the barrel on Kirmani's forehead. He pulled the hammer back and pressed the barrel harder into the captain's head. "I told you we meant you no harm, but only if you cooperate."

"I believe it is seaman Nazari, there," Kirmani said, pointing at a man near the middle of the line of captives.

Tsaryov lowered his pistol and walked up to the man. "Ask him," he said, looking at the commando who spoke Farsi.

The man complied, and said in Farsi, "Are you the youngest?"

"I...I...think so," the seaman stammered.

Tsaryov walked up to within a foot of the young seaman, leveled his pistol, fired, and put a hole in the middle of the man's forehead.

As blood, brain matter and skull fragments flew everywhere and *Blossom's* crew recoiled in horror, one man retching and emptying his stomach, the Spetsnaz commander walked up to Kirmani and barked, "*Kapitan vremeni?*"

Moments after Dmitry Tsaryov's senior sergeant had made his call to the Antonov to stop jamming, he had made a second call. That call was to a ship making bare steerageway near the Egyptian town of Ras Sedr, on the western coast of the Sinai Peninsula, near the northern reaches of the Gulf of Suez. Soon after the call, that ship headed north at flank speed.

Aboard *Blossom*, the crew had been completely cowed, and Kirmani stood in front of Tsaryov, whimpering.

"Pull yourself together, Captain. *The time!*" he roared.

Kirmani stammered, "Yes...yes...now I remember. It is early in the morning tomorrow...at 0400. We are supposed to embark the pilot an hour before that."

"Much better, Captain." Tsaryov motioned toward a few of his commandos. They took the crew below, hog-tied each man, and locked them in an empty storage room. Other men completed a variety of tasks, putting the ship back on a course and speed to make their Canal rendezvous. One commando took the ship's helm while the Farsi speaker stood by the ship's radio.

With a nod from Tsaryov, his senior sergeant threw the bodies of the two murdered crewmen over the side.

The Egyptian resort city of Ain Sukhna lies one hundred and twenty kilometers east southeast of the nation's capital. Its location near Cairo, only an hour away on Egypt's modern motorway, makes it the premier weekend destination for Egyptians fleeing the capital's intense summer heat. It is the crown jewel of Egypt's Red Sea Riviera.

None of that mattered to Dmitry Tsaryov. What *did* matter was that the Egyptian coast south of Ain Sukhna was completely uninhabited and represented the widest point of the Gulf of Suez. That was where *Blossom* now rendezvoused with another ship, well away from the traffic lanes, where no one would see what was occurring.

It had been three hours since Tsaryov and his squad had taken over the Iranian tanker. The seas were dead calm as one of the Spetsnaz commandos operated *Blossom's* small utility crane. The crane operator first transferred sturdy steel dollies from the alongside vessel to *Blossom*. Then, he grasped other objects and hoisted them from the other ship onto the dollies. As he did, other commandos pushed them to *Blossom's* fantail, dumped them on the deck, and then returned to the vicinity of the crane to repeat the process.

Even in the midday sun, the commandos finished their task in just a few hours. That complete, *Blossom* steamed northeast at 14 knots to rejoin the northerly shipping channel while the other vessel hugged the Egyptian coast and steamed north. As that vessel approached Ain Sukhna, it made a wide seaward turn to avoid being seen by beachgoers. Its captain had his orders to remain no more than two hours behind *Blossom*.

As *Blossom* continued to head north in the shipping channel at best speed, Dmitry Tsaryov huddled with his senior sergeant on the ship's starboard bridge wing. Nearby, with the rest of his crew locked up below decks, Farid Kirmani was handcuffed to a stanchion on the bridge. The Spetsnaz commander wanted him there just in case.

"We underestimated how much of the deck they would cover," his senior sergeant began. "We've used all the tarps and every other cover we could find, but almost half of them are still visible."

"That's not good enough," Tsaryov said, shaking his head. "What about the crews' quarters?"

"The crews' quarters?"

"Yes, strip their beds and sow their blankets and bed sheets together. It won't be perfect, but it will keep prying eyes away just long enough."

"I'll see to it," the man replied.

"Whatcha got, Charlie?" Laura Peters asked Captain Charles Johnson. The two were standing watch in SACEUR's anticipatory intelligence cell, looking for something that would help them nail down where the Belarusian vigilantes intended to take their stolen weapons. They were fairly certain that the Chechens had contracted for a ship but didn't know much else beyond that. That longer-range issue was now pushed aside by Johnson's frantic signaling to Peters to have her look at his computer monitor.

"Don't know if this means anything," he began, "but both DoD and the IC reported some odd jamming in the area of the Northern Red Sea several hours ago. It came on suddenly and stopped about three hours later, just as quickly."

"Are they sure it's no-kidding jamming, not atmospherics or something else?" Peters asked.

"Yep, the reports are pretty clear. It's described as 'military-grade' jamming."

Peters looked unconvinced that it was something they needed to worry about.

"And I figured you'd ask, so I checked," Johnson continued. "There are no military exercises going on nearby. Nothing in Egypt, Saudi Arabia, or Israel. CENTCOM is at a loss, but they're investigating."

"Okay Charlie, if you think it's important, let's push it up to Pat Cook's queue. And why don't we start running some anticipatory intelligence and see if it leads us anywhere."

"Good idea," Johnson replied.

Blossom steamed north in the Gulf of Suez traffic separation scheme as it approached the city of Port Tewfik at the southern terminus of the Suez Canal. Over the last several hours, they had been receiving instructions from the Suez Port authority regarding when and where they would pick up their pilot, when the day's only northerly transit of the Canal would begin, and how many ships would be in that convoy.

Dmitry Tsaryov had studied the history of the Canal, as well as its operations. Even though he and his men were about deadly business, he wanted them to know something about the engineering wonder they were about to enter. Tsaryov had put his senior sergeant in charge of telling his squad about the history of the Canal, while the Spetsnaz commander took on the task of explaining its operations.

Tsaryov had to admit that the history of this ditch fascinated him. The idea of a canal linking the Nile River and the Red Sea had been a dream since the days of the Pharaohs four millennia ago, his senior sergeant had told his men. But each attempt to build a canal was inadequate to accommodate large ships, and whatever was dug silted up quickly. The modern "ditch," as it was typically called, had been conceived by the French diplomat, Ferdinand de Lesseps, built under the auspices of the Suez Canal Company, and had been in operation since 1869.

Part of the history of the Suez Canal involved warfare. Tsaryov ensured that his senior sergeant made the men keenly aware of the violence that had surrounded the Canal during the Suez Crisis, the Arab-Israeli wars of 1967 and 1973, and especially the mining and clearing operations that had accompanied that latter crisis. After his senior sergeant had finished telling his men about this bit of history, Tsaryov segued into telling them about the Canal's operations.

Tsaryov first explained that the Suez Canal carried more traffic than any other canal, even the Panama Canal and that the ditch was essentially flat, with no locks. He told them it was about two hundred kilometers in length and could accommodate almost one hundred ships a day. Then, he showed them a picture of the Canal and explained why its width was such that it could support only a one-way flow of traffic. He showed them the passing lanes at Ballah Bypass and the Great Bitter Lake. Much to his delight, his men had many questions.

Dmitry Tsaryov, his senior sergeant, and the squad's Farsi speaker were on *Blossom's* bridge, dressed in clothing they had taken from the ship's crew, who were still bound and gagged below decks. They had also taken the captain below and locked him up with the crew. In the distance, they saw the pilot boat emerging from the Port Suez finger piers.

"The information you shared with us said the Egyptian pilots usually speak at least passable English," his senior sergeant began,

247

"do you think this one will?"

"Probably," Tsaryov replied. "We both know enough English and Farsi. We can say a few words in Farsi and then switch to English. But if he doesn't speak English, I've studied enough Egyptian that I can communicate with him well enough until he gets us into the southern end of the Canal. Once we're there, we won't need to communicate any longer."

His senior sergeant and the other commando on the bridge just smiled.

He had been ordered to stay close to *Blossom*, and as he saw the pilot boat approaching the ship his countrymen now controlled, the captain of the Russian vessel slowed his speed and hugged the Egyptian coast, paralleling the Suez-Ain El Sokhna Road. He planned to hold a position just south of the huge breakwater jutting out from the coast and pointing at the finger piers of Port Tewfik. His ship had been fitted out to look like a fishing vessel, so it blended in with the rest of the small-ship traffic along the coast.

It was shortly after midnight when the Egyptian pilot embarked aboard *Blossom* in the same way he had climbed aboard other ships thousands of times in his long service for the Suez Canal Authority. He scampered up to the bridge, where Tsaryov greeted him in Farsi. "Welcome aboard, Captain. Do you speak English?"

"Yes," came the reply, as the men exchanged handshakes and the senior sergeant approached with an envelope and delivered the bribe that all pilots expected and received for their "cooperation" during the fourteen-hour transit.

The pilot opened the envelope and looked at the bundle of rials, the Iranian currency, and smiled. Then, he conveyed his instructions. "You can see the other ships in front of and behind us. Our convoy will have thirty-six ships. We'll be..." he continued, and then paused to look at the piece of paper in his hand, "...ninth in line. We'll steam at six knots. That's slow, but there have been complaints about shore erosion, so there's nothing I can do about that."

"We understand, Captain," Tsaryov replied. "What time does our convoy begin its transit?"

The pilot looked annoyed that *Blossom's* captain hadn't done his homework. *These Iranians are all alike, expecting others to do their work for them,* he thought to himself.

"At 0400, Captain—just as we always do."

Tsaryov took the rebuke and then continued. "This man," he began, pointing at his senior sergeant, "will be your helmsmen. My other seaman will yield control of the radios to you. They both speak enough English that you can give them orders. I will be here for the entire transit."

"Fine, Captain. I'm curious, though. When I came aboard, I noticed that large military-style RHIB tethered to your port side. An odd boat for an Iranian oil tanker to have, no?"

Tsaryov had anticipated the question and didn't look shocked. "That, yes, we found it in the middle of the traffic separation scheme, near the southern end of the Gulf of Suez. We thought it presented a hazard to navigation so we took control of it. We will dump it when we make our port call in Constanta, Romania."

"Hmmm...," the pilot began, doing the math in his head about how much he might fetch if he sold the boat. "It might be better if I helped you get rid of it," he continued, smiling. With that, the two men entered a spirited conversation about the RHIB's disposition. Tsaryov's senior sergeant did as the pilot had instructed him to do and made bare steerageway as he nudged *Blossom* toward the entryway of the Canal.

Laura Peters' watch rotation was over. She had pushed the information about the military-grade jamming up her chain, and thus far, their anticipatory intelligence programs had not made any connections.

She was getting as impatient as Rick Holden and his team. They knew the Chechens wanted the weapons, but what were they going to do next? They had to get a ship to a port somewhere. But what ship? And when?

As a Navy intelligence officer, she had a huge degree of confidence in what the sixteen agencies that were part of the national intelligence community could do. She counted on something useful coming down the chain soon.

Aboard *Blossom*, the northbound convoy was progressing as planned, if plodding along at 6 knots could be called progress. It annoyed Dmitry Tsaryov that the pilot barked orders at his senior sergeant as if the decorated commando were some hired hand and then snatched the radio mic out of the other man's hands like he was taking a toy from a truculent child. But he would have to put up with it only a bit longer, and it would make what they planned to do even sweeter.

As *Blossom* passed the northernmost reaches of the Port of Suez, at a place where the width of the Canal was only about three hundred meters, Tsaryov looked at his senior sergeant and shouted. "All engines stop!"

The pilot stared at the Spetsnaz commander for a split second, then walked up to the senior sergeant and said, "Don't obey that order; keep your course and speed."

But the man had already backed down *Blossom's* engine controls, and they could feel the ship start losing way.

"I said don't obey that order; maintain your speed!" the pilot shouted, his brain in overdrive trying to comprehend why these Persians weren't doing what he told them to do. Nothing in his over twenty years of work as a Canal pilot had prepared him for this.

The senior sergeant just stared straight ahead.

The pilot came right up to him, his face just two feet from the man's, and yelled, "I said, bring the engines back on line, and do it *now!*" Spittle from his mouth hit the Russian in the face.

In his rage, the pilot had not noticed the other commando, the man from whom he had snatched the radio mic while verbally abusing him. The commando now stood directly behind him. With a nod from Tsaryov, he withdrew a garrote from his pants' pocket, flipped it around the pilot's neck, and pulled.

As the pilot flailed and tried to grasp at the hands pulling the garrote tighter and tighter around his neck, the Spetsnaz commander moved to within a foot of the struggling man, "Thank you, Captain. We won't be needing your services any longer."

As the ships in the convoy behind *Blossom* saw the Iranian ship slowing down, they had no choice but to do likewise. Moments later, there was a loud babble of voices shouting over the radios in several languages, surprised by what had happened and demanding to know what was wrong.

A few minutes later, a voice that identified itself as the Suez Canal Authority came on the net and demanded to speak to the pilot aboard *Blossom*. The pilots controlling ships farther back in the convoy line idled their engines, making bare steerageway, trying to figure out what to do next and scrambling not to hit any other vessels or the coastline.

Aboard *Blossom*, Dmitry Tsaryov knew precisely what to do next. He had sent his senior sergeant below to get the rest of the commandos, have them finish their work, and then have them get ready to jump into their RHIB. He stood next to the commando on the radios, put his hand on the man's shoulder, and told him to begin.

The man began reading from the script Tsaryov had spelled out on his tablet, speaking in Farsi. "This is the Iranian vessel *Blossom*. We've had a fire break out in our engine room. We are fighting it now, but we have lost all power. Our pilot is talking with our captain, and they have decided to drop anchor immediately."

The Spetsnaz commander's team sprang into action and went through their well-rehearsed procedures. One commando simultaneously reversed *Blossom's* engines and dropped the ship's anchor, bringing the vessel to an abrupt stop. Other commandos were on the fantail, pulling the tarps off their cargo and breaking down the chains and ropes that held those objects fast to the deck. Two commandos were already in the RHIB, one manning the tiller and the other with a tablet in his hand.

Within minutes, Tsaryov and his senior sergeant were the only two commandoes still aboard *Blossom*. The rest of their squad was aboard the RHIB, where the helmsman was idling the engine.

"How long did you set them for?" Tsaryov asked.

"Twenty minutes," his senior sergeant replied.

"Good, that's more than enough time. Signal the other boat and have them meet us just south of the Port Suez finger piers."

As they left the bridge and the roar of confused radio transmissions and headed for the RHIB, the senior sergeant spoke a few words into his secure radio. Within two minutes, they were in the boat and heading south.

———

The captain of the other Russian vessel had seen the long line of ships that were still in the Gulf of Suez slowing down and had anticipated the call he had just received. He pulled out from his spot behind the breakwater and headed for the finger piers.

———

Even in the early morning darkness, Dmitry Tsaryov wanted to attract as little attention as possible from the ships in the northbound convoy. As they travelled south in their RHIB, he had his helmsmen hug the western edge of the Canal. He glanced at the luminous dials of his watch from time to time and waited.

Suddenly, the morning sky was lit up by a huge detonation aboard *Blossom*. Flames shot a hundred feet into the air, and a cascading series of explosions continued to boom in the Canal. The pilots of the vessels in front of and behind the Iranian ship heard the deafening noise and felt the shock waves as secondary explosions continued and flames consumed the *Blossom*. They maneuvered their ships as best they could in the narrow confines of the Canal, trying to avoid getting too close to the inferno.

As *Blossom* slipped beneath the Canal waters, the cargo on her fantail floated free. As it did, the slowly moving currents in the waterway began to move the round objects. Less than ten minutes after the initial explosion, there was nothing left of the Iranian ship.

The explosion aboard *Blossom* was heard for more than thirty kilometers in all directions. That is to say, the sound propagated for that distance. Much of the land along either side of the Canal near the ship's last position was trackless desert, and no one—save a few Bedouins—was there to hear the detonations that doomed the ship.

The pilots, captains, and crews aboard the ships closest to where the Iranian ship had blown up quickly recovered from the shock and began trying to put lifeboats in the water. But this wasn't something they did routinely, and they struggled to do so.

At the Suez Canal Authority building in Port Suez, the small watch team heard the pilots of several vessels close to *Blossom* report the explosion and the sinking. In short order, those watchstanders had pinpointed the location where *Blossom* went down.

A half hour later, an Egyptian Coast Guard Crestitalia-class patrol boat, the only one in Port Suez that was manned and ready, was headed toward the last known coordinates of *Blossom* to search for survivors.

As they exited the mouth of the Canal and approached the Port Suez finger piers, Dmitry Tsaryov saw their rendezvous ship in the distance, about two kilometers south of them. He called them on his secure radio and told the captain to make bare steerageway so they could bring the RHIB alongside.

Twenty minutes later, the Spetsnaz squad was aboard and the ship began making preparations for their long journey back to their home port. For the moment, the vessel made bare steerageway along the Egyptian coast so they could monitor the chatter on the Canal radio circuits while they waited for the objects they had taken aboard the doomed Iranian tanker to do their deadly work.

At SACEUR headquarters, phones began ringing as calls from the Suez Canal Authority for assistance were picked up by U.S. military networks.

Major Pat Cook was standing watch in the anticipatory intelligence cell. Only hours before, he had read the report Laura Peters had sent regarding the military-grade jamming in the same area.

Cook didn't believe in coincidences. He texted Peters and Johnson and told them to make a beeline for the watch floor.

CHAPTER FORTY

In the Suez Canal
(October 19, 0615 East Africa Time Zone)

As morning twilight began to creep over the Canal, the scene was still chaotic, and the chatter over the radios was reaching a crescendo. The ships in the vicinity of where *Blossom* was lost struggled to get boats into the water and look for survivors. A helo from the Egyptian Air Force's 545th Tactical Helicopter Wing was ordered to fly to the scene to aid in the search, but as the French-made SA-342 Aérospatiale Gazelle engaged its rotors and got ready to launch, it developed a massive hydraulic leak and was forced to shut down.

Had the Gazelle made it overhead near *Blossom's* last known position, even in the partial pre-dawn light, it would have spotted a substantial number of large, round objects bobbing in the water near where the Iranian ship went down. And even the greenest Egyptian pilot would have instantly recognized the objects as floating mines.

———

The Russian-made MKB mine was one of the simplest and cheapest naval mines in the inventory of the Iranian Navy. That, and the fact that Russia had sold hundreds of these deadly weapons to Iran, made them the weapon of choice for Dmitry Tsaryov and his commandos to unleash as *Blossom* went down.

The MKB moored contact mine is typically set to float just below the surface of the water or as deep as five meters. A steel cable connecting the mine to an anchor on the seabed prevents it from drifting away. The explosive and detonating mechanism is contained in a buoyant metal or plastic shell and, once activated by a passing ship, triggers eighty kilograms of explosives.

When the mine case is disconnected from its anchor, the MKB becomes a floating or "drifting" mine. Used extensively during World Wars I and II, drifting mines are now banned by international law. The Russian commandos who unleashed the MKBs from *Blossom* when it went down had cut the anchors of some of the mines, and now they drifted in the Canal.

As the Egyptian Coast Guard Crestitalia-class patrol boat arrived on scene, it plowed directly into one of the MKB mines. The weapon did its deadly work. It broke the back of the rescue craft and sank it to the bottom of the Canal with all hands.

The disaster was witnessed by the other ships in the ill-fated convoy, and soon the chatter on the Canal frequency radios reached an even higher crescendo.

———

Within hours of the explosion that sent *Blossom* to the bottom, the international news media was on the scene over the Canal and on nearby banks on either side of the waterway. While the Egyptian Air Force could not get their Gazelle airborne, the news agencies based in Cairo had no such problem. Soon, the sky was filled with small, nimble news helicopters broadcasting the disaster worldwide.

That swarm of helicopters saw and reported on the dozens of floating contact mines. What they could not see were the bottom and moored mines that had also been seeded. Had they been able to see through the water, just twenty-four meters to the bottom of the Canal, they would have seen those far more deadly mines.

———

Colonel Martin Sauter had assembled his entire team on their anticipatory intelligence cell watch floor. Everything their algorithms told them, as well as their collective professional experience, led them to only one conclusion: The sinking of the Iranian ship *Blossom* was no accident. It was a carefully staged effort by Russia to block the Suez Canal and make it impossible for oil from the Middle East to reach Europe.

"I appreciate the analysis," Sauter began. "We've pushed our information up to the command level. What just happened will have serious repercussions. What we need to focus on now is getting that CIA team all the help we can give them tracking down those stolen nukes. Somebody tell me something."

"Boss, we're getting real-time feeds with everything the NSA knows," Pat Cook replied. "We know the Chechens have contracted a ship. We are pretty sure it's moving to a port either here or here," he continued, focusing his laser pointer on a map of Europe he'd pulled up on the large screen display.

"We're waiting for them to communicate with the Belarusian vigilantes," Charles Johnson chimed in. "Once they tell them what port to make for, Holden and his team will set up an intercept course."

There was a momentary silence as Sauter shook his head.

Laura Peters spoke up. "Holden's team has been mapping the local roads and highways. There aren't that many routes whoever stole those nukes can take. Once they commit to heading for either the Lithuanian or Ukrainian border, they'll be on them."

"The IC has done their job," Sauter replied. "We're pretty sure we'll be alerted to any calls the Chechens make. What about the other half of those calls? Can we do anything to pinpoint where those calls are going and maybe zero in on where those Belarusian vigilantes are holed up?"

'If you give us the go-ahead, we can hack into the big Belarusian cell providers," Johnson said, looking down at his tablet. "There aren't that many of them, and most share the same cell towers. When we get an alert from the NSA of a Chechen call to the vigilantes, we can walk back the exact time of the call and see what cell towers were pinged. That will help nail down their location."

"Can we do it without fingerprints," Sauter asked.

Johnson stifled a smile. "No problem."

"Then do it," Sauter replied. "Peters," he continued, "tell Holden what we're planning to do, and tell him his team needs to be ready to move instantly."

"Got it, Colonel."

At the Suez Canal Authority Administration Building in Port Said, the chairman of the Authority, Admiral Omar Koury, sat in his small command module. It was nothing more than a fifty-inch flat screen in a conference room, but it was where he and his key leaders had met during their training sessions on how to cope with emergencies impacting the Canal. Now it was the real thing.

Shortly after the explosion aboard *Blossom*, the watchstanders at the Canal Authority building at Port Suez had called Koury at his home. Others were awakened too, and in the pre-dawn morning, the most senior Canal Authority officials were streaming toward their administration building.

It took Koury and his staff only a few minutes on a conference call with the watchstanders in Port Suez to come up with a complete picture of what had happened: An Iranian VLCC tanker had sunk in the southernmost reaches of the Canal, an Egyptian Coast Guard boat had hit what was most likely a mine and had also sunk, and aircraft flying over the scene had spotted dozens of mines in the water.

Koury had no choice. He gave the order to clear the Canal of shipping. Within minutes of his issuing this command, the ships north of where *Blossom* had gone down continued north, toward Port Said, and those south of incident scene carefully backed down out of the Canal and re-entered the Gulf of Suez. The captains of those ships radioed their owners and waited for instructions.

———————

It was late morning in Port Suez when Omar Koury stood on the banks of the Canal with Egypt's defense minister. Both men had helicoptered here, Koury from Port Said and the defense minister from Cairo. The few staff members they brought with them kept a respectable distance from the two men as they tried to make sense of what had happened.

"The ship was an Iranian VLCC," Koury began. "It reported that it had a fire in its engine room and said it was dropping anchor. A short time after that, there was an explosion, the ship was consumed in flames, and it went to the bottom."

"And no survivors?" the defense minister asked.

"We're still doing an airborne search, and we'll continue until nightfall—but, so far, none."

"No survivors from our Coast Guard boat either?" the minister asked.

"Sadly, none. We lost six brave men."

"I had my pilot fly over the site where the ship went down, and I saw the mines floating in that area. It looked like there are at least three or four dozen. Do we think they came from the Iranian ship?"

"At this point, we don't know," Koury replied. "Maybe it was a mine that the Iranian ship hit and it started a fire. We're still trying to sort things out."

The defense minister's face grew hard, and he paused before replying. Finally, he spoke. "Someone dumps dozens of mines in your Canal, and you have no idea how they got there? You are chairman of the Suez Canal Authority." As the defense minister continued to speak, he grew more annoyed at Koury's lack of answers. He began raising his voice. "It's your *job* to protect the

Canal! Do I need to remind you how long it took to clear mines the last time this happened?"

The defense minister didn't need to remind the chairman of anything. Koury, as well as every Egyptian who had read a history book, knew how devastating mines, or even the threat of mines, could be to any canal. During the 1973 Yom Kippur War, the Suez Canal was seeded with mines as the Egyptian and Israeli armies fought for control of the Sinai Peninsula. It took a nearly-two-year international effort to clear the Canal of mines, and it wasn't until 1975 that it was reopened. Now, over four decades later, it was happening again.

"I have to get back to Cairo to confer with our president," the defense minister said. "We need to get our minesweeper force here immediately, and we need to ask for international help to clear these mines."

Omar Koury just stood there and nodded. He knew Egypt's small mine hunting force, vintage ships bought from the United States and the former Soviet Union, were in poor repair and their crews were ill-trained. Absent international help, the Canal would be closed for a long time.

"Why don't you go back to Port Said," the defense minister snarled. "Your work here is done." After casting a look of disdain at Koury, he turned on his heel and strode toward his waiting helicopter.

Hours later, the NATO secretary general, alerted by his staff of the urgent request from the Egyptian defense minister, placed an equally insistent call to the SACEUR Commander. His question was straightforward: How quickly could General O'Sullivan get NATO mine-hunting and mine-clearing ships and aircraft moving toward the Suez Canal?

For O'Sullivan, the call wasn't unanticipated, and his staff had armed him with a list of assets in the inventory of NATO nations, including their locations and states of readiness. The general provided the NATO secretary general with a thumb-nail sketch of what could be brought to bear to clear the mines.

"Is that it? Is that all we have?" the man answered, unable to hide his shock.

"I'm afraid so," O'Sullivan replied.

———

"Two-plus-two!" Laura Peters exclaimed as she got up from her chair in the nerd nook's watch center.

Every head in the room turned toward her.

"What?" Pat Cook asked.

"Do you remember when I told Colonel Sauter that Holden's team has been mapping the local roads and highways so they could try to figure out what route the vigilantes might use to head for either the Lithuanian or Ukrainian border?"

"Sure. You said they had driven a number of the roads to get their arms around how many routes there were and which ones seemed the most likely paths the vigilantes would take."

"Yes, and Holden told me one of his guys is a bit of a geek, so he took all that information and put it on Excel spreadsheets."

"Sounds reasonable, but they can't act on that information until we get a cell phone tower hit."

"Maybe; but maybe not. We've been tracking the cell phone tower info here, and our algorithms have done all they can with that information. But what if we take what Holden has learned about possible routes and feed that information in as well?"

"I think I see where you're going with this," Cook replied.

"If we mash those two streams of data together, we can help them get ahead of the problem and maybe set up an ambush once we get a cell tower hit."

"Let's do it," Cook said excitedly. "Get Holden to upload that info and send it to us ASAP."

Peters texted Holden and told him they needed to talk right away.

Ryan Garrett entered the Oval and sat in the conversational area in front of the president's desk. He had gotten closure on a task he had been working on for just over a week. He knew the answer that President Miller hoped to hear, and he was about to deliver that news.

"Ryan, I understand you're here to tell me what we've learned from Mayor Safronov," the president began.

"I am, Mr. President. He has been thoroughly questioned over the past several days, and his story has been verified by one of our top people at State—"

"There can't be any doubt, not with the issues at stake," the president interrupted.

"There is none. I can arrange for him to meet with you personally. He will tell you precisely what he told our State Department rep and what he told me."

"Fine. We don't need to take it to that level. He and his wife have been through enough. I want to be sure that they are well looked after and made comfortable wherever they decide to go in our country. And what he told you goes no further than that one person at State, you and me. Not until we need to use the information.

CHAPTER FORTY-ONE

Office of the Russian Federation President, The Kremlin, Moscow, Russia
(October 19, 0930 Moscow Standard Time)

Vladimir Putin found it difficult to hide his glee as he watched the reporting on the Russia 24 network. He had arrived at his Kremlin office early that morning, "guessing" there might be international news that merited his attention.

The news of the disaster in the Suez Canal was spreading like wildfire, and talking heads were speculating on exactly what had happened to the Iranian VLCC. Several hours later, Putin met with his chief of staff.

"It looks like we've achieved precisely what we wanted, Mr. President," the man began.

"Yes, I'm pleased. Are we certain our Spetsnaz commander and his men got away cleanly?"

"Yes, sir, and without any injuries. They're aboard the mother ship now."

"Good, when they return, I want them flown to Moscow. I'll recognize them in a ceremony here—a *private* ceremony, of course."

"I'll see to it."

"I've already been asked what we should do next," Putin continued. "It will take the West a while to flail around and figure out how to respond. For now, we'll just watch it get colder in Europe."

———

Vladimir Putin's delight was not felt elsewhere, especially in the European Council president's office in Brussels. While others dealt with the immediacy of the disaster in the Suez Canal, Erich Becker had to consider the long-range impact if the Canal was impassible for an extended time. He had called an emergency meeting of his cabinet, and his principal ministers soon had their staffs generating position papers, proposed responses and contingency plans.

"Ladies and gentlemen, while reports are still coming in, it is clear the Suez Canal will be blocked, perhaps for an extended period," Becker began. "I have asked the energy minister to brief us on where we stand."

The minister strode to the front of the room, holding a single sheet of paper. His staff had not had time to build a presentation for him, so he was making do with one page of notes. If Becker looked grim, the minister looked apoplectic as he began, looking only occasionally at his paper.

"What happened in the Suez Canal this morning clearly was no accident. Although there has been no attribution for the sinking of the Iranian VLCC, the mines that now bob in the Canal are not there by chance. This was a hostile act, and given how well known our energy needs are, one targeted against the European Union...." The energy minister continued to drone on, not getting to the point Becker wanted to hear.

Becker stopped him mid-sentence. "How long, Mr. Minister, before our energy needs become acute?"

"I was getting to that. We are one-third of the way into our reserves. Unless or until we can get oil by some other means: persuade the United States to start shipping again, end our sanctions against Russia and have them reopen their pipelines, or ask our

Gulf suppliers to ship us oil via the Cape of Good Hope, we will be in desperate shape in as little as two weeks, three at the outside."

"I don't think we have a choice," one woman said. "How soon can they start shipping us oil around Africa?"

"It's not that easy," the energy minister replied. "First, routing the oil that way adds almost seven thousand kilometers to the journey. Time and distance are money to shippers, so we'll have to renegotiate prices with our suppliers. And insurance rates have gone up as well—"

"The price of oil has spiked already," Becker interrupted. "Brent crude is up eight Euros, and the day isn't over yet."

"We know the Gulf States have us over a barrel," the energy minister continued, not even bothering to apologize for the poor pun. "But at the moment, we are out of options."

As the fractious meeting continued, Erich Becker felt whatever control he had slipping away.

―――――

Laura Peters had taken the data Rick Holden had sent her, fed it into the nerd nook's anticipatory intelligence algorithms, and told the systems to merge it with the cell phone analysis that was already underway. She asked the system to deliver a prioritized list of roads for Holden's team to cover.

She had pushed that information to the CIA team, and that had instigated a furious dialogue. Holden and Peters discussed, even argued, about the pros and cons of staging at various intercept points. One thing they did agree on was that once the Chechens told the vigilantes what port to make for, they would likely head that way immediately.

Peters thought they were done, but Holden had another ask.

"Regardless of how accurate the cell tower triangulation turns out to be, we've got a number of roads we have to watch. We sure could use that second Global Hawk. My operator, Mia Yeager, can control two of them easily."

Peters had anticipated that this was coming. Holden had brought it up in a text earlier. She knew he wouldn't like her response.

"We've talked about it here, and the decision was for us to keep control of that second bird. Our commander wants us to anchor it over where the cell phone tower triangulation points to and keep it there to watch for suspicious vehicles hitting the road in a hurry.

"Don't they understand the risks if they do that? If we keep flying a Global Hawk over their posit, even at high altitude, they will likely see it, and that will spook them. Who knows what they'll do if that happens?"

"It wasn't my call—"

"I don't care whose call it was," Holden interrupted. "This is an Agency operation. SACEUR is supposed to provide support, not tell us how to do our job."

"Look, Rick, we're supporting you with all the assets we can bring to bear. Just hear me out, will you? I'll explain how I think we can make this work."

Peters began a detailed plan on how they could coordinate their efforts. Slowly and deliberately, she walked Holden back from the edge of the cliff.

———

The director of National Intelligence was frustrated. His job was to ensure he was never surprised by world events and that the president knew what was going to happen before the event occurred. He'd had two phone conversations with President Miller earlier in the day, and now, as evening twilight began to envelop Washington, he sat with the president and his national security advisor in the conversational area in front of the president's desk.

"I've read the daily briefing reports Ryan's staff has sent me, as well as your memos," the president began, "but I have to confess,

I'm a bit perplexed about how this crisis in the Suez Canal snuck up on us like this."

The DNI began carefully, "We are just beginning to do our analysis, Mr. President. I expect we will know more soon. Right now, we're ramping up to support SECDEF. Egypt has already asked for mine-hunting and mine-clearing help from NATO and, by extension, from us."

"We have assets in Bahrain that Fifth Fleet can send that way," Ryan Garrett added. "There are two Littoral Combat Ships with mine-countermeasures packages, as well as several MCM ships—"

"I know that," the president interrupted. "But whoever did this found it damn easy to do. And it happened right under everyone's noses. We can pluck every mine out of the Canal, but the day after that, whoever did this can do it again. I want to find out who's behind this."

The three men embarked on their serious conversation, trying to divine who would mine the Canal and, more importantly, why they would do it. As they talked, they recognized that until divers could examine the wreck of the Iranian ship, they wouldn't know whether the ship sank after hitting a mine or for another reason.

What they found most perplexing was the Iranian fingerprints on this incident. An Iranian oil taker had sunk in the middle of the Canal, completely blocking traffic, and naval mines the former Soviet Union had sold to Iran years ago now floated in the southern reaches of the Canal, posing a deadly hazard to navigation.

But no matter how many possibilities they considered, they had trouble coming up with any plausible explanation why the government of Iran would sink their own ship and seed the Canal with mines. Iran had brokered lucrative contracts to ship energy to Europe, and the Suez Canal was the best route.

"One of our analysis teams floated the idea that the Iranian Revolutionary Guard did this to embarrass the Iranian government," the DNI offered.

"Why, because the government is cozying up to the West?" the president asked.

"Exactly. The IRG leadership could care less if most of the Iranian people live on the ragged edge of poverty. They're making money on the black market day in and day out. But if billons of Euros flow into Iran from oil they're selling to Europe, and Iranians' standard of living goes up, the whole notion of permanent revolution isn't attractive any longer."

"Interesting theory," the president replied. "Let me know what you uncover once you dig into it."

While the DNI held forth on his theory, the national security advisor was just shaking his head from side to side. Finally, he couldn't take it any longer. "Mr. President," Garrett said. "There is only one nation that stands to gain anything if the Canal is blocked, and that's Russia. I think that is where we need to look for culpability."

"I hear you," the president replied. "They can't be happy Europe is getting oil from the Gulf. Let's let the investigations run their course. And you're both right—we need to know more."

CHAPTER FORTY-TWO

Supreme Allied Commander Europe (SACEUR) Headquarters (October 20, 1430 Central European Time)

"It's Lithuania!" Staff Sergeant John Sundstrum shouted as he shot out of his chair. "The NSA says they're sure of it."

"Where?" Charles Johnson asked.

"Klaipeda State Seaport," Sundstrum replied as he maneuvered his mouse and brought up a map of Lithuania. "It's about thirty-five klicks south of the Lithuanian-Latvian border."

Text messages flew, and soon, every member of Sauter's team filled the command center.

"Talk to me, Peters," Sauter began. "Now that we know this, give Holden the best cell tower triangulation we can. He'll want to move his team to an intercept point."

"Already on it, Colonel," she replied. "There's one more thing, sir. I talked with Holden at length regarding our plans to anchor our Global Hawk over the spot where those cell phone towers triangulate. His team will have control of the other bird and will look ahead on whatever route they take, while ours will look for vehicles traveling north and east from wherever those towers point to."

Sauter considered this for a moment. "I want them to have all the advantages we can give them, so make sure our comms with them are bulletproof. If we see a suspicious truck or something else big enough to carry those weapons, they need to know about it."

"Roger that, Boss," Peters replied.

Peters was happy she had resolved that issue. She didn't have a good batting average in convincing her leadership to buy her other ideas. Early on in the crisis, she had floated the idea of having the Lithuanian military guard their border to intercept the vigilantes in the event they eluded the Agency team. She stressed the fact that Lithuania was a NATO member and had as big a stake as anyone in keeping the nukes out of the wrong hands.

Colonel Sauter had pushed the idea all the way up the chain of command to General O'Sullivan. The SACEUR commander had considered but ultimately rejected that initiative. The imperative to hide the fact that there were nuclear weapons missing in the first place was too strong.

It was another desultory day. Rick Holden and his team sat in the great room of their villa on the western outskirts of the city of Baranavichy—watching yet another European soccer game.

"Do these Euros play any other sport," Jimbo Folga groused. "It's the middle of football season back in the States."

"I hear they're pretty good at cricket, too," Mia Yaeger replied with a smile. "I can cycle through the channels and find a cricket match if you like."

Folga just flipped her off.

Holden knew his team was restless. Chapo Chavez had suggested they start going house-to-house to see if they could find the missing weapons. Holden knew if they were coming up with ideas that were that off-the-wall, they'd been cooped up way too long.

His phone buzzed, and the text from Laura Peters said, "Call me. Urgent."

Seconds later, Peters' secure phone rang.

"Rick, the Chechens just called the vigilantes," she began after answering on the first ring. "They told them to head for Klaipeda State Seaport in Lithuania. That's where their ship is."

"It's there already?" he asked.

"Yes, and they told the vigilantes to be there in the next twenty-four hours."

Holden scrolled through his tablet.

"That's almost five hundred klicks," he said.

"I know, but that doesn't matter now," she urged. "They'll be on the move immediately. I just sent you the coordinates of where the cell phone tower triangulation tells us the call from the Chechens was received. It's not a point solution, but the area isn't that large. Whatever vehicle emerges from that area will likely be the one you need to intercept."

"Your info just popped up. We've got it."

"Are you loaded up?" Peters asked.

"We are. We can roll out of here in ten mikes."

"Hurry, Rick."

―――――――

Rick Holden and his team weren't the only ones tired of waiting. Ilia Novik had something the Chechens desperately wanted and something for which they were willing to pay top dollar, yet they kept his team in the dark for days about when or where they were to go. All the while, the Belarusian Army, and likely the Russians too, were scouring the countryside looking for his team and their stolen weapons.

Now the call had finally come, and his handler was insistent, telling him he had to move. The man had even told him he didn't have time to take a leak—just move now.

Novik wasn't the man's puppy dog. *He* had what *they* wanted. He would control what his team was going to do—not them.

Still, he wouldn't get his payday until he delivered the nukes to the Chechens, and the money he was going to get would go a long way to ridding his country of the Russians. He would put up with his handler's abuse if it got him what he wanted.

He pulled his woman companion aside and told her to load the camper as they'd discussed. He told her to bring extra ammo for their weapons and enough food and drink for a day-long dash to the Klaipeda State Seaport.

That done, he spoke with his number two and reviewed the rest of their plan.

Other than what Laura Peters had told him in texts and phone conversations over the past several days, Rick Holden had little understanding of the capabilities of SACEUR's anticipatory intelligence cell. He didn't know what it did or how it did it, so he had no trust in whatever its software had spit out.

But he trusted Peters absolutely. He knew she had taken the data he had sent her, melded it with whatever else she had, and given him a location where she thought his team could best intercept the Belarusian vigilantes.

Within minutes of getting Peters' call, Holden's team was loaded up in their three Dartz Nagel Dakkar SUVs. Holden drove one vehicle, and Mia Yeager rode shotgun. Jimbo Folga drove the second SUV. Chapo Chavez drove the third. Blake Mason rode with Folga, and Darko Markovic rode with Chavez. The team was equipped with low power UHF radios that broadcast on a discrete frequency.

As they rolled out of the villa, Holden looked toward Yeager. "We know their vehicle, or maybe several of them, are supposed to get to Lithuania in a hurry, so they'll likely be moving at high speed. And these weapons are pretty big, so you can ignore anything on the road that is really small."

"Got it, Boss. So, discount all the Yugos, right?" The quip referred to the super-mini hatchback variant of the Fiat, which was widely ridiculed as one of the worst cars ever made.

"Yep, no Yugos. You're on the right track. Why don't you send the Global Hawk over Slonim?"

"You got it," she replied. "SACEUR is going to keep theirs anchored over the area where they got the cell phone hit?"

"That's their plan. We got shot down when we asked to control both, but I'm counting on Peters and her team feeding us everything they have in real time."

"Sounds like you really trust her."

"I do. Just lemme know when you've got our bird repositioned."

Peters' information put the location of the vigilantes in the vicinity of the city of Vawkavysk, about sixty klicks to their west. They counted on the fact that whoever had the stolen nukes didn't have the time to work their way north and east on poorly maintained local roads. They would likely take the east-west road that intercepted the main highway that headed northeast, toward Minsk. Slonim was just twenty klicks from that intercept point.

Belarus was one of the poorest countries in Europe and, as a result, had little to offer in the way of attractions other than the capital of Minsk.

Those Belarusians who had the means to travel spent whatever vacation money they had visiting other countries in Europe. As a result, most had little knowledge of their country other than the town or village where they grew up.

That wasn't the case with Ilia Novik. Years of maneuvers with the Belarusian Army had familiarized him with most of his country. That, coupled with the reconnoitering they had done while they waited for the call from the Chechens, along with his study of digital maps, convinced him he had the most effective and efficient routes planned whether they were told to head for Lithuania or Ukraine.

That plan had to be adjusted, though not completely blown up, when his handler had told him to get to Klaipeda State Seaport ASAP. Novik put waypoints on the digital map on his tablet.

As Novik and his female companion rolled out of their hideout in their heavily laden camper, their beach equipment was piled high on the roof rack. The woman held the tablet and began issuing turn-by-turn navigation orders.

Her first command took them onto a little-traveled country road.

CHAPTER FORTY-THREE

East of the City of Slonim, Belarus
(October 20, 1545 Central European Time)

They had rolled out of their layup house twenty minutes ago and were speeding toward Slonim, their best guess as to where they might intercept the vigilantes.

Rick Holden drove the lead vehicle as Mia Yeager rode shotgun and multitasked. She looked at one tablet and gave Holden waypoints to get to Slonim while she controlled the Global Hawk from another tablet. She needed to do two things with her bird: locate the vigilantes' vehicle and scan the roads ahead for Russian or Belarusian troops.

Yeager knew her job would be infinitely easier if she had control of both UAVs, but they had fought that fight and lost. She hadn't worked with Holden that long, but she knew better than to grind him and grouse about the fact that SACEUR still controlled one of the two available Global Hawks.

"Anything yet, Mia. Are you seeing any suspicious vehicles on that east-west highway?"

As she fed him information from her bird, she nudged him, gently, about what the SACEUR UAV was seeing. "Nothing, Boss. Anything from Peters?"

"Nope."

They were a few klicks east of Slonim when Holden called his team on the secure radio.

"Mia hasn't spotted any suspicious vehicles yet, and neither has SACEUR. We're going to continue west so we at least get closer to where they got that cell phone hit."

The drivers of the other two SUVs clicked their radios twice as they pressed on. They kept a spread of about a kilometer between their vehicles so as not to attract attention.

They discussed, disagreed really, as to whether to head in separate directions so they could cover more roads. But Holden vetoed that idea. He knew whoever had those weapons had killed several soldiers when they stole them and, now that they had a payday coming, would likely fight it out with his team rather than surrender. He wanted the odds stacked in his favor, even at the risk of not spotting the escaping vehicle.

Their old camper bounced along almost violently on the north-south country road they had been on for almost a half hour since rolling out of their hideout.

"Did someone remove the shocks from this piece of junk?" Ilia Novik's female companion asked.

"They were probably shot already, and loading them up with thousands of pounds of weapons probably didn't help. Don't worry; we'll be on a regular road in a few more klicks."

Novik knew that most, maybe all, of his team didn't agree with his decision to take bad roads for their initial journey toward the Lithuanian border. But he knew the countryside, and he counted on the fact that the Russians did not. Their pursuers would likely stay on main highways. This was their best shot.

They were about ten klicks west of Slonim when Holden asked Yeager, "Anything yet?"

"Nothing. The bird has picked up a few sedans and some mini-cars on the east-west highway but nothing that could even vaguely hold the kind of weapons we think they're transporting."

"Show me your tablet, would you?"

Yeager turned her tablet toward Holden, and he looked at the map.

"Maybe we're looking too far east. We assumed they'd take this east-west road because it got them to the M1 highway fastest—"

"Ummm...," Yeager interrupted. "Is this the part where we talk about what 'assume' means?"

"Ass of you and me...yep...I think you're right. How about moving your search west? And look a little bit north of Vawkavysk. We need to cover our bases if they picked another route."

"On it, Boss."

Holden was on the secure radio moments later, sharing the new search plan with his team.

———————

Ilia Novik rolled off the rutted country road and onto a highway, if one could call it that. It had a number which identified it but, like most roads in his country, was in a state of neglect and disrepair. This one pointed generally northeast.

"Better riding?" he asked his companion.

"Yeah, but not much. I hope my sister nursing the baby in the back doesn't have too many bite marks."

Novik smiled. The woman was reminding him that she knew what their cover story was in the event they were stopped. As he looked at the way she was cradling her weapon, he guessed she would prefer a firefight with whoever tried to intercept them.

———————

They were just over twenty klicks west of Slonim and going a bit slower than the speed limit.

Rick Holden tried not to ask Mia Yaeger an endless string of questions, but until she located something they could roll in on, they were flying blind. "Where is the bird now, Mia?"

"I've got it doing racetracks around the city of Ros, here." She turned the tablet toward him.

"Looks like as good a spot as any."

"Yeah, I think so. Nothing from the SACEUR bird yet?"

"Nope, and you hear me quiz Peters every ten minutes or so."

"And they're adamant they want to keep it anchored over Vawkavysk?"

"I asked that question, but they were adamant. That's what they want, and we'll have to live with it."

Yeager's momentary silence told Holden she was still pissed that SACEUR hadn't bought her plan. He knew he had to keep her in the game. "I've worked with Peters before, Mia. She's a pro. I know she's giving us everything she's got."

"All right, I've widened the search aperture on the Global Hawk's cameras," Yeager replied. "What it gives us won't be as high fidelity, but it will cover more real estate. I think that's what we want now, right?"

"You know what these birds can do. We'll follow your lead."

Laura Peters *was* trying to give Holden and his team everything SACEUR had and kept pressing her Global Hawk control cell for information, but they had nothing to give her.

It was easy to see why the vigilantes had picked Vawkavysk as a place to lay up. The ancient town adjoining the Wołkowyja River traced its roots to the eleventh century and was a farming and manufacturing center that, like the rest of the country, had fallen on hard economic times. It would have been easy for the vigilantes to find an abandoned warehouse or farmer's barn to hide out.

Still, she had to trust her chain of command that their decision to anchor the bird high above the city center would give them their best chance of finding a suspicious vehicle heading north.

―――――――

"I think I may have something!" Mia Yaeger shouted. "Look at this." She turned the tablet toward Holden.

"I see a camper loaded with what looks like beach stuff. Is that what you want me to look at?"

"Yes," she replied. "It's on this minor road that heads generally north-northeast. It's not moving that fast."

"Looks good size, I think it can hold those weapons."

While they had laid up, Holden had extracted every detail he could from Peters regarding the nukes that were stolen from the Belarusian Army base at Brest. Based on the size of the weapons and the carrying capacity of the camper he was seeing, he figured all, or at least most, of those bombs could be in the camper.

Holden was on the radio in seconds. "Chapo, put your radio on speaker. I want to ask Darko something."

"Go ahead, Boss. He's listening."

"Darko, Mia spotted an old camper loaded up with beach gear about a dozen and a half klicks northwest of here. It's heading northeast and looks like it's going less than the speed limit; other cars are passing it by."

"You said beach gear?" Markovic asked.

"Yeah, that's what seems strange. There sure as hell aren't any beaches around here. What about lakes, that sort of thing?"

"Sounds suspicious to me. There are no lakes of any size nearby. Plus, remember, this is a poor country. People don't take that kind of a vacation—and especially not this time of year. The water would be damn cold."

"That's enough for me," Holden replied. "We need to roll in on these guys." Turning toward Yeager, he continued. "Keep the

279

Global Hawk overhead that camper and give me a vector to intercept."

"You've got it."

Holden keyed the radio to update Peters on their contact.

CHAPTER FORTY-FOUR

Northwest of the City of Slonim, Belarus
(October 20, 1615 Central European Time)

Rick Holden had told Laura Peters what they were doing and had radioed Jimbo Folga and Chapo Chavez to close the distance so they could provide mutual support when they intercepted the suspicious camper.

They had discussed how they wanted to do the takedown and had finally agreed that Holden would drive right up behind the camper and nudge it with his SUV.

If it *was* a family on a vacation trip, he figured the camper would pull over and stop. The driver would likely rail at him for his bad driving. If that were the case, and they were certain it wasn't the vigilantes, he'd offer cash on the spot to repair any damage they had done.

But if the camper kept going, and especially if it sped up, he would have Folga and Chavez close, and they would box it in and try to run it off the road.

———

We've got trouble!" Mia Yeager shouted.

"What?"

"I had us taking this road here," she began, turning her tablet toward him. "But I see a convoy of military vehicles traveling south. Looks like about a half dozen of 'em. Can't tell if they're Russian or Belarusian, but I think we need to avoid them."

"I agree. Can you reroute us so we can keep clear?"

"Wait," she replied as she buried her head in her tablet. "Okay," she said as she popped her head up. "We can take the next exit up ahead and wait on the north-south road. It will only take about five minutes for them to get south of us. I'll keep the Global Hawk anchored on the camper and then we'll just have to see how much power these SUVs have. We'll be in a tail chase for sure."

———

Far from where Rick Holden and his team were trying to intercept the vigilantes and their weapons, President James Miller met with his national security advisor.

Ryan Garrett's staff had reached out to the Joint Staff as well as SACEUR and CENTCOM to try to determine how long the Red Sea mine clearing operation would take and when Europe could start receiving oil from the Gulf.

Garrett's people had pressed those military commanders, wanting to know why they couldn't deliver faster results. The answer was always the same—cordial but direct: There simply weren't enough assets to do the job quickly, and even the closest ones were days away.

Garrett had his own network within the U.S. military, and after his staff had delivered the disappointing news, he had reached out to those contacts himself. The answer was still the same, with those officers even piling on and reminding him how mine-hunting and mine-clearing was something the U.S. military had neglected for decades. There was always lip service given as to how important the capability was, but at the end of the day, there was a limited inventory of gear to perform the mission.

They did tell him that General O'Sullivan was pressing NATO allies to move their mine-hunting and mine-clearing assets to the Red Sea but that the situation with the allies was much the same as with the U.S. military. Mine work was a mission that wasn't a priority.

Worse, when Garrett bypassed his contacts and telephoned the SACEUR commander directly, O'Sullivan told him less than one in three of the allies' mine-hunting and mine-clearing ships could physically get underway—and many of *those* simply weren't mission ready.

O'Sullivan was savvy enough not to lecture Garrett on the predictable results of NATO's failure to achieve even its low threshold of funding (2% of each nation's GDP). The SACEUR commander ended the call with the national security advisor by suggesting that the chances of the Red Sea being clear for safe transit within the next month was next to zero.

Now Garrett sat in the Oval, delivering the bad news to the president.

Miller tried not to let his anger boil over and splash on Garrett. The man was loyal to a fault and seemed to be the only one trying to help him find a way out of this mess.

Instead, the president turned his rage toward Vladimir Putin. The Russian president had attacked America as surely as if he had flown a bomber over the United States. The cyberattack on the Port of Corpus Christi was a cowardly act that had killed U.S. citizens and, along with the attack on the Port of Lake Superior, had forced the United States to stop shipping energy to its European allies.

The EU had tried to goad Putin into getting out of Belarus and begin shipping energy to Europe again, but every effort, even those offering huge concessions, had been spurned by the Russian leader. He was already shipping energy to new markets in Asia.

But it was the sinking of the *Blossom* and the mining of the Red Sea, actions that flouted every norm by which civilized nations live, that demonstrated just how far the Russian leader would go to try to control world events. Miller had learned via back-channels that nine Iranian sailors were presumed dead and likely went to the bottom of the Suez Canal with *Blossom*.

Miller and Garrett had been talking for just over a half hour, recounting the litany of ways in which Vladimir Putin was sticking it to the U.S. and its allies. Finally, Garrett had had enough.

"Mr. President, we've taken, not just the first punch—but multiple punches, and some of them have been body blows. It's time to take the gloves off and punch Putin in the face."

"What did you have in mind?"

"Here's what we can do, Mr. President. But we have to move quickly...."

CHAPTER FORTY-FIVE

Highway P51, North of the City of Mosty Vtoryye, Belarus (October 20, 1645 Central European Time)

The Russian convoy had passed by, and Holden's team was now back on the north-south highway in pursuit of the camper.

"How far, Mia," Holden asked.

"Only about six klicks, and it's still traveling slowly. The Global Hawk is trailing them."

"Many other vehicles travelling along the highway?"

"Only a few, and they're just zipping past the camper."

"Good, that tells me they're carrying a heavy load. Are you thinking the same way I am?"

"Yep," she replied.

Holden sped up, and the other two SUVs did as well. As planned, they were now only a few hundred meters apart, ready to overtake and box in the camper once they caught up with it.

"Do you think that was a Belarusian Army convoy that passed us by a few klicks back?" Ilia Novik's companion asked.

"No, they were definitely Russians. Those vehicles looked almost new—not like the decrepit shit our army has."

"Are you sure we're okay on these highways? We know the Russians are looking for us."

"I think we've disguised ourselves as best as we can, and we have a good cover story. If we get stopped, you know what to say."

285

"They're just about one klick ahead, Rick. You'll see them soon," Mia Yeager said.

"Got it," Holden replied. He radioed the other two SUVs. "They're about one klick ahead. Close up on me and get ready."

Two double mic clicks told him that Folga and Chavez heard him.

"I see them!" Holden shouted.

Holden closed the distance and then decelerated slightly. The other two SUVs were close on his tail, ready to box in the camper if it accelerated once he bumped it.

They were in position, about fifty meters behind the camper. It didn't look like they'd been spotted. Holden accelerated.

Ilia Novik noted the SUV getting larger in his rearview mirror and was trying to get his brain around what was going on. Was the idiot texting or…?

There was a jolt as Holden's vehicle crunched into their bumper.

"What the hell?" his female companion shouted as her head shot up.

"Stupid fucker," Novik yelled.

"What's going on?" she asked.

"This guy just crushed my bumper, and he's still on my ass."

"What are you going—" she began, but another crash, this one more violent, jolted them.

"Shit, this isn't some fool with his head up his ass texting!" Novik shouted. "Someone's on to us."

As he spoke, he spied two more SUVs closing them at high speed.

286

"We can't outrun them on this highway. Tell me what's up ahead—what exits?"

She buried her head in her tablet.

"Just under one klick ahead, there's an exit for Patoka."

Novik paused a moment. "We'll take it!" he yelled. "It's heavily wooded and has campgrounds, and it's our best chance to lose them!" He pushed the accelerator to the floor and got on his cell phone.

"Guess we know they're our target," Mia Yeager said.

Rick Holden stayed a few meters behind the camper as Chapo Chavez and Jimbo Folga closed the distance. Chavez was in front, with Folga close behind. Chavez was going to jump in front of the camper and slow, while Folga was going to pull right next to it to box it in.

They had started to execute their maneuver when, suddenly, the camper turned sharply right and careened off an exit ramp.

"Chapo, Jimbo—follow me!" Holden shouted. "We'll box him in on whatever road he's on. Get ready for a firefight. These guys are likely desperate to get rid of us."

Ilia Novik drove the camper down the two-lane country road, making the best speed he could.

"Ilia, I counted three SUVs. Who are they, and how the hell did they find us?" His female companion knew that Novik didn't have those answers. And she also knew they would never outrun their pursuers. They had two choices: surrender—or fight it out. Novik was the leader, and he would need to make that decision, but she needed to know right now.

"*Ilia?*" she implored.

"I know, I know. We're not giving up without a fight. They'll likely try to box us in here, just like they did on the highway. I can't get my gun in the fight if I'm driving. I'm going to pull over on the shoulder of the road up ahead. Once I do, roll out with your weapon and mine. I'll get out and act like we have engine trouble, and then I'll join you over there."

It wasn't much of a plan, but it was the best they had at the moment. But all he had to do was buy time. He counted on help coming soon.

Rick Holden drove the lead vehicle, with Chavez on his tail and Folga close behind him.

"The camper's slowing!" Mia Yeager shouted. "They're pulling over onto the shoulder."

"I see it," Holden replied. He radioed Folga and Chavez. "This is it, he's either going to surrender or fight it out. Keep close to me, and don't start shooting unless I do."

Ilia Novik's female companion was already crouched behind the camper's right quarter panel with her gun in her hand. She had Novik's weapon and a pile of ammo laid out on the ground next to her.

As they'd planned, Novik got out of the driver's seat, stood in front of the camper, and looked at their old vehicle in disgust. As he did, he saw the three SUVs slowly approaching them.

He scurried behind the camper next to his companion and picked up his weapon.

CHAPTER FORTY-SIX

Country Road, North of the City of Mosty Vtoryye, Belarus (October 20, 1710 Central European Time)

"What now?" Mia Yeager asked as she cradled her gun in her lap.

"This confirms that there are two of them, and it looks like they're ready to fight it out," Holden began. "Can you use the Global Hawk to see behind the camper?"

"Nope, it's blind and no help to us while we're in this wooded area. I anchored it in a lazy orbit overhead," she replied.

They had stopped about seventy-five meters behind the camper. All three Dartz Nagel Dakkar SUVs bunched up, every team member with weapons at the ready.

Yeager looked at Holden. For a moment, he was lost in thought. He was trying to get his brain around how to approach their target. Even though they were on a country road, he figured anyone driving by would see an innocent-looking camper on the shoulder and three large SUVs close by and be overcome by curiosity. He didn't need some Good Samaritan caught in the crossfire.

Finally, he keyed the radio. "Jimbo, Chapo—back up a few meters and pull off the road as far as you can. Darko, sprint down to me and jump in my back seat, I need you to talk to these guys. Then the rest of you get ready to go into the woods and come up behind them. Mia and I will pull up a little closer and see if we can goad them into giving up."

"I don't think that's a good plan, Boss," Folga replied. "You're going to be exposed, and they can take you out."

"We'll use the SUV for cover. These things can take a hit."

289

"Don't like this either," Chavez added. "If you wait, we can come up behind them and maybe surprise them."

Holden knew his team and trusted their instincts, but he still wasn't absolutely certain these were the vigilantes. He needed to be the one to take the hit if they started shooting.

Markovic arrived in a sprint and climbed into the back of Holden's SUV. Holden drove a few meters closer to the camper.

"Mia, Darko—get out and take cover behind the left fender. I'll creep up on them."

Ilia Novik saw two of the SUVs backing up and the third one approaching them at a crawl. It took him only a moment to assess what was happening.

"That one will approach and likely confront us. Whoever is in the other two will probably try to flank us."

"And they *will!*" his female companion barked. "I say we take out the close SUV now."

"Not yet. Once we start shooting, they'll pound us with everything they've got. We only have to buy a little more time."

When Rick Holden had told Laura Peters that the camper they were chasing had exited the highway and headed off toward a country road in a heavily wooded rural area, she passed the information to the rest of her cell. She also told Colonel Sauter, as diplomatically as possible, that asking Holden for a play-by-play of what was happening would only distract him from his mission.

Sauter told her he would hold off his chain of command as they pressed him for information.

Rick Holden was hunched down in the driver's seat and drove his SUV at a crawl as it approached the camper. Darko Markovic and

Mia Yeager were crouched down, walking beside the vehicle's left quarter panel as it moved forward. Markovic held a pistol while Yeager held her submachine gun.

Holden stopped about thirty meters from the camper, figuring that was as far away as he could be and still have Markovic hail the camper's occupants in the native language.

"Hello, in the camper! We're sorry we bumped you and hope no one is hurt! *Do you need help?*" he shouted.

"Now?" his female companion asked.

"Not yet," Ilia Novik commanded.

He stood up and carried his weapon in his right hand as he shuffled to the back of the camper and peered around the corner at the SUV and Markovic.

"We don't know who the hell you are or why you crashed into us!" he shouted. "We're simply driving to a vacation spot, and your shitty driving has injured my wife! I've called the police and they should be here soon. You and those other two SUVs need to clear out!"

Markovic interpreted for Holden and Yaeger and then looked at his leader for guidance.

"Tell them *we're* the police and we were told there was a kidnapping in the area. We need to inspect their camper and ensure that they aren't the culprits."

"You sure about this, Boss?" Markovic asked.

"*Damn* sure," Holden snapped. "Do it."

Markovic did as instructed as Holden began to inch the SUV closer to the camper.

"Incoming," Mia Yeager shouted as a rocket-propelled grenade streaked toward them.

Rick Holden had caught sight of the RPG zooming at them a split-second before Mia Yeager's warning. He had mashed the accelerator, and the grenade glanced off the right rear bumper of the SUV. Holden, along with the two outside the vehicle, were shaken but intact.

He slammed on the brakes as Yeager and Markovic ran to catch up with him. He flung open the driver's door and rolled out of the SUV. "Let's head for the woods there!" he yelled, pointing at the opposite side of the road from the camper.

As soon as they heard the RPG explode, Jimbo Folga, Blake Mason and Chapo Chavez knew that Holden and the others were outgunned. They crashed through the woods and got ready to rush the camper.

"Okay, they obviously have heavy weapons, so these two aren't tourists," Folga began. "If we flank them, we can get the drop on them."

"Pure, fucking genius," Chavez offered.

Folga bared his teeth and snarled. Then, on the radio, Folga continued. "Rick, are you all okay?"

"Pretty much. We've taken cover in the trees on the other side of the road. Are you all getting close to flanking these guys?" he asked.

"Close—" Folga began.

Darko Markovic's shout drowned him out. "Watch out! Up the road a few hundred meters. There's a pickup truck barreling toward us at high speed. These assholes probably called in the cavalry."

Ilia Novik had indeed called in the cavalry. Once he knew their cover had been blown, he had called the house where they'd laid up and told his men there that he needed help—and fast. He explained what direction to head and said he would pinpoint his location as soon as they were on the road. Once he told them he was in a firefight, he didn't need to tell them to bring heavy weapons.

"Any doubt?" Darko Markovic asked Rick Holden.

"None," Holden replied, as they took up firing positions behind whatever cover they could find. Then, he keyed the radio. "Jimbo, you're our best shooter. Come out of the woods, take cover, and help us take this guy out. Have Chapo and Blake continue trying to flank these assholes."

"Got it, Boss."

When Ilia Novik had called for help, three of his comrades had piled into a pickup truck and sped toward the coordinates he gave them.

But beyond that, he didn't have much of a plan. He just wanted to try to even the odds against whoever the hell had tracked them down. Once Novik had the pickup in sight, he told his men to take out anyone in the SUVs near them.

Rick Holden wanted to wait until the pickup truck was closer to them to ensure that the people inside it were in league with the camper's driver and passenger and not just some teenagers out joyriding.

That plan was blown up once the pickup was about fifty meters away and someone in the bed of the truck began wildly firing at Holden's SUV.

"Take him out!" Holden shouted.

Jimbo Folga took the first shot, and the others quickly brought their guns to bear.

The combined fire of Folga, Holden, Markovic and Yeager did its deadly work. The pickup's windshield shattered, and it went careening off the road, smashed into a tree and flipped over, sending the shooter in the back of the pickup flying.

Seconds later, Holden was on the radio. "Jimbo, approach the pickup carefully and make sure they're all dead. Then circle back here and join us on this side of the road.

"Blake, Chapo, are you in position in the woods behind the camper?"

"We're about a hundred or so meters from them," Chavez began. "It looks like two shooters, a man and a woman. Do you want us to close and open up on them?"

Holden considered this for a moment. There was now little doubt these were the people who had broken into the Belarusian Army base at Brest. They had shown all the hostile intent they needed to, and they clearly had reinforcements in the area, how many more he could only guess. If the missing nukes were in the camper, they had already accomplished the first part of their mission, seizing them before they got to the Klaipeda State Seaport. But the next step, getting them to a safe spot, likely a Belarusian Army base, was important as well.

He knew Laura Peters and SACEUR were working on the "what do to next" part. He also worried that the camper's occupants could have many more confederates in the area. Trying to capture, vice kill, the two of them came off the table.

"We're going to open fire from here and keep them distracted and pinned down. Once we do, close in and take them out!" Holden ordered.

———

As Rick Holden and the others opened up on the camper, pouring heavy fire in its direction, Ilia Novik's female companion stared blankly at him.

"There are likely as many as a half dozen of them, and some of them are probably in the woods behind us," Novik began. "But they're all dismounted now. I say we crawl back into the camper and drive. We may find a spot to hide in the woods up ahead."

"I don't want to die like this, Ilia."

They continued to hear bullets plinking off the camper.

"Neither do I," he said as he rose and started for the camper's door.

Just then, bullets started flying toward Novik and his companion as Chavez and Mason opened fire from behind them. The shots were continuous and did their deadly work. The two were cut down within seconds.

Chavez approached cautiously and kicked both bodies. Then over the radio, "Clear here."

The second they heard Chavez's call, Holden and the others rushed across the road to the camper. When they got there, they found that Chavez and Mason had already opened the camper's side door and were staring at the nuclear weapons.

"Guess this was the right target," Markovic offered.

"That's for sure," Holden replied.

Folga arrived on a dead run. "All the assholes in the pickup truck are dead," he said. "Looks like we found what we're looking for."

Holden was about to reply when he noticed a frown on Chavez's face.

"Chapo?" he asked.

"How many nukes did they say these guys stole? Chavez asked.

"Nine, total."

"Well, we've got a problem, Boss. There are only six here."

CHAPTER FORTY-SEVEN

Supreme Allied Commander Europe (SACEUR) Headquarters (October 20, 1930 Central European Time)

Laura Peters had returned home to get a bite to eat when she received the call from Rick Holden on her secure phone. She listened, first with relief and then disbelief, as he related what had happened. She asked Holden if the camper was drivable, and he told her it was. She texted him the location of the nearest Belarusian Army base and said the SACEUR staff would coordinate with the Belarusian Army so they would be ready to take custody of the weapons. She then called Colonel Sauter at his home.

Within thirty minutes, the entire anticipatory intelligence cell was mustered and Peters brought them up to speed on what Holden and his team had done.

On his way into SACEUR headquarters, Sauter had called his boss, and soon, key SACEUR staff members were pouring in to deal with the crisis.

Rick Holden and his team were on the move again. They had left the dead vigilantes where they lay. He'd put Darko Markovic at the wheel of the camper, with Blake Mason riding shotgun. He drove the lead SUV ahead of them, with Mia Yeager riding shotgun. Chapo Chavez and Jimbo Folga trailed in the other two SUVs.

They were headed for the 11th Guards Mechanized Brigade base outside the city of Slonim, a temporary storage site for the nukes that had been agreed upon after a series of frantic phone calls between General O'Sullivan and the Belarusian defense minister. Holden had Yeager fly the Global Hawk ahead of their convoy, scanning the highways for Russian troops.

It was close to midnight at SACEUR Headquarters, and the relief that was felt there after learning Holden and his team had found six of the missing nuclear weapons was soon erased by the knowledge that there were still three missing nukes.

General O'Sullivan had his two- and three-star officers assembled in his secure conference room. Conspicuous by the fact that he was the only person in the room not wearing general's or admiral's stars, Colonel Martin Sauter sat at the end of the long table as the senior officers discussed the current crises.

After an earnest, but frustrating, conversation with his senior commanders, O'Sullivan looked toward Sauter. "Colonel Sauter, I guess this brings us back to you and your cell. Kudos to you all for getting us this far and helping the Agency team find those six weapons. And I understand they did so without any injuries. That's a win."

"Thank you, General," Sauter replied.

"My staff tells me that Holden and his team delivered those weapons to the Belarus Army base at Slonim, and I'm inclined to believe their defense minister when he tells me that they will be closely guarded. Now I need you all to help them find those three missing nukes. I suspect you have a plan, and we're anxious to hear it."

Sauter strode to the podium and began to recount the actions his cell had already taken. He began by admitting that once they had intercepted the call from the Chechens telling the vigilantes to make for Klaipeda State Seaport, they had stopped reading the transcripts of those conversations. But once Holden and his team had reported that there were nukes still missing, they had replayed the more recent conversations between the Chechens and the vigilantes.

Those tapes had revealed that the vigilantes had been instructed to take six of the weapons to Klaipeda State Seaport, where their ship was waiting, and the other three to the Ukrainian port city of Yuzhne, on the Black Sea, northeast of the major port of Odessa.

Sauter's team had also learned that the ship in question would not arrive in Yuzhne for at least three days. The Chechens had contracted a ship to make that pickup, but a day out of Yuzhne, the ship's owner demanded an exponentially greater amount of money than the Chechens had agreed to pay.

After an angry series of phone calls, the Chechens told the man to go to hell and looked for another ship to do the job. They had finally found one, but it was still days from Yuzhne.

The Chechens hadn't given the vigilantes explicit instructions as to when they were to arrive at Yuzhne in the same manner that they had insisted that they sprint toward Klaipeda State Seaport.

Sauter's report set off a spirited discussion among the senior officers. The biggest unknown was when the vigilantes would begin the more-than-one-thousand-kilometer dash toward Yuzhne from wherever they were laid up in southwestern Belarus.

O'Sullivan was mindful the Agency was leading this operation and SACEUR was providing support, but he also knew that Holden's team was flying blind without substantial help from his command.

"There are still a lot of unknowns, but here's what I think we know," O'Sullivan began. "Colonel Sauter, Holden's team reported that there were two vigilantes in the camper they tracked down and three in the pickup truck. Those three were likely summoned by the camper driver when our Agency team rolled in on them. The big question is how many they left behind to guard the other nukes."

O'Sullivan's ops director chimed in, "The Belarusian Army reviewed the security camera tapes of the break-in at the base at

Brest. It looked like there were a total of ten vigilantes who attacked the base. Their best guess is they were just looking for heavy weapons to fight back against the Russians and discovering the nukes was a bonus. They must have found out they could get an easy payday selling them to the Chechens."

"Makes sense," O'Sullivan replied. "That likely leaves a half dozen or fewer men with the three missing nukes. We need to find out if they're still laid up in the area of Vawkavysk or are on the move toward Yuzhne."

"General, my people tell me you've kept the Global Hawk anchored over that area. Has it had continuous coverage all this time?" Sauter asked.

O'Sullivan looked toward his ops director, and the man said, "Yes, General. It's getting near the end of its mission time, but we've had its cameras on a wide-angle scan of that area."

"If that's the case," Sauter continued, "I think we can pinpoint their location. We have to assume that when the camper got stopped by Holden's team and they asked their confederates for help, the pickup truck came from that spot. If we walk back the Global Hawk's tapes and see the pickup, we can pinpoint their location."

"Let's do it," O'Sullivan said. "And I want to know immediately what they tell us. I have a raft of people above my pay grade, up to and including the president's chief of staff, asking me questions. I owe them answers, and none of them are patient people.

———

Rick Holden and his team had turned down the invitation from the commander of the Belarus Army 11th Guards Mechanized Brigade to spend the night at the base outside of Slonim. Now that they knew there were still nukes missing, and that they were likely somewhere near Vawkavysk, they wanted to get back to their layup house at Baranavichy so they could be prepared to move in on the vigilantes once they nailed down their exact location.

The sixty-kilometer drive from Slonim to Baranavichy on the M1 and P99 highways would normally take just over an hour. But at 0130 on a moonless night, and with a heavy fog enveloping the roads, they proceeded slowly. Mia Yeager flew the Global Hawk ahead of their route looking for Russian convoys or roadblocks, but the bird's infrared sensors had a limited field of view. Still, it was better than nothing.

Holden was weary from the previous day's gunfight, the tense dash to Slonim, and now what he hoped was the final drive for the night. He was being lulled into a near stupor as he led their three-SUV convoy toward Baranavichy when his secure phone chirped.

"Holden," he answered on the third ring.

"Rick, its Laura. Where are you right now?"

Holden looked toward Yeager, who had heard Peters' voice coming through the phone. She turned her tablet toward him.

"We're on the M1 highway," he began, "about fifteen klicks from Baranavichy. We're going to lay up for the night and wait for instructions. What do you have for me?"

Peters began a detailed summary of the multiple SACEUR meetings, especially the instructions the vigilantes had received from their Chechen handlers regarding where, and approximately when, to deliver the three remaining weapons. She related the plan to mine the Global Hawk tapes to see if they could pinpoint the location of the vigilantes.

Holden listened impassively, asking no questions. When she was finished, he said, "I think the most important thing you've told me is that we'll likely be able to nail down the location where these guys are holed up, roll in on them, and grab the remaining nukes."

"Not exactly, Rick. I'm told you'll get instructions from your people at the Agency, but General O'Sullivan said he's getting stick and rudder from the White House. There's a larger issue they're dealing with, and grabbing the nukes isn't what they want to do—at least not yet."

There was a long silence before Holden replied. "I get what you're saying, Laura, and I want to be a team player with you and everyone in your command, but I need to hear this from the Agency. Otherwise, once you feed me a location, we're rolling in on these guys."

"You will, Rick. I'm sure of it." But in reality, Peters *wasn't* sure that would happen.

CHAPTER FORTY-EIGHT

**White House Situation Room, West Wing, Washington, D.C.
(October 21, 0815 Eastern Daylight Time)**

Ryan Garrett's national security staff had worked throughout the afternoon and night as they received updates from the SACEUR staff. Garrett arrived at the Sit Room shortly after the watch officer called him to report that only some of the missing nuclear weapons had been intercepted.

It had been less than twenty-four hours since he had told President Miller that they needed to punch Vladimir Putin in the face. He was surprised that the president was warm to his suggestions as to the multiple ways the United States could do just that.

James Miller had been amenable to hearing the various ways that his country could force Russia to leave Belarus and begin shipping energy to Europe again. Miller also wanted to convince Putin that conducting more cyberattacks against U.S. oil and gas facilities would be cost prohibitive for the Russians. However, he wasn't yet ready to take the sorts of draconian actions Garrett had posited.

But what had just happened in Belarus presented Garrett with a trump card that could potentially make Putin roll over. Two things needed to happen first: The Agency team needed to pinpoint the location of the vigilantes with the remaining nuclear weapons, and he needed to convince the president to take the action he wanted him to take.

Rick Holden and his team were laid up at their house in Baranavichy, leaning into whatever tasking they would get next. He didn't want to argue with Laura Peters, but he was stumped as to why his team wasn't going to assault the vigilantes as soon as SACEUR reviewed the Global Hawk tapes and nailed down their location.

Holden wanted to ensure his team was ready when called, so he took the first watch rotation and put the rest of his people to bed. He looked at his phone constantly, hoping that his handlers at the Agency would tell him what the hell was going on and why they weren't being told to roll in on the vigilantes as soon as they were located.

With thousands of military and civilian people working at SACEUR, having the entire command singularly focused on one function was something that fell somewhere in the range of highly unlikely to completely impossible.

But that wasn't the case now. General O'Sullivan and a few of his most senior officers were huddled around the workstation of Air Force Captain Amy Gillingham as she carefully reviewed the tapes from the SACEUR Global Hawk during the time it was anchored over Vawkavysk.

Gillingham's boss, an Air Force major who had years of Global Hawk experience, stood at her shoulder and kept up a running commentary as the tape ran. The two officers traded comments back and forth, assessing what they were seeing and what it meant. They had a printed photo of the crashed vigilante pickup truck that

Holden had uploaded to them, and they were comparing it to all vehicles near Vawkavysk.

To their credit, the senior officers queued up around the two Air Force officers kept quiet and didn't badger the pair with an endless string of questions. They knew that would only complicate their job and might cause them to miss something, and there was too much riding on finding the vigilantes to risk having the two Air Force officers miss seeing the pickup truck.

———————

President James Miller had built his political career on consensus building, and that was how he ran his White House staff. It was also how he dealt with cabinet secretaries and other agency heads, as well as his senior advisors. While some who worked for him occasionally groused that it took the president far too long to make a decision because he conferred with a multitude of advisors, most appreciated the fact that Miller rarely failed to consult them.

President Miller had broken that practice in dealing with the current crises. Ryan Garrett was the only one sitting with the president in the Sit Room. Garrett had insisted that the Sit Room watch commander brief them every half hour on SACEUR's efforts to nail down the location of the remaining missing nuclear weapons.

Each time the watch commander delivered a negative report, the two men became increasingly anxious.

CHAPTER FORTY-NINE

**Supreme Allied Commander Europe (SACEUR) Headquarters
(October 21, 1430 Central European Time)**

"Right here, General. This is it, we're certain." Captain Amy Gillingham hovered her cursor over a villa on the outskirts of Vawkavysk. "A white pickup rolled out of there at this time stamp you see here." She pointed to the upper left corner of her screen. "Add transit time, and that corresponds to the time when the Agency team said they took that vehicle out."

"Great work, Captain," Major O'Sullivan began. "Now we need a real-time view of what's going on there. How far away is the Global Hawk?"

"Just a few klicks. We'll have it there right away." There was silence as Gillingham maneuvered the bird to the location their tapes had indicated. "We're overhead now—exact match with the villa we saw on the video."

O'Sullivan, Sauter and the other senior officers looked at the grainy picture. They could make out a walled villa and a few vehicles but waited for the two Air Force officers to help interpret what they were seeing.

"We're sure this is where the pickup truck came from," Gillingham said. "We've had the bird anchored over Vawkavysk for a while, and this place is pretty standard for this area. There's a main house...and this outbuilding here...and it looks like three vehicles inside the walls of the compound."

"Can you tell us more about the vehicles?" O'Sullivan asked. "They all look about the same to me."

The senior officers did not have the thousands of hours staring at pictures like these that Gillingham and her boss had, and to the layperson, there didn't appear to be any differences.

"I know the dissimilarities are hard to discern, General," Gillingham said as she moved the cursor around the screen. "This one here looks like a small sedan, much like many we see in this area. This other one is a small SUV, not sure what European model it is, but it's about the size of a Toyota RAV4. This third one is quite a bit bigger than that—"

"How big?" O'Sullivan interrupted.

"About as large as a Chevy Tahoe, maybe a bit bigger," she replied. Then anticipating his question, she continued. "Likely big enough to hold those three weapons."

O'Sullivan turned to Sauter. "Colonel, your cell is communicating with the Agency team. You're going to pass this information to them, but I'm interested in hearing what you think they should do next."

"General," Sauter began, "as we anticipated, the Agency communicated with Holden's team and told them not to assault the vigilantes, but to determine, for certain, the location of the three missing nukes. Now that we've pinpointed where the vigilantes are likely laid up, we need to see if those weapons are in one of those vehicles, most likely the last one Captain Gillingham pointed to."

"You think they're in a vehicle and not inside the house?" O'Sullivan asked.

"Those bombs are damn heavy and they probably used lifting equipment at the base at Brest when they loaded them up. Maybe a bunch of strong men could carry them inside, but they're probably just as secure in the vehicle," Sauter replied.

"That makes sense," O'Sullivan said.

"We should keep the Global Hawk overhead to see if we spot people moving around outside the house. We know they've been told to wait, and it's likely they will just stay inside."

"What do you think Holden's team will do?" O'Sullivan asked.

"We'll keep feeding them information, especially if we see people outside the house. But my guess is that once Lieutenant Peters passes this information to them, they'll want to get eyes on the villa themselves and watch it. Again, it's the Agency's call, but I think they'll wait until after dark and then scale the wall of the compound and look inside that large SUV to see if the weapons are there. If they are, that gets reported to the Agency and to us. And then...well, General, as they say, all that is above our pay grades."

"It sure as hell is, Colonel."

As soon as General O'Sullivan and the others had left, Colonel Sauter sprinted back toward his anticipatory intelligence cell. Once there, he debriefed his team on what the Global Hawk surveillance had discovered.

Within minutes, Laura Peters was on the secure phone with Rick Holden. She asked him to reconfirm that his team was to reconnoiter, but not assault, the villa.

"That's what I got from the Agency, Laura. We'll head that way and get eyes-on. I think we agree with your assessment that those weapons are likely in the large SUV you told us about. More when we get there, but we'll probably wait until nightfall and then sneak in and confirm. Once we do that, we wait."

President James Miller had cancelled most of his appointments as he and Ryan Garrett waited for the news they hoped they would hear so the president could make the phone call he wanted to make.

The call from General O'Sullivan had provided Garrett with the first link in that chain. While he was frustrated that they would have to wait until nightfall for Holden's team to find out whether the nuclear weapons were where they thought they were, the national security advisor understood the operational constraints.

Garrett knew he had to do a delicate dance between having the president confront Putin as soon as possible and not tipping their hand, in case this was a false alarm. Nevertheless, he was mindful that calls between the leaders of two superpowers are not spur-of-the-moment events but rather carefully planned and orchestrated occurrences, typically preceded by days of staff work.

Garrett didn't have time for that. He needed to move quickly if Holden's team discovered the three remaining nuclear weapons. He called the chairman of the Joint Chiefs of Staff and told him to be standing by once it was nighttime in Belarus and get ready to call his Russian counterpart on a secure link otherwise known as the hotline.

Rick Holden's first action after his conversation with Laura Peters was to have Mia Yeager fly her Global Hawk over the villa to get their own eyes-on.

Once they had determined it was the right location, they searched the surrounding area to find a spot where they could hide their three SUVs while they watched the house.

That done, Holden and his team packed up their gear and drove the short distance from Baranavichy to Vawkavysk.

They stashed their vehicles in a heavily wooded area a little over a kilometer away from the villa. Holden was mindful that the vigilantes could be told to drive toward Yuzhne at any moment and that his team needed to be ready to follow. That meant they wanted to have most of the team in or near their vehicles. Only Holden and Jimbo Folga dismounted and made their way to a small hill, a few hundred meters from the villa.

"Looks pretty much like it did on the Global Hawk video, Boss." Folga continued scanning the area through binoculars.

"Yep, no surprises," Holden replied. "There's the big SUV. Based on the size of the weapons we found in the camper, do you think that could hold three of them?"

"Looks like it to me," Folga replied. "We'll know for certain tonight."

The call from the national security advisor had surprised the chairman of the Joint Chiefs of Staff. The hotline was a little-used device located in the National Military Command Center, the NMCC for short. In June, 1963, at the height of the Cold War, the United States and the Soviet Union agreed to set up a "hotline" between the leaders of the two superpowers. The connection, established later that summer, would be reliable and available any time of day. The hotline linked the Pentagon in the United States and the Kremlin in the Soviet Union. The Washington-Moscow hotline was still in use, only the technology had changed.

The original hotline was a teletype machine, was later replaced by a fax machine, and now was a tightly secured e-mail link that sat in a corner of the NMCC. The hotline had been used only sporadically, most notably to clarify American and Soviet (later, Russian) military maneuvers in conflicts such as the Six-Day War, the Turkish invasion of Cyprus, and the Soviet invasion of Afghanistan.

While the chairman would do what the national security advisor told him to do, he expressed some skepticism that his Russian counterpart would be alerted to the call quickly, let alone tell President Putin that the American president needed to speak with him immediately. Even though he was the most senior officer in the U.S. military, the chairman found it necessary to remind himself that if there was one thing he had learned in thirty-nine years of military service, it was the need to follow orders.

CHAPTER FIFTY

Outside the Villa Near the City of Vawkavysk, Belarus
(October 22, 0115 Central European Time)

As they waited for nightfall, Rick Holden and this team had discussed the options for sneaking over the wall and looking in the big SUV to see if it contained the three missing nuclear weapons.

To no one's surprise, Holden had said he would be one of the two who would do this reconnaissance. In the hours that they had waited, Mia Yeager had kept the Global Hawk anchored over the villa and had seen no sign of people coming or going. Still, they were working on the strong suspicion that the vigilantes were holed up inside.

After a spirited discussion during which all the members of his team, including Yeager, volunteered to go with him, Holden had picked Blake Mason. He was the smallest and lithest member of the team, and Holden figured he would be best equipped to slither into the SUV without being seen. And, if the vehicle was locked, Mason had offered that he had "certain skills" that could let him gain entry quickly.

The other big decision Holden had to make was when to do this. He needed to balance the urgency of determining if the missing nukes were here, something he understood was being driven by the White House, with the advantages of waiting long enough to be reasonably sure that the villa's occupants were asleep. He picked the second option.

Holden and Mason left the wooded area and headed for the villa. They crossed the road adjacent to the compound and scaled the wall on the side closest to the large SUV.

Once inside the wall, Holden whispered to Mason," I don't see lights on anywhere inside the house. Even if someone inside gets up to take a leak and randomly looks out the window, I think you can get into the passenger door without being seen."

"Roger that. Here I go," he replied.

Mason crept up to the SUV and pulled himself up with the door handle. He swung the door open, crawled into the passenger seat, and looked into the back.

Seconds later, he was back at Holden's side.

"Bingo—three big ones," he said.

Within minutes, Holden and Mason were over the wall and back with their team. Holden called Peters and delivered his report.

That done, they laid up and continued to watch the villa, ready to follow the occupants if they made for Yuzhne.

All organizations have their unique strengths and weaknesses. The U.S. military is no exception. There are some things it does well and others that are not done as well.

One of the things it does exceptionally well is communicate up, down and across the chain of command. Within minutes of getting Holden's call, Laura Peters called Colonel Sauter. Sauter, in turn, called his immediate boss, Admiral Morton, and then called the SACEUR Commander.

General O'Sullivan made one call before calling the national security advisor. He knew that the JCS Chairman had been instructed to be prepared to call his Russian counterpart on the hotline. Now that he knew the chairman would receive that order from Ryan Garrett, O'Sullivan's ethos to follow orders precisely was trumped by his desire to keep a fellow senior military officer in the loop. He called and gave the chairman of the Joint Chiefs of Staff a heads-up.

O'Sullivan then called Garrett, who in turn called the chairman. The JCS chairman made the hotline call, and to his great surprise, he was soon connected with the Russian defense minister. The minister assured him that President Putin's chief of staff would call Garrett shortly and set up a call between the Russian and American leaders.

Just over an hour later, Vladimir Putin's chief of staff called Ryan Garrett. The man was insistent, even abusive, demanding to know why the American president wanted to speak with his boss so urgently.

Garrett was polite, but firm, and told the man that he wasn't at liberty to discuss the particulars of why President Miller wanted to speak with his boss.

Putin's chief of staff unleashed a stream of invective at Garrett, demanding to know more. Garrett listened with as much composure as he could muster and then simply said, "If you're unable to perform this simple task, the president will summon your ambassador. We have already alerted your embassy to have him standing by, and we'll get this done another way. Then, of course, you won't be necessary."

Garrett quickly pulled the phone handset away from his ear as Putin's chief of staff slammed his phone into its cradle.

CHAPTER FIFTY-ONE

Office of the Russian Federation President, The Kremlin, Moscow, Russia
(October 22, 0830 Moscow Standard Time)

The call had been set up for a while when Vladimir Putin arrived at his office at the usual time. After peppering his chief of staff with questions, most of which the man could not answer, the Russian president agreed to take the call. The fact that it was the middle of the night in Washington, D.C., caused him some concern, but only for a moment.

Once he had some time to think about it, Putin looked forward to the call. He held all the cards. He had cut Europe off from Russian energy, and his sources told him that the European nations were now deep into their reserves and strict energy rationing was in place throughout Europe. He had cowed the United States into not sending energy to Europe and had made it clear that his cyber-warriors could attack other American energy ports at will.

He had laughed as he received reports of the feeble efforts the United States and its so-called allies were making to clear the Suez Canal of mines. He had recently given a carefully orchestrated speech at the headquarters of the Russian Black Sea Fleet, at the naval base at Sevastopol, on the occasion of the christening of a new Alexandrit-class minesweeper. He told the assembled officers, sailors and dignitaries that mine warfare was a serious business and one that their Navy already excelled at but needed to continue to take even more seriously than other nations did.

There was little doubt anywhere that the speech was a thinly

313

veiled threat that even if the mines in the Suez Canal were eventually cleared, another "accident" could occur there, or in the Strait of Hormuz, and Europe would get no energy. They would be on their knees begging that he ship them oil and gas again. They would then have to lift their sanctions before their citizens froze to death.

Even given the odd hour of the call, Putin figured that was what his American counterpart was going to do: beg him to let the United States help Europe meet their energy needs. The Russian president would string him along and then lower the hammer. Then he would get on with the rest of his day.

He picked up the phone on the fourth ring, all the better to let Miller twist in the wind just a bit longer.

"Good morning, President Miller. My staff told me we needed to speak urgently, but I must confess you've kept the reason for the call quite mysterious. Am I safe in assuming it has something to do with Europe being in dire straits regarding their energy needs?"

"It has everything to do with that, as well as with another matter, President Putin."

Miller paused, and Putin waited for the begging to begin.

"I'm listening, President Miller. You asked for this call, so don't expect me to carry the conversation."

After a longer pause, Miller continued. "President Putin, I'm curious as to your relationship with Chechnya?"

"Chechnya?" Putin asked, completely surprised by the question. He couldn't get his brain around why Miller was asking this open-ended query. After stalling for a few moments, he finally gathered himself and said, "Surely you know your history, President Miller. Chechen terrorists were doing things that needed to be stopped. We took actions that were necessary."

"Including murdering tens of thousands of civilians?" Miller shot back.

Putin responded with virulent bluster, spouting the party line, blaming everything on Chechnya and nothing on Russia. The

314

Russian president spit out venom about its leaders, its citizens and all the rest. Finally, he said, "So, President Miller, does that answer your question about Russia's *relationship* with Chechnya?"

It was precisely what Miller wanted to hear. "I hear you, President Putin, and so I think you are saying these people still harbor animus toward you and toward Russia."

"Yes, President Miller, that rat hole of terrorists still harbors animus toward us, but what the hell does that have to do with anything or with the problems our two nations are having at the moment? You call me in the middle of the night in Washington; surely it's not just to discuss geopolitics and a place most of your citizens can't locate on a map."

"No, President Putin, it isn't. Would it surprise you to learn that a Chechen group has agreed to buy nuclear weapons and is about to have them shipped to their republic?"

Putin's chief of staff was listening on another line and the Russian president looked toward him for some sign that he knew what Miller was talking about. Much to his consternation, the man looked back at him blankly.

"That would surprise me, President Miller. But I suspect you're about to tell me more."

Miller began laying it out for Putin, starting with the break-in at the Belarus Army base at Brest and the theft of a "certain number" of nuclear weapons. He told him how the vigilantes who stole the weapons had negotiated to sell them to a Chechen group. He continued with a detailed accounting of how the U.S. Agency team had intercepted the weapons destined for the Klaipeda State Seaport. He then explained how those weapons accounted for only some of the nukes stolen from Brest.

Putin tried desperately to connect the dots and looked toward his chief of staff to see if Miller's story had elicited some epiphany—but the blank stare continued.

"I suspect you want to tell me more, President Miller." Putin was growing impatient. "Go on."

"President Putin, I told you that our team intercepted some of those bombs bound for Chechnya, but there are more. We know where they are, and we know where they are headed.

"I think we agree that both our nations are united regarding the dangers of nuclear proliferation. Under normal circumstances, I would have my team seize those weapons and return them to the Belarus defense forces, just like they did with the others—"

"That's what you *must* do," Putin interrupted.

"Unfortunately, President Putin, these are far from normal circumstances. You have chosen to hold seven hundred and fifty million people hostage for reasons that still elude me...."

Miller then began his own monologue, listing all of Russia's hostile actions: the crucifixions, the cyberattacks, the kidnapping of the American reporter, the sinking of the *Blossom*, the mining of the Suez Canal and all the other nefarious deeds Russia had perpetrated. When he had finally finished, he delivered his ultimatum.

"President Putin, I can take actions to try to intercept these weapons, or I can step aside and let them reach the Chechens, who are eager to get them. The choice is yours. You can withdraw from Belarus immediately, begin shipping energy to Europe, close down your cyberattack facilities and clear the damn mines you sowed in the Suez Canal. But I suggest you move quickly. It's not that long a journey to get those weapons to Chechnya. Once they are there, I can no longer help you."

Putin was about to respond, but Miller abruptly ended the call.

Putin looked toward his chief of staff for some guidance, even for a hint of what he should do—but the man was as shocked as he was and had nothing to offer.

Finally, Putin barked, "Get everyone who matters in here immediately. You know the drill!"

"Yes, Mr. President."

CHAPTER FIFTY-TWO

Office of the Russian Federation President, The Kremlin, Moscow, Russia
(October 22, 1015 Moscow Standard Time)

Ryan Garrett had listened in on President Miller's call with Vladimir Putin. As soon as the call ended, he validated the president's impression that he had shocked the Russian president with the story about the Chechens wanting to get their hands on the stolen nuclear weapons.

He stayed with the president for an hour after the call ended, trying to intuit how Putin would react. All logic pointed to the Russian president having no choice but to ask the United States to intercept those weapons and keep them from falling into Chechen hands.

Had they had this call a week or two earlier, with thousands of Russian troops still spread throughout Belarus, they would have bet that Putin would figure his army could find those weapons. But soon after deciding to stop shipping energy to Europe, the Russian president acceded to the wishes of his generals and began withdrawing most of the Russian soldiers from the country. They counted on the fact that the Russian Army couldn't redeploy and surge back into Belarus before the vigilantes got their cargo to Yuzhne.

Garrett insisted that the president get some sleep, reminding him that he would likely have an eventful day ahead of him. The national security advisor elected to stay in his office and wait for a call that he was certain would come once Putin processed what could happen if Chechnya got their hands on those weapons.

It was mid-afternoon in Moscow when one of Garrett's staffers told him that President Putin's chief of staff needed to speak with him immediately.

Garrett picked up the phone's handset and pushed the blinking button. "Good afternoon —"

"*Has your president gone mad?*" the man interrupted, breathlessly spitting his words out. "Do you realize this is an act of war? There are unguarded nuclear weapons and you refuse to intercept them."

"We did intercept a number of them. We almost lost some of our citizens in doing so. The only reason that team was in Belarus in the first place was to rescue an American reporter your president had kidnapped, tortured and left hanging on a cross to be eaten by wild animals. Don't lecture me about what's right and what's wrong—"

Putin's chief of staff interrupted again with a lengthy screed, as Garrett anticipated he would.

The national security advisor listened impassively until the man was finished. "I'm mindful we each were listening in when our principals talked earlier today. I am giving you the courtesy of being the only one on this line. Can you tell me that this is a private conversation on your end as well?" Garrett asked.

"Yes, I can. My president knows I am calling you. He insisted I do so. He wants me to persuade you to talk some sense into your president. I am in my office with the door closed."

"Is it fair to say that the troubles between our two nations began with your invasion of Belarus just over a month ago?"

"You know why we entered that country. What point is there in dragging out that history? And you know damned well that we have withdrawn most of our troops almost as quickly as we sent them into Belarus. What the hell is your point?"

"We know that your excuse for attacking a peaceful country was supposedly to protect your energy shipments to Europe. But the vigilantes had been attacking those pipelines for a while. What about the assassination attempt on Ambassador Baryshev? Wasn't that what really triggered your invasion?"

Putin's chief of staff's head was spinning. What did this have to do with stopping the nukes from falling into Chechen hands? He had to stop Garrett from dredging up this history and get back to the business at hand.

"Yes, there were several reasons we felt we needed to move into Belarus, and that attempt on our ambassador's life was one of them. But I think you would agree that it was the final straw that proved to us that President Sechenov couldn't control her own country. The ambassador's residence and our embassy are in the most secure part of Minsk. If that can happen *there*, all of our diplomats are in danger. Surely you can understand that we needed to ensure that our other envoys weren't at risk from whatever Belarusian terrorist group tried to assassinate Iskra Baryshev."

"Would it surprise you to know that we have incontrovertible proof that your president ordered Ambassador Baryshev's assassination—?"

"That's outrageous," the man interrupted. "How dare you!"

"No, how dare *you*. President Miller knew you, and perhaps others, were listening in on his call with your president and chose not to confront your boss with what we know while others could hear what was said. So, he told me to tell you this: We have a man, as well as his wife, who recently defected from your country. They have told us, and will tell the world, that Vladimir Putin's fingerprints are all over this. President Putin can deny this all day long, but no one will believe him."

The conversation dragged on for another ten minutes, with Putin's chief of staff denying and threatening. But Garrett could tell that the steam had seeped out of his arguments.

Finally, the man stopped talking, and Garrett concluded by saying, "I'll count on you to convey this to your president, and quickly. We know the general timeline these vigilantes have to deliver these weapons, and my guess is that if you wait as much as a day, it may be too late."

With that, Garrett ended the call.

CHAPTER FIFTY-THREE

Office of the Russian Federation President, The Kremlin, Moscow, Russia
(October 22, 1530 Moscow Standard Time)

After Vladimir Putin's chief of staff revealed what Ryan Garrett had told him: that the United States knew he had ordered Iskra Baryshev's assassination and would reveal the truth to the international community, Putin fumed and blustered and was as enraged as the man had ever seen his leader. But once Russia's president gathered himself, he knew he had no choice. He told his chief of staff to call Garrett and arrange the best terms he could. The man didn't bother waiting until it was morning in Washington, D.C. He made the call immediately.

Russia had little leverage, and Garrett delivered his terms: The United States would intercept the ship contracted to carry the nuclear weapons and then capture the vigilantes holding those weapons and ensure their safe return to the Belarusian government. In return, Russia would begin shipping energy to Europe immediately, withdraw its army from Belarus but leave behind all their equipment so President Sechenov's army could use it to deal with any remaining vigilantes who tried to attack the pipelines, pledge not to conduct any further cyberattacks on American ports, and sortie its substantial mine-clearing assets to the Red Sea to clear the mines it had sowed. Putin's chief of staff grumbled and countered, but Garrett would have none of it. Finally, the Russian accepted the offer.

The next day, northwest of the island of Crete, the Arleigh Burke destroyer USS *Farragut* cut through the pre-dawn Mediterranean waters at 30 knots. Named for David Glasgow Farragut—whose order during the Civil War Battle of Mobile Bay, "Damn the torpedoes, full speed ahead," forever enshrined him in the paragon of U.S. Navy heroes—DDG 99 was closing in on the Greek-flagged merchant ship, steaming east at 15 knots.

"Hold this course and speed until you're within a quarter mile of her and then back it off to match her speed," *Farragut's* captain ordered.

"Aye, aye, Captain," the officer of the deck replied.

SACEUR's anticipatory intelligence cell had worked closely with the IC. They had found the ship that the Chechens had contracted to transport the nuclear weapons from the port of Yuzhne.

Farragut's captain had received his top-secret orders, executed an emergency sortie from a port visit in Naples, Italy, and had made best speed to catch this vessel. They had been in a tail chase all night and were now ready to intercept the ship.

They crept up on the merchant and came directly abeam on the vessel's starboard side. *Farragut's* captain called on the bridge-to-bridge radio, "This is U.S. Navy warship USS *Farragut*. We have orders to intercept your ship. Heave to and prepare for boarding."

The ship's master wanted his payday, but he was no hero. Seeing *Farragut's* five-inch gun and 30 mm canon pointed directly at his bridge, along with hearing the MH-60R helo hovering off his port side, it's crew-served weapons also trained on his bridge, convinced him to stop his engines.

Farragut's boarding team maneuvered their eleven-meter RHIB to the merchant's starboard quarter and were quickly aboard.

The lieutenant in charge of the team proceeded to the bridge, where the ship's captain approached him.

"What is the meaning of this?" he demanded in broken, but understandable, English.

"Captain, we mean you and your crew no harm. But we have reliable intelligence that you have been contracted to carry stolen weapons in violation of international law. If you cooperate, we will escort you and your vessel back to your home port of Patras, and the video you are about to provide will not be revealed to your government."

The ship's master quickly recognized that he had no options. Somehow, he had been found out. He agreed to comply.

Once the boarding team set up their camera on his bridge, the man revealed that his owners had told him to pick up weapons at Yuzhne and deliver them to the Batumi seaport in Georgia. He told them he had no idea how they would be transported overland to Chechnya, but that wasn't his worry. He was to get his payday when he delivered the weapons to the Chechens who he was told would be waiting at the port.

Once the video was complete and uploaded to a secure website, the lieutenant in charge of the boarding team and one of his petty officers remained on the ship as the rest of the team got in their RHIB and returned to *Farragut*. Then both ships turned north for the journey to Patras as the crew of *Farragut's* MH-60R helo filmed the ships steaming together.

———

Later that day, cameras were rolling as Russia's energy minister went on the Russian-language Russia 24 network and announced that, "After due consideration of the plight of their fellow Europeans, Russia was immediately resuming energy shipments to Europe."

Soon after that, Russia broke the contracts to ship energy to new customers in Asia. Long-accustomed to being one of the world's most reliable energy suppliers, Russia now had another international black eye to deal with.

Several hours later, the Russian defense minister called the NATO secretary general and told him that the remaining Russian troops in Belarus would be pulled out "on an accelerated timeline." He also said that President Sechenov would be compensated for her military forces that Russia's army had destroyed, that the Russians would leave behind whatever equipment the Belarusian Army considered useful, and that Russia would also provide the gear President Putin had initially offered—but without Russian operators.

CHAPTER FIFTY-FOUR

The Villa Near the City of Vawkavysk, Belarus
(October 24, 0500 Central European Time)

At 0500 the next morning, the Belarusian vigilantes in their villa outside the City of Vawkavysk, Belarus, were startled awake by the loud honking outside of their front gate. Rick Holden was mashing the horn of his Dartz Nagel Dakkar SUV as it sat idling. Darko Markovic stood at the front bumper and called out, "Inside the house, come out please."

Holden and Markovic wore side arms but kept them holstered.

Two sleepy men stumbled out into the courtyard brandishing assault rifles.

"Who the hell are you, and what to you want?" one of the men shouted.

"We need to talk with you. We are armed, but haven't drawn our weapons. However, our friends have," Markovic replied as he swept his hand left and right.

The vigilantes looked up and saw two other SUVs with their headlights on, each one on a different rise a few hundred meters away. The vehicles' headlights framed shooters with their guns aimed at the courtyard.

"Get in here then, you and your friend," one vigilante said.

Holden and Markovic entered the compound. Holden carried a small satchel. The two armed men confronted the Americans in the courtyard. One man snatched Holden's package, saw that there was just a tablet inside, and handed it back. He then took their side arms. The two men escorted the Americans into the house where the rest of the vigilantes were assembled.

With Markovic speaking in their native language, Holden powered up the tablet and showed them pictures of the camper with the six nuclear weapons his team had intercepted, along with pictures of the camper's dead occupants. He then showed them photos of the ship the U.S. Navy had seized. Next, he played a video of the intercepted ship steaming in company with USS *Farragut.*

The Americans saved the best for last, and showed them the merchant ship's captain making a full confession. Markovic then told them that they had snuck into their compound and knew the remaining nukes were in the large SUV.

There was a crescendo of loud voices as the vigilantes embarked on a furious discussion. Finally, their leader spoke. It was easy to see why he had taken charge. He was a brute of a man, well over six feet tall and built like a linebacker, with red hair and a full red beard.

"We still don't know who the hell you are or what business this is of yours. And as to these photos and videos, who knows whether they're legit or not. We could kill you right here, and we have enough weapons to take out your friends too."

Markovic interpreted for Holden, who nodded and scrolled through his tablet.

After a few seconds, Holden handed the tablet to Markovic, who walked over to the vigilante leader. "You could do that, although it would be unwise," Markovic said as he handed the leader the tablet. It showed an aerial view of the villa, with the Dartz Nagel Dakkar SUV parked in front.

"This is the video from an American UAV anchored above us as we speak. It's an infrared picture, but you can clearly see that it is us. This aircraft, and several other UAVs we have under our control, will chase you wherever you try to run."

The vigilante leader still looked unconvinced, so Markovic continued. "Call your Chechen handler and ask him where your ship is. He'll tell you that your deal is off. Or get in your vehicles and drive to Yuzhne if you like. We'll follow you, of course. You really have no options here but to turn the nuclear weapons over to us, tell us where your confederates are holed up with the rest of the weapons you stole from the base at Brest, and surrender.

"We don't know what kind of justice the Belarus government will extract from you, but your only other choice is to fight it out with my men. Our comrades surrounding your villa are getting itchy trigger fingers, as are our UAV operators. They get medals for every enemy they kill."

The last statement, referring to the unarmed Global Hawk, was a lie—but it was the one thing that triggered the vigilante leader.

He turned to his men, and another spirited discussion ensued with men shouting and gesticulating. When the voices finally quieted, the leader turned to Markovic and said, "You have no idea how we have been oppressed by the Russian minority in this country and what they and these invaders have done to us. We only broke into that base to try to get enough weapons to even the score. We never intended to kill those soldiers, and finding the nuclear bombs was a complete accident."

Markovic interpreted for Holden and they exchanged a few words.

"We understand all that," Markovic replied. "And we will not turn you over to the Belarusian authorizes until they assure us that you will be dealt with fairly."

"Look," the man replied, "you still haven't told us why this is any of your business. If you and your friends have been in our country for a while, you know that there are many of us who have been attacking these pipelines and that we have paid a heavy price in blood thanks to these damned Russians—"

"You heard the TV announcement, they are leaving your country already," Markovic interrupted.

"But we still have issues with the Belarusian government, and again, that is no business of yours. You killed our leader and another four of our comrades. I'm the leader of the small group you see here, but Ilia Novik's number two is now making the decisions for all of us. I will contact him and give him your terms—"

Markovic began to interrupt again, but the man would have none of it.

"*No*, you listen for a change!" he shouted. "We won't negotiate with you under the barrels of your guns." Then turning to one of his men, he continued. "Give them their side arms and give them your cell phone."

The man complied, and then the first man spoke to Markovic again. "You and your friend get the hell out of here and move your other vehicles away too. I will call you on the phone we just gave you soon, once I talk with our leader. I promise I will present your terms fully, and he and a number of his men may come here to talk with you in person. That's the best I can offer. Otherwise, we fight it out right here."

Markovic grabbed Holden's arm and walked him to the other side of the room. He related what the man offered, and the two Americans had an animated conversation.

Markovic moved back toward the vigilante leader and spoke. "I have related your offer to *my* leader, and he says you have four hours, and not a minute longer, to meet our terms. We are not going to wait until you bring men from all over to try to overwhelm us. And don't forget, we still have those armed drones overhead. Don't make us take you down."

"Four hours it is," the man replied. "Now leave and wait for my call."

The two Americans left the house, hopped into their SUV and drove away. As they did, Holden called the others and told them to drive away as well. He gave them coordinates for their meet-up point.

———————

Ten minutes later, the three SUVs converged on a small, wooded rise a half kilometer from the house where they had just confronted the vigilantes. They had a clear sight-line to the house.

"What's the 411, Boss," Jimbo Folga asked.

"We thought you'd get them to surrender right there," Blake Mason added. "We had them under our guns."

"How many of them are in the house?" Mia Yaeger asked.

Rick Holden patiently explained all that had transpired and what was going to happen next, emphasizing his desire to avoid further bloodshed.

"That's all fine, and I don't want to kill any more of these guys than we have to, but do you really trust them?" Chapo Chavez asked.

"Only as far as I can throw them. That's why we'll stay here, keep an eye on them, and be ready to move if they bolt. Let's hope they're not that stupid."

"You said there are only four of them," Chavez replied. "We can take them out now."

"I know we can, but our job is to grab and safeguard the nukes, not kill as many of these vigilantes as we can. We've killed five already. Maybe that's enough. Let's just keep an overwatch and do what I learned to do when I was with the SEALs, hope for the best but plan for the worst."

"We get it, Boss," Folga chimed in. "I'll take the first watch looking at these guys, and Mia will keep them bore-sighted with the Global Hawk."

"Roger that," Holden replied.

"Boss, a minute?" Darko Markovic asked. The others stood and listened.

"What's on your mind, Darko?"

"The guy who's their leader, Big Red, the dude with the red hair and beard—I get a bad vibe from him. I thought he was going to kill us right there. I don't think he wants any of what we're selling. I think he's gonna bolt."

"Like I told Chapo," Holden began. "We gave them an ultimatum and made it as easy as possible for them to digest. We need to wait it out."

"You're the boss," Markovic replied without enthusiasm.

Now on the secure sat phone, Holden called Laura Peters. He related what had happened at the house and especially the timeline they had given the vigilantes.

"It's your call and your mission," Peters replied. "Are you pretty confident they'll surrender?"

"I think we convinced them that they don't have a ship to meet, so I don't know where they would run to. I am worried that they may have unlimited resources to call on to take us out. Sure would help if you gave us control of the second Global Hawk so we can watch our six while we anchor it over the house and keep an eye on them in case they decide to try to escape."

"I'll work that here and get back to you ASAP. I wish we could somehow call in the cavalry to help you all out."

"I'm afraid it's too late for that. I've got a good team. We'll make it work."

As Holden and his team were watching the vigilantes, at 0730 Moscow time, while Muscovites were enjoying a breakfast of *vareniki* (Russian dumplings) or other traditional dishes, the talking heads on the Russia 24 network breathlessly said, "We have breaking news—an announcement by the Russian defense minister."

The minister appeared on the screen and began, "Russia is fully committed to helping the international community ensure the safety and security of the world's waterways, especially chokepoints such as the Suez Canal.

"To that end, since the Russian Navy has the most modern mine-hunting and mine-clearing ships in the world, as well as the best-trained crews, we intend to lead the effort to remove the deadly mines that international terrorists have sowed in the Suez Canal. We welcome other navies to join our efforts."

The minister stopped speaking, and the screen was filled with a video. It showed Russian Navy Aleksandrit-class and Natya-class minesweepers leaving their home ports on the Black Sea and Baltic Sea, steaming toward the Suez Canal.

CHAPTER FIFTY-FIVE

**Near the Villa Outside the City of Vawkavysk, Belarus
(October 24, 0940 Central European Time)**

"How much longer do they have?" Blake Mason asked.

Rick Holden looked at his cell phone, "Two hours and twenty-six minutes."

"We gonna hold them to that timeline?"

"Damn right, we are," Holden replied.

Holden and Mason engaged in an extended conversation regarding trust. Mason didn't want to second-guess his boss, but it was clear he had no confidence the vigilantes would surrender peacefully.

Their conversation was interrupted by a shout from Chapo Chavez, who was standing overwatch with his binocs pointed at the house.

"Boss, these guys are piling out into the yard. I count four of them...." Seconds later, he continued. "Fuck, two of them are jumping into the big SUV. Looks like Big Red is riding shotgun, and one of the others is driving. The other two are getting into the smaller truck. These assholes are making a run for it, and they're armed to the teeth."

Mason flashed a condescending smile toward Holden "That shoots the shit out of hope for the best, Boss."

"Let's mount up!" Holden yelled. "Mia, keep one Global Hawk on top of them and don't lose them. SACEUR gave us control of the other bird; have that one watch our six, in case they have friends on the way."

The small SUV led the larger one carrying the nukes out of the villa compound. Once clear of the house, they turned northeast, heading for the P44 highway.

As he had promised the two Americans he would, the vigilante leader at the house had contacted his leader at the main vigilante layup house at Astravets. But that was as far as it went. There was no talk of surrendering—far from it.

Ilia Novik's second-in-command had contacted their Chechen handler, who told them that even though their designated ship had been intercepted, they would contract for another ship. He told the Belarusian that he just needed to evade capture for a few days.

When their confederates in the villa had asked for instructions, Novik's second-in-command told them to leave the house before the Americans' timeline ran out and head north toward Astravets. He would have several vehicles and many men speed south to meet up with them and overwhelm the small American team.

The leader of the vigilantes at the villa knew that there were at least three American vehicles and maybe more. He did not know how well armed they were, but he felt that he had enough heavy weapons to deal with whatever his pursuers might throw at him.

He and his men had argued about the American threat to rain down destruction from the air with armed UAVs. But at the end of the day, they counted on the fact that the U.S. team was likely bluffing. Ilia Novik had explained military matters to them, and they were convinced that it was extremely unlikely that the U.S. military had armed drones on standby anywhere in Europe.

They had been on a secondary road for just ten minutes when they intercepted the P44 highway.

Rick Holden and his team had, indeed, "planned for the worst." They had leveraged all that Laura Peters and SACEUR's anticipatory intelligence cell could give them.

Using the same cell tower triangulation process they had employed to locate the villa near Vawkavysk, the team at SACEUR had monitored the calls between the two groups of vigilantes. They knew there was a group, and likely a large one, holed up at Astravets and that they would probably barrel south-southwest to support the vigilantes trying to escape with the nukes.

Peters had passed their analysis to Holden and his team and had suggested that if the vigilantes at the villa did make a run for it, they would likely head north-northeast to meet up with their comrades.

Holden had agreed with the analysis and had staged his team northeast of the villa. He had counted on the Global Hawk's ability to give them a clear view of any hostile movements.

When the vigilantes left the compound and moved onto the secondary road, his team paralleled their route. Once they rolled onto the P44 highway, he knew that he needed to intercept them before the group coming from Astravets, two hundred and thirty kilometers away, converged on them somewhere between the two cities.

Holden drove the lead SUV, with Darko Markovic riding shotgun. Mia Yeager rode in the back seat, controlling the Global Hawks and keeping them focused on the two fleeing vehicles. The two other SUVs followed behind. They were in a several-kilometer loose trail when Holden turned to Markovic. "So much for promises," he began. "I worried that they would make a run for it, and now they have. Call them."

Markovic called on the cell phone the vigilantes had given them. Even though Holden didn't speak the language, he could tell Markovic was slamming the vigilante leader for trying to escape and was threatening to take him down. Then, Markovic stopped talking. After listening quietly for several seconds, he broke the connection.

"What did he say?" Holden asked.

"He told us to fuck off and that his pals were just a few kilometers away."

"It's a bluff!" Yeager shouted. "I've got the second Global Hawk anchored well north of here. There's no gaggle of vehicles heading this way, at least not for the fifty-plus kilometers I can see."

"That squares it," Markovic said. "I say we take out these guys now."

Holden didn't reply. He mashed the accelerator and headed toward the two fleeing vehicles as the other American SUVs closed up behind him.

———————

Vladimir Putin had slept little since his chief of staff had related what he and Ryan Garrett had agreed to. The Russian leader was still angry that he had been thwarted, but he knew the American plan was still the best chance of keeping the nukes out of Chechen hands.

He had been in his office since 0630, waiting to hear that the weapons had been wrested away from the Belarusian vigilantes. Now, it was late morning, and he summoned his chief of staff.

"*Well?*" he asked impatiently as the man entered his office. "What has your American counterpart told you? Do they have the weapons in hand yet?"

"Evidently, not yet, Mr. President."

"*Dammit!*" Putin shouted as he shot up out of his chair. "We've met every one of their requirements and broadcast those facts on national and international media. Did you send him the overhead photos showing the empty parking lots at our two cyber facilities?"

"Yes, I did that yesterday, and he acknowledged that we were complying with their demands."

"Then what's the holdup? You spoke with him two days ago. Either they've taken custody of the nukes, or they haven't. Which is it?"

His chief of staff paused before continuing, knowing that the news he had held back from his leader would likely send Putin over the edge. He proceeded with extreme caution, bending the truth. "Mr. President, I've just received news about communications intercepts our intelligence services have made. It seems that even though the Americans intercepted the ship the Belarusian vigilantes were to rendezvous with, those terrorists elected to run with the nukes and try to meet up with a larger force of vigilantes. We think the Americans are giving chase—"

"You think? We don't know?" Putin interrupted. "I'll be damned if I'll let some ragtag group of bastards deliver those nukes to the Chechens. Do you have any idea what will happen if they do?" His chief of staff knew full well what that would mean. But before he could speak, Putin continued. "You said our intelligence people had made comms intercepts. Do we know where these vigilantes are now?"

"We do. They've left their hideout near the city of Vawkavysk and are heading north-northeast. The Americans are in a tail chase and will likely intercept them.

"They're monitoring them with one of their Global Hawk UAVs, and we're tracking that drone with our satellites."

"And we don't know whether the Americans will catch them?"

"We don't, but we do know that there is a large group of their fellow vigilantes moving toward them. We believe they intend to overwhelm the American group chasing them."

"*That's it*—I've had enough! I'm tired of waiting for someone else to do what I can do myself. Where is our nearest military airfield to the Belarus border? Show me."

His chief of staff scrolled through his tablet and brought up a map. "Here, sir." He held the tablet in front of his leader. "It appears that Kubinka Air Base is the closest one."

"Does it have fighters and bombers?"

His chief of staff scrolled to another page. "Yes, sir—a squadron of MIG-29M fighters and two squadrons of SU-25 attack aircraft."

"Get the chief of the general staff on the line and tell him to launch four attack aircraft with fighter support immediately and have them head west. Once they're airborne, I want to talk with him. We're going to blast these Belarusian vigilantes to hell."

His chief of staff gasped. "Mr. President, the Americans are in pursuit and will likely catch them and take custody of the weapons. Our pilots may not have a way to sort out who is who if we try to take out the Belarusians. And if we attack a vehicle carrying the nukes, they may be unstable and detonate."

"I don't give a damn. It's not my worry if Maria Sechenov couldn't safeguard her weapons or if the Americans can't do what they promised they would."

Putin's chief of staff was searching for something—anything—to say to have his leader come to his senses and not escalate an already volatile situation. He was about to speak, but Putin preempted him, jabbing his finger at the man. "I told you to get the chief of the general staff on the phone, and I meant it. Now leave me and do what I told you to do, or I'll find someone who will!"

His chief of staff beat a hasty retreat.

CHAPTER FIFTY-SIX

Supreme Allied Commander Europe (SACEUR) Headquarters, Mons, Belgium
(October 24, 1130 Central European Time)

Laura Peters was on watch in SACEUR's nerd nook, manning the command console. Major Pat Cook was monitoring the stream of conversations going into and out of the Kremlin. The cell's focus was on Holden and his team at the moment. Suddenly, Cook shouted, "*What?* Are you shitting me?"

Peters and the other two watchstanders in the cell converged on Cook and looked over his shoulder.

"Right here," he began, hovering his cursor over a paragraph in the transcription of the call between Vladimir Putin and his chief of the general staff. "Putin just told his top general to launch fighters and bombers out of Kubinka Airfield. He has orders to take out the Belarusian vehicles fleeing Vawkavysk."

"Can they find them?" Peters asked.

"Evidently they can. Look at this," Cook replied, pointing his cursor at another paragraph in the conversation. "They discussed the intel they have about where the vigilantes with the weapons are, as well as the ones coming down from Astravets. Putin told him to take them all out."

"Holden's team is going to get caught in the crossfire for sure," Peters replied.

"I know. Call Holden and tell him to back off for now. I'm calling General O'Sullivan."

338

Rick Holden, Darko Markovic and Mia Yeager were discussing how they planned to take down the vigilantes who were still several kilometers ahead of them on the P44 highway when Holden's secure cell phone chirped.

"Rick, its Laura. Where are you now, and where are the vehicles you're chasing?"

Holden gave Peters the information and wondered why she was quizzing him. She had to know what they were doing and that they needed to focus on the task at hand. Was he going to get micromanagement from SACEUR?

"Here's what's happening," she continued, describing how Russian aircraft were launching from Kubinka Airfield and that U.S. Air Force F-22A *Raptors* were launching from Ramstein Air Base in Germany to intercept them. She told him that SACEUR recommended that he and his team back off from the fleeing vehicles to avoid being caught in the crossfire if the U.S. military aircraft failed to intercept and turn back the Russians.

Holden was dumbfounded. "Are they trying to start World War III?" he asked.

"Damned if I know," Peters replied. "Our team here thinks that now that our commander has aircraft moving to intercept the Russian jets, the next call he'll make is to the JCS chairman. He'll probably tell him to get on the hotline with the Russian defense minister and let him know their aircraft will be dealt with if they penetrate Belarus airspace."

There was momentary silence as Peters waited for Holden to tell her that they were backing off from the vigilante vehicles until what she had just described was sorted out.

Finally, she couldn't wait any longer.

"Rick?"

"I need to talk this over with my team."

"You're standing into danger!" she shouted. "If those Russian jets make it through, they won't even try to discriminate which vehicle is which. They'll just blast away and take out anything on that highway."

"I *know* that. We need to talk it over. I'll get back to you."

Peters was about to marshal her arguments for Holden's team to back off, but the connection was broken.

There was ice in his voice as the chairman of the Joint Chiefs of Staff told the Russian defense minister what would happen if Russian aircraft crossed into Belarus. The Russian stalled, protested, and insisted that his government had met all the conditions that the American's had imposed.

The Chairman listened, showed little empathy, and told his counterpart that the Agency team was on the heels of the fleeing vigilantes and *would* intercept them and recover the nuclear weapons. He reminded him that it was none of Russia's business how that occurred and that if any of the few remaining Russian troops in Belarus tried to interfere, they would be dealt with. He ended the call abruptly.

"That went well...or not?" Darko Markovic asked.

Rick Holden related Peters' end of the conversation.

"Whew, just when I thought this couldn't get any more complicated," Markovic replied.

Holden paused before responding. Throughout his entire professional life, he had prided himself on planning his missions carefully, whether as a CIA operative or as a Navy SEAL. Now there was no time to plan, and he was momentarily stuck. He knew the vigilantes had no intention of surrendering and were armed to the teeth. He also knew the dangers if Russian and American jets got into a fur ball over Belarus.

"We need to take them out now, Darko. I'm calling the others."

It had taken the Russians almost an hour to scramble their warplanes to carry out the no-notice orders of the Russian president. Now they streaked west, waiting for further instructions as to what direction to head to take out the threat that had only been vaguely described to them.

Two formations, each with four U.S. Air Force F-22A *Raptors*, flew at thirty thousand feet, high above the Polish countryside. Their orders were to continue into Belarus airspace and turn back any Russian aircraft that crossed into Belarus.

Rick Holden had made his decision: If he backed off the fleeing vigilantes and waited for the U.S. and Russian aircraft standoff to resolve itself, even if it didn't start World War III, the vigilante group traveling south from Astravets would converge on them and overwhelm his team.

He transmitted his on-the-fly plan to his teammates in the other two SUVs, and now they were within a kilometer of the fleeing vigilantes. His team had their heaviest weapons ready for the showdown.

Air Force Lieutenant Colonel Alan Zerbe was the flight leader for the eight F-22A formation. Many American pilots assigned to the European theater had basic Russian language training. They were sixty kilometers from the Russian aircraft when Zerbe began his scripted transmission.

"Russian aircraft heading west at twenty-six thousand feet, this is U.S. Air Force flight leader. I have a multiple-aircraft formation, and we are tracking your flight with our radars. Each of my aircraft is armed with long-range air-to-air missiles, and we have orders not to allow you to penetrate Belarus airspace."

Zerbe paused, waiting for a response.

"We have our orders, and we intend to carry them out," the Russian flight leader replied.

Zerbe anticipated the response. He called the other aircraft in his flight and said, "Light 'em up."

The pilots in the Russian aircraft formation heard the unmistakable warble of the American fire-control radars. As they did, the size of the American formation came into full view on their own radars. There were eight blips.

The Russian fighter lead had only one wingman.

Moments later, the Russian pilots watched their systems degrade as the Air Force EC-130H *Compass Call* aircraft trailing Zerbe's *Raptors* began to jam their systems.

"Nikolay?" the leader's wingman asked. There was a tremor in his voice. He could see the American jets on his radar. The odds were overwhelmingly in the Americans' favor.

The Russian flight leader was no coward, but he knew when he was outnumbered and outgunned.

"Break off," he replied. "We're turning around."

Zerbe and his flight watched as the Russian aircraft executed a hundred-and-eighty-degree turn and headed east. Then over the radio, he called the Air Force E-3 *Sentry* AWACS control aircraft monitoring his flight and asked for instructions.

———

While one of his men drove the large SUV with the nuclear weapons, the vigilante in charge of that small team was furiously texting his leader, who was speeding south from Astravets, urging him to go faster. They were now just one hundred and twenty kilometers apart, and he knew if he could just keep the Americans from catching them, they would be home free. If not, he counted on his comrades to win the firefight.

Suddenly, his windscreen was filled with the body of an aircraft coming south on the P44 highway. "What the hell!" he shouted to his driver as he tried to get his brain around why this aircraft was at a dangerously low altitude and was descending.

They looked up in horror as the Global Hawk, the size of a small commuter plane, landed on the highway less than a kilometer in front of them. The bird's gear collapsed and fifteen tons of aircraft came barreling toward them. Shredded metal flew everywhere and the UAV's fuel tank exploded, sending flames high into the air.

"Pull off the road, *now!*" the leader shouted, as both vehicles braked hard and lumbered across the shoulder and into the wooded area, crashing into a stand of trees.

———

"Well, it worked," Mia Yeager said with a crooked smile.

"We need to see if any of them are alive," Darko Markovic offered.

The U.S. team approached the scene cautiously, as the highway was strewn with wreckage of the crashed, and still-burning, Global Hawk.

"Mia, you know these birds," Chapo Chavez called on the radio. "The fire looks like it's consuming that thing. Should we worry about secondary explosions?"

"I think we're good," Yeager replied.

"Jimbo, Chapo, keep closed-up on me. We need to head for where these guys ran off the road," Holden said.

Both men complied.

Holden had struggled with how to stop the fleeing vigilantes before they were either met by their comrades or attacked by Russian aircraft. He didn't like their chances if they got into a rolling shootout on a main Belarus highway. Not only would he be putting his team at extreme risk, but other vehicles on the highway might be hit as well.

Holden had at first expressed shocked disbelief when Mia Yeager proposed crashing one of the multi-million-dollar Global Hawks on the highway ahead of the vigilantes. She figured that if she flew it head-on toward them and at an extremely low altitude, other vehicles would clear out of the way, and when she crashed it ahead of them, they would be forced to run off the highway. They would have little choice unless they wanted to be crushed by the crashed aircraft or consumed in flames from the burning fuel disgorged by the ruptured fuel tank.

The plan had worked, and now Holden's team, in their three SUVs, was picking its way through a debris-strewn highway.

"There they are," Folga called on the radio.

"I see them," Holden replied. "Keep close on me."

The Agency team continued to creep along, keeping the two vehicles in their sight. As they got closer, they could see that the smaller SUV had flipped over and impaled itself on a tree, while the larger one had crashed into a large tree and looked basically intact.

"I figure the ones in the small SUV are dead, don't know about those in the large one with the nukes. What do you think?" Yaeger asked.

"Let's approach, but have the others—"

"Rick, let's talk about this," Markovic interrupted. "When we took down their pals in the camper we got hit with an RPG. These guys are likely armed to the teeth too. Shouldn't we just wait it out for a bit? They won't just sit there forever. Maybe they're worried their SUV will explode."

Holden considered this. Markovic had a point, but the urgency of the situation was too great. They had to secure the nukes before the other vigilantes reached them.

"I roger what you're saying, Darko. But it's a risk we have to take. We've got six guns in the fight; they only have two. I like our odds."

"Your call," Markovic replied.

Holden keyed the radio. "Blake, hold back and get ready to give chase if these guys somehow get rolling again. Chapo, stay on my bumper, and we'll close to about fifty meters. Then we'll dismount and take cover behind the SUVs. They took hits before, and we came out of it okay."

Double mic clicks signaled the men in the other vehicles understood.

"Chapo, can Jimbo hear me?"

"Roger, Boss—I've got you on speaker."

"Jimbo, you're our best long shooter. I want you to dismount before any of the rest of us, take cover behind your vehicle, and set up a sniper overwatch. If they open up on us, it will probably be as soon as our feet hit the ground. Keep your mic hot, and let us know what you see."

"Will do," Folga replied.

While Mason hung back, Holden and Chavez crept ahead, keeping an eye on the intact SUV. There was no sign of movement by the driver or passenger.

"We're stopping here," Holden said once they were in position. "You're first out, Jimbo."

Folga climbed into the back seat and got out on the left side of the SUV to shield himself from the vigilantes' SUV. He laid his Barrett M82 sniper rifle on the hood of his vehicle and looked through his Leupold 4.5–14×50 scope, searching for movement. There was none.

"Nothing moving. Do we want to approach?" Folga asked.

"I want Darko to call out to them first," Holden replied. As he did, Markovic crawled out of their vehicle and crouched down behind the left quarter panel of the SUV.

"In the SUV—" Markovic began.

But as he did, Folga came over the radio. "Watch it, Big Red's getting out of the vehicle, and he's got what looks like—"

Before he could finish the sentence, the man opened up on Holden's team, and the driver slipped out of the truck and began firing as well. Big Red was lying prone and blasting away with an RPK-74M machine gun, while his companion hefted a Bullpup assault rifle.

The fusillade of fire peppered the three American SUVs. The rest of the Agency team bailed out, took cover behind their vehicles, and began returning fire. Holden was the first to blast away with his weapon.

Suddenly, there was a shout. "*Jimbo's hit!*" It was Chavez. He rushed over to Folga, who was bleeding profusely from his right shoulder.

"Lucky bastards," Folga said through clenched teeth as Chavez dug under his coat to find the source of the blood.

Holden, Markovic and Yeager opened up on the vigilantes on full-automatic.

The Americans poured out a withering fire as Mason also dismounted and got his gun into the fight.

The combined fire of the four Americans shredded the two vigilantes, and both dropped like sacks. Finally, it was quiet.

As Chavez continued to tend to Folga's wounds, Markovic started to move toward the big SUV. Holden thrust his arm in front of him. "I've got this," he said.

Holden approached the large SUV and kicked both men to ensure they were dead. Then he moved to the flipped-over vehicle and saw the other two vigilantes were dead as well.

He went back to the SUV with the nukes, looked at the mangled engine compartment, and looked in the back to ensure the nukes were there. They were.

It was clear to him the truck wasn't drivable, and he knew the weapons would never fit in their vehicles. As much as he understood that this was an Agency operation, he also realized they needed help.

Holden returned to where their vehicles were stopped and made a beeline for Folga. He could see that he was sitting up and leaning against one of the SUVs. He had a huge bandage on his shoulder and his right arm was in a sling. Folga looked like he was going to be okay.

"Doc Chapo fix you up?" Holden asked.

"Yeah, but he said don't wait for a pretty nurse to hold my hand."

Now, Holden knew that Folga was fine. "We'll get you to a hospital, and then you can worry about who's tending to you," the leader replied.

The rest of his team was in a tight circle around him as Holden told them what they already knew. They had only one option to safeguard the weapons they had risked so much to secure.

As soon as Laura Peters came on the line on the secure radio, Rick Holden poured out his story, telling her that they had stopped the vigilantes and recovered the nukes, but that they had no way of carrying them away. He said that they would use the one remaining Global Hawk to watch the highways to the north for the vigilantes he knew were streaming toward them, but for the moment, staying where they were and preparing for a standoff was his only option.

As Peters listened, she was forming a plan. "We'll get you help...and soon."

CHAPTER FIFTY-SEVEN

In the Skies Above the Belarus Countryside
(October 24, 1415 Central European Time)

The E-3 *Sentry* AWACS mission commander had told Lieutenant Colonel Alan Zerbe he was putting two fly-to points into his system. The first was a rendezvous point to meet up with two KC-46 *Pegasus* refueling tankers at thirty-two thousand feet north of Minsk. The second was a moving fly-to point anchored over the Belarusian vigilante vehicles moving south, toward Holden and his team.

After a furious series of telephone calls between the U.S. secretary of defense and the Belarus defense minister, the army colonel in charge of the Belarus Army 11th Guards Mechanized Brigade base outside the city of Slonim had rolled every serviceable vehicle, each with heavily armed troops, out of the base's main gate. Their orders: Make a beeline for where the U.S. Agency team was guarding the three remaining nukes.

At SACEUR headquarters, Laura Peters was walking a fine line between keeping her multiple bosses, up through and including General O'Sullivan, updated on what Holden's team was doing and not interfering with his mission by peppering him with questions. She counted on the AWACS mission commander to keep all informed as Colonel Zerbe's flight approached the vigilante convoy.

"What the hell?" the vigilante leader shouted to his driver. He was in the lead vehicle of their convoy and saw multiple jet aircraft rapidly descending right over them.

The trucks shook as four *Raptors* passed directly overhead at less than a hundred meters. Just as the vigilantes began to recover from the shock, four more jets jolted their vehicles as they streaked above them.

The group continued south as the leader got on his cell phone and called the vehicle right behind him. "They look like American jets. I don't know how they found us, but if they're doing this, they're probably trying to scare us into turning around. We keep moving—tell the others."

The man complied, and the vehicles continued.

Suddenly, the highway about two kilometers south of them exploded as small diameter bombs from the American jets rained down, chewing up huge swaths of the roadway and making it completely impassable.

The convoy screeched to a halt. The vigilante leader looked at his driver and said, "Creep along on the shoulder over there; I think I see a clear path."

The man began to comply, only to see another salvo of bombs chew up more of the highway.

The driver looked pleadingly at his leader.

The man was trying to decide what to do next when another salvo of missiles exploded less than two hundred meters in front of them. Chunks of broken roadway rained down on their vehicles.

"Dammit—we're next!" the driver shouted.

The vigilante leader uttered a curse and told his driver to turn around and head north.

Less than an hour later, a convoy of Belarus Army trucks arrived at the spot where Rick Holden and his team were guarding the remaining nukes.

"You're a sight for sore eyes, Colonel." A smiling Holden shook hands with the senior Belarusian officer.

The colonel smiled back at Holden. "You delivered the other weapons to us, so I thought we'd save you the trip and come to *you* this time. Are all of your people okay?"

Holden walked him over to where Jimbo Folga sat propped up.

The colonel summoned one of his men, a field medic, who began examining the wounded American. He's basically okay," the medic said, "but we need to get him some proper medical attention. Our clinic back at the base can fix him up."

"Will you and your team accompany us back to our base?" the colonel asked Holden. "We'll get your man patched up, and then I suspect your mission is complete and you'll want to return home."

"That would be great, Colonel. We'll follow you there. Then, we're all anxious to wrap this up."

News of the successful mission to secure the remaining nuclear weapons passed quickly up multiple chains of command. At the urging of General O'Sullivan, two senior leaders—the secretary of defense and the CIA director—talked on a secure line. In less than ten minutes, they made a decision to do what O'Sullivan had suggested.

Unbeknownst to Rick Holden and his team, the decision meant that they would not be returning home—at least not yet.

CHAPTER FIFTY-EIGHT

Supreme Allied Commander Europe (SACEUR) Headquarters, Mons, Belgium
(October 24, 1630Central European Time)

Once they had loaded the stolen nukes aboard the Belarusian Army trucks and begun the journey toward the base at Slonim, Rick Holden was finally able to relax. He had debated whether to call the Agency aircraft pilots and have them head toward Minsk airport, but his concerns over Jimbo Folga's wounds overrode that idea. He'd get his man patched up first—then worry about heading home.

Holden was still en route to Slonim when Laura Peters called him on the secure sat phone. "Rick, it's Laura. Are you all okay?

"Yes, one of my men got hit, but we're heading to the Belarusian Army base to get him patched up. Thanks for sending in the cavalry."

"Easy day. We can thank the Air Force for turning around the vigilantes heading your way."

"How did they do that?" he asked.

"I'll tell you more when I see you."

"See me?"

"Your Agency people talked with the folks at DoD. General O'Sullivan thought that it was important to recognize the amazing work you all did here and do so in theater. Your Agency aircraft will be en route to Minsk as soon as you get your man patched up and ready to fly. You and your team will be flown here to our headquarters in Mons. We have a celebratory dinner planned."

For one of the few times in his life, Rick Holden was lost for words.

———————

The Belarusian Army doctors had been able to tend to Jimbo Folga's wounds quickly and ready him for transport. Within a few hours of arriving at Slonim, Rick Holden and his team headed toward Minsk International, escorted by a large convoy of Belarusian Army trucks.

After that, it was a whirlwind. When they landed in Germany, they were whisked to the VIP quarters on base where they were able to get cleaned up and don fresh sets of clothes the SACEUR staff had produced for them.

The dinner in their honor was attended by General O'Sullivan, his senior staff, and each member of Colonel Garrett's nerd nook team. As dinner ended and the last toasts were given, Laura Peters leaned close to Holden and said, "Get some sleep. I've got the general's tennis court reserved for 0900 tomorrow morning. Someone has already dropped a racquet and tennis gear in your room."

———————

By 1030 the next morning, they had played two sets of intense tennis on SACEUR's well-kept tennis courts and now were taking a breather.

"Holden, you're not as rusty as I thought you'd be," Peters quipped.

"I was running hard to keep up with you. With these courts right here on your base, you probably play every day."

"I wish. I don't think either one of us will be as good again as we were when we were at UVA—but a girl can dream I guess."

"Did we both almost wind up in the middle of World War III?" Holden asked.

"I think so," she replied. "People underestimate Vladimir Putin, and when they do, things go off the rails."

"Do you think we have him back in the box now?"

"Hard to say. I do think he over-reached when he had his ambassador murdered, and our country was able to leverage that to force him to make the concessions he did. But I'm afraid Putin will likely view it as a momentary setback."

"I think you're probably right."

There was a short silence before Holden continued.

"Your cell bailed us out a number of times, and I'm grateful that you went to the wall to help us out. You must really enjoy your work here."

"I do. It's the best job ever. How about you? Back to the Agency...or?"

"Whew, dunno. I've got a lot to process, and I'm ready to unwind a bit. For the moment, I think I've got some vacation time coming."

"Europe is great this time of year, and these courts really don't get much use," Peters replied, smiling.

"I just may take you up on that—another set?"

"You're on."

Epilogue

Pavel Safronov completed his speech, with his wife, Olga, sitting in the front row of the Heritage Foundation auditorium. The crowd that had listened to his remarks rose and delivered a thunderous ovation.

Like other speeches he had given here at Heritage, where he had been installed as a distinguished fellow, Safronov had blasted Vladimir Putin as an international criminal who would stop at nothing to try to fulfill his megalomaniacal goals.

The former mayor of Petersburg and his wife had been granted political asylum in the United States. While his home base was now at this conservative think tank, he had already given speeches across the country. Safronov had one passion, and it was to do all he could to bring down the man who was ruining the country he loved.

"Brian, would you please tell our viewers why the people behind you are protesting. Hasn't the government acceded to most of their demands already?"

"Yes, Patricia, they have." The young correspondent began following the carefully built script Patricia Bailey had sent him.

After her harrowing ordeal in Europe, Bailey had been given time to reunite with her parents and then brought back to CNN headquarters. After a thorough debriefing, she was told that the network's CEO was giving her an anchor spot in Atlanta. It was something to which she had always aspired, but after her rescue from Vladimir Putin's henchmen, she had intended to spend some more time as a field reporter, building her brand. The network, however, had different plans for Bailey. They wanted to capitalize on her instant fame, as well as keep her out of the field, lest anything untoward happen again.

While Bailey enjoyed her time in the limelight, CNN's field reporters were already bristling over her micromanagement of every aspect of their reporting.

Maria Sechenov and her government had been shaken to the core by what happened in their country. The president of Belarus had used the military equipment Russian troops left behind to put a security blanket over the pipelines snaking through her country. Energy was now flowing to, as well as through, Belarus.

But beyond this immediate triage, Sechenov did two other things. Slowly, and deliberately, she worked with her parliament to pass legislation that would ensure that the Belarusian majority in her country received a bit more of the country's limited resources. But more importantly, now that Vladimir Putin had been thwarted, she put her country on a path to join the European Union.

Rick Holden and his team received a warm welcome when they returned to CIA Headquarters at Langley. As anticipated, they were absorbed into the ops directorate.

All were given responsible desk jobs—but with a twist.

Holden had asked, and his bosses had finally agreed, that while he and his team would do their standard nine-to-five jobs, once a month—for an extended weekend—they would go to their training facility at The Farm and keep their skills sharp.

Laura Peters had told Rick Holden that working in SACEUR's anticipatory intelligence cell was one of the best jobs she'd ever had, and she meant it. Once Holden and his team left to return to the United States, she folded back into the nerd nook—but not before she took some well-deserved leave.

While she was away, and unbeknownst to her, Colonel Sauter met with General O'Sullivan. Sauter's message was simple and direct—and one that O'Sullivan agreed with: While Peters was a valuable member of the anticipatory intelligence cell, she could make an even bigger contribution to the U.S. military, and to the nation, in another role.

Sauter had the action to tell her this as soon as she returned from leave.

Afterword

This story has painted Russia and its leader in stark, unflattering terms. While this is fiction, one thing undergirding the high concept for this story is that Russians are spectacular grudge holders. If you tick a Russian off, the chances of him forgetting about it and not seeking revenge asymptotically approach zero. Perhaps the best way to explain this is by way of a story that has been retold countless times:

> An angel appeared to three men, a Frenchman, an Italian, and a Russian. The angel tells them that tomorrow the world is going to end and asks them what they each want to do with their last night on earth. The Frenchman says he will get a case of the best champagne and spend his last night with his mistress. The Italian says he will visit his mistress and then go home and eat his last meal with his wife and children. The Russian replies that he will go burn down his neighbor's barn.

Other than writing thrillers, I like nothing more than connecting with readers. You can follow me on Facebook and Twitter, and learn more about my books, blogs and other writing on my website: http://www.georgegaldorisi.com/—especially a series "Writing Tips"—which offers useful advice for all writers from established authors to future best-selling writers.

Also from Braveship Books...

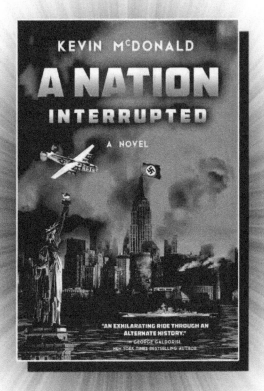

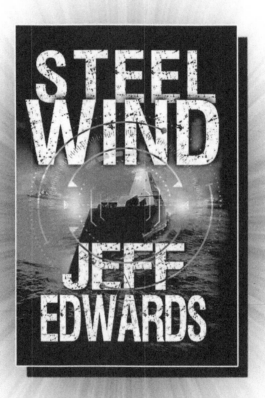

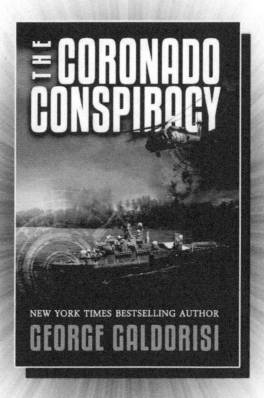

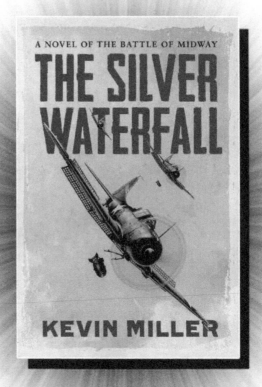

Made in United States
Orlando, FL
11 June 2023